Readers who hunger for a great espionage thriller with an extra helping of romance will devour *The Rules in Rome*. A.L. Sowards is at the top of her craft with this terrific WWII suspense/spy novel. It is definitely a book not to be missed!

—Gregg Luke
author of *Bloodborne* and *Do No Harm*

The Rules in Rome has it all: romance, adventure, and epic themes illustrating the unconquerable human spirit. From the moment Gracie met Bastian, I knew I would love this book. He's the perfect hero, and Gracie is his match. I fell in love with these characters over and over again. Thank you, Sowards, for another fabulous read!

—Stephanie Fowers
author of The Twisted Tales trilogy and *Jane and Austen*

THE RULES IN ROME

OTHER BOOKS AND AUDIO BOOKS
BY A. L. SOWARDS

Espionage

Sworn Enemy

Deadly Alliance

THE RULES IN ROME

A. L. SOWARDS

AUTHOR OF SWORN ENEMY, DEADLY ALLIANCE, AND ESPIONAGE

Covenant Communications, Inc.

Cover images: *Marine*, courtesy of Corbis Images, *Coliseum* © Phant courtesy Shutterstock, *Peaceful Woman with Long Wavy Hair* © Masterfile Corporation.

Cover design copyright © 2015 by Covenant Communications, Inc.
Map copyright © 2015 by Briana Shawcroft

Published by Covenant Communications, Inc.
American Fork, Utah

Printed in the United States of America
First Printing: February 2015

21 20 19 18 17 16 15   10 9 8 7 6 5 4 3 2 1

ISBN 978-1-62108-882-0

For VaLynn and Elaura

Because being the oldest has its challenges, and being the youngest does too. Plus, I know you both like "kissing books," and this story is about as romantic as I get.

ACKNOWLEDGMENTS

First of all, I'd like to thank the readers who connected with me on Facebook and helped name my characters. Thank you, Lane, Randa, Tracy, Elaura, Vanessa, Lela, Mark, and Suzanne, for your suggestions. I apologize if I missed anyone.

A special thanks goes to the members of my writer's group: Linda White, Terri Ferran, Kathi Oram Peterson, and Nikki Trionfo. Their feedback made this book far better than it would have been without their help. Likewise, I'm grateful to my test readers: Melanie Grant, VaLynn Woolley, Candice N. Toone, Ron Machado, Stephanie Fowers, and Carli White. They not only got rid of typos but also gave suggestions that added depth to this story. Special thanks to George Evans Jr. for looking over the motorcycle scenes.

Thanks also goes to my publisher, Covenant Communications, especially my editor, Sam. This was a fun story to write, and I'm grateful for their help in getting it to the public.

Special thanks also to my mapmaker, Briana Shawcroft, who graciously fit my project in despite a very busy schedule.

And I couldn't have written this without the support of my family, who have courageously put up with years of lazy cooking while my mind and fingers have been busy with the 1940s.

USEFUL TERMS

Carabinieri—Italian military policemen loyal to the Italian king and disbanded by the Germans

Gappisti—Members of the Patriotic Action Groups, mostly Communist, working to rid Italy of the Nazis

Hauptmann—German Army officer, rank similar to a US Army captain

Kriegsmarine—German Navy

Obersturmführer—Nazi officer, rank similar to a US Army first lieutenant

OSS—Office of Strategic Services. US intelligence and sabotage agency that operated from June 1942 to January 1946

Partisans—Armed fighters resisting Nazi occupation

Sturmbannführer—Nazi officer, rank similar to a US Army major

Untersturmführer—Nazi officer, rank similar to a US Army second lieutenant

Wehrmacht—German armed forces

ITALY, SPRING 1944

ITALY

CIVITAVECCHIA

ROME

TIBER RIVER

ALBAN HILLS
▲MOUNT ARTEMISIO

SACCO RIVER

CAESAR LINE

GUSTAV LINE

ANZIO

NETTUNO

HITLER LINE

RAPIDO RIVER

CASSINO

LIRI RIVER

GARIGLIANO RIVER

TYRRHENIAN SEA

N

VOLTURNO RIVER

CASERTA

NAPLES

50 mi
100 km

PROLOGUE

November 1943
Forty-five miles north of Rome, Italy

BASTIEN LEY GRIPPED HIS TOMMY gun in the darkness, listening for the Nazi convoy scheduled to pass along the narrow country road ten yards ahead of him.

Marcello, positioned mere feet to Bastien's left, lifted a hand and tilted his head to the side.

"You hear something?" Bastien asked his friend in Italian.

Marcello nodded, and after a moment, Bastien heard it too. He hoped whatever was coming was large enough to be worth their effort but small enough that it wouldn't overwhelm their four-man team. As the noise grew closer, Bastien could pick out the roar of motorcycle engines.

"It seems the hunters have become the hunted." Marcello stood and signaled to the two men stationed across the road.

Bastien followed Marcello into the thicker underbrush while they waited for the motorcycles to pass. The Nazis were getting smarter, and Bastien's group was getting smaller. Bastien had parachuted into Italy a month ago to help local fighters harass the Nazis. Every truck they ambushed meant fewer supplies for the German Army; every guard assigned to protect convoys was one less soldier on the front line. Throughout October, their work had gone smoothly. Their attacks had been quick—a few grenades thrown, a few clips of ammunition emptied. And before the Germans could organize a response, Bastien and his men had melted into the night, regrouping at dawn in a nearby barn to plan their next raid.

That had changed when the Nazis started using motorcycles. Bastien and his men chose their ambush sites where trucks would have a difficult time leaving the road to chase them. But the motorcycles could follow them through the fields, and three days ago, they'd gunned down two of Bastien's men. Attacking a convoy with motorcycle escorts involved more risk than Bastien and Marcello were willing to take tonight.

As the motorcycles and the five trucks they guarded rumbled past, Bastien frowned. He needed to rethink his strategy because the US Office of Strategic Services hadn't sent him to Italy to watch Nazi trucks roll south with supplies. He was supposed to be helping the war effort. If he couldn't do it here, he needed to do it elsewhere.

When the convoy's sounds faded, Bastien and Marcello found the other members of their team, Roberto and Giovanni.

"He drove within three feet of us," Roberto said. "I almost shot him, but I didn't think I'd be able to outrun his partner, and then the guards in the trucks would've been alerted."

"Can we get more men? If we have teams for each motorcycle, plus men to attack the convoy at the same time—" Bastien stopped when Marcello held up his hand. It took him a few seconds, but then Bastien heard what had caught Marcello's attention: another motor. "Back to your stations."

The men climbed into position. They had already agreed on their plan: Marcello and Bastien would attack first, then Roberto and Giovanni would join in. The vehicle came into view, traveling at the maximum speed it could safely navigate the small, winding road. Marcello hurled a grenade at the vehicle the way star pitchers threw baseballs, and the resulting explosion instantly halted the machine's progress. The driver scrambled out and tried to escape, but either Roberto or Giovanni shot him. Bastien also fired a few shots, but his went through the vehicle's canvas cover, so he couldn't tell if he'd hit anyone.

"One car. Hardly worth our time," Marcello said.

Bastien nodded but knew hitting something without taking any losses would at least be good for morale, and maybe someone important was inside.

Marcello covered Bastien as he approached the transport, a Kfz.1 personnel vehicle that reminded him of an American jeep. Bastien took out his flashlight to check inside. The lone occupant lay dead in the rear seat. Bastien gave the corpse a superficial glance before focusing on the leather attaché case on the floor. He grabbed it and stepped to the side of the road to look through the papers, letting the others finish their search of the wreck.

The documents were in German, but Bastien had lived in Germany until he was in his early twenties. He sat and skimmed a letter of introduction. The man they'd shot was on his way to join a German headquarters staff in Rome. He'd somehow earned an Iron Cross during the siege of Leningrad, and his specialty was building fixed defenses, like gun emplacements, bunkers, and mine fields. Bastien was glancing through the man's engineering achievements when Roberto distracted him with a string of Italian profanity.

"You look as if you've seen a ghost, Roberto. What is it?" Marcello asked.

"Look at him." Roberto pointed inside the car.

Marcello examined the corpse with his light, then aimed the beam at Bastien.

Bastien turned away from the glare. "Stop shining that in my eyes."

"Capitano Ley, you didn't leave a twin in Germany, did you?"

"No, of course not."

"Come look at this. He looks just like you."

Bastien rolled his eyes as he got to his feet. He didn't doubt there were plenty of tall German officers with blue eyes and light-brown hair, but that hardly made any of them his twin. Yet as he studied the man's face, Bastien was shocked. It wasn't like looking in the mirror—not exactly—especially with the hole from a .45-inch bullet in the man's temple, but all the same, the resemblance was startling.

The four of them stared at the dead soldier. "Roberto, go keep lookout," Bastien said.

Roberto nodded. As the team's youngest member, he was used to following orders. His eyes flitted between Bastien and the dead German a few more times before he climbed the rise at the side of the road.

"What did the papers say?" Marcello asked.

"You interrupted me before I could finish. He was heading to Rome."

"Returning, or going for the first time?"

"Transferring. Looks like the poor man just recovered from an injury on the Eastern Front. He's an engineer. Probably sent to build up the Gustav Line."

Marcello walked around the car to stand next to Bastien. "So no one in Rome has ever met him before?"

Bastien shrugged. "How should I know?"

"How's your German?"

"Better than my English or my Italian. Why?" But Bastien already had an idea of what Marcello was about to suggest.

"Do you have any idea how valuable it would be to have a plant inside German headquarters in Rome?"

Bastien shook his head. "I'd be dead in two days, Marcello."

Marcello fingered the thin black mustache on his upper lip. "No, I think this could work."

"It's not your neck on the line, is it?" But even as his instincts argued against it, Bastien could see the value in having intimate knowledge of the massive defenses being built to stall the Allied push north. And what other information could a German officer learn? Which convoys to attack? Weaknesses in the supply chain? Battle plans? Impending roundups targeting Italian partisans and the OSS men working with them? *I want to do something more effective than watch Nazi convoys drive by, don't I?* It was a calculated risk; if caught, he'd be killed. But the potential was huge, and in comparison, the value of Bastien's life seemed small. "Find his papers."

Marcello dug through the man's tunic and handed Bastien a pay book and an ancestor pass. Bastien opened the pay book. Adalard Dietrich, the man they'd killed, was an Evangelical Christian, on paper anyway, and had owned a construction company in civilian life. He'd been recently promoted to hauptmann—the same rank as Bastien. He was from Ingolstadt, on the Danube. Bastien had grown up in Frankfurt am Main. He'd only been to Ingolstadt once. He remembered some of the buildings, but if he was really going to do this, he'd need to avoid conversation with any Ingolstadt natives. The eye and hair color were right. *Could this work?*

"He's the wrong blood type," Bastien said.

Marcello chuckled. "So stay out of the hospital."

Bastien looked back at the papers. No wife listed; no minor children. Bastien checked the man's date of birth: 1911, two years earlier than Bastien's. He figured Dietrich wasn't old enough to have any grown children, so that meant he had no family. Dietrich was an inch taller, but would anyone notice? And if they did, would they be suspicious or let it pass as evidence of an overinflated ego? Dietrich's shoe size was listed too—bigger than Bastien's but only by a half size.

The other pages concerned Bastien far more than the minor physical discrepancies. "What do I say if someone asks me about the siege of Leningrad?"

"Curse the Communists, and complain about the weather."

"That will work for two sentences. What do I do after that? And what do I say when someone asks me about the invasion of France?" Dietrich had been at war for years.

Marcello put his hand on Bastien's shoulder. "What you're doing here with us, it could get you killed. Pretending to be him could also get you killed, but you're risking your neck anyway." Marcello tapped Dietrich's pay book. "More danger in Rome, maybe, but think of all you could learn. The other veterans, if they were in Russia, won't want to talk about it. If they weren't there, they won't know anyway. And you read enough about France in the newspapers to know what happened there."

"I don't even know who was in command of which division—this thing could fall apart in seconds."

"What was his injury?" Marcello asked.

Bastien read through the book again. "It doesn't give details. Just says it happened in April."

"You were caught in a fire after a shell burst." Marcello pointed to Bastien's hands. They'd both been burned when Bastien was a child. "You also injured your head, and it affected your memory. Everything before waking up in the hospital is a blur of cold weather and loud Russian rockets."

"How convenient." Bastien glanced through Dietrich's ancestor pass. He had a genealogical record that would make Himmler proud. *So do you*, Bastien reminded himself. *But actions are more important than blood.*

"Look, Capitano, just set yourself up as a quiet man who keeps to himself. That won't involve much pretending." Marcello smoothed his mustache again. "Most people like to talk about themselves, so ask them a few questions and listen. Chances are, they'll keep talking."

"I'm not a real engineer."

Marcello shoved his hands into his pockets. "Maybe the officer who promoted you valued party loyalty over occupational competence."

Bastien had worked on projects with the Army Corps of Engineers during his initial enlistment, then studied architecture for two years before the National Guard called him back and gave him his commission. Would that be enough? He glanced at Marcello. "You really think this could work, don't you?" Bastien pictured himself in Rome, pretending to be a German officer. Then he thought of how quickly he could mess it up. "You're crazy. And this scheme of yours is crazy too."

"So crazy that it just might work?"

"No. So crazy that it's going to get me killed. Maybe if I had a few weeks to prepare, but if I'm going to be Adalard Dietrich, I only have until the next car comes barreling down that road to assume a new identity. I might feel better about it if I could contact headquarters and talk it over with them."

"Anyone with half a brain at your headquarters would tell you to go for it. A chance like this doesn't come along every day. Maybe once a war."

Bastien looked through the papers again. "I'm not supposed to speak Russian or anything, am I?"

"I don't know. I can't read German." Marcello laughed again.

Bastien wondered if he'd still be laughing if their roles were reversed. He stared at Dietrich's pay book. His chances were slim, but what if it did work? The information he would gain could change the course of the war. And Bastien did want to change the war, make it end before he lost another brother. He looked at the scars on his hands as he thought about his family. His mother, two sisters, and youngest brother had depended on him the last eight years. They *wanted* him to return alive, but they didn't *need* him, not anymore. If he died, they would grieve, but they wouldn't starve. And few others would notice his absence. Bastien had little to lose, and the Allies had all of Italy to gain.

"Giovanni, take his clothes off. Check his skin for scars—anything that might explain his injury." Bastien turned to Marcello. "You'll need to hide that body where it will never be found."

Marcello nodded.

"Does the car still work?"

Marcello turned the ignition, but the engine didn't start. Bastien strode to the front of the vehicle and opened the hood. He could see black scorch marks along the engine's right side, and the grenade blast seemed to have repositioned most of the internal parts. He frowned, wondering if he could somehow slide the parts back into proper alignment.

Marcello stepped beside him and waved a hand. "Leave it alone. A broken car works to your advantage. Wait here until the next German patrol comes along, then act like an arrogant officer and demand they take you to Rome."

"And what if some partisans come along and shoot me?"

"We'll stand guard, make sure the initial act in your play goes according to plan."

Bastien walked to the trunk, opened it, and searched through the luggage. He retrieved a clean pair of Dietrich's underwear, because pulling on the dead man's underclothing was more than he was willing to do, and stared at the framed picture of Dietrich in uniform. It could have been a picture of Bastien. He held back a shiver. He had almost ended up in the German Army. Were it not for his father's convictions, Bastien would be fighting on the other side of this war.

Giovanni handed him Dietrich's clothes.

"Did you notice any scars?" Bastien asked.

"No. Maybe he just got sick."

Bastien looked at Dietrich's face one final time. Dietrich's chin wasn't as pointed, but they both had detached ear lobes, the same cheek structure, and similar eyebrows. The resemblance was uncanny. Bastien removed the cord with Dietrich's oval ID tags and placed them around his own neck. He hesitated for an instant before handing Giovanni the dog tags that identified Bastien as a member of the United States Army. "Take these. Get rid of them. And I want Smitty's radio."

Sergeant Smith had parachuted into Italy with Bastien as the team's radio operator. They'd worked together almost a month, until a German patrolman riding a motorcycle had killed Smitty. Bastien wasn't great with the radio, but he'd managed to encode one message and get it to headquarters, and if he discovered anything worthwhile as Adalard Dietrich, he wanted his information to reach the right people.

"You should change," Marcello said. "Then if traffic picks up, you'll be ready. Giovanni, get the radio. We'll deal with the body later."

Marcello went to check on Roberto as Bastien dressed himself in the dead man's uniform. The road sustained only light travel most nights, and Bastien hoped the pattern would hold. He needed more time. The rhythm of his heart seemed loud, and although the night was cool, his skin felt slick with sweat. He knew he had to seize this chance while he could, but it was happening too fast.

Marcello returned, and Bastien handed him his Thompson submachine gun and his Colt pistol. "Roberto gets the tommy gun." The boy had been eying it for weeks. Bastien thought Roberto had probably watched too many Hollywood movies about gangsters, but he knew the weapon would be in good hands. Roberto was young—not yet twenty—but his aim was impressive. Bastien strapped on Dietrich's Luger, then took the pistol out to check the clip.

When he was satisfied with his sidearm, Bastien retrieved the personal letters from Dietrich's bag and skimmed them by flashlight. There were only three, and they were all from his mother. She seemed to write weekly and began each letter with an admonition for her son to write more often. *Perfect, she's not used to hearing from him regularly.* The letters were short, but he picked out that Dietrich's father was dead. *Something else we have in common.*

"I was thinking, Capitano . . ." Something in Marcello's voice made Bastien think the Italian man was about to suggest something he wouldn't like.

"What?"

"You look good for someone who just survived an ambush and a car wreck. There's blood on the back seat of the car but none on you."

Bastien snorted. "You want to shoot me in the arm or something? Bad idea. I'm supposed to stay out of hospitals, remember?"

"I was thinking a bump on the head, a little cut, nothing more. Then you could complain of a headache and maybe have a day to rest before you report for duty. A day to prepare."

Bastien considered it. He didn't want Marcello to whack him in the head, but if it would help their plot . . . "What are you going to hit me with?"

Marcello held up his Sten gun.

"No."

"A torch, then?" Marcello pointed to Bastien's flashlight.

Bastien frowned. "All right."

It took every bit of Bastien's self-control not to flinch when Marcello rammed the flashlight into his forehead.

"Ow! Are you trying to knock me out?" Bastien put his hand to his forehead, although that didn't diminish the sharp ache's intensity.

Marcello pulled out his knife. "Not finished yet. Sit down."

Bastien sat inside the personnel vehicle and closed his eyes. He felt a sting as Marcello's knife bit into his hairline.

"There, just enough to make a mess."

"I hate you."

"No, you don't."

Marcello was right. Bastien didn't really mean it, but he was itching to bash something into his friend's head. It wouldn't contribute to the scheme's success, but it would make him feel better.

Marcello handed Bastien the flashlight and the leather bag with Dietrich's papers. "Someday you'll thank me."

"Don't expect that day to come anytime soon."

Giovanni returned. The radio he carried was in a suitcase, so Bastien pointed to the trunk. "What happened?" Giovanni asked.

"Marcello is getting back at me for all the times I interrupted his drinking. But if you ask him, he'll tell you he's giving me an excuse to look groggy."

Bastien thought he saw smiles on the two Italians' faces as Marcello and Giovanni stowed the radio and went to watch the road. Bastien spent the next few hours going over the papers in Dietrich's attaché case. His head pounded, so eventually, he stretched out on the bloodstained seat and fell asleep.

Marcello woke him before dawn. "A car's coming. We'll wait in case there's trouble, but there won't be. This is going to work. I'll meet you in two days, the bar north of Castel Sant'Angelo. I'll be there all evening. Come when you can." Marcello left, darting across the sunken road and up the bank that bordered it.

As Bastien waited for the German car to reach him, he silently repeated what he'd told himself all night long, at least until he'd dozed off. *My name is Adalard Dietrich. I am a soldier in the Nazi Army, and I am loyal to Adolf Hitler. Bastien Ley no longer exists.*

CHAPTER ONE

February 18, 1944
Switzerland

GRACIE STARED INTO THE FIREPLACE, watching the flames dance along the logs, forcing herself not to fidget.

"He's probably dead."

Gracie glanced across the common area of the luxurious cabin in the Swiss mountains to where American Captain Vaughn-Harris stood by the window, gazing into the snow. Gracie didn't say anything. Vaughn-Harris was talking to Colonel Ambrose, not to her, and he'd already predicted the death of the agent they called Centurion multiple times.

They'd waited all of yesterday and all morning. Ambrose had said they'd wait until nightfall for the agent's arrival, but Gracie was beginning to agree with Vaughn-Harris's pessimism, which was a pity. She'd heard so much about Ambrose's mysterious super-spy that she wanted to meet him. She half expected him to look like Captain America or Superman or one of the other comic book heroes her nephews loved. She tried to picture Clark Kent as a corpse but couldn't see it, so she went back to watching the fire. Agent Centurion would either come as he'd been ordered, or he wouldn't, and there wasn't anything she could do but wait.

She hoped he'd come. If he didn't, she wasn't sure when she'd get another chance for real field work. This was her best shot to really make a difference, to show her mother and everyone else that being smart was better than being beautiful and that her college degree hadn't been a waste. *Not that I'll be able to tell anyone about my assignment if Centurion shows up and I join him in Italy.*

Gracie picked up the Italian-language Swiss paper and skimmed through the articles. The paper was dated February 16, 1944, so it was a few days old, and she'd already heard most of the news on the radio: American Marines fighting in the Marshall Islands, the Red Army capturing large numbers of German soldiers in the Ukraine's Korsun Pocket, continued Allied failure to move north of Cassino and the Gustav Line, and unending hell on the Anzio beachhead, where the Allies had landed in an attempt to bypass the Gustav Line but had instead gotten stuck. *I can help with the fiasco at Anzio if Centurion shows up.*

"Well, I'll be," Captain Vaughn-Harris said. "I owe you dinner, Colonel."

Gracie put her paper down, assuming the agent was in sight if Vaughn-Harris was admitting he'd have to pay up on the bet he'd made with Ambrose over supper the night before. She looked toward the window. Ambrose had joined Vaughn-Harris in front of the glass, so she couldn't see anything from where she sat, but she stayed where she was, not wanting to appear overeager. She wanted the men to think she was professional.

It seemed like an eternity before Ambrose returned to his chair and Vaughn-Harris walked to the door. He waited just inside, his hand inches from his holstered pistol. Gracie wondered about his defensive posture. Centurion was late, but there were guards outside to deal with any security problems.

Two firm knocks sounded on the cabin door, and Vaughn-Harris opened it. A tall man stood in the doorframe, skis balanced on his shoulders, ski poles clutched in one hand. Vaughn-Harris stepped back to let the agent come inside.

"Welcome, Captain Ley. We saved a seat for you by the fire." Ambrose motioned to the empty spot on the sofa next to Gracie.

Ley leaned his ski equipment in the corner behind the door and put the bag strapped to his back and his winter clothing in a wardrobe near the cabin's entrance. His nose and cheeks were red from exposure, but instead of taking the seat between Gracie and the fireplace, he perched himself on the edge of the seat farthest from the fire's warmth, closest to the cabin's exit.

"You remember Captain Vaughn-Harris?" Ambrose asked.

"Yes." Ley's eyes followed Vaughn-Harris as he sat next to Ambrose. Ley was five yards away, but Gracie could pick out the bright blue of his eyes and the dark shadows beneath his lower eyelids.

Ambrose motioned to Gracie. "Agent Graziella Begni, recently arrived in Europe after the usual OSS training. One of the best radio operators I've ever seen."

Ley met her eyes briefly before turning back to Ambrose. *He didn't stare at my birthmark*, she thought with relief. Most people did—it was on her right check, the size of a dime, brown like her eyes. Her father had called it an angel kiss. Gracie had believed him until she'd turned thirteen and overheard her mother and one of her sisters lamenting her marred complexion.

"Did you have any trouble at the border?" Ambrose asked.

"No. I went across on skis."

Gracie added *accomplished skier* and *heavy German accent* to the list of things she was learning about Captain Ley. He pronounced his *W*'s like *V*'s. Ambrose had told her agent Centurion had been born in Germany, and she supposed he wouldn't have survived his current assignment if he didn't still sound German.

"Any chance you're being tailed?"

"No."

"Are you sure?" Captain Vaughn-Harris studied Ley with suspicion.

"Yes. That's why I'm late. It took some time to lose him." Ley gave Vaughn-Harris a less-than-friendly glance and ran a hand through his light-brown hair, still matted down from the stocking cap he'd been wearing when he'd arrived. His *TH* sounded like a *Z*.

"So someone did follow you?" Vaughn-Harris asked.

"Not far."

"Just one tail?"

Ley nodded.

"And what happened to him?"

Ley looked at his hands. They were discolored with patches of what looked like dark-pink scar tissue. "You don't need to worry about him anymore," Ley said. Gracie had run into several men who kept a running total of the Nazis they'd killed. To his credit, Ley was calm about the run-in, but he didn't seem pleased by it.

Vaughn-Harris snorted. "Wonderful. I'm sure disappearing Gestapo agents won't cause any suspicion."

"I'm not the one who requested this meeting," Ley snapped. "He was SD, not Gestapo. I made it look like an accident."

Gracie shivered, even though her seat near the fire was warm. Being followed by someone in the Gestapo sounded bad, but being pursued by someone from Himmler's SS Security Service sounded even worse.

"Well, after your putting us off for two and a half weeks, we're glad you could finally fit a trip to Switzerland in," Vaughn-Harris said.

"The German Army has been a little busy lately," Ley said. "I couldn't ask for leave when it looked like an Allied invasion of Rome was imminent."

"What did you tell your unit?" Ambrose asked.

"I'm on leave for an aunt's funeral. I'm supposed to be somewhere in the Ruhr. I don't know if Hauptmann Dietrich has any aunts, let alone dead ones in the Ruhr, but I don't think anyone else in Italy knows that either, so it should be fine."

Gracie assumed *Hauptmann Dietrich* was the name Ley was going by in Italy. He'd been undercover for months, and Ambrose seemed to think his Centurion could return to Rome and continue the ruse.

"The SD man . . . Do you think you're being investigated?" Ambrose shifted in his seat.

"Possibly."

Ambrose frowned. "So is it safe to send you back?"

"Safe?" One corner of Ley's lips pulled into a smile. "I doubt any of your assignments are *safe*, but I plan to return if you want me to. You certainly need me to. Do you know what the Germans are calling your little beachhead at Anzio? The world's largest self-supporting POW camp. What type of idiot do you have running the invasion?"

Vaughn-Harris's eyes narrowed. "*Captain* Ley, I think you forget yourself. Or maybe you've been out of touch a little too long. Captains don't insult generals, not in our army, anyhow. Perhaps the Germans do it differently, but here you will show respect for your superiors."

"No, the Germans don't insult their incompetent generals; they relieve them. Which is what you should have done—any green second lieutenant with the right intelligence could have done better at Anzio."

"General Lucas didn't have the right intelligence," Vaughn-Harris hissed through his teeth.

"I told you the Germans weren't ready to counterattack. But instead of pushing on to better ground while there was time, your commander holed up on the beach, and now he's stuck there, surrounded by German artillery focused in from the Alban Hills—the high ground your commander had plenty of time to take *before* the Germans regrouped and counterattacked."

Vaughn-Harris stood and started pacing. "Your message of January twenty-seventh included an incorrect security check. We couldn't be sure you hadn't been turned, so we couldn't trust it or any subsequent reports. Perhaps you remember. The word was *counterattack*."

Ley's eyes followed a few of Vaughn-Harris's strides. "Last I checked, counterattack ends with a *CK* and has three *T*'s, not two."

"Oh, you mangled the spelling sufficiently," Vaughn-Harris said. "But you were instructed to misspell one word in each message and were told to choose the word based on the date your message was sent. *Counterattack* was, in fact, the twenty-sixth word of your message, not the twenty-seventh."

Ley's jaw went slack for an instant. "You've ignored three weeks' worth of messages and let our army get trapped on the beach because my misspelling was off by one day?"

"No, *you* let our army get trapped on the beach because *your* misspelling was off by one day."

Gracie was shocked. Agents made coding errors all the time. A simple error like the one Ley had made should have resulted in a few follow-up questions, not in discarded messages.

Ley frowned, and his eyes narrowed. "When I sent that message, I hadn't slept since the twenty-fifth."

"Yes, it's no doubt a challenge to be a full-time German soldier and a part-time American spy." Vaugh-Harris slowed his pacing, his words sympathetic but his tone patronizing. "Which is why you will take Agent Begni with you when you return to your post so she can handle your reports and ensure you don't make the same mistakes again."

Gracie did her best not to flinch as Ley's glare shifted from Vaughn-Harris to her. She didn't think Ley had known why she was in the room until that moment, and he didn't seem pleased.

Ley turned back to Vaughn-Harris, his voice calm but cold. "I have enough to do without babysitting one of your rookie radio operators."

CHAPTER TWO

BABYSITTING? GRACIE WAS TWENTY-THREE YEARS old—she was hardly a child anymore. She'd managed to graduate near the top of her class from both Brigham Young University and a tough OSS training program. Her eyes narrowed as Ley looked at her and automatically dismissed her as a liability. She was about to say something in her defense, but Vaughn-Harris spoke instead.

"You will follow orders, Captain Ley, or I'll have to start questioning your loyalty."

"The Nazis murdered my father, remember? I'd be the last person on earth to assist them."

Vaughn-Harris's face pulled into a sneer. "You might not intentionally aid them, but your incompetence when it comes to coding your reports has helped them whether you meant it to or not."

"Incompetence? I suppose that's an easy accusation to make from behind a desk. It's a bit of a different story in the field—"

"That's enough," Colonel Ambrose said.

Ley looked toward the window, his face drawn into a scowl. "Why did you bring him, sir? We always butt heads. You know that."

"That's just as much your fault as it is his. I have good reasons for selecting all the men I have working for me." Ambrose paused and turned toward Gracie. "And the women too."

Ley studied Gracie again, his face calm instead of angry. Then he turned to Ambrose. "Sir, I'd prefer to send in my own reports as I've done in the past. I'll double-check my work and triple-check the calendar. I've sent in dozens of reports without errors, haven't I? I'll just be a little more cautious."

"Caution from you will mean reduced speed, and that would make it easier for the Gestapo to find you. You're much too valuable to put behind a radio. From now on, you'll give your reports to Agent Begni. She'll encode them for you and send us the information."

Ley sighed. "With all due respect, sir, I don't think that will work."

"Why not?" Ambrose asked. "I think it will work splendidly."

Ley glanced at Gracie. "You're just shifting part of the risk from me to her. That's not improving the situation. Throwing another agent into the mix will just complicate things."

"Actually, since her radio skills are vastly better than yours, I'm not just shifting the risk; I'm reducing it."

"I don't like working with strangers."

Ambrose looked from Ley to Gracie. "You have the evening to become better acquainted. And I can fill you in on the important things. As I already mentioned, she's the best radio operator I've ever seen."

"But does she have any experience?"

Gracie did her best to meet Ley's eyes as he evaluated her. "This is my first assignment, Captain Ley, but I can promise you I'm ready."

"Oh? And what makes you think you're ready, Miss Begni?"

"I've had the normal training, of course."

Ley's eyes seemed to laugh at her. "Field work is different from training."

"Her OSS instructors gave her high marks, Captain. And don't underestimate her intelligence. She was second in her class at Brigham Young University," Ambrose said.

"And what did you study there, Miss Begni? Home economics? Fashion?"

"Mathematics." Gracie noted a bit of surprise in Ley's eyes as she responded and maybe a touch of respect. *Good.* She was tired of his hints that he didn't want or need her. She'd worked hard for her degree and even harder to follow her father's suggestion that she score higher than any class-mate who doubted a woman could succeed in a male-dominated field.

"At least she has a college degree," Vaughn-Harris said.

The muscles in Ley's jaw hardened. "I'd have a college degree too if the National Guard hadn't asked me to return to duty. Or do you think I should have asked my father to use his influence so I could sit out the war while I completed my education?"

Vaughn-Harris glared at Ley, but then his eyes relaxed and his lips turned into a smirk. "At least I have a father. What happened to yours again? Captured by the Gestapo and slaughtered like an animal?"

Ley flinched.

Gracie held back a gasp, surprised that Vaughn-Harris would say something so cruel. She understood a little of Ley's pain. "What were you studying, Captain Ley?" she blurted out, hoping to distract him. His left hand was balled into a fist, and Vaughn-Harris's arrogant grin was practically begging for a few jabs.

Ley turned to her, a confused look on his face, but his hand slowly relaxed. "Architecture." He paused, his eyes downcast. "Miss Begni, you no doubt have a knack for mathematics and codes, and you've just shown yourself capable of diffusing tense situations, but how do you plan on surviving in Fascist Italy?"

"I was born in Italy. I lived there until I was eleven."

"Where?"

"Nettuno."

Captain Ley's foot began to bounce up and down rapidly while he considered her answer. "And after you left Italy, where did you settle?"

"Salt Lake City, Utah."

One corner of his lips pulled down. "And then you attended BYU?"

"Yes."

Ley pinched the bridge of his nose as if he were in pain. "What on earth is a good little Mormon girl like you doing in Switzerland with a trio of OSS officers? Go back to Utah, Miss Begni."

Gracie felt her mouth hang open. Had Ley really just ordered her home? And wasn't it a bit presumptuous of him to assume she was a good little Mormon girl? He was right, but she didn't like that he'd jumped to that conclusion based on her answers to two questions. She forced her lips together and inhaled deeply before speaking, her words clipped and precise with anger. "There's a war on, Captain Ley. I'm in Europe because I want to help end it. And I'm in Switzerland because you're going to take me to Italy so I can make sure your information gets to the right people without any mixed-up security checks."

His jaw hardened when she mentioned the security check, but she didn't care. It may have been an easy mistake, but it was one she wouldn't make, and he obviously needed help, even if he didn't want to admit it. "What makes you think you can survive in Italy if you can't even get in by yourself?" Ley asked.

Gracie wasn't sure how to reply, but Ambrose spoke up again. "This isn't just about your information. The Gestapo arrested some of our people in

Rome recently, including a radio operator. There are still two members of the cell gathering information. When you arrive in Rome, Agent Begni will find them and turn in their reports as well as yours."

"Why do I have to smuggle her in? Can't you drop her off by parachute?" Ley sat back in his chair and folded his arms, still tapping his foot so quickly that it was almost a vibration.

"Are you saying you're incapable of smuggling her in?" Vaughn-Harris returned to his seat, a smug smile on his face.

"More brave words from an armchair warrior?"

Vaughn-Harris stood and took a few threatening steps toward Ley. Gracie didn't even try to distract them—she had no idea what to say, and she now thought both of them deserved a good blow to the face.

"Captain Vaughn-Harris," Colonel Ambrose said. "Perhaps it's time for a few drinks."

Vaughn-Harris gave Ley a final glare before walking over to the bar. He poured something for Ambrose and turned to Ley. "Something to drink?"

"No."

"Take it," Ambrose ordered.

Vaughn-Harris filled a shot glass with amber liquid and placed it on the small table next to Ley, but Ley didn't touch it, Gracie assumed out of spite. Vaughn-Harris handed her a bottle of soda, then poured something significantly stronger for himself.

"Even if I manage to get Miss Begni and myself back into Italy without blowing our cover, how am I supposed to explain my sudden, frequent contact with an Italian civilian?"

"She can pose as your mistress," Vaughn-Harris said.

Ley's foot stopped moving. "You plan to have a good little Mormon girl play a woman of loose morals? I think that's a bit of a stretch."

Ambrose sighed as if weary of arguing. "Mistress, girlfriend—I don't care how you define it or how serious you make it appear, but a romantic relationship is a simple, believable solution." The colonel waved toward the stairs. "Go ahead and show him the wardrobe we picked out for you."

Gracie stood and walked past the two captains and up the stairs to her room in the loft. She tried to shake off the sting Ley's words had left. He didn't want her. She knew she shouldn't be surprised; no one ever wanted her. No one except her father and Michael and a few OSS men—but the OSS recruiter and Colonel Ambrose didn't really count. They didn't want her, just her talents.

She slipped out of the sapphire-blue dress cut to emphasize her chest instead of her hips, frowning as she remembered all the effort her elegant, refined mother had spent trying to make Gracie look more like her petite older sisters. *This dress will help camouflage those hips, Graziella. Don't pull your hair back, Graziella. It makes your birthmark stand out.* She had always been too tall and too curvy, but maybe here, away from the other women in her family, Gracie wouldn't seem so far from graceful.

She dug through her luggage, glad her mother was on the other side of the world, where she'd never see the bland black rags OSS had provided to help Gracie look like an impoverished Italian civilian desperate enough to become a German officer's consort.

Her old boyfriend had described her mother and sisters as fragile wraiths. She smiled, remembering his feigned surprise that they hadn't blown away with the napkins during a picnic with her family. Michael was the only person who'd ever made her feel beautiful, and she missed him. She blinked away a tear as she rearranged her hair. The last thing she needed was to get all weepy and give Ley or the other men the impression that she'd been upstairs crying.

She pulled on her least favorite outfit, deciding she might as well get used to it. If Ley thought she looked too wholesome to date a Nazi, the dress's neckline would prove him wrong. *It's not that low,* she told herself as she glanced in the mirror. But she still wished the OSS officer in charge of her wardrobe hadn't laughed at her when she'd suggested altering it.

Ambrose and Ley were talking about the weather forecast as she came down the stairs. She almost laughed that they were discussing such a trivial subject until she realized how relevant it was.

"If you can't get us in by air, which looks like the case, we'll have to take the train," Ley said. "I'd prefer to travel at night."

"Why?" Vaughn-Harris asked.

Ley jerked his head toward Gracie, who was descending the final half of the stairs. "She's not exactly nondescript, is she? Tall, gorgeous, dynamite legs, and a birthmark that looks like a thumbprint on her right cheek? There can't be many women who meet that description, and I don't want someone reporting her departure from Switzerland and linking it to her arrival in Rome."

Gracie paused, one foot on the bottom step. She would have been flattered by Ley's description if his tone hadn't been so condescending. When he said *dynamite legs*, he probably meant tubular and shaped like a stick of TNT.

"Do you ski, Miss Begni?" Ley asked.

Gracie returned to her spot on the sofa before answering. "Not as well as you do, I imagine. I've done some downhill skiing but not much cross-country." She straightened the neckline of her dress but pulled the fabric in so it wouldn't slip off her shoulders and hang lower in the front. She hated the dress and was beginning to regret wearing it just to prove a point to Ley.

"That leaves us with the train or a car. Or a combination."

"I'm sure you'll figure out something by tomorrow evening," Ambrose said.

Ley frowned but didn't disagree.

The men all seemed more relaxed now—Gracie wondered if the alcohol had done the trick, but Ley's glass still looked untouched. She adjusted her dress again.

"Miss Begni, may I give you a few tips?" Ley asked.

Gracie nodded.

"More lipstick and more fabric."

Gracie wasn't sure what Ley meant, but Vaughn-Harris asked for clarification before she had to. "What's wrong with her dress? Have conditions in Italy improved so dramatically over the past few months? Do all the women have new clothes now?"

"There's nothing wrong with the dress or its well-worn appearance. The problem is *her* in that dress. She hasn't stopped fiddling with the neckline since she sat down. It's obviously cut lower than she's comfortable with, and if I can tell, a Gestapo agent would notice too. Get her some different clothes. Have her smear on an extra layer of makeup if you want her to look the part."

Gracie felt a strange mix of gratitude that she might not have to wear such skimpy clothing and embarrassment that her discomfort had been so obvious.

"Or better yet, I can go back alone. She may be smart, but I don't think she's up to playing the role."

The gratitude vanished. "What is wrong with you?" she asked, her hands flying up in her anger. "You need help, and I'm willing to help you, and you're acting like I'm some ball and chain instead of an asset. Those men on the beach need information, and I can make sure that information is delivered accurately." She forced her hands back to her lap, even though she really wanted to adjust her neckline again.

Ley leaned forward. "Miss Begni, I am reluctant to bring you with me because despite your talk of assets, you still seem more of a liability. You may be able to operate a radio, but I've yet to see evidence that you can act. If you're arrested as a spy and I'm associated with you, I'll have a very difficult time not joining you in front of the firing squad."

"I can act. And I'll stop playing with my dress since that has you so worried."

Ley huffed. "Fiddling with that dress is the least of your problems. Everything about you screams wholesome religious American. Have you even been kissed before?"

Gracie ran her left thumb along the inside of her ring finger. There wasn't a ring there, not anymore. "Yes, I've been kissed before, Captain Ley. But I don't see how that's any of your business."

Ley stood and walked over to her, holding a hand out. She took his hand and let him pull her to her feet. "Let me guess. Something like this?" He leaned forward and pressed his lips to hers for a few brief moments.

When he pulled away, she could still feel the imprint of his mouth. Surprised but remembering his question, she nodded. Ley's kiss had been a lot like Michael's: soft, sweet, and affectionate.

"In Italy, if you're pretending to be my girlfriend, I'll be kissing you often but not like that. Like this."

He slipped one hand to the back of her neck, the other to her waist, and pulled her close for another kiss. She was startled at first but soon realized she didn't want to resist. His lips were insistent and inviting, making her heart race. She was glad when Ley's hand moved from her waist to the center of her back, because her legs were starting to feel unstable. She wanted to fall into him, into his kiss. The way he maneuvered his mouth over hers was making her lose all sense of place and time, and she found herself wishing he'd never stop. When he began to pull away, she wanted to lean her head on his chest and catch her breath, but then she remembered she'd just met Ley and wasn't even sure she liked him.

She took a step back, staring at him, wondering what had just happened.

"You see, that won't do at all," Ley said. "The Gestapo will be all over you. You're acting like you've never been kissed before."

Gracie sat on the sofa, her eyes still fixed on Ley. She hadn't ever been kissed like that.

"I thought it was convincing," Ambrose said. "You have your orders, Captain Ley. As long as Agent Begni is willing to go, you are required to take her."

CHAPTER THREE

Bastien paced the floor of his room in the cabin. It was over Captain Vaughn-Harris's, so he didn't bother avoiding the squeaky board in the center as he analyzed the day's events.

He wished he had thought up an excuse to postpone the meeting and stay in Italy. *I could refuse to go back.* There had been that SD man tailing him—sufficient reason to assume his cover was shaky. Two and a half months was a good enough run, wasn't it?

Bastien thought of his little brother. Lukas would finish high school in a few months, and after graduation, he wanted to join the Air Corps and become a pilot. More than anything, Bastien wanted the war to end before Lukas finished his training, and there were few ways Bastien could contribute more usefully to the war effort than by going back to his life as Hauptmann Dietrich. Bastien was just one man, and he had no illusions that his work would dramatically turn the course of the war, but the military intelligence he gathered and the tips he passed to the partisans were significant. He was more effective and influential as Hauptmann Dietrich than he could ever be as Captain Ley. Bastien had said countless prayers pleading for a way to help his brother. He couldn't very well walk away now that God had given him this chance.

He didn't want to take Miss Begni with him. He trusted Ambrose's assessment of her intellect and radio skills. He'd tested her Italian that evening, and she sounded like a native, but even if she managed to play a convincing Italian civilian—in love with him, of all people—he still didn't want her.

In his high-stakes world, Bastien had to be ruthless. If Marcello or Roberto or Giovanni were ever arrested and there was no realistic chance of helping them, Bastien wouldn't hesitate to act the part of a Nazi soldier in their execution. And he knew Marcello would do the same—both would maintain their cover or their freedom at any cost, even if it meant turning on a friend who could no longer be saved.

Bastien didn't want to take a woman into that world. There were female partisans, of course, but that was different. Their country had been taken over by Fascists—first by Mussolini, then by Hitler. Bastien suspected Miss Begni didn't have a clue what she was volunteering for or what sacrifices she'd be forced to make as she lived a lie. *Why is she so insistent on coming?* He tried to shrug off the other thing that was bothering him: the way Miss Begni reminded him of Julie.

Your first chance in four months to sleep without worrying about the Gestapo, and you're worrying about women instead? Bastien sighed and walked to the bed. When he pulled back the covers, he realized there was only one thin blanket. Logs were piled in the fireplace and matches lay on the mantel, but a roaring fire wouldn't help him sleep.

He quietly opened his bedroom door. The other men had been sitting in the main room when Bastien excused himself a few hours ago, but the room was empty now. Ambrose and Vaughn-Harris had the two larger bedrooms on the main level, and Bastien had been assigned the middle of the three rooms in the loft. He assumed Miss Begni was in the far room, with the guards sharing the room at the top of the stairs. Perhaps the guards had spare blankets.

Bastien knocked softly on the door, expecting one of the off-duty men to answer. He waited for perhaps half a minute, and then the door opened, revealing Miss Begni wrapped in a robe, with her black hair falling loose across her shoulders.

He took a step back. "I'm sorry. I thought you were in another room."

"If you're looking for Captain Vaughn-Harris, his room is down there." She waved her hand toward the stairs.

"Why would I be looking for him?"

She folded her arms and shrugged. "I thought you might want to finish your argument in private. It was fairly obvious the two of you wanted to take a few swings at each other this afternoon. What happened between you two?"

Bastien ignored her question. "I think it would show poor sportsmanship on my part if I were to slug an inebriated man half a head shorter than me. I was actually planning to ask the guards if they had any spare blankets. Sorry to disturb you, Miss Begni."

"I have extra blankets." She left the door open and walked back into her room. She pulled several blankets from a wooden chest pushed beneath the window and brought them to him.

"Thank you for the blankets, Miss Begni."

"Most people call me Gracie."

"Gracie, then."

She seemed to be waiting for something. "What's your given name, Captain Ley?" she finally asked.

"In Italy, I'll be Hauptmann Dietrich. I suppose we'll soon pretend we're on good enough terms that you'll usually call me Adalard."

"But what's your real name?"

Bastien tucked the blankets under his arm. "If you don't know my real name, you won't accidentally use it in the field."

She scowled at him and placed a hand on her hip.

Bastien remembered Ambrose's instructions. As long as Gracie was willing to go, he had to take her. But what if he could convince her to withdraw? "You've never been in the field?"

"No," she said. "But I've had all the training."

"Training is different. How will your conscience react to lying all the time?"

"That's part of being a spy. I'm prepared for it."

"Oh? And what if you have to kill someone?"

She hesitated. "I've read enough about what the Nazis are doing to consider it justified, if it's required during the course of our mission."

Bastien stepped toward her, deliberately trying to intimidate her. "And have you heard what the Gestapo will do if they catch you?"

She looked away, and he thought he saw a hint of fear in her downcast eyes and tensed shoulders. "One of the instructors went over their likely techniques, yes."

He leaned in even closer. He was so near that if she moved her hands like she normally did while she spoke, she'd bump into him. "The reality is much worse than anything they talk about in the classroom. The stuff of nightmares, Miss Begni. Go back to Utah."

She stiffened, glaring up at him. "If you're trying to scare me, it won't work. I'm coming with you, even if you don't want my help. Good night, Captain Ley." She closed the door firmly in his face.

Bastien returned to his own room and spread the blankets on his bed. The night's attempt to convince Gracie to stay behind may have failed, but he had another day to change her mind. He still wasn't sure why she wanted to go to Italy, but he'd learned enough. She was nervous about the possibility of killing someone and was worried about the Gestapo's interrogation techniques. He had until the next evening to play on her fears.

CHAPTER FOUR

GRACIE SLAMMED A NEW CLIP into the P 38 pistol, pinching a bit of skin in the process. She shook her fingers, trying to fling the pain away. Captain Ley reached for her hand and examined it, then turned it over and studied her fingernails.

"You know, sometimes Gestapo guards like to rip out a prisoner's fingernails during interrogation." Ley released her hand. "It hasn't happened to me yet, but I hear it's quite painful."

"I'm sure it is." Gracie took the pistol in her right hand and aimed for the bull's-eye on the target strapped to a tree. They'd been at their makeshift firing range for an hour. Ley had insisted she dismantle, reassemble, load, and fire half a dozen rifles, machine pistols, and light machine guns. He scrutinized each move she made as if hoping she'd mess up. She hadn't hit the center of the target on each shot, but she was close enough that he hadn't yet criticized her marksmanship.

"The Lord gave you two hands and two eyes, Miss Begni. Use all of them to aim your pistol."

Gracie gripped the pistol with both hands and fired a few shots at the target.

"Of course," Ley continued, "the Gestapo has been known to blind its prisoners." He brushed a finger across her cheek, under her eye. "How would you like to go through the rest of your life blind, Gracie? Or should I start calling you Concetta?"

Gracie smacked his hand away. She didn't like her new alias, and she didn't like the confusion his fingers and lips both seemed to stir up whenever they came in contact with her skin. "I know what you're trying to do, Captain Ley, and it won't work. I have a healthy fear of the Gestapo—I'd be a fool not to. But despite that fear, I'm going to Italy. If you'd rather stay behind, so be it. You aren't the only agent in Rome who needs me."

"And when the Gestapo beats you until your bones are broken and your blood is staining the floor, what then?"

Gracie swallowed back a shudder. "They'll have to catch me first, won't they?"

"I think I heard somewhere that the average radio operator lasts six weeks. Some last only days."

"Well, if the average is six weeks and some last less, some must last longer." Surely with her thorough training and natural abilities, she had a better-than-normal chance of surviving until the Allies reached Rome.

Ley chuckled. "Don't assume you'll be the one to go beyond the average."

"Are we finished here?" Gracie gestured toward the weapons. "I passed all my OSS firearms training. Have I passed your tests as well?"

Ley picked up the P 38 and smoothly reloaded the clip. "We're done shooting, yes. But I want to make sure you're aware of all the risks involved in this assignment. The Third Reich is heavily dependent on slavery. Some of the slaves are petty criminals; others are political dissidents or members of the wrong race. But the Nazis aren't picky. When they need workers, I've seen them round up ordinary civilians. They ship the men off to dig trenches or work in a factory and force the women to cook or wash laundry—or work in a brothel. I know a little of your background, Gracie, and I want you to be fully aware of the possibilities. Even without anyone suspecting you, the Nazis might pick you up. And they wouldn't send you to work in the kitchen or the laundry. Nor is the Gestapo above raping their female prisoners. Do you fully understand what could happen to you in Italy?"

Gracie knew the Gestapo could be positively fiendish, but she chose not to dwell on the worst that could happen. She planned to be careful, and if things took a wrong turn, she was just as likely to be killed as captured. Listening to Ley, she thought being killed might be preferable. "I'll expect the worst from the Gestapo should things end badly. In the meantime, I want your word that you won't take advantage of our cover story."

"Take advantage of our cover story?"

"I understand the need to pretend we're in a relationship, but I don't want it to go beyond the necessary show of affection." Gracie had been nervous when Ley had knocked on her door the night before, then was relieved that he only wanted blankets.

"Miss Begni, I promise I will never kiss you unless there's a high probability of someone seeing us. Nor will I expect us to have joint sleeping arrangements."

Gracie was relieved but surprised that he'd given his consent so easily. She couldn't get his kiss from the day before out of her head. Hadn't he enjoyed it? Or was she so inexperienced that he'd found their moment bland?

She turned to go back to the cabin. As she walked away, she heard Ley emptying the P 38's clip. She glanced at the target on the tree a few yards beyond the one she'd been aiming at. Each of his shots had hit the bull's-eye.

Show-off.

Captain Vaughn-Harris was watching from the window when she returned. He nodded a greeting. "Did you run out of ammunition?"

"No, but we're finished."

Vaughn-Harris smirked. "He's something else, isn't he?"

Something else? Yeah: arrogant, irritating, and confusing. Gracie wasn't going to gossip about her new partner with someone who obviously didn't like him, but she wasn't above asking a few leading questions. "Have you known each other long?"

Another burst of small arms fire sounded. Gracie wondered if Ley had hit the bull's-eye again.

"Since our initial OSS training," Vaughn-Harris said.

"Why don't you two get along?"

"He's not the most likeable person. Rude, haughty, thinks he's better than everyone else. On a more personal note, we were both engaged to marry the same woman—my wife now. He's a sore loser."

Colonel Ambrose stepped into the cabin's common room. "I seem to remember you two having troubles long before Annie."

Vaughn-Harris flushed slightly.

"It's almost time to leave," Ambrose said.

Vaughn-Harris nodded and went to his room.

The colonel turned to Gracie. "Just remember there are two sides to every story, Graziella. I suppose it's time for you to gather your things."

"Yes, sir." Gracie walked to the stairs but lingered on the second step. "Why is Captain Vaughn-Harris here?" Ambrose was giving the orders, Ley and Gracie were receiving them, and Vaughn-Harris seemed like an unnecessary complication.

Ambrose smiled. "Two reasons. I need someone with luxurious taste to find me the best available liquor. And Captain Ley's assignment is difficult. No one could blame him for not returning to what, in all likelihood, will end in an unpleasant death. But I want his information, and I didn't think he'd back down in front of Vaughn-Harris." The colonel winked at her. He seemed to have a knack for reading people, and Gracie wondered how well he understood her. Did he accept her stated desire to serve her new country? Gracie sincerely wanted to help the war effort, but she was also running away—away from her mother's expectations, away from the twin tragedies that had shattered her hope and security. Did Ambrose know?

She went upstairs and finished packing, then stared out the window, wondering if she was making a mistake. A knock sounded on her door, and when she opened it, Captain Ley stood in the hallway.

"Are you ready, Miss Begni?"

"Yes," she said, hoping her voice wouldn't betray how nervous she was.

Ley's blue eyes locked with hers. "Miss Begni, you're a very intelligent woman. Your Italian is excellent, your marksmanship competent, and your radio skills no doubt outstanding. Will you please reconsider risking your lovely neck?"

Gracie shrugged off his compliments, certain they'd been given in an attempt to manipulate her. "I'm not going to back out, Captain."

"Why not? Because you're stubborn? Concern over what others think is a poor reason to sneak behind enemy lines. If you refuse, the only people who might think less of you are Ambrose and Vaughn-Harris, and their opinions aren't worth dying for."

Gracie felt her temper flaring. "I'm not doing this to gain their approval."

"Then why are you doing this?"

"Because I want to help end the war."

Ley crossed his arms. "You could help end the war in a different capacity. Rome isn't the only place you can serve."

"I won't be withdrawing from this assignment, Captain Ley."

"I wish you would, Miss Begni," he whispered.

Gracie put a hand on her hip. "Most of us don't always get what we want."

Ley sighed. "No, we most certainly don't." He looked beyond her to the suitcases on her bed. "Are your things ready?"

"Yes."

Ley stepped past her to her luggage. At first she was impressed, thinking he would carry her things downstairs for her.

"Is this the radio?" He pointed to the smaller of the two suitcases.

She nodded, and he proceeded to open and check everything inside.

Ley ran his fingers over the transmitter, receiver, and power source. "An SSTR-1?"

"Yes."

"Have you used it before?"

Gracie forced herself not to roll her eyes. "Of course."

"No modifications?"

"No." It was a standard Strategic Services Transmitter Receiver Number 1.

"Good. We can share spare parts, if necessary." Ley closed the suitcase containing the radio and reached for the second piece of luggage. "These are your personal things?"

Gracie nodded again.

Ley opened her suitcase, found the secret compartment, and checked her two handguns and the transposition keys printed on silk handkerchiefs.

"You encode with double transposition?" he asked.

"Yes." Messages encrypted with double transposition were like word scrambles but with several hundred characters. They were hard to break without the key, especially if the encoder used a different key for each message.

"And I suppose you have some type of security check?"

"Yes, but in training, we were told not to share it."

Ley replaced her weapons and her handkerchiefs. "I'm not asking you to share it with me. I just want to make sure you remember it."

Gracie bit her tongue to keep from speaking out loud. *Of course I remember my security check.* Before scrambling the letters of her report, she was to add dummy letters in the third, fourteenth, fifteenth, ninety-second, and, if the message was long enough, six hundred fifty-third slots. The positions were based on the value of π so they'd be easy for her to remember. If forced to transmit under duress, she could remove the extra letters and anyone reading her transmission would know it couldn't be trusted.

Ley closed the secret compartment in her suitcase and, to Gracie's horror, started going through her clothing. He unfolded most of the items, then refolded them and set them on the bed.

"What are you doing?" she asked.

"Making sure nothing inside will attract the wrong kind of attention."

Gracie glared at him, but he wasn't paying attention to her. "OSS carefully selected each of those items."

Ley grunted but didn't stop his inspection.

Gracie crossed her arms, her anger rising each time he lifted out another piece of her clothing. "I think that's enough," she said when her luggage was nearly emptied. Her underclothing was at the bottom of the suitcase, and she didn't want him handling it.

He didn't stop. When he reached her underwear, he examined it just as he'd examined all her blouses, skirts, and dresses. "OSS approved this? It looks awfully new."

Gracie's face felt hot, and she thought it was probably red too. "No one will inspect my underwear while we're in Rome."

"We can hope such an intimate inspection will never occur, but there's no guarantee. Miss Begni, you can't let yourself slip up on even the smallest detail when you're pretending to be someone you aren't. I assume OSS gave you more appropriate underclothing. Where is it?"

Gracie stomped over to the chest of drawers and opened the top one. The underwear was inside, old, discolored, and obviously used. The thought of putting it on made her skin crawl.

"Pack it."

Gracie folded her arms. "No one will check my underwear, and if they do, I'll tell them my German boyfriend pulled a few strings and got newer items for me."

"I won't be your boyfriend for a few days at least. And just because I'm an officer doesn't mean I can pull off miracles."

"You're being ridiculous. And rude. And improper. You shouldn't be looking through my things in the first place." Gracie shut the drawer with a firm thud.

Ley grabbed her almost-new underwear, walked over to the fireplace, and threw the panties into the fire.

Gracie's jaw dropped. "How dare you!"

"If you want to come to Rome, Miss Begni, you will have to deal with every aspect of espionage, even the unpleasant ones."

Gracie shook her head. She couldn't believe he'd burned her underwear. Didn't he know how hard it was to get new clothing? He probably did but didn't care. If she hadn't known how badly he wanted her to quit, she would have considered it. Someone as rude as him was the last person she wanted to work with.

"What are you wearing under that dress?" Ley asked.

"That's none of your business."

Ley exhaled deeply. "Actually, since we're working together, everything about you, including each item of your clothing, is my business. If you'd rather not continue this inspection, feel free to withdraw from the mission." He strode to the chest of drawers, brushed her to the side, and handed her an old bra and a pair of panties. "Change into these. I'll be back in five minutes."

Gracie had never wanted to hit someone so badly before, but she refrained from a physical assault. That was beneath her dignity, and Ley was well over six feet tall and looked like he was made of solid muscle. She tried a verbal onslaught instead. "Captain Ley, you are the rudest, most insufferable man I've ever met. No wonder your former fiancée chose Captain Vaughn-Harris instead of you."

She'd hoped her words would sting, but Captain Ley laughed. "Allotment Annie? She had a goal to be married by winter. Vaughn-Harris is just upset that I was her first target and that I was relieved instead of jealous when he told me they'd married a few weeks after I left for Europe. Five minutes, Miss Begni."

When Ley shut the door behind him, Gracie threw the underwear after him in frustration. Dressing like a pauper would be infinitely easier than pretending she was in love with *him*.

CHAPTER FIVE

As THE TRAIN BEGAN ITS ascent through the Gotthard Pass, Bastien left the compartment he shared with three other German officers and walked to the dining car. Gracie wasn't there, so he checked the other cars. They'd both purchased tickets and boarded the train at the same station but at different times. As was expected of a German officer, Bastien had purchased a first-class ticket. After giving her a final opportunity to withdraw from the mission, he'd suggested she purchase a coach fare. It wasn't very chivalrous, and Colonel Ambrose had no doubt given her enough cash for a more expensive ticket, but Gracie needed to play her role, and an Italian civilian in well-worn clothing would blend in best while sitting in third-class.

He hoped she'd backed out before boarding, but he continued his search and finally found her in the last compartment before the luggage car. She met his eyes for an instant before turning toward the blacked-out window. They weren't supposed to have met yet, so she was acting appropriately, but he wondered if it was playacting or her anger that had prompted her to look away.

Bastien continued to the rear of the train before going back to his sleeper. By the time he passed her again, she had pulled the collar of her jacket up so it covered more of her neck, and her arms were wrapped tightly around her body. OSS had outfitted her for Rome, not for the Alps during winter. The compartment was heated but not very thoroughly. He felt guilty walking to his superior accommodations while she shivered the night away sitting on an old bench crowded with strangers.

It's her decision, he reminded himself. He'd done his best to make her say no. He'd tried to shock her with a kiss, scare her with stories of the Gestapo, irritate her with endless target practice, and infuriate her with his wardrobe check. He felt he'd succeeded in drawing out each desired response, but none had been enough to make her quit.

Bastien lay on his bed, hoping the movement of the train would lull him to sleep as it left Switzerland for Italy. He felt a hint of regret as Gracie crossed his mind again. He hadn't meant to kiss her that thoroughly, but something about her and her lips had created a momentary lapse in his judgment. The confusion and vulnerability he'd seen in her face just after stung his conscience. He'd tried to provoke several emotions, but he hadn't meant to toy with her heart.

* * *

Bastien and Gracie switched trains inside the Italian border early the next morning. Bastien walked around the platform, pretending to stretch his legs as he made sure Gracie was in the right place.

Winter weather had slowed traffic on the Brenner Pass between Italy and Austria, making the Gotthard Pass through Switzerland busier than usual. Axis trains sent through Switzerland were supposed to contain no weapons and generally brought coal south and slaves north. With the heavy traffic on the rail system, less important trains were often forced to side tracks to make way for trains with more vital supplies. Bastien passed one such sidetracked train, its cars locked and guarded by members of the SS, and recognized its human cargo.

The prisoners' hands were jammed into the cracks between the doors and thrust through the mesh covering the small windows. Bastien could hear their pleas in haunting Italian, begging for water. The Nazis frequently rounded up Jews, Gypsies, and Communists and sent them to camps. They gathered up other civilians too, sometimes bribing them with the promise of work or cigarettes, other times simply taking them. The car looked like a forty-and-eight boxcar—meant to transport forty humans or eight horses. Usually, far more than forty people were shoved inside, leaving the passengers with insufficient room to even sit down.

The SS guards ignored the requests. The Nazis often locked people in trains for days with no food or water; they did it to POWs, to civilians, and to undesirables. Bastien had long ago concluded that the best thing he could do for Italian civilians was help the Allies break out of Anzio and kick the Nazis back into Germany, so even though he wanted to help the unfortunates on the train, he fully intended to walk past and do nothing.

An elderly Italian woman, her gray hair showing under the black scarf she wore on her head, approached the train. She had a bag slung over her shoulder, and she reminded Bastien of his grandmother, the one his family had lived with when his father had gone away to war. Bastien had no memories of his father prior to his sixth birthday. His grandmother had been the one who had taught him to tie his shoes, spell his name, weed the garden, and do a hundred other things.

The woman opened her bag and handed potatoes to the Italians trapped inside the locked train.

"Stop! What are you doing?" One of the SS guards brandished his pistol and rushed over to the woman.

As the guard ripped away her sack and raised his hand in preparation for a strike, Bastien interrupted. "What seems to be the problem?"

The SS man was only a guard, not even an NCO, so Bastien, acting as Hauptmann Adalard Dietrich, clearly outranked him. The man lowered his hand and turned to face Bastien, anger written on his face.

Bastien glared back. Acting like a conceited officer was one of the few perks of his current assignment. "Put your pistol away. This cargo is to do work for the Reich, no? Well-fed slaves are better workers."

"Italian scum. Plenty more where they came from. If a few die on the journey, it's an insignificant loss."

Bastien glanced at the sack lying on the ground, still half full of potatoes. "You will go draw water for them, *sturmmann*." Bastien stressed the last word, emphasizing the soldier's low rank.

The SS man's face twisted with defiance.

"Now, sturmmann. You may do it yourself or release a few of the prisoners and have them do it."

The guard marched off, though Bastien didn't think he'd really fetch water for the prisoners. Bastien handed the bag back to the woman. "Quickly, Signora. I think it best if you leave before he returns."

The woman was just finishing her mission of mercy when the SS guard came back, his officer by his side. It was an obersturmführer, so Bastien was still the ranking man, but the officer would be more difficult to deal with. Bastien shooed the old woman away.

The officer stopped a few feet from Bastien and tilted his chin up. "Hauptmann, it appears we have a misunderstanding."

"Oh? And what would that be, Obersturmführer?"

He gestured toward the train with his hand. "I am escorting these criminals to Germany. I will allow no interference."

"And what are their crimes?"

The obersturmführer seemed surprised by the question. "Too numerous to enumerate."

"Hmm. I'd wager most of them committed the simple crime of being born in the wrong place." Bastien glanced behind him, making sure the

Italian woman had disappeared into the crowd. "I have finished my so-called-interference. I assume this cargo will be transported through Switzerland?"

"Yes."

"Then feed them and give them water. We wouldn't want the Red Cross to notice anything amiss, would we?"

The obersturmführer snorted. "The Swiss don't care what we transport as long as we continue to line their bank vaults."

"For your sake, I hope you're right, Obersturmführer. Good day." Bastien turned to leave, hoping he'd successfully bluffed his way out of a volatile situation.

He shouldn't have done it. Of the six boxcars full of Italian civilians, the woman had fed less than one. For all he knew, the men inside were strangling each other for a bite of potato. Her gift could have easily made their journey more, not less deadly. And Bastien had his cover to maintain. At all costs, he had to maintain his cover, even if it meant one old woman was beaten by an SS guard.

"Just a moment, Hauptmann."

Bastien turned to meet the man's arrogant blue eyes. "Yes, Obersturmführer?"

"Your name, please."

Bastien unfastened the top buttons of his overcoat, exposing Dietrich's Iron Cross. "Hauptmann Adalard Dietrich. And your name?"

At the sight of the award hanging from Bastien's neck, the obersturmführer lost some of his confidence, and his lips trembled slightly as he spoke. "Obersturmführer Fritz Meyer."

"Carry on, then, Meyer." Bastien strode from the boxcar, hoping Dietrich's decoration would deter Meyer from filing a report.

And if it doesn't? Bastien shivered in the early morning chill. He was supposed to have gone to the Ruhr for an imaginary aunt's funeral. If questioned, he could perhaps claim he'd acted under the influence of her compassionate nature. Travel through Lombardy was reasonable, especially with the transportation disruptions air raids, sabotage, and winter weather caused, but drawing attention to himself had been a mistake.

"Stop!"

It took Bastien a few moments to recognize the feminine voice.

"Stop! Thief!" At least Gracie had remembered to shout in Italian, but now neither of them was blending in like they should.

CHAPTER SIX

Bastien found Gracie in the crowd, chasing a young man who was running off with her suitcase—the one with the radio. He hesitated. Stepping in would only draw more attention to himself. Bastien still had Smitty's radio, so Gracie could use that if she lost hers, but if the thief reported the radio to the Gestapo, Gracie would be in trouble. And while Bastien might not be eager to work with her, he didn't want her to get caught.

Bastien moved to cut the man off at the edge of the platform, but someone else intervened first. A shot sounded, the young man fell, and Obersturmführer Meyer, his pistol still drawn, approached the thief and kicked him in the ribs.

Bastien pushed his way through the crowd forming a circle around Meyer and the thief. The man on the ground wasn't dead yet, but his wound looked fatal. Bastien considered asking if there were any doctors in the crowd, but although death was a severe punishment for stealing a suitcase, interrogation by the Gestapo, followed by death was even more severe. And there was the radio to worry about.

Bastien reached for the dropped luggage, but Meyer beat him to it. Bastien swallowed. Suitcases packed with radio parts were heavier than they looked.

Meyer hefted it by the handle, scrunching his eyebrows together and staring at the piece in surprise. "Weighs more than I expected."

Bastien reached for it. Meyer pretended not to notice. "I'll take that, Meyer."

Meyer reluctantly handed it over.

"Thank you, Obersturmführer. I assume you can deal with this." Bastien gestured toward the dying man.

"I think it best that we take every precaution, don't you? We should question him and search the suitcase, see if the man or the woman has partisan connections."

"He looks young for a partisan." That wasn't true—the wounded thief looked about Roberto's age, a teenager, and Bastien had seen other partisans far younger than any of Marcello's men. "He's probably just a pickpocket trying to move on to larger items."

Bastien met Gracie's gaze and walked toward her. She was breathing hard, and despite the chill, a few dark hairs were matted across her forehead with perspiration. Her face was pale, and she looked ill. Bastien wasn't sure if that was the result of the theft or of what had happened to the thief, but in either case, she didn't look up to an interrogation by Obersturmführer Meyer. "I'll investigate the suitcase and its owner," he told the SS man. Turning back to Gracie, he lifted the suitcase and switched from German to Italian. "Is this yours, Signorina?"

Gracie nodded.

"Do you have any other luggage?"

She looked around as if she'd completely forgotten her other suitcase. "Yes."

"Well, let's find it before someone runs off with it."

Gracie retraced her steps, and Bastien stayed nearby, carrying the radio for her. Her other suitcase still sat on the platform.

"I'll need to search your things," Bastien said. Meyer would be suspicious if he didn't, but Bastien wasn't sure where he could perform the search without everyone seeing what was inside. He spotted the ticket office and, taking Gracie's other suitcase, led the way.

The small building was closed to the public, but he was a German officer, and neither of the railroad employees objected when he stepped inside, Gracie right behind him. He turned the suitcases so no one but he and Gracie could see the contents and glanced at her. The incident had left her shaken. *So now that there's no turning back, she finally realizes what she's gotten herself into.* Bastien pretended to examine the contents of her luggage, and this time, she didn't protest.

He closed both suitcases with a snap. "All seems to be in order, Signorina." He spoke loudly so the rail workers could hear. "I'll help you to your train."

Bastien planned to escort her all the way to her seat, but he ran into Meyer again outside the train. He handed the suitcases to Gracie and watched her board.

"Anything suspicious?" Meyer asked.

"No."

"What was in the small suitcase?"

"Sewing machine parts." Bastien glanced around the platform. The crowd had dispersed, and the thief was gone. Bastien saw two SS men carrying away something wrapped in a blanket. It was the right size to be a body. "And our thief?"

"He died before I could ask him any questions."

Bastien glanced once more at the covered bundle. "Probably a random robbery. Good day, Meyer."

Meyer saluted, then followed his men.

Bastien turned toward the Rome train and briefly met the eyes of a stocky, middle-aged man. Before boarding the train, Bastien looked back again. The man was still watching him, and according to his uniform, he was SD.

* * *

Gracie was exhausted when the train finally pulled into Rome's Termini Station a day and a half after leaving Switzerland. In good times, a passenger train could cross the border into Italy and make it to Rome the same day, but her route had taken much longer. She'd had to switch trains twice, and her last train had stopped for several hours somewhere between Milan and Bologna to fix a problem with the engine.

Because the train arrived during curfew, the passengers weren't allowed off until nearly dawn. Gracie hadn't slept since boarding the first train, but she couldn't sleep now. She was too cold. At first it had been the winter chill, but after her radio was stolen, it was fear that left her shivering. Her cover had almost been blown, so easily, even though she hadn't made any mistakes. She'd never seen someone shot before, and the memory was horrible. She wouldn't have said anything, preferring to let the thief get away with her radio, if she'd known what would happen to him. And she was worried. Had it been a random theft, or had something about her or her suitcase made it a target?

When light from the still-hidden sun illuminated the station, she saw Captain Ley through the window. They'd planned no contact until the next day, and she supposed the robbery wouldn't change that. He strode away, composed, confident, perfect for his assignment.

As Gracie left the train not long after, she dreaded what might happen next, what bad luck or her own inadequacy might bring. She'd been so eager to work behind enemy lines, but unlike Ley, she wasn't perfect for this assignment. She had pictured herself calmly meeting with informants, then competently transmitting vital intelligence, doing something that would really make a difference for the army. She hadn't even been able to handle the thief without help. She whispered a prayer, pleading for divine protection. She had a feeling she was going to need it.

Colonel Ambrose and Captain Ley had given her the names of several buildings where she could seek lodging, all of them a long walk from Termini Station. She grabbed her luggage and began her trek. At least the scenery was pleasant. Rome was an open city, so although it had been bombed a few times, most of its structures were still intact, and the buildings, piazzas, and statues she passed were beautiful, even behind piles of sandbags. She'd been to Rome a few times when she was younger, and despite the years, things were mostly the same. Except for the occupying army. German soldiers were everywhere.

The first two places she approached had no spare rooms. The third, by far the dingiest of her options, gave her the choice of two apartments after she'd shown the landlord her forged paperwork.

"Would you like the room on the second floor or the one on the fifth?" he asked.

"The fifth, please." Gracie hoped she'd have more warning from that floor if she needed to hide the radio. The room was small, furnished only with a bed and a chest of three drawers topped with a porcelain pitcher and bowl. The bathroom was at the end of the hall, to be shared with the residents of the other five apartments on that floor.

According to her papers, Gracie was Concetta Gallo, a student. Her supposed studies would give her an excuse to come and go at irregular intervals, but she thought she should collect a few books so her room looked the part.

She unpacked her clothes and the other items she'd brought, then checked the radio. The lightbulb that indicated signal strength as she transmitted was cracked. She replaced it with a spare and hoped the spare would last. If it broke, she'd have to ask Ley for his, and she didn't want to ask him for any more help. Her radio's transmitter, receiver, and power source were each about the size of a skinny shoebox. They'd be easy to carry in the suitcase, or she could wrap them to look like packages or hide them in a bag of groceries. For now, she wrapped them in cloths and hid them in the bottom drawer behind some clothes before she slid her empty secondhand suitcases under the bed.

She picked up her silk handkerchief printed with two hundred sets of transposition keys and slipped it into her bra. No one would feel it in a pat-down, and she wanted to keep the radio and the silk separate. She slipped a second handkerchief and a sheet of instructions for its use into her pocket so she could leave them at a dead drop for one of her contacts. The last things she checked were her pistols, both Italian Berettas so they couldn't immediately be tied to US forces. She hoped she would never have to use either of them. She wasn't even sure how often she'd carry one because civilians weren't allowed to own firearms.

The bed had only a single, threadbare blanket, but at least the sheets looked clean. Gracie sat on the thin mattress and then lay down, telling herself she'd just rest for a few minutes.

She woke to the sound of someone in the stairwell and glanced out the window. The sun was sinking toward the western horizon, and she had work to do before the five o'clock curfew. She took a sheet of paper and a pen and wrote what looked like a love note. *Amore mio, it's been so long. I've missed you. Please let us return to how things were last summer.* Then she grabbed her lightweight coat, slipped the note and a piece of chalk into her pocket, and left, locking the door behind her.

Whomever she'd heard in the stairwell must have found their floor because the building was now quiet. She descended the rickety metal staircase quickly at first, then slowed, trying to make her passage less noisy. She didn't want half the building's occupants to hear her every time she came or went in her clunky black loafers.

Maybe a different pair of shoes would be better? Gracie almost laughed at herself. She was posing as a poor Italian student; she was no longer the daughter of a fashion-conscious, upper-middle-class mother, and she would have to get by with one or two pairs of shoes rather than one or two dozen. She quieted her footsteps and left the complex, heading north and passing a bakery. Her room had no kitchen, so she'd have to purchase most of her meals in nearby shops. She slowed her pace outside the bakery, inhaling the aroma of fresh-baked bread. The line was long, so she couldn't stop now, but maybe she'd have time to buy something later.

The fountain she'd been told to find was in an open plaza, and one of her contacts passed it every evening. Gracie hoped she wasn't too late, that the agent would see her mark tonight. A chalk triangle drawn on the west end of the fountain was a signal to meet the next morning at a nearby waterline. Bombing had damaged the water ducts, so most civilians had to wait in line for their water. If everything went according to plan, Gracie would find the agent in line the next day and recognize her contact by the red patch sewn on his or her left sleeve near the elbow.

She waited until a pair of Italian Fascist policemen left the area, then drew her triangle. The fountain was dry, which was a pity. She thought it would have been lovely otherwise. The marble figures looked almost real but too pale and perhaps too perfect. She circled the fountain once, admiring it, then moved on toward the other agent's address. She slipped her note under the door to alert her contact that she was in Rome, able to pick up any information left at a specified dead drop. She was tempted to leave the silk transposition keys and instructions under the door too, but her contact had been out of touch with OSS headquarters in Caserta for several weeks. It would be better to follow procedure and use the dead drop.

She was back on the street and had walked nearly a block when she glanced behind her and took in about a dozen faces. A few blocks later, she checked again, recognizing one face from her previous glimpse, a handsome Italian civilian. Gracie turned left at the next intersection and increased her pace. Two blocks and two turns later she glanced back, and the man was still there, roughly the same distance behind her despite her rush.

Stay calm, she told herself. *He's Italian; it's not like the Gestapo's on your tail.* Her training had covered what to do if she was followed. She could confront him or try to elude him. She turned into a more crowded street in the hopes of losing him and rushed along, trying to put more people between them.

She'd just passed an alley when someone grabbed her arm from behind and yanked her off the road. A hand slapped over her mouth before she could scream, and within seconds, she'd been dragged into the deserted foyer of a dark building.

CHAPTER SEVEN

"Easy, signorina," a voice whispered in Gracie's ear as she struggled to pull away. "The change in weather could bring rain."

Gracie relaxed as she recognized the code phrase. "I'll be sure to carry my umbrella when I go out," she replied, reciting the memorized counterphrase.

"The dead drop's been compromised."

"So you tracked me down?"

He nodded, his dark eyes never leaving hers. His face broke into a grin, causing slight lines to appear around his lips. "You didn't make it easy though."

Gracie returned his smile. She was glad she hadn't been too easy to track but grateful he'd managed to do it before she blundered into a Nazi trap.

Her contact slipped his hand into a well-worn shirt pocket and brought out several sheets of paper folded into quarters. "My reports. The last several of them."

Gracie slid them into her own pocket and brought out one of the silk handkerchiefs. "I was asked to deliver this. It's for encrypting your messages, and it's more secure than your old system."

He ran the smooth fabric between his fingers. "So I use these numbers for the transposition keys instead of words from my poem?"

"Yes, and after you've used each set, cut them off and burn them. That way they'll only be used once, and if the Germans catch you, they won't be able to read your previous messages."

"Fine. I was getting sick of Catullus anyway."

"If the dead drop's compromised, how will I get your next report?"

A slight frown appeared on his face as he thought. He was silent as a pair of civilians entered the building from the street and went into one of the offices on the north side. "Come with me."

She followed him outside and walked beside him for a few blocks. When the foot traffic thinned and no one was within earshot, he slowed his stride. "I'm Angelo, by the way."

"I'm Concetta," Gracie said.

"Pleased to meet you, Concetta. I'm glad you're here. It's been frustrating not knowing who to pass my reports to." He motioned with his head to an apartment complex as they walked past. "In a week, meet me there, on the roof. Noon. I'll give you another report then." He took her hand, brought it to his lips for an instant, and winked at her. "I'll see you next week." He turned back the way they'd come and strolled away.

Gracie watched him until he turned a corner. His steps were confident, his clothing old but clean, and his smile friendly. She wondered how and why he'd started working against the Nazis and what he was like when he wasn't being a spy. She shook her head, knowing her primary concern should be whether or not his information was of any use to the Allies.

* * *

The next morning, Gracie walked along the water queue, wondering what her next contact would be like. So far, she was working with two men, both around thirty years old, both handsome. Of course, one of them had manhandled her into an office building and the other had burned her underclothing. *I don't care how old or ugly the next agent is, as long as they're easy to work with.*

The line stretched more than a block. She'd known water service in the city was sporadic and unpredictable but hadn't expected so many civilians to turn to public fountains for their water. As she walked along the untidy line, she looked at everyone's elbows, hoping to see a patch, hoping her contact would be there. She moved slowly, acting like she was trying to find a friend rather than somebody's elbow.

A block from the pipe, Gracie saw a woman with a maroon patch near her left elbow. Like most of the women in Rome, she was otherwise dressed in black. Gracie's own wardrobe was three-quarters black items, even though she preferred color. As Gracie drew near, the woman straightened, and Gracie realized her contact was pregnant.

"The sunset was lovely yesterday, wasn't it?" Gracie said.

The woman's lips curved upward as if she found the code phrase humorous. "Yes, I watched it from a street near the Pantheon."

Gracie tried to judge the distance between the woman's place in line and the water pipe, wondering how long of a wait she had.

"The line begins farther back."

Gracie had unintentionally cut in line, and the two women waiting behind her contact paused their gossiping long enough to cross their arms and glare at her. Gracie wasn't even sure which one had spoken.

"I need water," her contact said. "Can we meet later? Noon?"

"Yes. Where?"

The woman smiled again, revealing a perfect set of teeth. "The Pantheon?"

* * *

The last time she'd been in Rome, fourteen years ago, Gracie had gone sightseeing. She hadn't expected to act the tourist on her OSS mission but didn't mind an excuse to gawk at Rome's ancient wonders again. OSS had provided numerous maps and photographs of the city for her to study, but pictures and paper couldn't do Rome justice.

She chewed pieces of the pane nero she'd waited an hour for. The bread tasted horrible, but it had been the only thing available when she'd made it to the front of the line. *So much for fine Italian cuisine.* There hadn't been a line at the bookstore next to the bakery, so Gracie had also bought a few books of Roman poetry and was carrying them now.

Gracie's contact was late but only by a few minutes. "Sorry to keep you," the woman said, twisting her luxurious dark hair away from her neck.

"It's fine. Did you get your water?" Gracie looked around to make sure no one was close enough to overhear their conversation.

"Yes. And I got it up to my flat without spilling any. Such a nuisance. I think I'm just about ready to leave Rome and join my husband's partisan band in the hills. It can't be much worse than living here." She looked down at her abdomen. "Except they might not have midwives there, and my mother lives with me now. She'd be furious if I left and she didn't get to see her first grandbaby."

Even though she was complaining, the woman's voice sounded cheerful. Gracie had a feeling this new contact would be a pleasure to work with. "I'm Concetta."

"I'm Otavia. I know some people in the country, and they know people. Word of what the Germans are doing outside Rome is brought to me, but for the last few weeks, I haven't been able to do anything with it."

"From now on, you can give it to me."

"Good." Otavia glanced at the bread still in Gracie's hand. "That's what you're eating?"

"It was all they had left by the time I got there. I don't have a kitchen, so I can't make my own food."

Otavia grinned as she waited for a few pedestrians to stroll out of earshot. "*Tesorina*, you're obviously new in town." Otavia used the term of endearment Gracie's grandparents had used. "Unless you want to starve, you're going to need to shop at the black market."

"But isn't trading on the black market punishable by death?"

Otavia laughed as she took Gracie's arm and led her away, then she whispered. "Yes, and so is operating an enemy radio or getting caught with a four-pointed nail or riding a bicycle or violating curfew."

"You can get shot for riding a bicycle?" Maybe that explained why Gracie had seen several bicycles with useless third wheels tacked on.

"The Gappisti had a few too many successful assassinations by bicycle."

Gracie had to think for a few moments before remembering that the Gappisti were Italian partisans, members of the Gruppi di Azione Patriottica, a resistance group working against the Nazis.

Otavia pointed across the street, and the two of them crossed to the other side, conveniently avoiding a pair of Italian Fascist police. "So today I'll show you where to get your food. And then Friday we'll meet again at the Piazza Navona, by Neptune's fountain."

"You like meeting by famous landmarks?"

"Gives us an excuse to loiter if one of us is late. And I love Rome. I know I talk about leaving, but I don't really want to. I miss my husband, but if I went to join him, I think I'd miss this city. So I'm doing what I can to help the Allies get here quickly so I can have both my loves at the same time." Otavia pointed out a quiet side street and turned onto it. "The Amis and Tommies are certainly taking their time. I expected them to be here by now."

"Us too." Gracie thought of Ley's anger that the landings in Anzio and Nettuno had been so badly botched. "Where's your husband?"

"Somewhere to the east. They were going to send him away for forced labor, so he joined a partisan band instead." Otavia sighed. "At least I get letters. It could be worse."

Gracie wondered how she'd react in Otavia's position. *Not as well*, she knew.

"Have you seen Rome before?" Otavia asked.

"Yes, but not recently. I grew up in Nettuno, then my family moved to the United States when I was eleven. My oldest sister had married a few years before and they had immigrated. My brother-in-law started his own business and convinced my dad to come work for him."

"Didn't you miss Italy?"

"For a while." And Gracie had missed it but not for very long. Utah had quickly become her home, and she'd felt like she belonged there. Or at least she had until six months ago. Gracie shook her head to clear it. "Is the black market expensive?"

"Depends on what you need." Otavia stopped in front of a store window, her eyes glued to the dress on display. It was black, with an empire waist and a hemline that hit the mannequin just below the knees. Tiny scarlet flowers were embroidered along the neckline and waist. "Oh, I love that dress. Not that I could pull it off, but you'd look wonderful in it."

"Me?" Gracie stared at the dress. It was beautiful, but it would accentuate rather than disguise her curves. "It's probably too fitted for me."

Otavia sighed again, walking away from the shop. "*Tesorina*, a shape like yours is meant to be shown off. What I wouldn't do to look like you . . . I finally have a few curves, but an extra one came along as part of the deal." Otavia patted her stomach.

No one had ever told Gracie she'd look good in a dress before. Her mother had sometimes told her she was smart, but that wasn't a compliment, not coming from Marisa Begni, who didn't think women needed brains. Otavia, on the other hand, with her radiant smile and pleasant form, lithe even when pregnant, would fit right in with Gracie's flawlessly beautiful sisters. Gracie glanced at her reflection in a window, wondering if she'd somehow changed because Otavia seemed to see her in a different light. But she still looked like ungraceful Gracie. *Why on earth would Otavia want to look like me?*

CHAPTER EIGHT

OBERSTURMFÜHRER KORNELIUS ZIMMERMAN SAT IN his normal chair at the café and sorted through the postcards he'd just purchased, wondering which he should send to his twelve-year-old son. The Trevi fountain? The Colosseum? St. Peter's Basilica? He would send them all eventually but wasn't sure which to mail first. As Untersturmführer Otto Ostheim sat down across from him, Zimmerman decided on St. Peter's. He'd already sent a few views of the church's exterior to his son, but this postcard showed some of the interior, and Klaus would like that. He was drawn to churches. *Taking after his mother . . .*

"Any luck today?" Ostheim asked.

"The usual. A few Jews, two suspected Gappisti members, one of the Carabinieri who helped arrest Mussolini last July." Zimmerman grinned with satisfaction as he spoke. It had taken Hitler less than two months to rescue his friend. And those who had dared stand up against Hitler's most valuable ally were made to pay a heavy price when captured.

"That should make for a busy night at the Via Tasso, eh?"

"Yes. For you." Though he had a desk at the joint Gestapo headquarters and prison at 145 and 155 Via Tasso, Zimmerman's responsibilities involved catching wanted people rather than questioning and torturing them.

"Maybe I should get back," Ostheim said. "Make sure my newest guests are being treated correctly."

Zimmerman put the postcards away, knowing Ostheim would stay and eat something before going back to his work of supervising interrogations until late into the night. "And for you? A good day?"

"Yes, and it's about to get better."

Zimmerman turned to follow Ostheim's gaze. A tall woman, probably in her midtwenties, with black hair and a curvy figure, had just walked through the door. Zimmerman and Ostheim shared a weakness for Italian beauty, but while Zimmerman was more interested in its art, Ostheim was most drawn to its female inhabitants.

Ostheim went over to talk to her, and a few minutes later, he brought her to the table. "Obersturmführer Zimmerman, may I present Fräulein Concetta Gallo."

Concetta nodded a greeting, then sat when Ostheim pulled a chair out for her. She seemed a little hesitant and somehow different from the usual type of woman Ostheim picked up. Like most Italian civilians, her clothing looked a decade old. She was pretty, to be sure, even with the birthmark on her right cheek, but she seemed less . . . desperate than most of the others.

"Do you come here often?" Ostheim asked, speaking Italian.

"No, but I think I should. It's lovely." Concetta gestured out the window. Zimmerman glanced at the street, but it seemed ordinary to him.

Ostheim and the woman continued their conversation, but Zimmerman promptly tuned them out to focus on his food when the waiter brought it. Zimmerman's Italian wasn't as good as his friend's, and he had trouble keeping up with the woman's rapid speech. *How does she talk so fast and move her hands at the same time?*

Zimmerman was halfway through his spiced mutton when a Wehrmacht hauptmann entered the café and stopped near their table. Zimmerman had spoken briefly with Dietrich before, long enough to know he was an engineer and, like Zimmerman, preferred to work away from his desk. He only remembered the hauptmann's name because an SD man had been asking questions about him a few hours ago. "Good evening, Hauptmann Dietrich. Looking for a seat?" Zimmerman pointed to the empty chair beside him.

"Thank you. I have other arrangements for supper, but when I saw the signorina, I wanted to stop and say hello." Dietrich turned to Concetta. "I don't suppose you remember, but we ran into each other at the train station the other day."

The Italian woman's face lit up in a smile. "Yes, of course I remember. Thank you for your help with my luggage."

"What were you doing at the train station?" Ostheim asked Dietrich.

"Returning from a short leave. A bereavement pass, but the journey did have its bright spots." Dietrich turned his attention from Ostheim to Concetta. "Actually, I seem to remember planning a walk along the Tiber with you."

Ostheim cleared his throat. "Fräulein Gallo and I were about to order—"

"Actually, a walk along the river sounds perfect." Concetta stood, then turned back to Ostheim and Zimmerman. "It was a pleasure to meet you both. I hope we'll see each other again soon."

Ostheim glared at the couple as they left. He wasn't used to losing, and Zimmerman could tell Dietrich had just made an enemy.

* * *

Captain Ley was silent for several blocks. Gracie was relieved that he'd shown up because drawn-out conversations that revolved around her cover story made her nervous. She was ravenous, though, and disappointed to miss supper. Whatever Ostheim's friend had been eating looked and smelled heavenly after eating nothing but bread for the last day and a half.

"Do you have any idea who you were sitting with?" Ley's face still held a pleasant smile, but his whisper was icy.

"Otto—I think his last name was Ostheim. And his friend was Lieutenant Zimmerman."

"I am fully aware of their names, ranks, and duties. What I'm wondering is if you noticed the silver *S*'s on their uniforms, like a pair of lightning bolts."

Gracie wondered why Ley seemed so upset. "Yes, but back in Switzerland you told me to be friendly with other army officers so it wouldn't look strange for me to be friendly with you when you arrived."

"*Army* officers. Obersturmführer Kornelius Zimmerman and Untersturmführer Otto Ostheim are not members of the German *Army*. They're members of the Allgemeine SS, and they specialize in arresting Jews, partisans, and spies and deporting or torturing them. They aren't the type of men you want to cross, and thanks to you, Ostheim, and probably Zimmerman too, now has a very good reason to hate me."

"Well, what was I supposed to do when Ostheim came up to me?"

Ley didn't answer, instead taking a pencil and a sheet of paper from his pocket. He wrote something on the paper, folded it, and handed it to her. "My report. And an address. If you're not under arrest, meet me there tomorrow for my next report. Sixteen hundred hours. And if by chance I'm late, don't flirt with SS officers while you're waiting." He turned abruptly and strode off.

She scowled at his departing figure. It wasn't like she'd had much of a choice. Surely flirting with an SS man and getting an invitation to supper was preferable to snubbing him and inviting close scrutiny of her papers. Gracie passed a clock and quickened her pace. She would have to head for her apartment at once if she wanted to make it before curfew.

Her stomach rumbled, but she didn't have time to wait in line for food. Maybe she shouldn't have turned down Ostheim's supper invitation. SS or not, he seemed more friendly than Captain Ley.

* * *

Bastien was still on edge when he arrived at the hotel on the Via Veneto, where he and a few dozen other officers were billeted. Since his arrival in Rome the previous fall, he'd done his best to maintain a low profile. Thanks to Ambrose and Vaughn-Harris, he'd drawn far too much attention to himself the past few weeks, first by requesting leave, then by the mandate to work with their inexperienced radio operator. Desk officers seemed to think the only qualifications a radio operator needed were language fluency and the ability to tap out Morse code, but the real requirements were more complex.

Bastien went straight to supper. He wasn't really hungry—not after spotting the SD man from the train station for the third time in as many days. He assumed skipping meals would only be suspicious, so he spread real butter on his bread and forced himself to eat as if he had an appetite, wondering why the SD was on his tail. Did they suspect he wasn't really Dietrich? That he wasn't loyal to Germany? Both?

He was nearly finished when he realized Obersturmführer Heinrich Vogel, the man sitting next to him, hadn't said anything the entire meal. He was usually more talkative and had a tendency to whistle "Lili Marlene" while coming to and from the dining hall. Bastien watched him for a few seconds. Heinie was moving food around his plate, but his meal wasn't making it to his mouth.

"Something wrong, Heinie?"

Heinie's brown eyes flickered to Bastien's, but he didn't speak for a while. The blood vessels in his eyes were more prominent than usual, and his lips formed a frown. "Had an interesting conversation with Sturmbannführer Scholz today."

Scholz was Heinie's commanding officer, but Bastien had gotten the impression that Scholz, though an adamant Nazi, was easy to work with. "Interesting as in bad?" Bastien whispered.

Heinie nodded, glancing around the table at the other officers.

Bastien didn't pry further, but he excused himself early, as usual, and Heinie followed him to their third-floor rooms.

"What happened with Scholz?" Bastien asked when they were alone in the hallway.

"I asked him for permission to get married."

"And?"

Heinie frowned again. "Maurleen can only prove her German ancestry back to 1787. That would be good enough if I was just an enlisted man, but because I'm an SS officer, she has to prove racial purity back to 1750."

Bastien knew the SS controlled its men like a supply officer controlled his best equipment, but he hadn't realized how strict the requirements for marriage were. "I'm sorry, Heinie. How is Maurleen taking the news?"

Heinie pulled a letter from his pocket. Bastien caught a hint of perfume and assumed Maurleen was the author. "Do you have any idea what the paperwork is like to apply for marriage? She had to fill all that out, then they did a medical exam—and it's not as if she's a lounge singer; she's a minister's daughter. It was humiliating for her." Heinie opened the letter and read from it. "'I wanted to be your wife so badly, but now I realize I am unworthy of such an honor. I trust our Führer to lead Germany to greatness, but perhaps I can best serve the Reich as a factory worker rather than an officer's wife. I would never want to damage your career or pollute the blood of your posterity. Yet my heart will always be yours. I shall have to go on loving you from afar, as a humble flower loves the sun but can never approach its glory.'"

Heinie put the letter away, his voice tight with emotion. "They've got no right to make Maurleen feel like that—she's beautiful and smart and kind, and she's a good German. Better than any of them. Who cares who her great-great-grandfather was? It's ridiculous. They have Waffen SS divisions made of Muslims from Bosnia, but they won't grant permission for me to marry someone like Maurleen? They don't come any better than her!"

Bastien unlocked his door and motioned Heinie inside. He didn't want someone overhearing Heinie's rant against the SS. Bastien could get in trouble for listening to it, and Heinie could get in even worse trouble for voicing it. "Can you appeal Scholz's decision?"

Heinie followed Bastien inside the one-bedroom suite and slumped into one of the wooden dining chairs. "I offered to resign my commission. Then they wouldn't care about any ancestors born before 1800."

"You'd do that for her?"

"Yes, but Scholz told me he'd consider my resignation an act of treason. I'm stuck." Heinie raked his fingers through his hair in frustration. "I shouldn't have listened to that arrogant SS recruiter. He promised us advanced training, newer weapons, superior uniforms. 'Join the Waffen SS and become the best of the best.' Me and my stupid ego. I thought being part of an elite unit would impress Maurleen, not keep us apart forever. I've known I wanted to marry her since I was eighteen, and now . . ." His voice trailed off.

"Then you've already waited six years. Wait a few more."

"What if the rules never change?"

Bastien sat across the table from Heinie. "Maybe we'll lose the war. I doubt SS rules will still be in force should that happen."

Heinie smiled and shook his head. "You could get reprimanded for saying that, Adalard." His smile broadened. "But not as severely as I could be reprimanded for calling SS regulations ridiculous." He lowered his voice. "Do you really think we'll lose the war?"

Bastien looked at the floor and realized his leg was rhythmically tapping the carpet. He forced it to stop. "No one's taken Rome from the south since the sixth century."

"But Italy isn't the only place we're defending. The Red Army is unending. It doesn't seem to matter how good our men are, the Communists just send more troops. And I ran into a cousin about a month ago. He's with the Kriegsmarine. Said our U-boats aren't sinking as much tonnage as they used to. What if the Allies invade across the English Channel?"

"They might try, but that doesn't mean they'll succeed." As Bastien said it, he knew it was true but wished with all his heart that a cross-channel invasion would come soon and result in a quick Allied victory. "Just do your best, Heinie. You can't control anything else. And write to Maurleen. She needs to know you still love her and that you'll wait."

"I worry about her. She's never been all that confident, so to have some slimy SS bureaucrat tell her she's not good enough to get married . . . And she's in Schweinfurt now. She promised she'll go to the bomb shelter as soon as the sirens sound, but sometimes I think my odds are better than hers when it comes to surviving the war. Saturation bombing—it's barbaric, and Schweinfurt seems to be a frequent target."

"Remind her to get to the shelter quick, then." Bastien didn't bring up the German bombings of Warsaw or London or Belgrade, but maybe Heinie was right—the death of civilians on both sides was tragic and was happening with far too much frequency. "Does she work at the ball-bearing plants?"

Heinie nodded.

"Well, I'm sure they have plenty of warning before attacks, and they have deep shelters."

Heinie was quiet for a while, so Bastien switched subjects, hoping his friend would give him additional information he could pass on to Gracie. It was a little odd, thinking of Heinie as a friend. They belonged to opposing armies, and Bastien never hesitated to gather information from him, but he liked Heinie. Even as he used him, Bastien hoped that someday Heinie and Maurleen would be able to wed. "How are those new flak batteries coming along?"

CHAPTER NINE

Bastien stared at the trench that had been carved into the mountain by a group of forced laborers, part of the Hitler Line, prepared to defend Rome should the Gustav Line fail. The workers weren't there—they were often forced to work at night when Allied air patrols couldn't see them. Most of the slaves had been kidnapped from the streets and were fed only enough to stave off starvation. Their taskmasters were cruel, so even with unskilled, half-starved men, the results were imposing. Italy seemed designed for defensive warfare, and Kesselring's Army—and the slaves they employed—were making it even worse.

It was Dietrich's job to inspect the finished entrenchments, and though Bastien often worked nights, the sun was high as he examined the lines cut into the rocky ground. He wasn't sure how well the latest pillboxes and slit trenches could be destroyed from the air, but at least the Allies would know where they were. *As long as Gracie can radio it in.*

Bastien continued his inspection, taking careful notes for Wehrmacht headquarters and for Gracie. He had to walk a fine line—if there were obvious defects, he had to point them out so they could be fixed. The result was something more difficult for the Allies to seize, but if he didn't report it, he'd be considered incompetent and lose access to the information he collected.

After a full morning, Bastien rode his motorcycle back to Rome. As was his habit, he took the long way home. If asked, he could say he was trying to avoid assassination by the Gappisti. That was partially true; he didn't want his allies to shoot him. The long route also allowed him to observe more of the German positions, and sometimes, like today, it gave him a chance to meet with old friends.

Bastien rode over a hill and pulled the NSU 351 off the road. He checked his watch. He was two minutes early, but so were his contacts.

"Do you have any idea how intimidating you look in that uniform?" Marcello asked from the shade of an olive tree. His arms were folded behind his head, his legs crossed at the ankles. Giovanni lay next to him.

"But you aren't one to let an intimidating officer interrupt your siesta?"

Marcello chuckled softly and propped himself up on his elbows as Bastien approached. "Nothing should get in the way of siesta. Except perhaps liberation. Where are all your American friends? They should have been here weeks ago."

Bastien sat beside Marcello and Giovanni in the shade, wondering the same thing. After the landings in Anzio and Nettuno, he'd expected Allied troops to reach Rome in days, not months. "Maybe if your country didn't have so many rivers and mountains and things like the Gustav Line. Why can't Italy be more like Kansas?"

"Kansas?" Giovanni's eyebrows wrinkled in question.

"Flat. I haven't seen it myself, but one of my sisters married someone from Kansas."

"Perfect panzer country," Giovanni said.

"Good thing the German Navy is almost kaput, eh?" Marcello pushed himself up the rest of the way.

Bastien wasn't sure the Kriegsmarine was really out for the count, but he doubted they'd be launching an invasion across the Atlantic, not for at least a decade. Kansas was safe, and so were his sisters, but if the war dragged on much longer, how many men like his brother, Lukas—still boys, really—would be brought into combat? "I have information about expected shipments to Rome. I'm not sure how large the escorts will be." Bastien handed a copy of the schedule to Marcello.

"Giovanni's brother looked over some of the fortifications north of Rome." Marcello gestured to Giovanni, who handed a paper to Bastien. "Not a bad trade, eh, Capitano?"

"No, not a bad trade."

"Ready to thank me yet for making you wear that uniform?"

"No, not yet. Especially not now that I've got a new radio operator to babysit and an SD man on my tail."

Giovanni and Marcello looked around as if they both expected the SD officer to suddenly appear and arrest them.

"I haven't seen him today," Bastien said. "I had an early start."

"So you think he'll be waiting for you back in Rome?" Marcello asked.

Bastien shrugged. "Maybe. I've been able to lose him twice so far. He's not exactly easy to slip past, but he's manageable."

"Your new radio operator, is he any good?"

Bastien didn't correct Marcello's assumption that the radio operator was male. It was better not to share details. "The new radio operator is good with the radio, inexperienced with everything else."

Giovanni cocked his head to the side. "Working with amateurs? That's not like you."

"Orders." Bastien had almost gotten used to the idea of working with Gracie until yesterday's fiasco. Now he was certain Vaughn-Harris had thought up the whole thing as one more shot at revenge. It wasn't right for Vaughn-Harris to try to get Bastien killed and risk the information he collected, nor was it fair for Gracie to be thrown into a mission she wasn't ready for. But Colonel Ambrose wouldn't allow Vaughn-Harris or anyone else to manipulate his agents. Ambrose, at least, thought the arrangement with Gracie would work.

"So you've got someone from the SD on your tail and a clumsy partner. Will we see you again?" Giovanni was still just as direct as ever. "Other than in prison?"

Bastien pursed his lips. "I'll plan on meeting you in a week. If I don't show up, I've either been arrested or killed or my cover's been blown and I've gone south."

Marcello stood as Bastien walked back to his motorcycle. "Take care of yourself, eh, Capitano? You've had a good run. Don't keep it up longer than you need to."

Bastien nodded. Marcello's advice was wise, but Bastien was afraid he wouldn't know he'd kept the charade up too long until it was too late to let it go.

* * *

The ride back to Rome was uneventful. Bastien avoided his office, going directly to his meeting with Gracie, and arrived at the hotel lobby before the appointed rendezvous. One of the hotel waiters offered to bring him coffee—he even claimed it was real coffee—but Bastien turned him down despite the temptation to order some just so he could see what Gracie would do when he handed her a cup.

She arrived right on time. Bastien stood as she came through the doors, quickly catching her attention. Doing his best to remember his manners, he motioned her toward a seat and remained standing until she sat down. She looked around the room and leaned into the cushions as if exhausted.

"Are you all right?" he asked. They were the only ones in the lobby, so he didn't bother with pretend formalities.

"I'm fine. It's just been a long day."

Bastien glanced at the large clock hanging over an unstaffed hotel desk. "Only four o'clock, and it's already been a long day?" Bastien had been up for twelve hours, working through most of them, but given the long curfew, he doubted that was the case for Gracie.

Her fingers, which rarely stopped moving, fiddled with the end of a decorative pillow. "Waiting for breakfast and sending my report in and standing in line for water took until now."

"Where did you transmit?"

"Today I went to a deserted apartment near the Vatican." She motioned with her hands in the appropriate direction. "I'll try not to use the same place more than once or twice."

"Good. They taught you something useful in training."

"I learned plenty in training." Before she could continue, her stomach rumbled. One hand flew to her mouth, and her cheeks grew pink.

"Hungry?" Bastien asked.

"I haven't had time to eat since breakfast."

Bastien stood and offered Gracie his arm. "Early supper?"

She nodded. "If you think we can finish before curfew."

"If we're late, I'll walk you home. I have permission to be out whenever I like." After seeing Gracie home, he'd have to write a report for his German superior about that morning's inspections and see if the SD man was still around. He hadn't seen him yet today, but the man had previously been near headquarters, not in random Roman hotels or pillboxes along the Hitler Line.

The hotel's restaurant host bowed slightly as they approached, and Bastien peeked at Gracie. "Pretend you're enjoying yourself," he whispered.

She glanced at him, startled, and tried to smile.

She was taller than Julie or Annie, but Bastien reminded himself that now wasn't a good time to think about the past and that Gracie's height was irrelevant to everything they were doing in Rome.

"Could we have a more private table?" he asked when the waiter led them to the most crowded corner of the restaurant.

The slight man hesitated only an instant. "Yes, sir. Of course, sir." He pointed to a table in the room's opposite corner, where the nearest patrons were at least three tables away. "Would that do, sir?"

"Yes, thank you."

When they were seated, the waiter gave them their choices.

"I'm hungry enough to eat anything," Gracie said.

"Two of the chicken dishes, then," Bastien said.

"And to drink?"

"A bottle of your house wine." As Bastien spoke, Gracie opened her mouth, no doubt to protest, but he met her eyes and held them, and she took the hint, saving her comment until after the waiter disappeared.

"I don't drink alcohol."

"Yes, I know. And I've no intention of making you drink it, but if you look around, you'll notice that every other restaurant patron has a glass of wine in front of them. We'd be drawing attention to ourselves if we didn't order some. If you like, we can pour it in the plant behind you."

"When in Rome, at least pretend to do as the Romans do?"

"Something like that."

Gracie studied the ivy behind her. "Will the wine hurt the plant?" She kept her voice down so no one would overhear her.

Bastien shrugged. "If it does, I doubt the effects will be noticeable before we've finished."

"Will you be drinking yours? We could switch glasses, and you could have mine too."

"And show up at German headquarters with half a bottle of wine in me? No, I think I'll donate mine to the plant. Best to keep a clear head in this line of work." He wasn't looking forward to writing his report and possibly facing the SD officer again, and he still wasn't sure if he'd offered Gracie supper as a way to stall the inevitable or out of genuine concern for his hungry radio operator.

"Where did you learn Italian?" Gracie asked.

"I spent time in Switzerland, about a year in the Italian-speaking part."

"What were you doing there?"

"I wasn't with the military." She looked at him as if expecting him to elaborate, but he wasn't about to give her any additional information. "You ask a lot of questions."

She rolled her eyes and flitted her hands in an irritated arc. "That's usually how people get to know each other. And since I was under the impression we're pretending the start of a romantic relationship, I thought questions would be part of a normal conversation. Or did you want me to sit silently all through supper? The other patrons seem to be talking with their table mates."

Bastien caught himself smiling. He was going to get into trouble if he underestimated Gracie's verbal sparring abilities. "You can ask any question you like about Adalard Dietrich, but I'm afraid I won't know many of the answers."

"I'd rather get to know someone real."

"Adalard is real; he's just dead."

Gracie's lips curled up at the ends, and she studied him as the waiter filled their glasses with wine. She watched the man leave, then turned back to Bastien. "You said *is*, not *was*. Does that mean you believe in an afterlife?"

"According to my papers, I'm an evangelical Christian. But since I didn't have a Bible among my things, I don't think I'm very devout." He wished Dietrich's belongings had included a Bible. Bastien had been forced to leave all his kit, including his scriptures, with Marcello.

"So Adalard's religious beliefs are hazy. What about the real you?"

"The real me doesn't matter. Not in Rome." The truth would probably surprise her, but he saw no reason to share unnecessary facts.

"Does it ever bother you, pretending to be someone else? I mean, I'm Concetta Gallo, but she's never existed, not in real life. Whereas you . . ." She gestured with her hand. "Do you think Adalard's ghost will try to haunt you or something?"

He fought back a laugh. "I'm not haunted by ghosts. And while I do believe some part of Dietrich still exists somewhere, I imagine his soul has more important things to do than worry about me."

"But didn't you kill him? Don't you think—"

"I'm sure he knows it was nothing personal." Bastien had long ago realized war called for different standards. He couldn't fight violence with mere words. Bastien's father had tried that, and it hadn't worked.

Gracie was quiet until the food arrived. She focused on her meal for a while, then paused and watched him cut his chicken. "Is Adalard left-handed? I noticed you were back in Switzerland."

"His pistol was strapped to his right side, so I assume he was right-handed. We're not a perfect match. We also have different blood types, so if I'm bleeding to death, don't bother taking me to the hospital."

"Do your tags have Adalard's blood type on them?"

Bastien nodded.

Gracie looked horrified. "But if they think you're a different blood type, you could die if you need a transfusion."

"I'll try to stay healthy. But better death in a hospital than death in a Gestapo prison."

"Do you think anyone will notice that you're left-handed when you're supposed to be right-handed?"

Bastien held both his hands up, palms facing her. The right one had more than double the scar tissue. "My injury caused a change in hand preference. That's true for both Adalard and the real me."

"What happened?"

"Adalard was injured outside Leningrad. I don't know the details of his injury, but if anyone asks, it included burns."

Gracie nodded. "And in real life?"

Bastien stared at his fingers for a few seconds before hiding them under the table. "It's probably best you don't know the real story. I wouldn't want you to get confused as to which version Adalard's girlfriend is supposed to know."

"I think I can keep two stories straight."

"Yes, because you'll only know one of them—the one you're supposed to know."

Her eyes narrowed.

Bastien glanced around the restaurant and handed Gracie his wine glass. "Will you pour half of that out for me? No one is watching us at the moment."

The distraction seemed to work. Her face showed less frustration as she returned his glass to him. They spent the rest of the meal talking about the weather and Roman architecture.

It was after curfew when they finished, so he walked her home. Normally, he wouldn't try to find out where she lived—it was better that he didn't know in case he was captured. But they were supposed to be dating—or soon would be. People would expect him to know her address, and her neighborhood wasn't completely crime-free. He'd hate for her to get robbed or otherwise attacked on her way home.

They crossed a busy intersection and walked past a man missing his left leg. Bastien watched him for a few moments. He didn't mean to stare; he just wondered what the man's story was. He looked like he could have been in the military: good posture even while using crutches, appropriate age. Bastien pulled his eyes away and held back a shiver.

He thought of a man his father had known from their army days. Bastien had met him a few times when he was younger. The man had lost a hand and an eye in the war and had been largely dependent on others the rest of his life. Bastien remembered accompanying his father to the man's funeral and the way no one would talk about how he'd died. Only after the service had Bastien's father explained the heavy toll his friend had faced every day of his life since the injury and that the fatal knife wound was self-inflicted. *We shouldn't judge him, Bastien,* his father had said. *None of us knows what he was dealing with.* At age twelve, Bastien had tried not to judge, but he'd sensed then that a life-changing injury was the end of a happy life, and what he'd seen since had done little to change his opinion.

Gracie walked into an apartment building, and Bastien followed her up the rickety steps. He could hear someone coming down the stairs when they reached her door, so he kissed her on the cheek. Her skin was soft and warm, and he was tempted to give her a more thorough kiss, but that wasn't necessary this early in their fictitious relationship. "Good night, Concetta. See you tomorrow." He slipped her his report, as well as one he'd made from Marcello's information.

As he returned to the hotel for his motorcycle, he thought it strange that one little kiss could instantly change his mood from brooding and gloomy to almost lighthearted. Had he met Gracie in different circumstances, he might have asked her to supper of his own volition, and he might have been more open when she'd asked about his past. He glanced at his scarred hands, then shoved them into his pockets.

His good mood was short-lived. The closer he got to German head-quarters, the more he wished he wasn't pretending to be Dietrich. *Think of Lukas*, he told himself. It was enough motivation to see him through his report on the morning's inspections, and to his relief, there was no sign of the SD officer.

CHAPTER TEN

When Gracie awoke Friday morning, she remembered instantly that she was in Rome, but for the first time since her arrival, that knowledge didn't fill her with panic. When she sat up in bed, she wasn't dizzy. Another first. *Amazing what getting enough to eat two days in a row can do.* On Wednesday she'd eaten with Captain Ley at the hotel, and Thursday evening, he'd given her some cheese. A gift of cheese wasn't the most romantic of gestures, but she didn't think he was trying to be romantic, just practical, and she appreciated his gift far more than she would have appreciated flowers. Roses or daisies wouldn't appease her empty stomach.

She washed and dressed, then waited in line for breakfast—pane nero again. She ate it as she returned to her apartment to pack the pieces of her radio. She'd encoded Ley's Thursday report the night before, so all she needed to do was find someplace private to contact headquarters. The biggest trick with her job was finding a new location every day, or at least enough of them that the Gestapo couldn't home in on her signal and begin stalking a frequently used neighborhood. As a further precaution, she tried to keep her batteries charged so she wasn't dependent on local electricity. More than one radio operator had been caught when the Gestapo had systematically turned off the power, block by block, house by house, until the transmission signal went dead and the Gestapo could guess exactly where it had been sent from.

Another catch was moving the radio to the call-in site without looking suspicious. During training, some of the men had smuggled pieces of their radios under heavy overcoats, but she'd tried imitating them, and it had been obvious she was hiding something. Hauling the set around in the suitcase was possible, but the Gestapo knew about suitcase radios, so she preferred alternate disguises. For today, she hid the transmitter in an oversized purse and the receiver and power pack in a paper sack. She topped the bag with a dress and a few blouses, said a quick prayer that she wouldn't be intercepted, and was on her way.

When she arrived at one of the empty apartments she'd staked out the day before, it took longer than normal to raise her OSS contact in Caserta. Someone was supposed to be listening for her transmission every morning from ten until noon, but she wasn't the only agent sending in reports. By the time she established contact and completed her message, she knew she wouldn't have time to stop for lunch and take the radio back to her apartment before her scheduled meeting with Otavia. She contemplated taking the radio to the meeting, but she didn't like carrying it around. It was heavy, and getting caught with it would be a death sentence. She sighed as she packed away the pieces. She would have to take it back, skip lunch, and hope her meetings with Otavia and Ley were finished in time for supper.

* * *

The fountains on the Piazza Navona released no water, but Neptune was still surrounded by a shallow pool, liquid that had taken on a green tint as it sat mostly stagnant, disturbed only by rainfall and the occasional insect.

"It's prettier when the water's running," Otavia said. The two of them had the plaza mostly to themselves. No one was close enough to overhear them.

Gracie closed her eyes, remembering. "I've seen it before. I always thought a god should be battling a larger octopus. Don't get me wrong—I wouldn't want to wrestle with an octopus like that, but if Neptune's supposed to be immortal, I think his monster should be larger."

"And I always thought Zappalà should have used a different model for the Nereids. Someone like you, maybe. But then you'd have to be nearly eighty years old, I suppose." Otavia giggled. "I'm glad he didn't use an old woman as a model for nude statues."

Gracie joined in with Otavia's laughter—it was hard not to. Even with the frequent hunger and the unending tension of being a spy behind enemy lines, Gracie found Otavia's cheerfulness contagious. "How's your baby?"

Otavia moved one of her hands to her abdomen. "I felt him—or her—for the first time yesterday. It made it more real. Sometimes I still can't believe I'm going to be a mother."

Gracie's sister had said the same thing before her first son was born, but she'd spoken to their mother, not to Gracie. She tried not to let it bother her, the way her older sisters still treated her like a child. They were, after all, ten and twelve years older than she, in a different stage of life. But Gracie had seen how close Michael's sisters were despite their age gap, and for a time, they'd included her in their circle. She wished she'd had that friendship with her own sisters.

"You'll be a good mother; I'm sure of it," Gracie said. It surprised her how quickly she felt a sisterhood with Otavia, how much she had looked forward to this meeting.

"I hope so. And I hope the Allies get here before my baby's born. That would be better—to bring the baby into a free world." Otavia looked around to make sure they were still alone. "If they could just crack through Cassino."

"Last I heard, that wasn't going so well."

Otavia sighed. "That's what I've heard too. But I get depressed talking about it." Otavia slipped her report to Gracie.

"Did you have any trouble with the new system?" Gracie had given Otavia a silk handkerchief with transposition keys at the end of their last meeting.

"No. It was actually a little faster." She turned from the fountain. "Have you seen the Fontana del Moro on the other end of the plaza?"

"Not for more than a decade. I'll have to hurry though. I'm supposed to meet another contact this afternoon."

"Bored of Otavia the tour guide?"

Gracie laughed. "No. Believe me, I'd rather spend time with you."

"So this other contact—a man? A woman?"

"A man."

"Young?" Otavia asked.

"About thirty, I think."

"Handsome?"

Gracie almost said no, but that wasn't true. "I suppose he is." Otavia raised her eyebrows expectantly, and Gracie felt herself blushing. "But he's also infuriating."

"How?"

Gracie took her time answering. Vaughn-Harris had called Ley haughty, but she'd yet to see that side of him, if it existed at all. A little prideful, perhaps, especially at the train station, but she thought that was more playacting than pride, and it had been to help her. Gracie almost told Otavia he was rude, but that wasn't right either. Ley wasn't impolite, just cold. Yet cold wasn't a good description either, not when she remembered his lips and their ability to make her knees weak and her head spin. What was it about him that irritated her? He'd been condescending in Switzerland

and again the day they'd met in the café, but not since then. "I suppose he's just a little high-strung." And she couldn't really blame him. Who wouldn't be uptight in Ley's position—living a lie, knowing he'd be tortured if he was caught? As they reached the fountain, Gracie wondered if maybe she'd been too hard on him.

* * *

When Gracie saw Captain Ley a half hour later, she was determined to show more sympathy. They met at a bridge, and when she approached, he kissed her on the cheek and wrapped an arm around her shoulders. For some reason, it felt natural for his arm to be around her as if they'd been dating for years, and it was easy to smile up at him and pretend she was happy to see him.

He returned her smile, waiting for a few pedestrians to pass. When he finally spoke, his voice was all business. "My report's in your pocket. When do you plan to send it?"

"Tomorrow morning."

"Any chance you could send it tonight? I heard of a few units heading to the front. They're passing through Rome in a few hours, could be attacking our troops tomorrow. I'd like them to have warning."

Gracie knew the information was important, but she wasn't sure how she could get her radio from her apartment, find a safe location, then code and send the information all before curfew. "It would involve being out past curfew."

"I can come with you, be your security."

Ley would be a perfect guard. If anyone tried to arrest her, he could say he'd already done so. But there was one other problem. "I don't know that anyone will be listening—it's not my normal transmission time."

"I had one scheduled before Switzerland. I doubt it's been canceled."

Gracie nodded.

"We're closer to my place than yours," Ley said. "Do you prefer your own radio, or would you like to borrow mine?"

Gracie studied his face, wondering if he was implying anything with his question. But he didn't seem to be asking if she was so simple that a different radio might thwart her transmission; he sincerely wondered what her preference was. Or was he just trying to get her into his hotel room? She didn't think it was that either. She believed his promise that he'd keep their relationship professional when no one was watching. "We can use yours."

They passed barbwire barriers and machine guns as they entered Ley's hotel, but the German guard either recognized Ley or trusted his uniform. The sentry came to attention and saluted but didn't ask for identification. Ley acknowledged the salute without slowing his pace. He led Gracie through the lobby and up the stairs to the third floor. As he was unlocking his door, someone from the room across the hall exited into the hallway. Gracie noticed the double S's on his uniform and stiffened. *Captain Ley lives next to an SS officer?*

"Good afternoon, Adalard."

Ley turned and smiled at his neighbor. "Heinie, how are you?"

Heinie shrugged. "I'm feeling a little more hopeful today." He pulled a letter from his pocket. "She's still writing to me."

"Good. Oh, um, let me introduce you to Signorina Concetta Gallo. She's the reason I wasn't at supper on Wednesday and the reason I'll be absent tonight as well. Concetta, this is Obersturmführer Heinrich Vogel."

Heinie inclined his head and shoulders in a polite half bow. "Good to meet you, Fräulein, er, Signorina."

"Pleased to meet you." Gracie forced a smile as she wondered what sort of work Heinie Vogel was involved in with the SS. Torturing captured Gappisti? Sending Jews to concentration camps?

"Well, I've got to be off. I'm working the next few nights but have to stop by headquarters for a couple hours first. See you around, Adalard, Signorina." Heinie walked away, and by the time he'd turned the corner, he was whistling.

Ley pushed his door open and motioned Gracie inside. The room was dark, but Ley flipped the light switch on as the door closed. It was a gorgeous room—one Gracie's mother would approve of. Each piece of furniture was a work of art. To the left of the doorway was a sitting area with a sofa, a carved sideboard, and two armchairs. To the right of the door was a table with two chairs, and beyond that, a wet bar.

"No windows?" Gracie asked as she admired the painting hung over the table.

"The bedroom has a balcony." Ley pointed to one of the two doors opposite the suite's entrance. Now that they were inside, his demeanor changed to cool and professional.

"So what was all that talk about avoiding contact with SS men?" She kept her voice quiet as she spoke, not knowing how thick the walls were.

"Heinie's Waffen SS, not Allgemeine SS."

Gracie tried to remember what the difference was.

He seemed to notice her confusion. "The Allgemeine SS is what most people think of when they hear Schutzstaffel—the political police. The Waffen SS is the military branch. Their primary role is that of a soldier, though most of them are also fanatical Nazis. Heinie's an exception."

"But Ostheim and Zimmerman aren't?"

"Most definitely not." Ley disappeared into his bedroom. While he was gone, she took out her silk handkerchief. She heard shuffling sounds, and he returned with a suitcase.

"Your radio?" She pointed to the brown leather suitcase with a sturdy-looking lock.

"Yes. Do you prefer encoding everything here or at the call-in site?"

Gracie considered the question before answering. "Here, I think. I doubt the Gestapo searches your apartment all that often."

Ley frowned in answer.

"What?" she asked. "Do they search your apartment?"

"I'm not sure what the Gestapo thinks about me, but I saw another SD officer on our way to Rome, right after your luggage was stolen. I saw the same man Monday and Tuesday. Haven't seen him since."

The room wasn't cold, but Gracie felt a sudden chill, just like she had in Switzerland the first time Ley had mentioned someone from the SD investigating him. "Do you know why?"

"No." Ley leaned against the wall and crossed his arms over his chest. "And I'm not sure if he's really gone or if he's using someone else to watch me." He shook his head slightly. "Still want my help at the call-in?"

Gracie hesitated but not for long. "If someone is watching you, he's probably already seen me." She tried to shake off the gloom she suddenly felt. "Can I have some paper?"

Ley grabbed a few sheets from the sideboard for her. She skimmed through Ley's report, written in a mix of English, Italian, and German to make it harder for the enemy to break. She looked at her key, drew a grid, added her security check, and put the letters of the report into their squares.

"So what does Heinie do with the SS?" Gracie looked at her second transposition key and made another grid.

"He's an engineer. Like Adalard, only Heinie supervises the actual building process. Adalard mostly inspects the finished product. And Heinie works on SS projects, not army projects."

"I guess I expected him to be a guard at a concentration camp or something."

"That's generally the Totenkopfverbände SS, not the Waffen SS, although that line can get a little blurry," he said.

"Does he usually work nights?"

"Yes. So do I, sometimes. Good thing, otherwise I'd be at an office until curfew most days."

"Are you qualified as an engineer, or do you just bluff your way through?"

Ley shrugged. "I picked up a few things during my first enlistment, and I was studying to be an architect. So far, it's been enough."

Gracie nodded and began filling in her second grid with the letters from the first grid, scrambling them in an orderly, managed method.

"I'll go see if I can figure out dining arrangements," Ley said. "If anyone knocks, don't answer. Take your papers and lock yourself in the bathroom."

Gracie worked diligently while he was gone but hadn't finished checking her message when she heard someone in the hallway. Not sure who it was, she grabbed her papers and shoved them under a blank sheet.

"It's me." Gracie recognized Ley's voice as he opened the door.

She spread her papers back out and started working again.

"Can you eat and work at the same time, or do you prefer not to?"

The scent of fresh bread drifted toward her from the basket he held. "I should concentrate on this first," she said even though she was ravenous. With effort, she turned her focus from the food to the report. She glanced up long enough to see Ley take a bottle of liquor from the basket and put it on the wet bar, unopened. As she checked her work, he removed all the food from the basket and packed the pieces of his radio into the bottom before replacing whatever smelled so good.

When Ley's report was encrypted, she cut the bottom line of keys from her handkerchief and held it up with her scratch papers. "Will you burn these for me?"

Ley went into his bedroom and returned with a matchbook, which he handed to her. "You can burn them in the bathroom. I'll put the suitcase away just in case the Gestapo really does search my rooms."

"If they did, would they find your radio?"

"If they looked hard enough."

CHAPTER ELEVEN

GRACIE TOOK THE PAPERS AND strip of silk into the bathroom and lit them on fire, holding them until the flames were within an inch of her fingers before dropping them into the toilet. The bathroom was tidy—cleaner that she'd expect from a bachelor.

He was ready when she returned. "Where to, Concetta?"

That was the constant question. "I'm not sure." She needed to spend more time scouting locations because she was running out of options. But her days were already filled with waiting in line for food or water, meeting contacts, and transmitting their reports.

"I have a few ideas." He motioned toward the door, and she led the way, holding the basket for him while he locked the door. Once in the hallway, he was all smiles again.

"These things are heavy," she said when he took the basket from her, balancing it on one arm so his other arm was free to rest on her shoulders.

"That's why I plan to borrow a car."

He led her to a back door rather than through the lobby again. The lot they entered contained several rows of cars and motorcycles. Ley made arrangements with a guard stationed by the vehicles, but the two of them spoke such rapid German that Gracie couldn't understand the details.

Ley finished with the guard and put his hand on Gracie's back, gently guiding her to a VW Kübelwagen and opening the passenger door for her. He put the basket behind the seat and walked around the car to climb in next to her. "Feel free to eat on the way."

Gracie decided to take him up on the offer, even if it was more polite to wait. The bread smelled too good. "How did you get this?"

Ley backed the car up and drove around the hotel's perimeter before answering. "I know the lady in charge of the kitchen. Around Christmastime,

I caught her selling food from the mess to civilians. At the very least, she should have lost her job for it, probably worse, but I didn't report it. I just told her not to let it happen again."

"Did she stop?"

"As far as I know. Today I slipped her more than her normal weekly salary and told her I wanted to take a woman on a picnic. And I suppose my regular compliments about her cooking helped a little too."

"I doubt they hurt." Gracie reached back and pulled out the loaf of bread. "My dad always loved whatever I fixed, and it made me want to cook for him more often." She'd made his favorite, spice cake, at least twice a month until wartime rationing hit.

Gracie ripped off pieces of bread and cheese as they drove past the buildings that bordered the Vatican. The bread was light and chewy, the cheese rich and smooth, and the view spectacular. *Maybe I should visit Rome again, when it's not occupied.*

Ley didn't speak as he drove, but the silence wasn't awkward. He pulled to a stop in a shadowy alley, grabbed the basket, then helped her from the car. She followed him through a dusty doorway, up five flights of stairs, and up a ladder into a warm attic. She was grateful she wasn't the one carrying the basket with all the radio equipment in the bottom. Ley kept the food off the floor's filth by setting it on a clean cloth packed in the basket, then got the pieces of the radio out for her and set them on a rickety table. One of the legs was broken at the end, so the surface wobbled.

"The floor would be better if the table's going to move with every keystroke," she said.

Ley sorted through piles of rubbish until he found a handful of wood scraps. He tried several combinations under the short leg of the table until the surface was solid.

"Thank you," Gracie said.

He dusted off his uniform and smiled. "Whatever it takes to get the information to the right people while it's still useful."

Gracie had charged the power source with one of the small six-volt batteries she'd brought with her from Switzerland, so she had almost two hours of operating time, longer than she'd need, even with Captain Ley's detailed report. She took out the antenna, connected it to the set, then strung the flexible wire around the room, looping it over the rafters for a better signal. Next, she plugged the transmitter into the power supply and the receiver into the transmitter. After checking the antennae again, she pushed the metal switch to transmit.

She looked up. Ley was watching her every move, and she suddenly felt nervous, even though she was normally confident when it came to codes and radios.

"I'm just watching how an expert does it," Ley said, seeming to sense her discomfort. "I have no intention of questioning Colonel Ambrose's assessment of your abilities."

Gracie went to work again and tried to ignore his gaze. She set the receiver dial to the correct frequency, turned on the power, and put on her headphones. Then she plugged the radio crystal into the transmitter and tested the tuning to make sure the signal was properly set. The indicating bulb was supposed to light up with each keystroke she made, but she had to be wary of setting it too brightly, or it wouldn't dim enough to show a weakening signal. Ley's SSTR-1 wasn't as sensitive as hers, so it took longer than normal to get it right.

"I'll go make sure the Gappisti aren't planting a bomb in our car." Ley's voice was quiet through the headphones, but she nodded as he disappeared down the ladder.

She sent her call sign, Gladius, with a request for acknowledgment, and switched to receiving mode, waiting for someone to answer. She'd thought her call sign appropriate when it was assigned to her—named after a Roman sword. It fit with Captain Ley's code name, Centurion, an ancient Roman officer. When she had information from Angelo, it was from Pugio, a Roman dagger, and if it was from Otavia, Signiferi, a Roman standard-bearer. If she was sending a report from one of Ley's other contacts, it was from the Scutum network, named after a Roman shield.

When the reply came, it was weak. She had to strain to make out each dot and dash, but she assumed they'd be able to hear her report. Their receivers were much larger than hers. She switched back to transmit and got to work on the reports, first Ley's and then Otavia's. There was something about the rhythmic long and short bursts that she found strangely satisfying. And though Gracie was often self-conscious about her birthmark and her hips, she knew her fingers worked as well as anyone's.

Ley returned partway through the transmission. Gracie paused for an instant, but his face was calm, so she continued transmitting, and he disappeared again, coming back as she finished hiding the radio in the bottom of the basket.

"Done already?"

"Yes. Where did you go?" she asked as she lifted her hair off her neck. The air in the attic was stale and humid.

"I was checking doorways, seeing if anyone looked suspicious. It's unlikely the Gestapo could track you down from one transmission, but it doesn't hurt to be careful, especially with what I thought was a long report." Ley put the food on top of the equipment again.

"You don't want to stay for supper?"

"I think it's best to leave as soon as possible."

Gracie nodded. Ley was right, but she was still a little hungry. The food she'd eaten on the drive over had cut the edge off her appetite but hadn't banished it.

Ley carried the basket again as they made their way down the ladder and staircases and into the alley. As they reached the Kübelwagen, two men left the building across the alley. They looked menacing, with hats pulled low over their foreheads and solemn expressions on their faces. When she saw the men raise pistols and point them at Ley, she screamed.

"Get down!" Ley dropped the basket and pushed Gracie to the ground, where the car shielded her from the gunmen. He crouched behind the Kübelwagen's hood with his Luger out, firing at the men across the alley.

Gracie pressed her hands over her mouth to keep from shrieking as gunshot after gunshot sounded. She wasn't armed, so she couldn't do anything other than huddle there while Ley fought the men off. Bullets hit the cobblestones and the Kübelwagen, but Ley held his ground despite being outnumbered.

She remembered how accurate his shots had been in Switzerland, so she was surprised when she heard the would-be assassins running away. She risked a glance and verified her suspicion. Ley had missed. The men didn't even look wounded.

Ley stayed in a low position and edged past her toward the rear of the car. He only stood when the assailants turned left down an intersecting road.

"Concetta, are you all right?"

"Yes." It came out as a whisper.

"Good." Ley looked the other direction and frowned.

She followed his gaze and saw two men in Italian Fascist uniforms, then she noticed the basket on its side with the radio partially exposed. She scrambled over to it and hid everything with a cloth just as the men arrived.

"What happened?" one of the patrolman asked as he saluted.

Ley returned the salute. "They came from there." He pointed toward the door they'd emerged from. "Tried to shoot me. Ran off. Turned right at the next street."

Gracie opened her mouth, then shut it again without saying anything. The men had turned left, not right.

"Are either of you hurt?"

"No," Ley said.

The two men sprinted off, trying to chase down the Gappisti. When they were out of sight, Ley walked her to the passenger-side door and opened it for her. He took the basket and put it behind her seat.

For someone who'd just been shot at, he seemed remarkably calm. "Let's get out of here, shall we?" he asked as he slid behind the wheel.

"You missed on purpose?"

Ley nodded and started the car.

"Even though they were trying to kill you?"

"They were trying to kill a German officer. I'm not taking it as a personal insult. Better for them to live and fight another day. Maybe next time they'll try for someone who's really an enemy."

Gracie was quiet as Ley drove to her apartment, trying not to think about how close she'd come to getting shot and how awful it would have been to see Ley gunned down right in front of her. There were so many ways they could get killed in Rome. Her hands started to shake, so she pulled them into fists, hoping Ley wouldn't notice her reaction.

"I need the basket, but feel free to wrap the rest of the food in one of the napkins and take it with you," he said as they approached her neighborhood. "Chew carefully. A few bullets made it into the basket."

Gracie turned and reached for the equipment. "Are you going to check the radio?"

"Yes, but I prefer to do that in privacy."

Gracie pulled her hand back, realizing how foolish it would be for her to examine the radio while they were driving through the streets. She caught another whiff of bread. "Did you eat anything tonight?"

"I'm not hungry."

She studied him as he drove, but his lack of appetite was the only sign of unease she could detect.

CHAPTER TWELVE

ONE OF THE FIRST THINGS Bastien had noticed about Marcello was his ability to always look relaxed. Initially, Bastien had found it disconcerting, making him doubt he could rely on the Italian man, but Marcello had quickly proven his competence.

"Ah, Capitano, how was your week?" Marcello said from the shade of a grapevine. This week, Roberto accompanied him.

Bastien dismounted his motorcycle and joined them in the vineyard. "Mostly the same, except for getting shot at by a pair of Gappisti a few days ago."

Marcello's head jerked around. "I take it they missed?"

Bastien nodded. "Shot my radio though. Broke the crystal. It's useless without a replacement."

"Has Hauptmann Dietrich been doing anything to merit execution?" Marcello asked. Most of the time, Italian partisans were selective about whom they shot—preferring Gestapo agents or Italian Fascist traitors over normal army men.

"Such as torturing the Gappisti or executing black-market dealers? No. Maybe they wanted my vehicle and my Luger."

"Do they really execute you for selling things on the black market?" Roberto asked.

"Depends on what you're selling and who arrests you. I think forced labor is a more common sentence. Not quite the same thing as execution. Usually ends in death, but a slow death by starvation instead of a quick one in front of a firing squad. Why do you ask? Have you been selling things?"

Roberto smiled, which was as good as saying yes.

Bastien grinned back. "Just see that you don't get caught."

"Do you have anything for us today?" Marcello asked.

Bastien took a few papers from his pocket. "Just a shipment schedule. No idea what type of escorts they'll have, except for the one tonight. It might be larger than you want to hit without help."

Marcello read the list.

"And I heard a rumor at supper the other night. I'm wondering if you've seen or heard anything along the same lines," Bastien said. "A Wehrmacht intelligence officer is convinced the Allies have given up taking Rome from the south. Doesn't think they'll ever get past Cassino or the Alban Hills. Expects them to launch another amphibious assault, this time north of Rome, near Civitavecchia."

Marcello tucked the list away. "I haven't heard anything. You, Roberto?"

Roberto smiled lazily. "Do I ever hear anything you haven't already known about for a few days?"

"If they send in patrols for reconnaissance, try not to shoot them, will you?" Bastien said.

"Ask questions first; shoot later. Sure thing, Capitano." Marcello shifted in the shade. "Have you seen that SD man lately?"

"Not in the last week." Nor had Bastien seen anyone who looked like he was picking up where the SD officer had left off, but he couldn't be sure.

* * *

Gracie had seen Captain Ley daily since the Gappisti attack, and the frequency of their meetings worried her. Her trainers at OSS would recommend more separation because if either of them was caught, both their missions would be compromised. Yet Colonel Ambrose himself had ordered them to act this way, and Gracie didn't think there was a manageable alternative, not with the extent of Ley's information, so she tried to shrug off her concern.

She also took reports from her other contacts. She supposed she should have made her exchanges with Otavia and Angelo quick, but she enjoyed their company, and she was lonely. She spent hours in lines each day, surrounded by other civilians, but she couldn't be friends with any of them. Her fellow spies were the only people she could talk to for more than a sentence or two.

On the first day of March, she wasn't supposed to meet with anyone but Ley, and the lighter schedule gave her time to shop around the black market.

She was nervous, but anything she could get legally tasted awful, and there was never enough of it. She bought enough food that even if Ley didn't give her any when they met that afternoon, she wouldn't have to go to bed hungry.

As she hurried home with her illegal purchases, she was shocked to recognize Angelo. She'd seen him two days before and didn't expect to see him again for another week.

"Concetta?" His eyes widened, and his mouth hung open when he saw her. He took her arm and led her off the main road. They'd only gone a few steps when she noticed his limp. "Seeing you is an answer to prayer."

"It is?" She glanced around to make sure no one was close enough to overhear them.

"Yes. The Germans are having a massive roundup in my neighborhood, taking anyone they think they can get a few days' worth of work out of. I barely got away." He smiled, but the expression lacked its usual warmth.

"What happened?"

"I jumped out a second-story window and ran. Did something to my leg." Angelo stopped to rest as they waited for someone to pass them.

"Do you think they're looking for you?"

He shook his head. "No, they didn't have a list of names or anything. But curfew is coming, and I don't have anywhere to go. Can you hide me until morning? Tomorrow I can find somewhere else, but today I don't have any way to contact the other Gappisti, and I'm not moving fast enough to outrun patrols when curfew starts. I figure seeing you is a sign."

Gracie hesitated, but she couldn't really say no to an injured contact. "I just have one room. It's not very big."

"It's better than being crowded into the back of a truck and shipped off to dig trenches. And better than a jail cell."

Gracie nodded. At least she'd bought extra food today. She slowed her stride to match Angelo's limp and tried to support him with her arm. They were only four blocks from her flat, but it took longer than usual to get there. When they reached the stairs in her apartment building, the ascension quickly proved the hardest part of their journey. Angelo winced every time his left foot touched the floor.

"Let me help," she said.

He moved an arm around her shoulders, but each stair still seemed to cause him pain. "Which floor are you on?"

"The fifth. I'm sorry."

THE RULES IN ROME

Angelo laughed softly. "Well, beggars can't be choosers."

A middle-aged woman Gracie had seen before passed them in the stairwell, and one of her neighbors left his apartment right when they arrived, but no one said anything. As soon as she unlocked and opened the door, Angelo stumbled over to her bed and collapsed on it.

"I'm glad that's over," he said. "Maybe tomorrow my ankle will feel better."

Gracie didn't know much beyond basic first aid but thought elevating his leg was wise. Angelo's head wasn't on her pillow, so she folded the nearly-flat cushion in half and propped it under his injured ankle, then looked through her drawers and pulled out one of the fabric pieces she normally used for wrapping radio parts. "Can I look at it?"

He nodded.

She undid his old shoe and pulled his sock away from his ankle. The skin was discolored and swollen, but she wasn't sure what to do about it. "I can wrap it," she said softly. Anything spoken above a whisper could carry into a neighboring apartment.

"Thank you." He watched her, and as she finished, he straightened on the bed so he was no longer sprawled across it. "I guess we'll be cozy tonight, eh?"

Gracie opened her mouth in surprise. Her bed was big enough for two people, but surely he didn't expect them to share it . . . or did he?

"I don't suppose you have a chess set or a deck of cards?"

"No. I haven't been here long." Gracie glanced around the room. Even for a student's apartment, it looked sparsely decorated. "I have a few books." She pulled them from the top drawer in her dresser and held them out to him.

He glanced at the titles and shook his head. "No, thanks."

What am I going to do with him until tomorrow morning?

CHAPTER THIRTEEN

"You look tired. Come on. Get off your feet," Angelo said.

Gracie was tired, and the only places to sit were the bed and the floor. She put the books away and hesitated. Angelo patted the bed beside him, and she took her shoes off, then sat on the bed with her knees bent and her feet curled up behind her.

"So where do you come from, Concetta?"

"Nettuno. At least originally."

"And since then?" Angelo's dark eyes met hers. He was a good-looking man, and somehow the stubble along his jaw made him even more attractive.

Gracie's OSS training kicked in. "It's probably best if you don't ask personal questions."

Angelo smiled. "I won't ask you about your past, then. But what about the future? What do you want to do after the war?"

"I have to survive a while longer before I worry about that." And to be honest, Gracie wasn't sure what she'd do when the war ended and OSS no longer needed radio operators. She'd thought her life was all planned out, but that had changed, and now her future looked murky and unfocused.

"Did I upset you, Concetta?"

"No, of course not."

"You were frowning."

"I was? Sorry."

Angelo's lips curved into another smile. "You don't have to apologize for frowning. I'm the one who said something wrong."

"You didn't say anything wrong . . . I was just thinking."

"What were you thinking about, Concetta? Or is that the wrong question to ask? And is Concetta your real name?"

"No." Gracie smiled. "Is Angelo your real name?"

"No." He laughed, and she joined in. "You know, Concetta, or whatever your name is, you have a beautiful smile." As he spoke, he rested his hand on her leg just above her knee and ran his fingers over the thin fabric of her skirt. She could feel the warmth and strength of his hand, and it made her feel like a mouse caught in a trap. Gracie couldn't stay with him in the apartment all night.

"I forgot. I have another contact I have to meet tonight." Ley would be waiting for her.

Angelo looked at his watch. "Curfew's in twenty minutes."

Gracie pulled her suitcases out from under the bed and opened the small one. She packed her radio inside, along with a change of clothes. "I really can't miss this information. I'll stay with a friend so you'll have the place to yourself. The bathroom's down the hall, and there's plenty of food in my shopping bag."

"Wait, Concetta. Did I do something wrong?"

Other than being entirely too handsome and friendly? "No. I just can't miss this meeting."

She hurried from her room before he could say anything else. Gracie was outside before it fully hit her that she didn't have a place to sleep now. Otavia would let her in, she didn't doubt, but Gracie had no idea where Otavia lived. *You have to see Captain Ley anyway. Maybe he'll have a backup plan.*

Like the other civilians still outside, she walked quickly, trying to beat the clock and make it inside before curfew. The guard in the hotel lobby nodded his recognition and checked his watch as she arrived. Gracie's fingers tightened around the handle of her suitcase. She hadn't wanted to leave the radio with Angelo. She trusted him, but the radio was her responsibility, her most important tool. She couldn't leave it with her houseguest, especially now that Ley's radio was damaged and she no longer had access to a backup set. But she also realized what the suitcase must look like to the guard who'd seen her with Captain Ley so often. *As long as he doesn't suspect what's really inside.*

Ley opened the door as soon as she knocked, and he leaned into the hallway to give her a kiss. Once they were inside with the door closed, he looked pointedly at the suitcase. "Is everything all right? You're later than usual."

Gracie flung her free hand up in a show of desperation. "I ran into one of my other contacts, and he needed help. He's hiding in my apartment, and it took a while to get him settled." She set her suitcase on the floor. "So he's there, and I couldn't leave my radio with him. And I can't very well go back to my place tonight, and I'm sure the guard thinks I'm bringing my luggage along because I'm moving in with you or something, and . . . and it's all a mess."

"This other contact—did anyone follow him to your apartment?"

Gracie let her hands fall to her sides. "I'm not sure. I looked around a few times, but someone could have followed us without me noticing." She dropped her eyes to the floor, expecting a lecture and thinking she probably deserved it.

"Why is he on the run?"

"There was a roundup of civilians today."

"So I heard. Seven hundred of them."

She shifted her gaze from the floor to Ley. "You knew?"

"I heard about it at headquarters after it happened, when I went to file my report."

"He was trying to keep it from being seven hundred and one, and he hurt his ankle and can barely walk."

"So not only did you neglect basic principles of watching your back, but you were with an obviously injured man, and he now knows where you live?" Ley's voice was quiet, as it always was in his suite, but the words stung.

She felt her face burn with shame and a touch of resentment. "Yes."

"Well, at least he's not wanted for spying. Sounds like he's just an anonymous face who slipped through the roundup net." He walked over to the sitting area. "Would you like to sit down, Concetta?"

Gracie followed him and sat in one of the armchairs.

"So you aren't planning to go back to your flat tonight?"

"No. You've seen how small it is, and . . . and I'm not sure what his, um, expectations are of a female hostess."

Ley laughed softly. "So where are you sleeping tonight?"

"I haven't figured that out yet."

"And your supper plans?"

Gracie shrugged. "I had breakfast and lunch today, so supper isn't all that important, I suppose."

Ley leaned forward. "How about this? I'll take you to supper. That's what the guard will expect, and it'll give us a chance to check if anyone's watching you. I'll sleep on the couch tonight, and you can have my bedroom."

"I couldn't take your bed."

"The maid comes on Wednesdays. You'll have clean sheets."

"Oh, no, I didn't mean to suggest you have bad hygiene or anything. You're cleaner than I am—my building only has running water a few hours each week." Gracie looked at her skirt. It wasn't dirty, but it wasn't exactly clean either. "I don't want to kick you out of your bed."

Ley's lips turned up in amusement. "It makes more sense for me to sleep on the couch. I plan to leave several hours before dawn, and if someone knocks, they'll expect me to answer the door. They'd be suspicious if you were sleeping on the couch when they looked into the room."

"Do you expect someone in the middle of the night?"

"It's unlikely. But if you hear a knock, make sure both sides of the bed look slept in, and be wearing something scandalous." He looked her up and down, and she felt her face go hot again. He stood and cleared his throat. "Supper?"

* * *

When Gracie woke the next morning, Ley was already gone. She had showered the night before, but knowing she had only a sponge bath to look forward to at her own flat, she showered again.

Ley had left breakfast for her: a pair of hard-boiled eggs lay in the wet bar's ice box, and there was a thick roll—real bread made with real flour instead of the substitutes civilians had to manage with—and jam wrapped in waxed paper so it wouldn't make the bread soggy while she slept in.

Gracie shook her head. Ley had been so civil yesterday at supper, then had withdrawn again as soon as they'd returned. She assumed the smiles at the restaurant were an act but wasn't sure how to explain the thoughtfulness behind the breakfast he'd left for her.

* * *

After his morning inspections and a trip to army headquarters, Bastien went to the Gestapo building on the Via Tasso. He hated going there because most of the people who worked inside had at least a small streak of evil, but there were times when it was unavoidable. He hesitated as the gray-and-yellow building came into view, then walked past the rolls of barbed wire meant to deter a Gappisti attack.

Zimmerman was easy to find on a Thursday afternoon. When Bastien walked over to him, Zimmerman stood and yelled out an enthusiastic "Heil, Hitler," and Bastien returned the greeting. As an army officer, he could get away with a standard military salute, but he didn't want anyone to question his pretended loyalty. If the wrong people doubted him, he'd be locked in one of the twenty cells in the building's north-wing prison.

"What can I do for you, Hauptmann Dietrich?" Zimmerman motioned to a chair and waited for Bastien to sit before he returned to his seat.

Bastien scanned the desk, seeing a few files, a pile of postcards, and a picture of a woman and a little boy. "Your family?" Bastien asked, pointing to the framed photograph.

Zimmerman nodded. "Taken a few months ago."

"It must be hard being away from them."

"I am happy to serve our Führer."

"Of course," Bastien said. "As am I."

Zimmerman relaxed, a smile forming as he looked at the picture. "Someday I hope to bring them to Rome. My son would love the buildings, and my wife would love the art galleries. But between the Gappisti and the train shortage, now isn't the best time."

"The Gappisti . . . Did they give you any trouble yesterday during the roundup?"

"No, nothing to speak of. I'm sure a few slipped away, but we met our quota."

"Good." Bastien hoped that meant no one would trace Gracie's contact and, by tracing him, find her. "All my crew leads are asking for more labor."

Zimmerman's glance shifted to someone beyond Bastien. When Bastien looked over his shoulder, he saw Ostheim. Bastien outranked Ostheim but saw no reason to make him wait, especially not after stealing Gracie from him at the café.

"Well, I just wanted to check on the roundup." Bastien stood, grateful for an excuse to leave. Family man or not, Zimmerman was a fanatical SS officer, and so was Ostheim.

Ostheim saluted as Bastien walked past him. The motion was above reproach, but Bastien detected resentment in the man's crisp blue eyes.

CHAPTER FOURTEEN

BASTIEN HAD NEARLY MADE THE building's front exit when someone called his name. "Adalard!"

Bastien turned to see Heinie hailing him. "Hello, Heinie. On your way out?"

Heinie nodded, and when they stepped outside, he lifted his eyes skyward as if he felt as much relief to be leaving the building as Bastien did.

"Long day?" Bastien asked.

"Vogel!" Sturmbannführer Reinhart Scholz called them back.

Heinie saluted sharply, as did Bastien. "Yes, sir?"

"Is that report finished?"

"I left it with your aide, sir."

"Hmm." Scholz scrutinized Heinie's uniform as if hoping something was sufficiently out of place to require a reprimand, but Heinie's uniform was immaculate. Scholz turned to Bastien. "Dietrich, isn't it?"

"Yes, sir," Bastien said.

"Are you on duty Saturday?"

"No, sir."

"Good. There's a curfew party tomorrow night. Over in the Parioli district. Contessa Tignorio's estate. Do you know it?"

"Yes, sir." Contessa Tignorio, still a fanatical Fascist, owned a mansion in one of Rome's more prestigious neighborhoods.

"Come." Scholz's request sounded like an order.

"Thank you, sir." According to rumor, the contessa wasn't intelligent enough to be a worthwhile contact, but she was rich enough to host dozens of useful sources.

Scholz looked at Heinie again but didn't extend an invitation. "Good day, men."

Bastien and Heinie saluted, relaxing only when Scholz was out of sight.

"I suppose he's still unhappy that I offered to resign my commission," Heinie said.

Bastien nodded. It made more sense for Scholz to invite Bastien to the party as a snub against Heinie than to invite him for his own sake. Before today, they'd only spoken once, briefly. "I'm sorry, Heinie."

Heinie shrugged, then grinned. "The only person I'd want to take to something like that is in Schweinfurt."

Bastien smiled back at his friend, then wondered why Heinie was at the Via Tasso. "What are you doing at Gestapo headquarters?"

"Scholz says he can liaise better with the rest of the SS if he has an office here. He dragged me along as unofficial penance, but I suppose it's not too awful. There's a window only five desks away." The smile fell from Heinie's face as they turned the corner. "That report, on the other hand, was real punishment."

"What was it about?"

"Busywork. Mind-numbing busywork."

It took only a bit of prying for Heinie to give more details. He'd been asked to catalog which fortifications had been hit by Allied air raids, then organize the data by month and severity. By the time they reached their rooms, Bastien had enough information for a report.

When Gracie came to his suite an hour later, Bastien wrapped an arm around her waist and kissed her as he pulled her inside. He was growing fond of her lips, but the instant the door clicked shut, he ended the kiss and dropped his arm. "Is your houseguest gone?"

"I went back around lunchtime, and he was just leaving. He's supposed to meet one of his comrades today and thinks he'll get more permanent help from him."

"Good." Bastien motioned to the report on his table. "Details of the new fortifications along the Rapido River. The workers should be finished within two days, so in three or four days, it should be on the list of bombing targets. And, ironically, German assessments of past air raids."

Gracie picked up the papers and began reading through them. "All right. I'll send this in tomorrow morning."

Bastien watched her read and hesitated for a moment before plunging ahead. "Also, I've been invited to a curfew party tomorrow. I expect a dozen or so other officers to be there, so it could be a good chance to learn something. I'd like you to accompany me if you can."

Gracie set the papers down and nodded her agreement.

"I don't remember seeing anything fancy in your luggage, so try to find an evening gown." Bastien took out his wallet and handed her some money. "Something you'll be comfortable in but something that will make men turn to get a second look." Bastien suppressed a smile. Gracie was lovely enough that most men would turn to take a second look at her regardless of what she wore.

She stared at the floor.

"Is something wrong?"

Gracie shrugged, then made a dismissive motion with her hands. "A nice dress won't turn me into a movie star. If you want a beautiful woman on your arm, I'm not the right person."

Bastien wasn't sure if she was fishing for compliments or if she really didn't know how pretty she was. "Actually, I'm hoping for a woman with a brain to join me since there might be useful information flowing about. The fact that you're gorgeous is a bonus."

"Gorgeous?" Gracie's voice was barely a whisper. "That's not what my mother thought."

His competent radio operator had somehow morphed into what reminded him of an insecure teenager—like his sister Hannah after she'd seen the boy she'd liked for years kissing someone else. Bastien was tempted to change the subject, but he wanted Gracie at her best during the party, and if she was self-conscious the entire time, he didn't think she'd be much help. "Well, fortunately for us, it's not your mother's opinion that matters tomorrow night. Given the fact that I'm male and most of the guests we want information from are also male, I think we can safely rely on my opinion over your mother's."

Gracie forced a weak smile but didn't look convinced as she lowered herself into one of the dining chairs.

Bastien sat opposite her. "You don't believe me?"

Gracie opened her mouth, then shut it again, a hand moving in frustration. "I just don't want you to be disappointed, and I don't want to ruin your plans if you need the other guests to find me attractive."

"The more attractive the woman, the more likely they are to talk to her, but most of them won't complain as long as the woman in question is between the ages of fifteen and forty-five and has bathed within the last week."

"Oh." She reached for his report, but he watched her eyes, and she didn't seem to be reading the papers in front of her.

Bastien wondered just what type of hornet's nest he'd stirred up. "What exactly did your mother say to you?"

She glanced up, then away before answering. "She didn't say anything to *me*. I just overheard a conversation once when I was thirteen. My dad hurt his back, so he couldn't fix a broken closet door. I tried, but I wasn't strong enough, and my mom was frustrated. She said if the Lord was going to send her a child at age forty, He should have had the decency to send a boy. My dad told her to be quiet, and she said he didn't need to worry about me overhearing because I was probably upstairs doing a crossword puzzle or reading a book. But I wasn't. I was in the next room still trying to figure out how I could fix the door. Then she talked about what a waste it was for a girl to spend so much time reading and what a shame it was that my hips were so big and my birthmark so ugly." She frowned and ran her hand along the edge of the table. "It was the only time I ever heard my dad yell at my mother."

Bastien remembered how sensitive his sisters had been about their appearances at age thirteen; he thought their reactions would have been similar. "Most women are far more beautiful at age twenty-three than they are at age thirteen. I'm sure even your mother would agree that you're no exception."

Gracie nodded but didn't look convinced.

"I guess I expected your mother to be different. I've known a few Mormon families, and their mothers were saints."

"My mother's not very religious. Not anymore. She used to go to church all the time because her parents were devout. But I made her sick before I was born, and she got out of the habit." Gracie's hands gestured again, the movement holding a hint of sadness. "My dad was the one who took me to church. We started going with some neighbors when we moved to Utah, and we liked their church so we kept going back, and eventually we got baptized, my dad and I."

"So you're closer to your father than your mother?"

"Yes," Gracie said, a smile forming. "I was always his little shadow. And he was always my champion."

Bastien recalled the times his own father had called him and the other children his little shadows. "Maybe it's time you started listening to your champions instead of your critics."

CHAPTER FIFTEEN

FRIDAY WAS A BUSY DAY for Gracie. Ley's report was long, and whoever was on the other end of the radio took his time replying. Then there was the problem of finding a dress. She didn't have much time to look for one, so she went back to the shop with the black dress Otavia had drooled over. The shopkeeper raised her eyebrows when Gracie asked to try it on, as if she doubted Gracie's ability to pay or didn't want to sell such a beautiful dress to someone with such an ugly birthmark. In the end, the dress fit, Captain Ley's money was sufficient to pay for it, and the shopkeeper cracked a smile.

Gracie had wanted to take a nap before attending the all-night party, but when she got back to her apartment, she barely had time to change and wash up. As she tried to make her water ration stretch, she was tempted to borrow Ley's shower again, but there wasn't enough time for that either.

At least the bathroom was empty so she could use the mirror without waiting. It wasn't a real mirror, just a piece of polished metal, and scratches on its surface made her face look like it was crisscrossed with scars. The edges were so damaged that it gave her neck a foggy appearance, but it showed enough for her to pin her hair up and apply lipstick. She stood away from the metal plate to give herself a final look, but all she could pick out was dark hair, two eyes, lips, and a birthmark. She grabbed her extra hairpins and lipstick tube from the cracked countertop with a sigh. By 9:00 p.m., most of the party-goers would probably be too tipsy to notice her anyway.

Captain Ley was in the hallway outside her flat when she left the bathroom. Even though he smiled when she opened the door, Gracie's initial glimpse of a stern Wehrmacht officer almost stopped her in her tracks. He looked so real. A Hollywood casting director would have had a hard time finding someone more fitting.

"You look perfect." He bent down and kissed her on the cheek. Gracie was tempted to kiss him back. He'd look less intimidating with lipstick smeared across his face.

She held her reply until he followed her into her room. "I was going to say the same thing about you. Sometimes you don't look like a person; you just look like a Nazi."

"Most Nazis are, in fact, human," he said, looking at the flimsy walls and automatically matching her low volume.

Gracie waved her hand. "I know. I just . . . Well, sometimes you look a little scary." Gracie put her unused hairpins in the top drawer of her dresser. "I'm sorry I wasn't ready when you arrived."

"I was early."

Gracie nodded. "Will you put this in your pocket for me?" She held out her lipstick. "My dress doesn't have any pockets."

Ley smiled as he took it and slipped it into his trouser pocket.

"Is something funny?" she asked.

"Not really. I just remember my sisters asking the same thing. My youngest sister was the worst—it was never just lipstick. If I'd let her, I think she would have had me carry around a complete change of clothing along with all her cosmetics, an address book, a novel, no fewer than three writing utensils, and enough food for five people."

Gracie couldn't remember Ley ever talking about his family before. "How many sisters do you have?"

"Two." Ley frowned. "But Adalard didn't have pictures of anyone other than himself, so I'm not sure about him."

"Do you have any brothers?"

"Two." Ley glanced at his right hand. Gracie followed his gaze, wondering why he'd chosen that moment to study his scars. "I probably made Stefanie sound like a pack rat. She just likes to be prepared. When she was fourteen, I picked her up from school and we went straight to the train station. I'd packed a bag for her, but I'd missed the diary she had hidden in the closet, and I didn't pack her favorite dress because it wasn't practical for traveling. My mother and I had been planning to leave Germany for a few weeks, but we didn't tell the others because we were afraid they'd let something slip. I think it was hard for them to leave Frankfurt with no warning, no chance for good-byes."

"How did you get out?" Gracie wondered if he'd always been competent with things like spying and sneaking people out of totalitarian countries or if it was something he'd learned gradually.

"That's a story for another day." He unbuttoned his uniform and took out a folded paper. "I have a few things for you. First, my report. It's not urgent, so it can wait until tomorrow." She took his paper and hid it under her mattress. When she straightened, he was holding something wrapped in brown paper and tied with a string. It was too big for a normal-sized pocket, and she wondered where he'd hidden it. "And a present."

Gracie's jaw dropped. Ley had a present for her? She hesitated long enough that the moment became awkward. "Should I open it now?"

"Yes. I mean, it's yours, so you can do whatever you want with it, but I'd planned on you opening it before we left."

Gracie fumbled with the string for a few seconds, then Ley took out a pocketknife and handed it to her, handle first. She sawed the string until it broke, hoping her face wasn't as red as it was hot. *You don't need to be embarrassed just because he's giving you a present and you're not good with knots.*

As she pulled the paper off, Ley continued. "It's not new or anything. I just wanted you to see how pretty you are before we go."

It was a hand mirror with a flawless surface and a decorative silver-colored handle. Outlines of birds and flowers were carved into the back and onto the hand grip. If it wasn't new, it was still in pristine condition. "Thank . . . thank you."

"You're welcome," he said softly.

She glanced at herself, focusing on the clearly reflected brown circle on her cheek. At least her hair had cooperated and her lipstick was on straight.

"So, um, about tonight," Ley began. "Wander wherever you want in the house or on the grounds. We're supposed to be a couple, but I think it's more effective if we split up, so don't feel like you have to hang on my arm all night. I'm not sure who will be there, but keep your ears open for anything useful. Don't ignore any potential sources."

Gracie nodded and placed the mirror next to the pitcher. Her fingers caressed the handle one last time. It was a beautiful gift.

Ley moved toward the door, and she followed. Once they were in the hallway, the thoughtful, sober look on his face disappeared, replaced by a confident, charismatic one. She wondered which was real and which was an act.

Outside, a car and driver waited. "I didn't want someone setting off a bomb while I was inside," Ley explained.

Gracie smiled at the driver, a German-enlisted man, as he opened the door for her. She slid across the seat so Ley could enter from the same side, and she sat close to him for the driver's benefit and to calm her nerves. She felt safe next to Captain Ley and hoped she could channel some of his competence and courage. She'd been trained on how to trick information out of people, but she'd never done it in the field.

As they drove through the city and into a residential area, the houses grew larger and larger. They stopped in front of a mansion with an exquisite lawn, a huge fountain, and a pair of marble lions guarding the entrance.

Ley helped her from the car and told the driver to return at oh six hundred hours. It was going to be a long party.

Imitating a dozen other couples, Gracie and Ley strolled along the grounds. The gardens were extensive, probably involving the labor of multiple servants. Gracie couldn't see so much as a single wilted petal.

"My mother would love the flowers," Gracie said. "She's never more content than when she's out in her garden." Ley slowed his pace, as if sensing her hesitation to go inside. *Maybe he's nervous too?* As quickly as the thought came, she dismissed it. Captain Ley, nervous? That was ridiculous.

An elegant woman greeted them when they arrived at the mansion. Her gold dress shimmered with a metallic finish and flowed gracefully to the floor. Her hair was jet black, but the lines around her eyes revealed her age. She examined Gracie from head to foot, stopping briefly to eye Gracie's very un-party-worthy shoes and then again to stare at her birthmark.

With the hostess was an SS officer, the equivalent of a major. "Hauptmann Dietrich, good of you to come."

"Thank you for the invitation, Sturmbannführer Scholz." Ley and Scholz shook hands, then Ley continued. "May I present Signorina Concetta Gallo?"

Scholz set a hand on the hostess's shoulder, intimacy hinted at in their touch. "This is Contessa Tignorio."

A contessa? Gracie's meager confidence disappeared completely. Captain Ley had told her the hostess was a rich Fascist, and though Gracie should have guessed based on the size of the estate, she still found the woman's nobility intimidating. Their hostess warmed slightly when Captain Ley took her hand as Scholz introduced them, but then she quickly turned her attention to the next guests.

The décor inside the mansion was part museum, part grand-hotel lobby. The other guests looked as if they belonged in a magazine. The men wore dress uniforms or tuxedos, the women formal gowns. Michael had taken Gracie to see the new Utah State Symphony Orchestra just before he'd left, and she had enjoyed getting dressed up and being surrounded by others in their best clothing, but the dresses the women in the mansion wore made the Salt Lake women look shabby. It was like a different world from the squalor she saw on the streets of Rome. She glanced down at the black sheen of her own dress and wondered if she measured up.

Michael would have made a joke about the excessive amount of skin the women in Rome were baring. Ley took two glasses from a waiter in a black uniform and handed one to her. "The houseplants will be thirsty," he whispered in her ear.

Gracie smiled but felt the momentary lightheartedness vanish as she glanced around the room and locked eyes with Otto Ostheim, the SS officer she'd flirted with at the café before Captain Ley had interrupted them. Ostheim's friend, Kornelius Zimmerman, stood next to him. Ostheim whispered something in his ear, placed his empty glass on the rim of an enormous marble planter, and strode toward her.

"Let's not split up yet," she whispered to Captain Ley. He glanced at Ostheim before looking back at Gracie and winking.

Ostheim nodded to Ley before giving Gracie an appreciative glance. "Concetta, you look marvelous." Ostheim tilted his head toward Ley. "Did you come with him?"

"Yes, she did," Ley said.

"If there's dancing, I hope you'll let me borrow her for a song or two."

"That will be entirely up to Concetta."

Gracie was tempted to kick Ley. She didn't want to dance with an SS officer. It would have been easier if Ley had just said no. Now she was the one who'd have to be rude and snub Ostheim again. *Or you could act like a professional spy and use the dance as an opportunity to learn something or at least open the door again after slamming it shut in the café.* Gracie took a deep breath and forced a smile. "If there's dancing, I'd be delighted to take a turn with you, Otto."

The upward curve of Ostheim's lips hinted at triumph more than pleasure. "Wonderful." He gave them each a curt nod. "Until then."

"I hope there won't be any dancing," Gracie whispered after Ostheim returned to Zimmerman.

"I'd be surprised if there wasn't."

Gracie frowned before she realized what she was doing.

"Don't look so unhappy." Ley took her arm and gently pulled her into another room. "We're supposed to be at a party."

Gracie poured most of her drink into a nearby plant, then left it on a polished, dark-wood table next to another glass, that one empty. Within a minute, one waiter had retrieved both glasses and another was offering her a second drink. Gracie took it, deciding it would be less awkward to hold the thing in her hand than to repeatedly turn down such persistent waiters.

As they mingled with the other guests, Gracie was separated from Ley, and although she would have rather stayed near him, she told herself to be brave and did her best to make new friends.

Roughly three dozen men and women filled the mansion. From the wife of the late Count Tignorio's business partner, Gracie learned that the Tignorios had earned their wealth in the munitions business. The luxurious mansion, purchased with profits earned by bloodshed, suddenly seemed less beautiful. She tried to learn more about the business but ended up with only snippets of information about weapons and enough secrets about the other guests to write lurid gossip columns on nearly all of them. It wasn't the type of information she was looking for, but it made the time pass quickly.

Captain Ley found her just before supper and offered her his arm. He led her to a long table covered in a crisp white tablecloth and set with fine china and silver. Just before the waiters served the first course, Zimmerman sat across from her and Ostheim sat beside her.

CHAPTER SIXTEEN

GRACIE DID HER BEST TO smile politely as supper was served, but she found Ostheim's presence eerie. His eyes held no warmth, and she couldn't forget his occupation as chief interrogator for the Rome Gestapo.

The meal began as an answer to all Gracie's culinary longings over the past two weeks, but she had to stop before the final two courses because she was full. She wondered how they got away with it: no ration coupons but more food than most people ate in three days, all at one meal. The other guests' chatter was constant, and though the ache in her head had left with the tomato bisque, she found herself longing for the quiet of her room or Ley's suite, especially when Ostheim turned his attention to her.

"What do you do, Concetta, when you aren't attending curfew parties?"

"I'm a student."

"How delightful. What are you studying?"

"Literature." Gracie took a sip of water. "And your duties with the SS?"

Ostheim waved a hand at her. "You don't want to talk about that, I'm sure. Who are you studying with?"

"Several different professors. One of them loves Dante; another loves Horace."

Ley interrupted, as if on cue, engaging Gracie in conversation before Ostheim could ask Gracie for the names of her professors. But as soon as there was a pause, Ostheim began asking her more questions. Gracie tried to be vague in her answers while sticking to her cover story, but Ostheim was specific in his follow-up. She nervously wrung the napkin in her lap as she concentrated on her answers. Ley seemed to instinctively know when Ostheim's questions grew too personal or detailed, saving her more than once before they finished the feast.

Zimmerman had been quiet most of the meal, but as the waiters cleared away the last of the dessert and began serving coffee, he turned to Captain Ley. "Hauptmann Dietrich, perhaps you could share with us how you earned your Iron Cross." Gracie had noticed Zimmerman eyeing the medal at Captain Ley's throat more than once that evening.

"Oh yes, a rousing war story would be perfect," the middle-aged woman sitting next to Zimmerman said.

"It's not very rousing, I'm afraid," Ley replied.

"Don't be modest, Dietrich." Despite their difference in rank, Ostheim's words sounded like an order.

"I was fighting the Communists outside Leningrad. The real credit goes to the men I commanded."

"Come now; more details," Ostheim requested.

"About Russia? It's a horrible place, especially in the winter."

As Ostheim and the woman next to Zimmerman pressed for more information, Gracie thought she'd return the help Ley had given her earlier. She reached for her water and tipped over her wine. The bright crimson liquid spread across the tablecloth, not spilling into anyone's lap but prompting the woman next to Zimmerman to push her chair back abruptly.

"I'm so sorry!" Gracie took the napkin from her lap and tried to sop up the spreading red pool. Other nearby diners added their napkins to the mess and one of the waiters hurried over. Gracie apologized to the waiter and stood to get out of his way.

Ley joined her and pulled her away, following some of the other guests leaving the banquet hall.

"Was that an accident?" he whispered.

"No."

"Well done. I haven't a clue how Dietrich earned his Iron Cross."

She grinned, happy the two of them were working as a team. "Before supper, I found out that the contessa's late husband owned a munitions business. I couldn't get many details about their actual work, but I picked up plenty of gossip about his partners and their wives."

Gracie had hoped Ley would be impressed with her discovery, but his smile was halfhearted. "Well, that's useful information, but Allied Intelligence knew about their company before the war began."

Gracie's excitement soured into disappointment. "And I suppose the gossip will be useless too."

"Maybe, maybe not. We can go over it later, see if anything sounds important. And don't feel bad—we still have hours to learn more."

"How are you doing?"

"Not bad so far." One side of Ley's face pulled into a grin. "How are you at dancing?"

Gracie glanced around the enormous ballroom they'd walked into. "I can follow well enough."

The dancing started not long after. Gracie danced a few numbers with Captain Ley and managed to shrug off most of the embarrassment from spilling her wine. It was silly for her to be ashamed when she'd done it on purpose, but the emotion lingered. Her mother wouldn't have approved, even knowing the reasons behind it. But as she followed Ley smoothly across the dance floor, she realized her mother was mistaken. Embarrassing herself to help someone else had been the right thing to do. And as she noticed a few admiring looks from the other male guests and remembered the way Ley and Ostheim had complimented her, she realized that maybe an aversion to embarrassment wasn't the only thing her mother had been wrong about.

"I think I detect a smile, Concetta. Does that mean you're enjoying yourself, or does it mean I'm an awkward dancer and you find my skills laughable?"

"I guess it means I'm enjoying myself because your dancing skills are perfectly adequate. Did they give you a class on that during training?"

Ley shook his head. "I was actually thinking I'm a little out of practice." He glanced beyond her as the song ended. "Are you feeling up to a dance with Ostheim?"

Gracie hesitated. "I may as well get it over with." She turned and forced a smile as Ostheim trod toward her.

"Concetta?" Ostheim held out his hand. She grasped it, and he led her a few steps away before placing his other hand on her back and pulling her in as the music started. She hoped her grin didn't look as frozen as it felt. He seemed content to dance without much conversation, and although he held her a little more firmly than Ley had, he was otherwise polite.

After two dances, an Italian officer interrupted them. Before releasing her, Ostheim leaned next to her ear; she could feel the moisture from his breath. "I suppose I'll give you up—for now."

As she walked away with her new partner, she glanced back at Ostheim and caught a look in his eyes that alarmed her. Earlier that night, she'd thought she'd seen respect and admiration in Captain Ley's eyes. Ostheim's eyes, on the other hand, revealed nothing but lust as they took her in from head to foot.

Hours passed on the dance floor, and Gracie was exhausted. She wasn't used to staying up late—with curfew so early, there was rarely a reason to—nor was she used to dancing with so many men. Her head pounded, and the dance floor proved a poor area for collecting intelligence. The music was loud and the dances short, so she never got beyond trivial conversation with her dance partners.

When an Italian officer asked her if she'd like to rest, she followed him from the ballroom. Unfortunately, he was more interested in pawing her than in telling her anything that would be useful to the Allies.

Gracie slipped away when he went to get drinks and ran into a friendly young German. His smile was promising, but his Italian was as bad as her German, and she didn't dare test his English. She put forth a valiant effort to communicate with him, and he reciprocated, but the only thing he seemed to catch was her complaint that she was tired. He found her a chair and spoke earnestly to her for about twenty minutes, but she only understood about one word in ten. After his monologue, he helped her to her feet, kissed her cheek, and used a few phrases of broken Italian to invite her to one of the mansion's more secluded areas.

"*Nein*," Gracie said, glad she knew at least that in German. He was disappointed as he left, but before long, she saw him pursuing a new target.

Gracie yawned, and her stomach growled. She found a clock and saw that it was two in the morning. No wonder she was hungry again. Upon returning to the dining hall, she found an impressive buffet of fruit, sandwiches, pastries, and alcohol.

Even after a snack, the pain in her head persisted. Music from the ballroom filled the dining room and all the sitting areas on the main floor. In the upstairs game room, a record blared. She needed somewhere quiet.

The noise finally faded when she found the library. It was empty and dimly lit, and the chairs and sofas looked far more comfortable than the cheap mattress in her apartment.

Gracie was considering a nap when a shadow fell across the doorway and Otto Ostheim followed her into the library.

CHAPTER SEVENTEEN

"Hello, Otto," Gracie said, trying to smile.

He returned her smile, but on him the expression looked venomous. "Your boyfriend had a bad night at the card table. I just won your company for the next two hours."

"What?" *Would Ley really do something like that?* She thought he would if it would help the men trapped at Anzio.

Ostheim stepped toward her and firmly grasped her arm. "Come with me." His breath reeked of alcohol.

She pulled away, but he easily grabbed her again, harder than before. "Let me go!" she said.

He laughed until her elbow caught him in the ribs. After that, he glared, catching her and pulling her toward a nook in the corner of the library. "Think you're too good for me, do you?"

"Leave me alone, Otto. You're drunk." Gracie tried to punch his face, but he blocked her jab, then gripped her arms. *Would anyone hear me scream?* She doubted it. All the other guests were drunk, asleep, or near loud music.

Ostheim laughed again. "No, for the next two hours, you're mine, and I intend to enjoy you."

He was holding her so tightly it hurt, and a growing fear gnawed at her stomach. As he forced her to march forward, she managed to twist one arm away. Then she smashed his nose with the heel of her hand, just as she'd practiced in training. He released her and stumbled back a few steps, one hand holding his nose. When he pulled his fingers away, they were covered in blood. The look in his eyes was murderous.

He seemed set to lunge at her, but before he could pounce, someone cleared their throat behind them. Gracie and Ostheim both turned toward the door, where Ley stood, pistol in hand.

"Untersturmführer Ostheim, I believe you've had too much to drink. Perhaps it's time for you to go home."

Ostheim glanced at Ley's Luger and nodded slightly. With one final glare at Gracie, he brushed past Ley, purposely bumping into his shoulder. Ley followed Ostheim with his eyes, holstering his pistol only after the SS man was out of sight.

"Well, I'm glad to see you can take care of yourself," Ley said as he walked toward her. "I daresay you broke his nose."

Gracie shook her head at his casual response. When Ley had asked her to dress up for the party, she hadn't realized he was setting her up as a poker prize. She was willing to sacrifice a lot for the army but not *that*. He could have at least told her about his plan before using her company as part of a bet. When Ley was close enough, she slapped him across the face as hard as she could.

He put his hand to his cheek. His mouth hung open in surprise, and the muscles around his eyes tightened in anger. "What was that for? I came here to protect you!"

"He said you lost a bet playing cards, and *I* was his prize. I can't believe you told him he could do whatever he wanted with me. Do you have any idea what his intentions were?"

"I wasn't even at the card table."

"Well, he said—"

"And who are you going to believe? Him or me?" Ley took his hand off his cheek. Even in the dim light, she could see the red mark from where she'd struck him.

Gracie felt her breathing grow ragged as embarrassment mingled with the terror she'd felt earlier. "You didn't tell him he could do whatever he wanted with me for the next two hours?"

"Most definitely not."

She closed her eyes and tried to control the tremors in her hands. "I'm sorry."

He didn't respond right away. She finally opened her eyes and saw him glance at his watch. "Look, it's late—or early. You're tired and scared, all the men I came to see have slipped from drunk-and-talkative to drunk-and-nearly-comatose, and there are still several hours before we should leave. Take a few deep breaths and relax. We've done enough for the night."

Gracie sank onto the couch behind her as her legs started to shake.

"Are you all right?" Ley asked.

She nodded and drew in a labored breath.

"Did he hurt you?" Ley sat next to her.

Gracie held her right arm out. "I'll probably have a bruise where he blocked my punch, and my hand is a little sore, but other than that, no. I'm . . . I'm sorry I hit you . . . I should have realized he was lying, but I was so scared . . ." She stopped when her voice cracked.

"It's okay." He brushed aside a lock of hair that had fallen into her face and put his arm around her quaking shoulders. She snuggled in next to his chest and closed her eyes, ashamed that she'd jumped to the wrong conclusion, relieved that he'd come when he had. Her headache still raged, but it wasn't quite as bad with her eyes shut. She knew the cuddle was just part of an act, but she didn't want to be alone if Ostheim returned, and for tonight, she didn't mind playing along.

* * *

Bastien slept in the morning after the curfew party, rising in time for the midday meal of sausage and potato soup.

"How was the party?" Heinie asked as Bastien sat next to him.

"You didn't miss much."

Heinie laughed softly. "I can tell when you're lying."

Bastien hoped that wasn't really the case. "Music, endless food, an elegant mansion, and a beautiful date. Not bad."

"Did you take that Italian girl? Concetta?"

Bastien nodded and looked at his watch. "We're actually meeting again this afternoon."

"Hmm." The noise was part speculation, part interest. "And what will you do together?"

"I'm not sure yet. Have you heard from Maurleen recently?"

Heinie's smile was answer enough, and he whistled "Lili Marlene" as he left the dining hall.

When Gracie came to Bastien's room a few hours later, he gave her his report. It was a long one because the excess alcohol had loosened more than one man's tongue at the party. There was continued suspicion that the Allies were preparing an invasion near Civitavecchia, complaints about inadequate supplies, even a few detailed contingency plans. The snippets Gracie had picked up were of questionable worth, but Bastien decided to include them. If nothing else, it might help the Allies track down Italian war criminals if they chose to hide in the homes of former mistresses.

Gracie sat at the table to encode everything, then looked over at him when she finished. She seemed more relaxed than the night before, partly because her dress was more casual and her hair was down, but it was also in her face—less nervous, less worried. "I'm sorry about this morning." She mimed a slapping motion. "I can't believe I did that."

"You already apologized," he said.

"I thought maybe I should apologize again."

"Once is enough. I'm not one to hold grudges."

"Unless it involves Vaughn-Harris?"

"That's more him holding a grudge against me than me holding a grudge against him. Besides, he never apologized."

He got a soft laugh out of her and a deeper smile.

Bastien leaned forward in his armchair. "Look, about this morning, I want you to know I would never ask you to seduce Ostheim in order to get information. I wouldn't ask that of anyone, especially someone like you."

Gracie nodded, looking at the table, and some of her dark hair fell forward across her shoulders.

When she stayed silent, he tried again. "I'm sorry it was even a question. I guess my actions haven't given you much confidence in me, and I apologize."

She met his gaze, her brown eyes solemn again. "It's not that I lack confidence in you. I can tell you're very good at what you do. It's just hard to trust you and a little frustrating because I know so little about the real you."

He was quiet for a while, thinking back to an earlier conversation. "My real blood type is A. Adalard's is B."

She raised one hand in frustration. "That's not very helpful."

"All right. What would you like to know?"

Gracie's mouth opened, then closed again as if she didn't believe he would really answer her questions. "We could start with your first name."

"Not that." He'd almost slipped a few times and called her Gracie instead of Concetta and assumed it would be equally difficult for her to call him Adalard if she knew his real name. Ignorance, in this case, would make her job easier.

She sighed, disappointed. "Do you always tap your foot like that?"

Bastien looked at his legs and noticed the left one was moving.

"You don't even realize you're doing it, do you?" Gracie asked.

"Not usually."

"Colonel Ambrose said something happened between you and Vaughn-Harris before Annie."

Bastien nodded.

"Well, what was it?" she asked.

"What was your final OSS training assignment?"

Gracie raised one eyebrow as if to chastise him for steering the conversation into a tangent, but she answered his question. "For my team assignment, we were told to go through the motions of sabotaging train tracks in Philadelphia. So we planned our routes, entered the city separately, then met in the middle of the night and wired the tracks." As she spoke, her hands moved along the table, tracing the routes each team member had taken, he supposed.

"Did you get caught?"

"No. It was scary, really. We could have paralyzed the city's entire transportation hub had we been German saboteurs."

Bastien leaned back into the chair again. "And your individual test?"

"I was asked to gather intelligence about the Sparrows Point Shipyard near Baltimore. I got a job as a telephone operator, under a pseudonym, and listened in on conversations for a few weeks. I ended up with information about what materials they needed, when they arrived, how much they cost. I also gathered the names of the most important people working there or working with them. I know it doesn't sound like much, but my trainer was pleased."

"Sometimes even mundane information is important when you piece it all together," Bastien said.

"Yes, but what do my tests have to do with Captain Vaughn-Harris?"

"For my test, I was asked to find out how a certain congressman would vote on a particular bill. So I broke into his office."

"That was bold."

Bastien shrugged. "My accent would have put everyone on alert if I'd tried to find out in person." There hadn't been much of an alternative.

"I assume you succeeded?"

"Yes. And in addition to discovering how he planned to vote, I uncovered evidence that he was accepting bribes from a defense contractor. A company owned by Vaughn-Harris's father."

Gracie's mouth opened in surprise. "Was there a scandal?"

"No, but the congressman didn't run for reelection, and the Vaughn-Harris family lost most of their contracts."

"So Vaughn-Harris thought he would take revenge on you by marrying Annie?"

Bastien knew few details of Annie and Vaughn-Harris's courtship—just that it had ended in marriage. "Maybe. She might have shown interest on her own. She wanted to be married, not just engaged. The government sends monthly checks to brides, not to fiancées. Of course, the only reason Vaughn-Harris was still around to date Annie after we finished training was because he relaxed a little too much at the OSS party celebrating the end of training. You had one of those, I suppose?"

"Yes."

"But you didn't drink anything?" he asked, even though he already knew the answer.

"No. And I figured out it was a hidden test fairly quickly."

"Vaughn-Harris didn't. He had to repeat some of his training, and I don't think Ambrose has ever sent him into the field. Doubt he trusts him."

"So you hurt his father's business and showed him up in training, and when he tried to take revenge on you by marrying your fiancée, you were relieved instead of heartbroken." Gracie smiled at him. "No wonder he hates you."

"Mmm."

Gracie tapped a finger on the table. "But how could you be engaged to someone and not care when she married someone else?"

"Getting engaged to Annie was an accident."

"How do you get engaged by accident?"

Bastien shrugged. "We'd been on a handful of dates. When I walked her home after a movie, she told me her roommate was out of town until Monday and invited me to stay the weekend. I told her I didn't think that would work since we weren't married. So then she asked me if I'd want to get married before I spent the weekend with someone, and I said yes, and then she said she accepted. It took me a minute to figure out that I'd somehow proposed to her."

"So why didn't you sort it out right then?"

"I was afraid if I stayed much longer, she'd convince me to stay the night. And I was leaving in a few weeks to go overseas. I guess part of me liked the idea of having someone waiting for me. I wasn't sure I'd make it home anyway, so I postponed dealing with it."

"And then Captain Vaughn-Harris came along and stole her from you?"

"Yes, thank goodness." Maybe Bastien owed Vaughn-Harris his thanks, first for taking an unwanted fiancée off his hands, then for forcing him to work with an unwanted but much-needed radio operator.

CHAPTER EIGHTEEN

ZIMMERMAN LONGED FOR AN ORDERLY. He'd rather pass in front of a sniper's nest than tackle the stack of paperwork waiting on his desk. *Maybe if I get another promotion.* That would make his wife happy, but he doubted it would relieve him of his paperwork. He had a few rungs to climb before he was the one doling out forms. Until then, he was on the receiving end.

Had he been home in Germany, he would have gone to church with his wife and son, then taken the family for a hike in the forest. Instead, he was spending his Sunday afternoon catching up on reports.

"Still here?"

Zimmerman recognized Ostheim's voice and looked up from his pile. "Yes. War might not be so bad if it wasn't for all this paperwork."

Ostheim sank into the chair in front of Zimmerman's desk. "I'd settle for eliminating the Wehrmacht."

"Excuse me?" What did Ostheim have against the German Army?

"I don't really want to get rid of it, just make it subservient to the SS and revoke commissions for current hauptmanns."

"Oh?" Zimmerman raised an eyebrow, waiting for Ostheim to explain.

"Not all hauptmanns. Just Dietrich." Ostheim thumped his fist on the desk. "What I wouldn't give to outrank him."

Zimmerman looked back at his report. Ostheim had already told him what had happened at the curfew party. "There are other women in Rome."

"It's not about the woman so much. It's about winning, or at least beating Dietrich."

"Leave it alone, Otto. He outranks you, and he's got an Iron Cross." Zimmerman glanced up long enough to see Ostheim fiddling with one of his pencils.

"You don't have any dirt on him, do you? Shoddy engineering? A Jewish cousin? Late entry into the Nazi party?"

Zimmerman tried to think of anything that seemed off about Dietrich, but nothing came to mind. He was quiet, professional, competent. Showed no signs of dissatisfaction with Nazi leadership or the army. "I suppose there was that SD man asking questions about him a week and a half ago."

"Why?"

"He didn't tell me the reason for the investigation, and I didn't consider it my duty to question the SD." Zimmerman stressed the end of his sentence, hoping Ostheim would take the hint and realize questioning Dietrich wasn't in his line of duty either.

"What type of questions did he ask?"

Zimmerman sighed and sat back in his chair. Ostheim was persistent. Usually, that was an asset, but as Zimmerman looked at his unfinished pile of paperwork, he thought even positive traits could sometimes become vices. "He asked if I'd seen another SD officer recently. Someone came out to investigate Dietrich, but he disappeared."

Ostheim seized the last bit of information. "An SD officer disappeared while investigating Dietrich? Surely that reflects poorly on Dietrich."

"Not necessarily. The SD man could have gone missing anywhere between Berlin and Rome. Might have gotten killed in a bombing, might have been murdered by the Gappisti, might have decided to go live in Switzerland."

"There's a file on Dietrich somewhere though, isn't there? Either here or at army HQ?"

"I'm not going to go looking through a *hauptmann's* files unless I have a better reason than his success in wooing Italian women. If you're so curious, why don't you send a letter to Reichsführer Himmler and ask him about Hauptmann Dietrich? Be sure to tell him how much time you've spent pursuing this and why." Zimmerman tried to focus on his paperwork, but he put it down when he heard his pencil snap.

"Sorry." Ostheim threw the broken pencil into the wastebasket.

"I'll keep my ears open, Otto, but I don't think this is worth your time."

Ostheim didn't say whether he'd take Zimmerman's advice. "Well, I have a few interrogations to check on." He stood. "I wouldn't mind having Dietrich locked in one of those cells."

Even after Ostheim left, Zimmerman had a hard time focusing on his paperwork. He stood in frustration, paced around the room, tried to ignore the beautiful weather beckoning him outside, and sat at his desk again. *Finish the paperwork now, then you won't have to worry about it tomorrow.*

On his fourth form, something finally caught his interest. It was a tip two sources had verified claiming a Catholic church in the San Lorenzo district was harboring refugees. The tip itself wasn't odd; Zimmerman saw similar tips day in and day out. Rumor was, half the city was hiding the other half. But when it came to churches, the SS walked a careful line. No one wanted to provoke a condemnation from the Vatican. So far, rumors of plans to kidnap the Holy Father and Vatican City's geography, surrounded by German troops, had kept papal memos vague. The Pope condemned the war and pleaded for peace but didn't publicly take sides. Yet there were concerns that papal neutrality might be tested to the breaking point if the SS began searching churches, especially if it ended up being a false alarm. *But with two sources?* Zimmerman smiled, thinking two sources might make it worth the risk.

* * *

On Monday morning, Zimmerman received permission for his search. He just had to notify the Wehrmacht and gather his team. As he approached German Army headquarters, he recognized Hauptmann Dietrich coming from the other direction.

"Heil Hitler." Zimmerman saluted.

Dietrich returned the salute and joined Zimmerman on the steps. "Beautiful morning, isn't it? Shame I have to spend it inside."

"Yes, perfect weather for a roundup."

"Oh, and who are you rounding up today? More men to dig trenches for me?"

"Maybe I'll send some your way, but I doubt it will be very many. I've finally convinced my superiors that we should risk Vatican disapproval and search churches if we have sufficient evidence they're hiding someone."

"And I assume you have sufficient evidence?" Dietrich asked.

Zimmerman nodded. "Two independent tips claiming the clergy in a San Lorenzo church are harboring Jews, probably a few Gappisti and escaped POWs too."

"And when will this roundup take place?"

"Just before curfew." If he waited until civilians were supposed to be off the street, it would be easy to spot anyone trying to escape.

Dietrich slowed, looking through his attaché case. He swore softly. "Forgot my report. I'll have to go back and get it." He shook his head. "It's a rotten day to be stuck behind a desk. Good luck with the roundup."

Zimmerman smiled his sympathy. It was indeed a rotten day to spend doing paperwork. As he walked through the door, Zimmerman considered telling Ostheim about the exchange. Maybe Ostheim would feel better if he knew Dietrich would pay for his weekend with the Italian woman by slaving over a pile of paperwork on a sunny day, but Zimmerman decided not to say anything. He wanted Ostheim to drop it. Dietrich didn't seem so bad—Zimmerman could sympathize with anyone who didn't like reports. Besides, he planned to have more exciting news. One successful raid on a church would make it easier to conduct another. Papal protests would be brushed aside if he found proof the churches were being used as asylums. By tonight at supper, Zimmerman planned to celebrate.

* * *

Gracie was going to be late meeting Otavia at the Sant'Angelo bridge, and all she had to show for it was a thin piece of dry black bread. *That has to have been the slowest line I've ever seen.*

"Concetta?"

Gracie recognized Ley's voice instantly, but she wasn't expecting to see him until evening. She turned and waited for him to catch up, worried because he wasn't one to change plans without reason. "Good morning, Adalard."

"Good morning." He leaned in to greet her with a kiss. It only lasted a second, but it somehow reached all the way down to her toes.

How does he do that? She concentrated on a response. "Is anything wrong?"

He nodded and slipped his arm across her shoulders, keeping her walking at an even pace. "The SS is going to raid a church in the San Lorenzo district this evening. Plan to pick up whoever's hiding there—Jews, Gappisti, escaped soldiers and airmen. I'm in staff meetings the rest of the day. Can you warn them? And tell them someone's been talking?"

"Do you know which church?"

"No."

"Do you have any idea how many churches there are in Rome?" Gracie couldn't warn all of them, not in one day.

"Close to a thousand, I think. But it's a church in San Lorenzo."

Gracie waited until a few pedestrians passed them and were out of earshot. "That cuts it down a little, but I don't know that district—there could be dozens of churches there."

Ley was quiet for a few long seconds. "If I ask for more details, it will look suspicious. I can't miss my meetings to help you, and the churches wouldn't trust me anyway. They'd see me as a German officer trying to flush them out. If you can't do it, so be it. A few dozen more Jews will be shipped off to concentration camps. Based on what I've heard, it won't make much of a difference, not percentage-wise."

Gracie felt her face grow hot with anger. It wasn't that she didn't want to help—she did—but he was giving her an enormous task. "You think it's no big deal if a few Jews get shipped off to their deaths?"

Ley shook his head. "No. I think it's tragic, but I'm not going to blow my cover for them. Thousands of Allied servicemen depend on my information. I wouldn't have asked for your help if I didn't think you could warn the church without giving yourself away. If you disagree, just pretend I wasn't here." He smiled at her, but she was close enough to see the frustrated look in his eyes. He slipped his arm from her shoulder to her waist and kissed her good-bye before striding away.

People would be arrested and probably killed unless she prevented it. She knew she had to try, but how was she supposed to warn every church in San Lorenzo all by herself? San Lorenzo was east of Rome's center, near the freight yards and the cemetery. She'd never been there. It might have five churches or five dozen.

She heard a church bell toll ten and thought of Otavia. Gracie was supposed to be at the bridge now, and it would still take her a while to get there. She walked faster, hoping something would work out. Maybe Otavia would at least know how many churches were in San Lorenzo. *Please let her know something that will help, or let me somehow find the right church*, she prayed as she rushed toward the bridge.

Gracie was afraid Otavia would be gone when she arrived, but she was still there looking up at one of the marble angels guarding the bridge. Her face was serene, like the angel she studied. One hand rested on her abdomen, and the other held a basket.

"I'm sorry I'm late," Gracie said.

Otavia smiled and put a hand on Gracie's shoulder. "It's fine. Is everything all right?"

Gracie's initial instinct was to grab Otavia's report and then move to her next assignment. It wasn't the job she'd been trained for, but someone had to warn those churches. Yet Otavia probably knew more about the San Lorenzo district than either Ley or Gracie did, and she would want to help the people in hiding. "The SS is conducting a raid this evening on a church. They'll arrest whoever's hiding there, so I'm supposed to warn them, but I don't know which church. I don't know what to do."

"Those poor people. Do you know anything about the church?"

"It's in the San Lorenzo district—that's the only clue I have."

Otavia slipped her hand through Gracie's arm. "We've got a lot to do, then. We'll go to San Lorenzo fuori le Mura first. Maybe they're hiding someone in the rubble."

"You'll help?"

"Of course," Otavia said.

"Thank you." Gracie blinked away the extra moisture in her eyes, relieved and grateful. "I wasn't sure where to start."

"How did the SS find out? And how did you find out?"

"The SS has an informant, so someone at wherever they're hiding the refugees is talking or let the wrong thing slip to someone they shouldn't trust." Gracie took a deep breath as she moved to Otavia's second question. She couldn't tell Otavia about Ley. "I found out from someone who wasn't able to warn them."

"Do you trust whoever you heard it from?"

"Yes." Gracie answered immediately. She was overwhelmed by Ley's request, but she knew his information would prove true.

Otavia reached into her basket and pulled out two dark scarfs. "These are dirty, but if there's an informant, we might want to wear them anyway."

They put the scarfs over their hair and walked to the Basilica of San Lorenzo fuori le Mura together. The church had been damaged in an air raid the previous summer, and there was still significant work to do before it was fully repaired, but that didn't mean there weren't plenty of hiding places inside.

"The frescoes were so beautiful," Otavia said.

Gracie followed Otavia's gaze but saw only rubble.

"They're gone now." Otavia frowned as she stepped into the church.

The basilica was one of Rome's best, and Gracie was in awe of the grandeur that shone in spite of the mostly missing roof and damaged walls.

She pulled her eyes away from an elaborately carved column and looked around for someone to confide in. Otavia had already tracked down a priest, and as Gracie joined them, she heard Otavia explaining the expected raid.

The priest was quiet, nodding at Otavia's words. His face was calm. Gracie wondered if he was naturally good at concealing his emotions or if perhaps he had nothing to worry about because he wasn't hiding anyone. *Or he doesn't believe us.*

"Thank you for your warning," he whispered. "I will do what I can to share the information with those who might be in danger." Gracie prayed that meant he knew where the refugees were hiding and that he'd ensure they were warned.

When they left the church, Gracie turned back and saw the priest motioning another man over to him. "Do you think he knows something?" she asked.

"Probably." Otavia glanced around to make sure they were alone. "Let's split up. We'll meet at the cemetery when we're finished. If we're quick, I think we can get to all of the churches while there's still time to move anyone they're hiding."

CHAPTER NINETEEN

GRACIE SPENT THE NEXT FEW hours searching out churches. Otavia divided the district by streets and told Gracie what to expect, but it was still a new area for her. Fortunately, although there were hundreds of churches in Rome, most of them weren't concentrated in San Lorenzo.

Otavia was already in the cemetery, sitting on the grass next to a headstone, when Gracie arrived. When she saw Gracie, she smiled up at her. "I'm sorry. I should have taken one more and given you one less."

Gracie waved her hand, dismissing any suggestion that Otavia had cause to apologize—in truth, she had probably saved a few people's lives. "I couldn't have done it without your help. Thank you."

Otavia pushed herself from the grass but stopped midway to her feet, still hunched over. A grimace of pain showed on her face, and one of her hands pressed against her abdomen.

Gracie rushed over to her. "Are you all right?"

Otavia took a few deep breaths before answering. "I'm not sure. It's not so bad now, but it was like those cramps I used to get if I did too much walking and didn't drink enough water. Except I'd get them in my calves, not all the way across my stomach."

"You don't suppose the baby's coming?" Gracie asked.

A look of panic crossed Otavia's face. "It's too early."

"Sit down again and rest. I'll find you some water, and then I'll help you home. Where do you live?"

"By the Villa Borghese."

That was a long way to walk. They could take the tram, but even that would involve a significant stretch on foot. Gracie helped Otavia back to the ground, noticing a few rivulets of sweat along Otavia's hairline. Gracie checked Octavia's forehead for fever, but she felt cool and clammy.

"I'll be back as soon as I find something for you to drink." Gracie left the cemetery, thinking she'd go back to the last church she'd been to.

"Excuse me, signorina. Is something wrong with your friend?"

Gracie turned around to see a young Italian of about thirteen. His clothes were old and slightly dirty, and he needed a haircut, but underneath a layer of grime, his face was earnest. "She's feeling ill. You don't know where I could find someone with a car or a horse-drawn cart, do you?"

"Depends on what you can pay."

Gracie wasn't sure if the boy wanted money for himself or for the driver, but she assumed she'd need to pay both. The tram would be less expensive, but trams were breeding grounds for lice, and Gracie wasn't sure how far Otavia should walk. She felt in her pocket, pulling out enough lira to buy several days' worth of food. "Will this do?"

"That's enough for me to find someone for you. What he charges is another story." The boy reached for the bills, but Gracie held them out of his reach.

"Find the cart first."

The boy nodded and ran off. Gracie checked her pocket again, grateful OSS had given her plenty of currency. Purchasing a ride home wouldn't be a problem. It was finding a ride that was a challenge. Gracie continued along the street until she saw a café. Deciding to skip the church, she went inside and convinced the owner to fill an empty wine bottle with water and sell it to her.

When Gracie returned to the cemetery, Otavia was waiting. "I had another one," she said, rubbing the side of her abdomen.

"Here, have some water. That should help."

Not long after, Gracie saw the boy again. He lingered outside the cemetery's entrance, so she walked over to him.

"I found something for you." He pointed down the road to where a cart pulled by a single horse plodded toward them. "He's a milkman."

Gracie handed the boy his money. "What's your name?"

"Neroli."

"Thank you for your help, Neroli."

He shoved the money into his pocket and grinned before running off.

When the cart pulled to a stop, Gracie negotiated with the driver on the price of a ride. He was less expensive than Neroli, but she didn't regret paying the middleman, or middleboy. Like most of the people she passed on the street, Neroli looked like he needed more food, and without his help, she wasn't sure she could have found a way to take Otavia home. Gracie helped her friend to the cart, and the two of them found places to sit on the floor. It wasn't very comfortable, but it was better for Otavia than walking or standing in a crowded tram.

The cart was slow—Gracie thought she could have beaten the horse in a footrace—but she didn't have anything else to do before curfew, other than collect Ley's report. Otavia had no additional contractions during the ride, but she grimaced as the cart jostled them about. Despite the discomfort, she managed to smile for most of the journey.

When they arrived, both women thanked the milkman, then watched him drive away.

"My apartment is a block back," Otavia said. "I gave him the wrong address, to play it safe."

Gracie nodded. "I'll see you in, if it's all right with you."

"Thank you, *Tesorina*."

The street where Otavia lived was old, with lush, ancient trees and buildings that reminded Gracie of palaces. She paid more attention to the architecture than to the inhabitants, but as Otavia led her inside, Gracie caught sight of a boy's head. She couldn't be sure from the back view, but for an instant, it looked like Neroli. Then Gracie lost sight of him and couldn't find him again. There were plenty of children in Rome who needed haircuts, and the dirty brown and gray of the boy's clothing was common enough. She almost suggested they walk around the block as a precaution, but Otavia looked tired. *It's just a coincidence.*

They took the stairs slowly, and as soon as they arrived in Otavia's modest apartment, Gracie had Otavia put her feet up. The view from the living room window was extraordinary, showing Rome in all its splendor.

"You said your mother lives with you?" Gracie asked.

"Yes, but my aunt isn't feeling well, so she went to stay with her."

"Do you want me to find her?"

"No, I'll be all right."

Gracie hesitated. She didn't want to intrude, and Otavia seemed better, but Gracie wanted to be sure. She glanced around the orderly kitchen, suddenly itching to make something. "Can I at least cook you dinner?"

"I don't want to be any trouble."

"I don't have a kitchen, and I miss cooking, so you'd actually be doing me a favor."

Otavia laughed. Gracie loved the way she laughed—as if she didn't have a care in the world. Gracie knew that wasn't true. Otavia's husband was away, involved in a dangerous partisan movement; her beloved city was occupied; and she risked execution if the Nazis caught her gathering and passing information to the Allies. Yet even with reasons to frown, Otavia consistently looked on the bright side. "Well, if you put it that way, I suppose I could let you borrow my kitchen. I think my mother went to the market before she left, so there should be something worthwhile to make."

Gracie found fresh fish, cicoria, and cheese. She looked through the cupboards and found basic baking supplies too. The flour wasn't as fine as she preferred, but she still thought her biscuits would be good if eaten while warm. Even Gracie's mother liked her biscuits. She seasoned the fish and cicoria with olive oil and lemon juice, and they ate the biscuits with slices of cheese.

"Do you want a job? I've never been a very good cook." Otavia helped herself to a second serving. "Not that I could pay you—we can barely afford rent nowadays."

"I'd be happy to come cook again," Gracie said. "And I left money and ration coupons on the counter to make up for what I'm eating."

"You don't have to do that."

"Yes, I do. Food's hard to come by, and I know I won't starve." Ley would give Gracie food if she asked for it.

"Thank you." Otavia wrapped the leftover biscuits in a cloth and put them in a breadbox. "Do you suppose whichever church was hiding people got them moved by now?"

"I hope so. But it can't be easy to find somewhere new on such short notice."

"Do you think the SS would search catacombs? Most of the churches have them. Plenty of hiding places down there."

Gracie shuddered. "I'd hate to hide there. It's so dark. And it would be so creepy with all those skeletons."

"They're just bones. Better to hide there than get arrested."

"But don't you think it's spooky? I mean, they used to be living, breathing people, and now . . . now they're gone."

Otavia looked thoughtful. "I don't think they're gone. They've just moved on to a better place."

Gracie nodded. That was what she believed too—she wouldn't have been able to survive the past year if she hadn't known with certainty that life continued after death. But she still hoped she'd never have to hide in the catacombs.

The afternoon passed quickly, full of conversation. They laughed a lot and even cried once when Otavia spoke of how much she missed her husband. Before Gracie knew it, a nearby clock struck five in the evening. Curfew had come.

"I should have left an hour ago." Gracie had missed her rendezvous with Ley. Otavia's apartment didn't have a phone, so she couldn't call to explain, and she'd probably be arrested before she reached his hotel.

"You can stay the night, if you'd like," Otavia said. "I'd hate for you to get caught out after curfew. If we warned the right refugees, the SS will be extra nasty to anyone they arrest tonight."

Gracie thought for only a moment before agreeing.

CHAPTER TWENTY

ZIMMERMAN STOOD IN THE RENAISSANCE-ERA chapel, fuming. "What do you mean you haven't found anyone?" he yelled at one of his squad leaders.

"I'm sorry, sir. We've searched everywhere."

"Search harder. Look behind the tapestries. Make sure no one is hiding in the priest's quarters or under the floor."

"Sir, we've already searched *everywhere*."

"Search again," Zimmerman said. But he'd worked with this squad leader before. Möller was thorough, not one to miss much. That meant there would be several indignant clergymen to deal with, as well as his own incensed superiors. Zimmerman was the one who'd convinced them to risk upsetting Vatican neutrality, so he would be the one to shoulder the blame.

He waited another two hours while his men went over everything again. He was tempted to let his men literally tear the church apart, but if no one was found—and he suspected no one would be—a ruined church and the political backlash it would cause could result in his demotion. What would his father, a decorated veteran of the Great War, think? And his wife—he wasn't sure if she'd be more disappointed that he'd demolished a church or that he'd destroyed his career.

When everything had been searched at least twice, Zimmerman dismissed his men and walked back to the Via Tasso. There would be no celebration supper tonight. Zimmerman had a report to write, then he would probably have to endure the most severe reprimand of his life. After that, he was going to find his sources and see what had gone wrong.

* * *

Bastien knocked on Gracie's door for the second time that evening. When she hadn't come to his suite as planned, he'd come to check her flat. There had been no answer, so he'd gone back to his hotel, thinking they might have missed each other. When he couldn't find her there, he'd returned to the old building where she lived.

There was still no response from behind the door. Bastien checked the bathroom at the end of the hallway, but it was empty. He didn't think she was in the building, but he wanted to know for sure. What if she was injured and unable to answer his knock? If she was hurt, it was probably his fault. He hadn't thought it very risky to warn a few churches that the SS planned to search them, but what if she'd been arrested? Or shot? Or killed?

Bastien went to the ground level and found the landlord. The old man saw the German uniform and backed into his office, knees trembling.

"I need the key for a room on the fifth floor." Bastien could break in, but he might damage the door. He wanted Gracie to be able to lock it again, assuming he found her.

"Why, sir?"

"That's not your concern. You can give me the key, or I'll kick the door in. The choice is yours."

"But, sir, my tenants have a right to some privacy." The landlord stood a little taller. "I must offer them an explanation."

"I am a Wehrmacht officer, and I want to see what's inside Signorina Gallo's apartment. That should be sufficient reason." Bastien held his hand out, hoping the landlord and any tenants who recognized him would think he was just a jealous lover. "The key."

The landlord mumbled an agreement but took his time finding the correct key. Then he followed Bastien up to the fifth floor and watched from the hallway while Bastien unlocked the door to reveal an empty room. Ignoring the worried look on the landlord's face, Bastien went into the apartment and shut the door behind him. He opened a few drawers and found Gracie's radio, so she wasn't out trying to contact headquarters. *Where is she?*

Bastien stayed inside less than a minute. He locked the door and returned the key to the landlord, dreading his next destination.

Gestapo headquarters never slept. The first person Bastien saw when he walked inside was Ostheim. Bastien cursed his luck. Of all the SS men in the city, Ostheim was the least likely to help him. Ostheim's salute was practiced and precise, but the hatred oozed from his eyes as he turned toward the prison side of the building, no doubt to begin his nightly interrogation sessions.

Bastien followed him from a distance. As he drew near the cells, he could hear moaning, and the air itself seemed oppressive. If Bastien were ever arrested, this was probably where he'd be brought. He held back a shudder and approached the desk of an SS NCO, returning a Heil Hitler and then taking a deep breath.

"I understand there was a raid on a church this evening," Bastien said.

"Yes, sir, but nothing came of it."

"Any new arrests today?"

"No, sir."

Bastien nodded. That meant Gracie wasn't here, and that was a relief.

Ostheim appeared again as Bastien was turning to leave.

"Anything I can help you with, Hauptmann Dietrich?" Ostheim's tone was anything but helpful.

"I'm just following up on a raid. Obersturmführer Zimmerman said he might have more labor for me, but it seems the raid didn't turn out as expected."

Ostheim frowned. "Obersturmführer Zimmerman is completing his report on the other side of the building, should you like more details."

"I think I've learned enough. Thank you, gentlemen."

As Bastien walked away, he was fully conscious of Ostheim's gaze following his every move.

Bastien's next stop wasn't quite as horrible as the previous one, but it was still a prison, and its inmates were still tortured. German jailers ran one wing of the Regina Coeli prison, and the Italians ran two. Like the Via Tasso Gestapo building, it was one Bastien normally avoided.

He recognized no one when he arrived, much to his relief. If no one knew who he was, his inquiry was less likely to come back later and jeopardize his mission. Bastien began with the Italian side of the prison, addressing a young soldier stationed at a desk. "I need to see the list of prisoners taken today."

"I'm not at liberty to disclose that, sir. Not without permission from my superior."

"Then call him."

The soldier nodded and picked up a phone, then told someone on the other end that a German hauptmann wanted to see him. Not for the first time, Bastien was grateful Dietrich had been promoted past the initial ranks—most people quickly cooperated with German captains.

An officer who looked as young as his clerk came through the doorway not two minutes later. "May I help you, sir?"

"Yes. I'd like to see today's prison manifest."

"May I inquire as to why, sir?"

Bastien walked to the side of the room, where the clerk wouldn't be able to overhear him, and the officer followed. "It's a delicate matter. I'm looking for a double-agent, someone working for us but pretending to work with the Gappisti. I have reason to believe the agent was arrested today. I'd rather not tell you the agent's name or alias in case I'm wrong. I don't want word to leak out that we've infiltrated the Gappisti."

The officer frowned as Bastien suggested the possibility of a leak from the Regina Coeli, but he cooperated. "Follow me."

He led Bastien to his office, opened a ledger, and turned it around for Bastien to read. Bastien skimmed through the page until the dates switched from March fifth to March sixth, then slowed. There were no women, so Gracie wasn't in the Italian portion of the Regina Coeli. "The agent's not here. Thank you for your help."

Bastien used the same story on the German side, with similar results. Knowing it was foolish to try, he went to Gracie's apartment again anyway, but no one answered the door, and when he returned to his hotel, his rooms were empty.

Even though he'd have to get up by 0300 hours, he spent most of the night pacing in his bedroom. Where else could he look? Rome was too big for him to check everywhere. Gracie didn't seem to be in prison, so Bastien's mission could continue. But if he'd sent Gracie to her death, he wasn't sure he'd ever be able to forgive himself.

***

Gracie rushed to Ley's hotel as soon as curfew ended the next morning, but he wasn't there. She wasn't surprised. He'd been working early mornings most of the past week, so he probably wouldn't be back until that afternoon. She hoped he hadn't learned anything urgent in his meetings the day before. She should have done a better job keeping track of time—there was hardly a place in Rome where you couldn't hear church bells, so it wasn't that difficult of a task. *At least Otavia is all right.*

She returned to her flat for a few hours and was about to leave for lunch when someone knocked on her door. The sound always made her tense because it could be the Gestapo. She took a deep breath before answering the door and was relieved to find Captain Ley in the hallway. He leaned in to give her a kiss, and her heart rate accelerated at his touch and his nearness. As he straightened, she noticed the shadows under his eyes.

She let him in, and as soon as the door closed, he leaned against it. "Where were you all night? I was afraid you'd been arrested, and when you weren't in any of the prisons, I didn't know what to think."

He searched the prisons for me? "I got stuck out after curfew."

"So where did you go?"

"I stayed with one of my other contacts—"

He frowned. "The one who spent a night here?"

"No. A different one. She's in the family way and had a bit of a scare. I helped her home to make sure everything was all right, and then I lost track of time."

"And your contact, is she in good health now?"

Gracie nodded. "Yes, she was fine this morning. I'm sorry I missed our meeting yesterday."

He didn't speak at once, and she braced herself for a lecture on the importance of being punctual. "I'm just glad you're safe. And good job. The SS didn't find anyone in their little raid, so whatever you did worked."

* * *

The boy standing in front of Zimmerman groveled, much like Zimmerman had done earlier that week when called in front of his superior to explain why the raid on the church had come up empty, embarrassing the SS and adding strain to the already-rocky relationship with the Vatican. It had taken Zimmerman a few days to find his second source, an Italian street urchin who liked to be paid for his information with cigarettes.

"You said there were Jews hiding in that church. Why was it empty when we arrived?"

The boy swallowed. When he finally spoke, his voice was a whisper. "There were two women, sir. One came to the church while I was cleaning and warned the priest."

"Then why didn't you send an update?" Zimmerman had looked like a fool. Had he known of the Jews' escape, he could have canceled his search and saved himself and the SS significant embarrassment.

"I was following the women, sir. And I know where they live."

Zimmerman leaned back in his chair and handed Neroli a carton of cigarettes. "Where?"

"A building in the Villa Borghese. A flat on the third floor. I can show your men."

"And what do the women look like?"

Neroli shrugged. "Women. One looked like she was expecting a baby; the other one had dirt or something on her cheek. They were wearing scarves so I couldn't see their whole faces."

"How old?"

"Not too old."

Zimmerman wondered what *not too old* meant to someone as young as Neroli.

It had been a bad week for Zimmerman. First there had been the fiasco with the raid. Then on Wednesday, the Gappisti had destroyed a fuel truck and 2,500 gallons of gasoline at the Via Claudia, near the Colosseum. Earlier today the Gappisti had attacked a parade of Italian Fascists, killing three of them and wounding others. The Gappisti were everywhere—a few steps ahead of his raid, destroying his supplies, and killing his allies. He'd had no leads on Wednesday's explosion or Friday's ambush and murders along the Via Tomacelli. Up until now, he'd also had no leads on Monday's failed raid on the San Lorenzo church, but maybe this new information would make the week end better than it had begun.

* * *

Bastien inspected new fortifications early Friday morning, so he was finished and exhausted by midafternoon. He glanced at his watch as he strode through the hotel lobby and figured he had just enough time for a quick nap before Gracie arrived for their meeting.

He'd only taken off his boots and unbuckled his belt when someone knocked on the door. When he answered, Gracie stood there, an hour early, but he didn't mind. He leaned out to welcome her with a kiss. Lately, he'd found himself keeping her in the hallway longer so he could lengthen his greeting, even if no one seemed to be watching. She fit perfectly in his arms, and her lips were soft and responsive. It was all part of the act, of course. Or was he carrying it too far? Enjoying it more than he should?

He gave her cheek a final caress and pulled her inside, then instantly wanted to kiss her again. But he'd promised he wouldn't take advantage of her, and he intended to keep the promise he'd made in Switzerland. Besides, the tense set of her eyes and downward curve of her lips made him think she was worried.

"Is something wrong, Concetta?"

"I was supposed to meet a contact over an hour ago, and she didn't show up." Gracie's hands moved in tense, antsy motions. "She's the one I told you about—she helped me warn the churches and then was ill. What if something happened to her? She lives with her mother, but her mother was away on Monday, and what if she's still gone and my friend needs help? She doesn't have a phone, so she can't call anyone."

Bastien noted that Gracie used *friend* in her explanation, rather than sticking with *contact* or *source*. It was unwise to get too attached to other spies—but he wasn't one to talk, not after he'd searched prisons and then paced away most of the night when Gracie had gone missing, not when that afternoon he'd been more interested in kissing her than in finding out why she'd been early. "You know where she lives?"

"Yes, but I'm nervous to go alone. I can't explain why—it's just a feeling. I was . . . I was wondering . . . if you'd go with me?"

Bastien had a quick internal debate. He didn't want Gracie's contact to know who he was, but she had helped warn the churches, and Gracie's eyes were pleading with him. *So much for a nap.* He fastened his belt around his tunic, shoved his feet into his boots again, and followed her.

"This is the contact expecting a baby?" he asked after they'd left the hotel.

Gracie nodded. "And she had pains on Monday after traipsing all along San Lorenzo. She loves Rome, and she likes to walk. Maybe she overdid it again."

"I don't know that I'll be much help if a baby's on the way. I was nearly thirteen when my youngest brother was born, but I wasn't there. My sisters and I were sent to my grandmother's house."

"I don't know anything either, but at least she wouldn't be alone. She's mentioned a midwife, so maybe she can tell us where to find her."

Bastien was relieved there was a midwife somewhere because he wasn't sure any of the German military doctors would offer their assistance.

They walked about fifteen minutes, then Gracie led him into an apartment building. As they entered, an SS enlisted man hurried out with an MP 38 slung across his shoulder. Beads of sweat dotted his forehead, and three parallel trails of blood were etched across his left cheek.

They climbed two flights of stairs, and with each step, it felt like an ounce of lead was being lodged in the bottom of Bastien's stomach. Gracie's face was tense, and her frown grew deeper the closer they got. Whatever he was feeling, she seemed to be feeling it too.

Outside the door, Gracie knocked. There was no sound from within, so she knocked a second time. After a long pause, Bastien tried the doorknob. It turned beneath his hand and opened into an eerie silence.

"Hello?" No one answered Gracie's call. She stepped past Bastien and turned down a hallway. "Her room's over here."

Bastien stayed near the entrance. If he was honest with himself, he was afraid of what he'd find. But women in childbirth usually made some sort of sound, didn't they? Or was the woman far enough along for the baby to come? Bastien couldn't remember if Gracie had said.

The apartment was as silent as a tomb. He walked toward the balcony, and as he passed the bathroom, he saw a frying pan on the floor. *Odd place for a frying pan.*

He stepped into the bathroom and stopped, stunned. Gracie's contact was in the apartment, but she wasn't having her baby. She would never have her baby.

CHAPTER TWENTY-ONE

GRACIE'S FRIEND LAY ON THE floor, one arm at her side, the other above her head, stretched across a cascade of dark hair. A line of bullet holes ran from her left shoulder to her right hip. Stepping around a pool of blood, Bastien bent to feel her neck. Her skin was still warm, but there was no pulse. He hadn't expected to find one, not with that many holes across her chest and swollen abdomen. He closed her eyes and swallowed back the bitter taste of bile before rising and stumbling into the flat's main room.

Bastien could piece together what had happened. The guard with the marks on his face would soon return with someone to help him deal with the body.

"Concetta?"

Gracie appeared at once from the hallway.

"It's time to go," he said.

"Just let me check the other rooms first."

He shook his head, not sure how to soften the blow. "I already checked them."

She seemed to sense something was wrong. "And?"

"She's dead."

"What?" Gracie's eyes opened wide, and her mouth fell open, showing the same shock he'd felt on seeing the slain woman. She tried to push past him to the bathroom.

"No, don't look." He reached out to grab her and usher her toward the door, but she dodged his arm and got around him.

"Otavia?" Gracie's face drained of all color, and she swayed to the side before catching herself on the bathroom's door frame. "Otavia!"

Gracie reached a trembling hand toward her friend and looked like she was about to kneel next to the body. Bastien knew she'd be covered in blood if that happened, so he wrapped an arm around her waist and kept her on her feet. "We've got to go. Now. Whoever shot her will be back soon."

"But . . . but we can't just leave her—"

"We can't help her anymore." He manhandled Gracie toward the door, and by then she was crying too hard to say anything else.

They'd made it to the second-floor landing when Bastien heard the door on the main floor crash open and the strike of military boots across the tile floor. Gracie's face was covered in tears, and her breaths were coming in sobs. He pulled her away from the stairwell and down a hallway, knowing she'd cause suspicion if the guards saw her.

"You've got to stop crying." Yet even as he said it, Bastien sensed she'd need more than a few seconds to turn the tears off.

"I'm trying." Her voice shook with emotion.

The hallway was straight, without any alcoves to hide in, and he didn't want to break into one of the nearby apartments. That might be loud, and even if it wasn't, he'd have some explaining to do if the residents were home. Depending on the patrol's size, Bastien might be able to finish them off with his Luger before they shot back, but he didn't want to risk a firefight with Gracie around, so he did the only other thing that came to his mind.

"Play along," he whispered. Then he pulled her closer and kissed her. He kept one arm around her waist and used his free hand to hold her face, hoping to hide her tears and her birthmark. He kept one eye half open as the men raced up the stairs. The patrol consisted of three soldiers, and he recognized the scratch marks on one of their faces.

One of the men paused, watching Bastien and Gracie. *Make him go away*, Bastien pleaded. Gracie trembled in his arms, whether from grief or fear, Bastien couldn't tell. The soldier yelled something to Bastien before following the other men up the stairs. Bastien hoped Gracie's German skills weren't good enough to understand the man's crass comment. He wished his kiss could somehow ease her pain, but seeing the murder—the double murder—had left him shaken, and he hadn't even known Otavia.

Gracie hadn't resisted his kiss, but the second the guards were gone and Bastien released her, she increased the distance between them. He wanted to hold her again, to comfort her, but when he reached for her, she stepped away and started down the last flight of stairs. He walked beside her all the way to her apartment, hoping the people they passed wouldn't notice the tears that silently slid down her cheeks. She didn't say a word to him the entire trip to her apartment. When they arrived, she kept her eyes on the floor, still sobbing, and shut the door to her room in his face.

* * *

Gracie leaned against the door and tried to control her weeping. She waited until Ley's footsteps faded down the hallway before she collapsed to the floor. Her cries echoed around the room, and not wanting her neighbors to hear, she moved to the bed and buried her face in her pillow.

A picture of Otavia's body was stuck in Gracie's mind. She and her baby deserved life, not a horrible death. *And what if the soldiers found her because I involved her in Ley's mission?* Overwhelming guilt joined the suffocating grief. It wasn't the first time she'd lost someone she loved, but what if this time it was her fault?

Gracie cried for a long time before turning to desperate prayer. *Father in Heaven, I never meant for Otavia to get hurt. I came to Rome to help, not to cause more harm. Please forgive me. And please don't let me hurt anyone else.*

* * *

Zimmerman's hopes for a better week were dashed when the man he'd sent to arrest the women came back with three scratch marks across his cheek and no prisoners.

"I held her there for almost two hours, waiting for the other woman to arrive. I turned my back for an instant, and she attacked me. I had no choice but to kill her."

"A good soldier doesn't let his guard down, not even for a moment," Zimmerman said.

The man stared at the floor. "I'm sorry, sir. Call of nature."

Zimmerman shook his head. *Excuses.* "My source seemed to think both women lived there. You shouldn't have left until the second one returned."

"I'm sorry, sir. I panicked and went for reinforcements."

Why would he need reinforcements to handle a corpse? Zimmerman cursed under his breath and kept his eyes away from the picture of his wife and son. A pregnant woman had tipped the churches off, and now she was dead. Zimmerman had wanted punishment for the women but not execution. Something inside him ached for the slain woman. Yet something else within him demanded revenge on the two women who'd thwarted his raid and lowered his standing with his superiors.

"Was there anything different in the apartment when you returned?" Zimmerman asked.

The soldier didn't answer.

"Well?"

"I closed the door when I left, sir. It was open when I came back."

Zimmerman swore again. "Left open by the other woman, no doubt. She won't be returning, not unless she has a death wish. Did you see anyone else?"

"Just an old woman outside when we came in and a couple on another floor kissing."

Life was strange like that: death on one floor, love—or lust—on another. "You're sure the woman outside was old and not in disguise?"

"Her wrinkles were deep enough to stall a panzer, sir."

"And the couple?"

"The man was a Wehrmacht officer, sir."

Zimmerman frowned. "Did you question any of them? Ask them if they saw a woman leaving the apartment?"

"No, sir," the young soldier answered.

Zimmerman leaned back in his chair, disappointed. The young squad leader's face still bled from the marks the dead woman's fingernails had left. Zimmerman had thought he could trust the man with a simple arrest, but the soldier had failed him. *I should have requested Möller or gone myself.* He was going to have to supervise everything directly from now on.

* * *

Gracie went to Ley's suite the next afternoon, just as she'd done nearly every day for the past two weeks. She'd been miserable all night and all morning, crushed by grief. Otavia was the most beautiful person she'd ever met, inside and out. What if Gracie was somehow responsible for her death?

Yet now, as she passed the guard in Ley's hotel lobby, she was also embarrassed. She'd lost control of her emotions yesterday. She should have been more logical, more professional. Before leaving her apartment, Gracie had checked her reflection in the mirror Ley had given her, so she knew her eyes were puffy and red. She kept her head down as she walked, hoping the guard wouldn't notice.

When she arrived and knocked on his door, Ley didn't kiss her like he usually did. No one was in the hallway to see them, so he didn't even bother smiling. He had every right to be disappointed in her, but she'd hoped for something different—compassion, understanding, forgiveness. Instead, she couldn't read his face at all.

As she came inside, she saw what she assumed was his most recent report on the table. She sat in front of the blank pages he'd left out for her and squared her paper in awkward silence. She knew she needed to say something, but she was afraid she'd start crying if she brought up what had happened the day before.

Ley sat across from her. "About yesterday . . . I want to apologize. I was desperate and didn't know what else to do. I know you've never asked for any of my kisses, but my timing yesterday was exceptionally bad." His voice was scarcely above a whisper, as was his habit when speaking of their mission.

Gracie squeezed her eyes shut. She understood why he'd kissed her like that. She'd been furious at him the evening before, then confused by how compelling his mouth could be after something as horrible as Otavia's murder, then angry at herself for reacting the wrong way to everything. "I . . . I owe you an apology too. And gratitude. Thank you for saving my life."

"Are you all right?"

Gracie shook her head. "It's wrong for her to have died like that. And I worry about her family. How long will it be before her husband finds out? What will her mother do when she sees all that blood? And I keep wondering if her death was somehow my fault."

He glanced at his scarred hands resting on the table, then pulled them into his lap. "Taking responsibility for someone's death is a heavy burden, one I don't recommend shouldering without absolute proof that it was your fault."

Gracie sniffed, and Ley handed her his pocket handkerchief and went to the wet bar to fill a glass for her.

"Most people would probably offer you a stiff drink," Ley said. "I'm just going to give you water and some advice." He set the glass in front of her. "Your contact was playing a dangerous game. We all are. She knew the risks. You haven't done anything with malicious intent, nor have you been careless while in Rome. Don't go down that road."

Gracie nodded, not sure she'd be able to follow his advice. Several times the previous night, she'd woken to a vivid image of Otavia's torn body. She took a few sips of water and started encoding Ley's report, hoping it would distract her. It did but only until she finished.

"Have you eaten today?" he asked after she'd burned his original report, her scratch paper, and her transposition keys.

Gracie couldn't remember eating anything, but food seemed so trivial. "I'm not really hungry."

"That doesn't mean you shouldn't eat. I know it's hard to lose someone you care about, but that doesn't mean you stop taking care of yourself. Especially out here in the field. Drawn-out grief is a luxury we don't have."

Gracie knew he was right. She couldn't let Otavia's death consume her. Nor could she just shrug it off, though that was the most professional way to act. And if she didn't act the way she was supposed to, the way she'd been trained to, she wouldn't survive. *I didn't think it would be so hard when I agreed to do this.* Gracie looked up and met Ley's eyes, wondering if he'd ever had second thoughts about his role in the war. "Did you always plan to be a spy?"

"No. The idea took a few years to fully form." Ley's leg made the table vibrate as he thought. "When my family was trying to leave Germany, one of my father's friends knew a father-and-son team from Great Britain, and they got us out by yacht. The son was about my age, and he mentioned how useful someone like me could be if war broke out. He offered to put me in touch with British intelligence. And don't get me wrong, I hated the Nazis even then, but I had my family to take care of first. It was only after I knew they'd be all right without me that I started looking for how I could best be of use." Ley described himself as if he were describing a tool. "I grew up with the enemy, so OSS seemed like a good fit. The rest just happened. You?"

Gracie was glad he'd opened up to her, at least a little, and decided to do the same. "Eight months ago, becoming a spy was the farthest thing from my mind. But I wanted to get out of Utah, so I let some OSS recruiter talk me into it." Gracie caught herself holding her left ring finger with her right hand. "A year ago, if you would have asked me what I'd be doing in 1944, I would have told you I'd be getting married."

"And I suppose you had a ring on that finger and a groom picked out?"

Gracie nodded.

"A nice Mormon boy?"

"Yes."

"What happened to him?"

"He joined the navy, and his submarine went down with all hands." Gracie paused for an instant, forcing her emotions back down her throat. Ley opened his mouth, but she cut him off, afraid he would tease her about her religion again. "You can ridicule me all you want about being a good little Mormon girl, but don't make fun of him." She'd never met anyone as wonderful as Michael. It didn't seem fair that he'd died at the bottom of the ocean, with no light and no air and no hope of escape.

"No, I never make fun of the dead. And I'm sorry. I know what it's like to lose someone you wanted to marry."

Gracie shook her head, surprised that he would compare Allotment Annie to Michael. "I thought you were relieved when Vaughn-Harris took Annie off your hands."

Ley leaned back in his seat. "No, I wasn't talking about Annie. I've been engaged twice. And the first time, I was really in love. Annie was a foolish attempt to fill the void left when Julie died."

"I'm sorry," Gracie said, looking at Ley in a new light. "What happened to her?"

"A car accident three weeks after I proposed." Ley fell silent, his leg tapping rapidly again.

"Julie—I suppose she was American?"

"Yes."

"How did you meet?" She wasn't sure he wanted to talk about it, but she wanted to know.

One side of his mouth pulled into a smile. "It's a long story."

Gracie gestured to the paper on the table. "It was a short report."

Ley was quiet for a few moments, looking beyond her. "When I was twenty-three, the Gestapo took my father away, and he asked me to take care of the family. I did the best I could, but when we found out he was dead, my mother and I decided to leave Germany. If we had stayed, Lukas would have had to join the Hitler Youth, and I would have been conscripted. It took all our savings, but we made it to America. And there we were, free, but almost out of money in the middle of a depression. My mom was a housewife; she didn't really have marketable skills, and as hard as I tried, I couldn't find steady work. My siblings were too young for outside employment but old enough that they didn't need me at home. So I joined the army. I sent my money home and learned a little more English, and none of us starved to death."

Ley glanced at his leg, seemed to notice its movement, and forced it to be still. "I got out three years later, and one of my sisters, Hannah, decided I'd spent too much time being responsible for the rest of them, so she encouraged me to do something I wanted. I bought a secondhand motorcycle and started restoring it, but she didn't think that was enough of an indulgence, so she set me up with one of her friends." Ley shook his head. "I didn't even want to go. Hannah's seven years younger than me, so I thought I was too old for her friend, but with Julie, it didn't seem to matter. When I dropped her off that night, I knew I had to see her again the next day. And the day after. It went on like that for weeks, months. I finally proposed to her about a year later, and then she died, and I just wished I'd asked her sooner."

Ley's face was calm as he spoke, with the exception of his eyes. Gracie could see the pain inside the melancholy blue, and she wished she could somehow erase it. She wouldn't have guessed Ley had a tragic love story in his past. Both of them seemed to be surrounded by death.

CHAPTER TWENTY-TWO

SEVERAL DAYS LATER GRACIE HAD a meeting with Angelo by the Pyramid of Cestius. She'd suggested that site when he'd left her apartment, before Otavia's death, and knew she'd chosen it because of Otavia's influence. It was a bit of a walk, but the weather was pleasant, and Ley was taking her out to supper that evening, so she didn't have to wait in line at the black market or at the legal one. But when Gracie arrived at the rendezvous, all she could think about was Otavia. What story would she have told about the pyramid? On a day like this, with such perfect weather, would conversation have revolved around her love of Rome? Or around her absent husband?

Gracie was fighting her grief and pretending to admire the pyramid's steep marble slopes when a shadow fell in front of her.

"*Buongiorno*, Concetta." Angelo's lips curved upward as she met his gaze. From behind his back, he brought out a bouquet of bright yellow mimosa and handed them to her.

Gracie smiled, surprised. "Thank you." The flowers were like a bit of sunshine in the middle of a storm.

"You're welcome." He motioned toward the Porta San Paolo and led her in that direction.

"How's your ankle?" she asked. It had been two weeks since their last meeting.

"Better." She studied him for a few steps and detected no limp. "Are you all right?" he asked. "You seem sad."

Gracie had tried so hard to keep her expression calm, but her emotions still felt close to the surface, as if they might betray her with the slightest trigger. "One of my other contacts was killed recently."

His hand gripped hers and didn't let go. "I'm sorry." They walked in silence for almost a block. "Were you there?"

"No, but I saw her body . . ." Gracie didn't know if she could tell Angelo anything else. She'd already broken one basic security rule: keep all your contacts and their missions separate. Over and over, the same question came to her mind. *Did Otavia die because I took her to San Lorenzo?*

Angelo squeezed her hand. "We'll take revenge on those who killed her. The Gappisti have a few plans. Meet me next Monday afternoon at the Quattro Fontane, and I'll show you. A quarter before two."

Gracie nodded. Then she wondered where his report was. "Do you have any papers for me today?"

"Yes. But first, I owe you an apology about our last meeting. That's why I brought flowers."

"You don't need to apologize, but the flowers are beautiful. Thank you."

"I do need to apologize," he insisted. "I didn't mean to put you in danger, and I certainly didn't mean to kick you out of your flat."

"I was glad to help." Gracie lowered her voice. "I'm sorry I ran off so suddenly. I forgot all about my other meeting until it was almost too late."

They strolled along in silence for a few paces, holding hands. "Does that mean you find me distracting?"

She glanced over his smooth face, dark eyes, and pleasant mouth, and felt herself blushing. Angelo was on the skinny side, but he was handsome. "I'm sure any colleague with an injury would be distracting," she managed to get out.

Angelo's lips twisted into a smile like he was about to laugh. "Well, I apologize for being a distraction and for kicking you out of your apartment. Thank you for helping me." He bent toward her and kissed her cheek. "My report's inside the flowers," he whispered. Then he straightened, focused on something behind her, and swore.

"What?" she asked.

"I've seen that man before. I was hoping it was just a coincidence, but this is the third time in the last two days."

Gracie was tempted to look behind her but knew that would make it obvious to whoever was tailing Angelo that he'd been noticed. "Do you know anything about him?"

"Italian. Not in uniform, but he looks like he knows how to handle himself. I'd guess OVRA or something like that."

Gracie could barely keep track of all the hostile entities that filled Rome. There were the Germans: the SS and the Gestapo, the army, and special task forces intent on anti-partisan warfare and Jewish roundups. The Italians had their counterparts in nearly every area. OVRA was Italian secret police.

"Keep walking," Angelo said, taking her arm. "Pretend nothing's different."

Gracie doubted she could completely hide her fear, but the Italian policeman was behind her, so he couldn't see her face. "What are we going to do?"

"I'm thinking." As they walked by an alley, Angelo dropped several objects into the shadows.

"What was that?"

Angelo showed her one of the objects before throwing it into the alley after the others. It was made of two twisted pieces of metal, with points at each end. "Any way you throw this, it will land with one point facing up. A dozen of these, and you can paralyze a German convoy. Take out the first vehicle and watch the others run into the back of it. Ambush the column while it's stalled. But the Germans know that, so they're particularly harsh if they catch you with these nails."

"Should I get rid of the report?"

"No. Most girls don't throw away perfectly good flowers." He led her into an apartment building's front lobby, and they ducked around a corner into one of two hallways stretching out from the center of the building.

Gracie went to her knees and peered through the leaves of a potted plant. A man hurried through the door and scanned the lobby. When a second man entered, the first man sent him to the left.

"There are two of them," Gracie whispered. "They're splitting up."

Angelo motioned her farther along the corridor and backed into a recessed doorway. He took a handkerchief from his pocket, rolled it up, and tied a knot in the middle. "Keep walking. Distract him, but make him come past this point."

Gracie didn't want to be a decoy, but the building was quiet and their tail was close, so even if someone let them into an apartment, the OVRA agent, or whoever he was, would hear them. She looked at the strip of fabric in Angelo's hands and shuddered as she stepped along the hallway. She knew the agent would turn the corner and see her within seconds.

"Signorina?"

Gracie tried to stay calm as she turned to face the round Italian man. "Yes?"

"Where's your friend?" he asked.

"What friend?"

He took his pistol out, gestured to the bouquet of flowers, then pointed his weapon at her heart.

Gracie forced herself to breathe, focusing on the man's face instead of his firearm. She let the flowers fall to the floor and raised her hands to about shoulder height in surrender. She took a slow step back, hoping the agent would come closer. In her periphery, she could see Angelo hidden from the man's view, but the agent stopped a few feet shy of the recessed entry. She took another step back, hoping she could keep a balance between obeying the agent so he wouldn't shoot her and luring him in. She swallowed hard. "He went on ahead."

"Show me."

Gracie nodded and slowly let her hands fall to her side as the man came toward her. He passed Angelo, and an instant later, Angelo sprang, wrapping the knotted handkerchief around the man's throat and jerking him back into the alcove. The man was unprepared for the attack and dropped his weapon, both hands going to the garrote around his neck.

"Get his gun!" Angelo hissed.

Gracie ran for it and heard the crack of a pistol as her fingers gripped the Beretta. She looked up to see the second agent a few doors down. She dove into the annex as he shot at her again. She fired back, and he ducked into an entryway, out of sight. Gracie waited for another clear shot, but the second agent stayed hidden.

"Shoot this one!" Angelo nodded toward the man he was strangling.

As the man's face twisted in purple agony, Gracie rammed the side of his head with the pistol. He stopped moving.

Angelo frowned and narrowed his eyes, took the pistol from her, and fired a round into the unconscious man's skull. Gracie bit back a scream as the dead man slumped to the floor. The second assailant reappeared, and Angelo turned his aim toward him. With Angelo's second shot, Gracie heard the other man cry out in pain.

Across the hall, a middle-aged woman opened her door a crack. As Angelo shot again, she quickly slammed it shut. Gracie was tempted to run across the hall and hide in the apartment, but she didn't know if the woman was sympathetic or just curious. And although staring at the dead agent was unnerving, Gracie was scared to cross the hallway again. The second agent's gun had left two bullet holes in her skirt.

Angelo kept his attention on their still-living opponent. "See if you can find more ammo. We'll kick a door in and escape through a window before reinforcements arrive."

Gracie dug through the dead man's pockets and found an extra magazine. "What about your report?"

Angelo slid the new clip into the pistol and glanced at the bouquet lying in the hallway. "We'll head across the hall, one door back."

She nodded. The dead OVRA man's eyes stared up at her.

"Ready . . . Now." Angelo let loose a series of shots, and the two of them ran, hunched over, toward the apartment they'd agreed on. Gracie scooped up the bouquet and pulled the piece of paper from the center of the stems as Angelo kicked the door. The door held. Angelo swore and fired a few bullets into the lock.

They rushed into the flat amid gunshots from the other agent and screams from the apartment's trio of residents.

"Get down," Angelo shouted, waving his gun around.

He and Gracie ran toward the window in the back of the apartment. As Gracie opened the window, Angelo fired a final shot.

"Got him," he said.

They climbed into the alley behind the apartment complex and ran until they reached the main road. Angelo slipped the Beretta into his pocket, and Gracie looked around. Everything seemed normal. No one was staring at them, nor did she see any police or military agents.

They walked in silence for several blocks, Gracie trying to calm her breathing and control the shaking in her arms.

"Next time I tell you to shoot someone, do it," Angelo said. "You think I want him waking up and finding me again? Who knows how long he's been tailing me—he could know everything about me. He had to die." Angelo shook his head in frustration. "I wish the other one was dead too, but I just hit his shoulder before he ducked back into the hallway."

Gracie nodded but couldn't picture herself pulling the trigger. She'd come to Rome to operate a radio, not assassinate OVRA agents.

Angelo's voice softened. "And I'm sorry I was followed. Next week, at Quattro Fontane, I'll make sure I'm clean before I come. You do the same. And you can consider your friend partially avenged."

Angelo turned left, and Gracie turned right. She still had an hour before she needed to set out for Ley's hotel, but she didn't want to go to her apartment. She kept doubling back, circling blocks, and stopping to hide, wanting to make sure no one followed her.

Taking the long route to Ley's hotel also helped her process what she'd seen in the apartment hallway. She pictured the dead man's eyes and remembered Angelo's parting words. It was one violent death in exchange for another. But Gracie had seen the soldier who had probably killed Otavia, and he was German. Even if it had been the same person, Gracie didn't think Otavia would approve.

CHAPTER TWENTY-THREE

BASTIEN HEARD THE AIRPLANE ENGINES and looked over his shoulder. As the white star on the plane's wing came into view, he drove his motorcycle into a ditch and threw himself to the dirt along the steepest side of the embankment. Bullets hit the ground all around him, but none of them slammed into his body. *All this to get shot at by my own side.*

The plane, a P-39, turned and came back for a second pass. The pilot couldn't know they were on the same side, but didn't he have more promising targets than German hauptmanns on motorcycles, like the targets Bastien included in nearly every report?

Bastien held perfectly still during the second strafing run, hoping the pilot would think he was dead. As the rat-tat-tat of the guns grew to a crescendo, he held his breath. He remembered how his father had described shellings in the trenches—the noise, the smoke, the confusion. *I wonder if he was ever scared.*

Bastien prayed, and the plane didn't come around for a third pass. He stayed in the ditch for several minutes to make sure the P-39 was really gone. When his breathing returned to normal, he stood and dusted off his uniform. The pilot had been on target with Bastien's motorcycle; it was destroyed.

A long walk back to Rome lay ahead, but first, he needed to meet with Marcello. Bastien was late, but Marcello and Roberto were still there, half asleep in the vineyard's shade.

"What happened to you?" Roberto asked.

"An American fighter decided a Wehrmacht officer was a good target for strafing. Sorry I'm late."

"Here's a list of alternative targets for your fighters." Marcello handed Bastien a paper, then laughed. "If that pilot's commander knew he was shooting at one of his country's top spies, he'd probably ground him."

Bastien read through the suggested targets on Marcello's list: newly repaired rail lines, hidden supply depots, camouflaged anti-aircraft guns. He folded the paper and slipped it into his pocket. "I'm hardly America's top spy."

"How do you know?" Roberto asked. He had a point—Bastien hadn't been briefed on any OSS operations other than his own.

"Common sense. And I have something for you." Bastien pulled a slip of paper from his pocket. "Weapons drop in a week, weather permitting. Came over the radio a few days ago." Gracie had passed the message to him yesterday: *Have Centurion inform Scutum group of airdrop, 0300 hours, March 22, drop zone 9C.* Bastien had needed to search the maps hidden with his radio to figure out where the supplies would be dropped, but it was a good location. He thought Marcello and his men would be safe there when the time came.

Marcello grinned. "Does this mean they expect the front to move closer? That maybe we'll be involved in the real fighting?"

"We can hope that's what it means." But Bastien had been requesting more weapons for the partisans since November. Perhaps the drop was timed to coincide with an offensive, or maybe it just took the OSS five months to fulfill requests. Bastien looked around. He couldn't see any bicycles. "Did you both walk?"

They nodded.

"I suppose that means I'll be heading back to Rome on foot."

"Watch out for the Gappisti, Capitano." Marcello stood and stretched his neck. "Solitary Wehrmacht officers are tempting targets."

"I know, but I'm closer to Rome than I am to any of the trenches I inspected this morning. Can't be helped."

Bastien was about to leave when he heard a faint sneeze. He looked at Marcello and Roberto, but they both shook their heads. Bastien took out his Luger, and Marcello did the same with his pistol. The noise they'd heard had sounded human and been close enough that whoever had made it would have heard every word of their conversation. They'd said enough to blow Bastien's cover and send all three of them to their executions.

Marcello pointed to the grapevines a few rows over and crept around to approach from the right. Bastien moved to advance from the left. As he squeezed past a grapevine, something dropped in front of his feet: a German potato-masher grenade. He kicked it away as hard as he could. When the explosion came, it knocked him to the ground, and he felt a wall of heat surge past him, stinging his eyes and stealing his breath. Flat on his back, he looked under a row of grapevines and saw their spy's feet, feminine and running toward him.

He had lost his grip on his weapon when the grenade exploded, but he found it in the grass, gripped it, and aimed. When the woman burst through to his row, her pistol was pointed at him. His finger on the trigger, he hesitated, not sure he wanted to shoot a girl. She was an adult but only barely.

A shot sounded, and the woman collapsed. Roberto, it seemed, had no scruples when it came to shooting women, and Bastien probably owed his life to that fact. He pulled himself to his feet, sore but uninjured, and gazed at the woman's lifeless body lying crumpled between the grapevines.

"I know her," Roberto said. "She lives near my parents' home. Isabella. Her father is the most enthusiastic Fascist in the entire village, but I never figured her for an assassin."

Marcello frowned. "So she followed you."

"I checked, and no one was following me."

"Maybe you need to check harder next time." Marcello turned to Bastien. "There's no way of knowing if this is the first time she's followed us. She might have accomplices. Perhaps we should meet somewhere else next week?"

"Wednesday still?"

Marcello ran his fingers along his mustache as he considered it. "Yes. Somewhere in Rome. That bar near Castel Sant'Angelo."

"We've already met there."

"Not since November. I'll think of somewhere new by next week."

Bastien left Marcello and Roberto to handle the corpse and started his trek back to Rome. He kept his eyes moving, watching for Gappisti ambushes, but the countryside was quiet. He thought of the two dead women he'd seen the past week. It seemed wrong for women to die like that.

As he walked, he wondered how he could possibly survive the war with both sides trying to kill him. *Is my life worth so much?* He'd give it up if he needed to, especially if his death could somehow save Lukas or Stefanie or Hannah. If it were possible, he'd go back in time and make a deal with God to take him instead of his brother Hans. But Bastien's survival instinct was still strong. He tried to tell himself he wasn't afraid to die, but the truth was, he wanted to live.

On the edge of the city, he caught a ride with a Wehrmacht officer returning to Rome in a staff car. "What happened to your head?" the man asked as the driver navigated the streets.

Bastien maneuvered himself so he could see into the rearview mirror. He had a cut along his left temple. "It's probably from when an American fighter chased me off my motorcycle."

"Should we take you to a hospital?"

"No. My hotel."

When they arrived, Bastien checked his watch. It was a few minutes past curfew, and he was two hours late for his meeting with Gracie. He wondered if she'd gone home or if she'd waited for him. Would she be as worried about him as he'd been about her when she'd missed an appointment a week and a half ago?

When he turned the corner to his hallway, he saw her sitting on the floor with her back against the wall and her arms wrapped around her knees. She stared up at him as he approached, and her eyes seemed deeper than he'd ever seen them before. He didn't care that he was dirty from lying in the ditch and dusty from the long walk back to Rome. He didn't care that blood was smeared across the side of his face. He took her hand, helped her to her feet, and pulled her to his chest. He kissed her for a long time, longer than normal. He wasn't quite sure why but thought part of it was his need to know that after everything that had happened that day, he was still alive. And maybe it was just part of the act, but she was kissing him back, almost as if she'd needed to see him as much as he'd needed to see her.

CHAPTER TWENTY-FOUR

SUNLIGHT STREAMED THROUGH GRACIE'S WINDOW early Saturday morning. She heard someone on the stairs and sat up in bed, hoping the footsteps would continue past the fifth floor. Instead, they came down the hall and stopped in front of her doorway. The knock that followed was gentle, but that didn't mean it wasn't the Gestapo.

"Just a minute." Gracie scrambled out of bed and reached for her clothes. After slipping into her dress, she grabbed a pistol and hid it behind her back.

She opened the door and found Ley standing in the hallway, dressed in civilian clothing. "Good morning," he said.

Relief that it was Ley and not someone else quickly turned to worry about what she looked like. She hadn't even glanced in the mirror before opening the door.

"Sorry, did I wake you?" he asked.

Her hair probably looked awful. "Um, I was awake. I just wasn't out of bed yet." She heard noise across the hall. "You better come in." He slipped inside before any of her neighbors peered into the hallway. "Is anything wrong?"

"No, I just had an idea. I'm not even sure it's a good one." He looked at the floor almost bashfully, which wasn't like him at all.

"Well, what's your idea?"

"I was wondering if you wanted to take a day off. Get out of Rome and not worry about anything for a few hours."

Gracie didn't even try to hide her surprise. "You'd do that for me?"

"You've had a hard week. I guess we both have. We'll be more effective if we have a chance to relax for a day, and the German Army isn't expecting me to do anything for them till tomorrow."

Rome was beautiful, but this past week, it had felt like a nightmare. The constant danger was wearing enough by itself, but the recent brushes with death haunted Gracie's memory and made everything worse. A day away sounded perfect. "I'd like that. Thank you."

"We can leave as soon as you're ready. I've got breakfast."

Gracie smiled and grabbed a hairbrush. Ley watched as she worked out the tangles. She normally adored men in uniform, but since Ley usually wore a Nazi uniform, Gracie liked his change into civilian clothing. Simple trousers, a blue button-up shirt with the cuffs rolled to the elbows, and suspenders. It felt almost normal for him to be there while she brushed her hair, but she wasn't sure she should feel so comfortable having him in her room while she got ready.

Ley seemed to notice her sudden discomfort. "I'll wait outside. I borrowed an Opel Blitz. It's parked near the front entrance. You can't miss it."

Gracie nodded as Ley let himself out. When she finished her hair, she wondered why he'd borrowed a troop transport. It sounded like a magnet for Allied fighters, but then again, most German vehicles were a target. She poured water into the small basin and washed, then tried on three different shirts and two different skirts. *Ley's the only one who will see you today*, she reminded herself. Yet it was his opinion she found herself caring about. *Did he really mean it, all the times he said I was pretty?* She searched her image in the mirror he'd given her. He often withheld information from her, but she didn't think he'd ever lied. She put the mirror away, eager to join him.

As she walked down the stairs, anticipation made her breathing more shallow than usual. *It's just because I need a break*, she told herself. But the nervous excitement in her stomach reminded her of how she'd felt when she went on her first date with Michael.

When she left the building, she scanned the street and saw Ley leaning against the passenger side of a truck. He opened the door for her when she arrived, then helped her up onto the seat.

He climbed in behind the wheel, and Gracie pointed to the machine pistol and box of ammunition piled on the floor. "Target practice again?"

"No. I just don't want to take any chances. If the Gappisti want to shoot my head off, that's one thing, but I'm not going to take you out to the country without the means to protect you." Ley started the engine. "There's a Walther P 38 under the seat in case you need it."

Gracie had thought the trip felt like a date, but the weapons quickly changed that.

Ley drove north. They passed through several checkpoints, but once the guards saw his papers and realized Ley was a captain, they asked few questions.

They drove perhaps an hour before Ley turned off the road and parked next to a large tree. He grabbed a pair of binoculars and opened his door. "Wait here," he said as he hopped out. He scaled the truck's hood and scanned the area. After a thorough visual search, he climbed down and walked out of her view. She heard him open the back of the truck, then saw him spread a blanket out under a trio of stone pines.

He'd told her to wait, but Gracie opened the door anyway, wondering what he had planned.

"Hungry?" he asked.

Gracie nodded.

"Good. The lady at the hotel put together a picnic." He went back to the rear of the truck and returned with a small basket. There were pastries inside and a container of whipped cream.

"How did she get cream?" Gracie asked.

Ley shrugged as they sat on the blanket. "Doesn't seem fair, does it? German officers can eat whatever they want, and the average person in Rome is slowly starving to death. I figure the more we eat, the less the real German officers can have."

She laughed, then ate three of the pastries. "I think this is the best breakfast I've had since the war started."

Ley offered her another, but she was full.

"Have you ever ridden a motorcycle?" he asked.

"No." Nor had she ever wanted to. Her clumsy bike riding as a twelve-year-old, combined with several very public falls, had earned her the nickname "ungraceful Gracie." Bicycles made her nervous. Motorcycles were even worse. When she was fourteen, she'd seen one of her neighbors break his arm when he'd crashed his Harley-Davidson.

"Come here." Ley led her to the back of the truck, where two motorcycles hid underneath the canvas cover. "They're DKW NZ 350s. Not too big, not too little."

Gracie thought they looked enormous, but at least they didn't have side cars.

Ley climbed inside and picked up a wooden board, then made a ramp out of it and brought the motorcycles down. "I'll be honest—I prefer British motorcycles. But getting two of these was tricky enough."

That meant he'd put considerable effort into their daytrip. Gracie wavered between pretending to be excited and telling him she'd rather sit under the tree all day than climb onto one of those motorized death traps. He was smiling as he brought the second one down, and she didn't want to ruin his mood after he'd tried so hard, so she kept silent. But it must have been written on her face.

Ley's smile disappeared. "I'm an idiot. I should have asked if you liked motorcycles. You don't, do you?"

"I've never ridden one. But didn't you almost get killed by an American fighter when you were out riding a few days ago?"

"It's overcast today. I think the Air Corp will take the day off." Ley looked up at the clouds as he spoke, then back at her. "I'm sorry. I wanted it to be a surprise, but maybe that wasn't the best idea. We can do something else."

"No, I'm willing to try it," she blurted out, not wanting to snub his efforts. Gracie glanced at the motorcycles. They had two seats. "Maybe you could take me for a ride to start with." That didn't seem quite so scary.

Ley hesitated.

"I should at least try, shouldn't I?" Gracie asked.

A hint of a smile appeared on his face. He reached into the truck and pulled out something made of fabric. "Here, put these on. They'll be too big for you, but they're the smallest size I could get without more notice." He handed her a rope too. "You can use that as a belt."

Gracie let the material fall open to reveal a pair of pants. Her face pulled into a grin as she thought of how horrified her mother would be. She preferred her daughters in dresses or skirts. But pants made more sense for riding a motorcycle.

"Let me help you up." Ley climbed into the covered truck bed and offered her a hand. After he'd pulled her up, he hopped down. "I'll wait by the cab. Call me when you're finished."

The pants were the right length, but the waist was too wide and the hips a little snug. She threaded the rope through the belt loops and thought it just as well that she couldn't see herself in a full-length mirror. "I'm finished."

Ley reappeared a few seconds later. "Have a seat on the edge of the truck." She sat as he climbed back into the truck and dug through one of the baskets. "I didn't even bother looking for shoes. I didn't think any would fit you." He pulled out a pair of gaiters and wrapped them around her ankles. "I don't want any loose clothing to get caught on the bike." His hands slipped to her waist, and he helped her to the ground.

They stood there for a few moments, only inches separating them, his hands still on her makeshift belt. The breeze blew his clean scent toward her. She guessed it was soap, but she couldn't see any stubble on his face, so maybe it was his shaving cream. She thought he was going to kiss her, and when he stepped away and climbed back into the truck, she realized she was disappointed that he hadn't.

"Almost forgot this." He handed her a helmet with a pair of goggles and fastened a similar one on his own head. Ley watched as she put hers on, and then he tugged once on the strap but otherwise kept his distance.

She followed him to the motorcycle.

"You always want to get on and off from the side with the kickstand. Then you won't pull the bike over on you if you catch it somehow." He swung onto the motorcycle and did something with his left foot. "I'm making sure it's in neutral. We'll go over that later." He smoothly dismounted again. "Do you want to try starting it?"

Be brave. "All right. How?"

He held up a key. "First you turn on the petrol cap. On a cold engine, you have to push in the tickler, then set the throttle and switch on the ignition. The kick start's over here." He showed her how to do everything, ending with the kick start. He slowly stepped down twice on the metal lever before pushing it down more quickly a third time, and the engine roared to life. He killed it after a few seconds. "Your turn."

Her first attempt failed. The second time she stomped on the kick start, the motorcycle started with a deep rumble. Even though Ley had already started it once, she flinched at the noise. She hoped he hadn't noticed.

"Not bad," he said, raising his voice so she could hear him over the engine. "I'll get on first. Watch out for the muffler. It's not hot yet, but it'll get that way. Then just lean with me."

Ley straddled the motorcycle, and she followed. She wrapped her arms loosely around his waist but quickly tightened her grip when he sped across the field. The wind blew all around her, and she gradually relaxed but didn't loosen her grip on Ley, even after he'd gotten them up to speed. His torso was firm and warm in her embrace. She closed her eyes and rested her head against his back, enjoying the moment.

Coding and transmitting reports was lonely work, but holding on to Ley, she didn't feel so alone. The countryside was beautiful—green and fertile. The air was fresh. It was easy to forget her mission, forget Otavia's death, forget the way Angelo had strangled the Italian man, and forget that Ley might have ulterior motives for his kindness. Gracie wasn't sure how long they rode around together, but she liked it more and more as they went along.

He slowed to a stop near the truck. "Ready to try it?"

Gracie eyed the other motorcycle, wondering how difficult it would be. He made it look easy, but he made a lot of things look easy. *Like being a spy and shrugging off death.* She swallowed hard. "I guess so."

She slid off his motorcycle, avoiding the muffler, and approached the other DKW from the left. She could find the kick start and the ignition switch, but beyond starting it and getting on, she didn't know what to do.

"Brakes are on the right. Right foot and right hand. Go easy on the handbrake at first; you don't want to lock up the front wheel. The foot brake's a little easier to control. You'll also use your right hand to control the throttle. Left hand is the clutch. Left foot switches gears." Ley swung onto her motorcycle and pushed a lever with his left foot. "You'll want to start out in neutral. It's there now. Go ahead and sit on it, get a feel for how everything moves."

Gracie was as nervous as she'd been at any other point on her mission. She mounted the motorcycle after Ley got off and went through the motions of feeling the clutch and the brake.

"You'll want to practice getting it started and moving through the first few gears." Ley knelt next to the left side of the bike and moved her foot to each gear's position. "You're in neutral now, step down into first, then lift through neutral to second, third, and fourth. You put the clutch in, switch gears, and then ease the clutch out as you open the throttle. Best way to learn is by trying."

Gracie wasn't sure she was ready. She took the key from Ley and tried to remember the first step. Ley pointed to the petrol cap. She turned it on, then primed the engine, checked the throttle, and twisted the key in the ignition. Ley worked the kick start for her.

"It's best to turn the engine over slowly a few times, then start it," he explained, leaning close so she could hear him over the engine. "Clutch in, then switch into first and slowly let the clutch out as you give it gas. We'll start with just getting it into first for now."

Gracie nodded, then choked the engine twice in a row.

"That's all right," Ley said. "It takes some practice. Try giving it a little more gas next time."

After five additional failures and only two successes, Gracie was frustrated. But Ley was patient. Gracie kept trying, and it got better—enjoyable even—as she slowly mastered shifting up and shifting down. By noon, her transitions were smooth, and when she took her first hill, Ley said she did it as if she'd been riding over hills for years.

He jogged over to her when she pulled to a stop past his position. "Take it back to the truck so I can get mine. It's getting hard to keep up with you. When you get the speed up, go straight. I haven't talked to you about countersteering yet."

Gracie nodded. She guided the machine through the first three gears but didn't push it any faster than that. She was content at that speed, feeling the wind on her face and the sensation of rapid movement as the grass swished past her legs. There wasn't any way she could control what happened in Rome, but out here, now that she'd figured it out, she could at least control the DKW. It wasn't so different from operating her radio—it took time and practice, but once she learned, she could use the machine the way it was intended, and that was immensely satisfying. She held in the clutch and moved into fourth gear, deciding to increase her speed after all.

She risked a quick glance at Ley. He was far enough back that she couldn't see his face, but his plan for a carefree morning was working. She was glad, for her sake, and for his. She felt a surge of gratitude for him. Somehow, in the last four weeks, he'd managed to convince her that she was beautiful despite her mother's disapproval, and today he'd taught her that a few decade-old mishaps with a bicycle didn't mean she couldn't master a motorcycle.

She spotted a hole in front of her and was there almost before she'd processed it. She turned to the right, but her motorcycle moved to the left—directly into the hole. She tried to shift down as she turned, thinking she'd have more control at a slower speed, but it only got worse. In desperation, her right hand clamped down on the brake, but she'd already lost control of the motorcycle.

The front wheel locked up, the DKW tilted toward the dirt, and she crashed. Hard.

CHAPTER TWENTY-FIVE

GRACIE'S HELMET BANGED INTO THE ground, and the weeds grabbed at her hair and clothing. A few of them ended up in her mouth. Everything happened quickly, but in the end, she was lying on her side with the motorcycle over her left leg. Her shoulder, head, and hip ached from the impact. The wind had been knocked out of her, and she gasped to fill her lungs with air again.

Gracie could finally inhale normally when she heard Ley running toward her. He knelt next to her, breathing hard from the run. "Can you move your neck?"

"Yes, but it hurts."

Ley stood and lifted the motorcycle off her leg. She knew it was heavy, but he moved it in seconds, then was on his knees at her feet. "Does it hurt when I move your legs?"

Gracie winced as he gently pulled her left leg straight. "Yes."

"Bruised or broken?"

"Just bruised." But it was probably the worst bruise she'd ever had.

He helped her to a sitting position, one hand supporting her back and the other cupping her neck. "Lightheaded?"

"A little."

"Just sit here for a while. It should get better. That was a nasty crash." He unbuckled her helmet and looked over her head, picking a few weeds from her hair as he checked for bleeding.

"I can't figure out what happened. I tried to go one way, and the bike went the other."

"That's what happens when you're going fast. If you turn the front wheel right, the back wheel drags the bike left. I'm sorry. That was going to be our next lesson. Along with tips like how it's unwise to downshift while turning."

Gracie hadn't realized there was still so much to learn.

Ley's fingers brushed along her hairline. "You've got a cut on your forehead." He took out his handkerchief and pressed it into her wound. "And a sore neck and a bruised leg. Anything else?"

"I hit my shoulder."

"I'm sorry. I should have been a better teacher. It just looked like you were having fun, and I didn't want to make you stop."

She had been having fun, but now she felt nauseated. "I think I need to lie down again."

Ley helped her back into the weeds. "Should I take you to a hospital?" He studied her eyes as he used his hand to shade her face, then expose it to sunlight again.

"No." Gracie felt too frazzled to keep her cover story straight.

Ley sat beside her for a while. Even with the clouds, it was hot staring up at the sky. "Would you be all right if I went and pulled the truck around? Or at least went and got the blanket for you to lie on?"

Gracie wanted him to stay, but a blanket sounded nice. The weeds kept poking the back of her neck. "I'll be fine."

He checked her motorcycle, but it must have been too damaged to ride because he walked back to the truck. When he returned, he found some shade, spread out the blanket, and helped her to it. Sometime while he was peering through the binoculars at a bicycle in the distance, she fell asleep.

"Concetta?"

She opened her eyes and found Ley leaning over her.

"I don't think you should sleep so soon after a crash like that."

"I didn't mean to fall asleep." Gracie sat up. "But a nap sounds nice."

Ley nodded, and she caught him yawning. "Maybe if we didn't have to worry about the Gappisti." He yawned again. "Sorry. I was up all night."

"You were? Why?"

"That's how I got today off."

Gracie was flabbergasted. He'd not only found the motorcycles, the truck, and the food, but he'd also given up his sleep to give her a break. And she'd ruined it.

"How are your bruises?" he asked.

"Still there."

"Well, we've got a while before we have to go back. They say when you fall off a horse, it's best to get right back on. I assume that holds true for motorcycles too."

The thought of getting on a motorcycle again made her stomach churn. The DKW had been fun for a while, until it had dumped her into the weeds. She was lucky she hadn't broken a bone or gotten burned by the muffler. "I'd rather not."

"Lunch, then?"

Gracie nodded, glad Ley hadn't insisted she try another ride. She didn't want to disappoint him more than she already had, but she wasn't ready to try again. She might never be ready to try again.

The meal wasn't as amazing as breakfast had been, but living in Rome was making her grateful for any food at all. "How much did you have to pay the woman for two baskets of food?"

Ley smiled. She liked the way his face softened when he was happy. "Not as much as I had to bribe the guard at the motor pool to lend me two motorcycles and a truck for nonofficial purposes."

"Do you think he'll get in trouble?"

"Not unless American paratroopers land in Rome and someone needs to move troops around. But if that happens, he might not be alive to be punished anyway."

Gracie sighed. "I wish the army would hurry up and get here."

"Italy's a hard country to fight in."

"And spy in."

Ley nodded his agreement. "They'll get here. Germany's going to lose this war."

"You're sure?"

"Yes. There are too many people like me who will never give up until Hitler is defeated."

"There are plenty of fanatical Nazis who will never give up either." Gracie thought of Ostheim and Zimmerman, wondering if they'd ever voluntarily surrender.

"Call it my blind faith, then."

"Faith that we'll win just because we're on the right side?"

One of Ley's feet tapped against the other. "I've lived under Hitler. I don't think God wants His children governed that way."

"So you do believe in God?" Underneath his talent for spying, Gracie sensed Ley was a good man, and she suspected he was more religious than he let on.

"I never said I didn't."

"No, you just change the subject whenever anything gets too personal." Gracie remembered his story about Julie and wished she could take back her words. Maybe he didn't want to talk about the past because it was painful. A murdered father, a dead fiancée, his fatherland taken over by a madman. "Well, most of the time."

"We have a job to do. Colonel Ambrose didn't send us here to gossip."

"Occasional conversations about you and your past hardly constitute gossip."

"Hmm."

Gracie couldn't decide if she found his noncommittal sound infuriating or endearing. "It's not like it's keeping you from doing your assignment. With all the information you gather, it's a wonder the Allies weren't in Rome weeks ago."

"My information can't help them get through the mud faster or crack Cassino." Ley frowned.

"If the Allies win, will you want to live in Germany when the war's finished?"

Ley scanned the horizon with his binoculars as he answered. "I like the United States. If I survive, I'll go back." The way he said his last sentence made Gracie think he thought his chance of survival was small. "You?"

"I'll go back to America. If I'm still alive."

He gently nudged her arm with his elbow. "Don't sound so gloomy about it. Your chances of survival are good."

"I seem to remember you telling me that radio operators normally last only six weeks. I've been here almost four, and I think the army is more than two weeks away."

"Most radio operators don't have me watching their backs." Ley winked at her. "And you're better than most radio operators, so you should last longer than average."

"That's not what you said in Switzerland."

"Maybe I've changed my mind after seeing you in the field for a while."

"So you think I'll survive, but you think your own chances are slim. It seems like we'd go down together if anything happened."

He frowned slightly. "If we're caught, I think you'll be sent to a camp. It would be horrible, but your faith would sustain you, and maybe an Allied Army would free you before you starved to death."

"And you?"

"I'd be executed."

Gracie shuddered, wondering which fate was worse. She felt Ley's hand on her arm.

"I'll do everything I can to make sure you aren't caught," he said. "First thing next week, I'll find you a new apartment so your other contact won't know where you live. He seems to have someone chasing him every time you meet him."

Gracie nodded.

"You know, we got matching cuts this week." He leaned closer to get a better view of the sliced skin on her forehead. "But I think yours will heal without a permanent mark."

Gracie hoped he was right. She already had a birthmark on her face. She didn't need a scar too.

"If it doesn't, I don't know what you're going to do when you get back to the States." Ley's words confirmed Gracie's fears, but he was grinning, so she didn't think he was serious.

"Why is that?"

"A scar might put a damper on your dating prospects. You'll be limited to men with their own fleshy anomalies."

Gracie glanced at Ley's scarred hands, then at his eyes, which seemed to laugh at her. He was teasing, but it was more fun to play along than to get upset over it. "I can think of worse fates." She could cut bangs if her forehead scarred, and she didn't think scars were that ugly, not compared to her birthmark. Since coming to Rome, she'd gradually realized that outward beauty wasn't as important as she'd been raised to think it was. She stretched out on the blanket, enjoying the pleasant weather and the even more pleasant company. "Are you going to tell me your real name yet?"

Ley shook his head. "Not yet. We should probably get back to Rome. How bad is your head?"

"It hurts, but not as much as it did right after I crashed."

"And your leg?"

Gracie bent her knee and flexed her ankle, wincing. "Still a little sore."

"Then I'll carry you to the Opel."

"It's only ten yards away."

"I won't be able to help you much come Monday, so let me do what I can today." He helped her sit up, then scooped her into his arms and straightened. She rested her head on his chest and listened to his heartbeat. She couldn't remember anyone carrying her since she was a little girl, and she liked it. She felt safe in his arms.

He set her down gently when they reached the truck so he could open the door for her. Then he brought his lips to within an inch of hers and stopped. They were in the middle of the countryside, so there was no one to see them kiss. As he pulled away with a sheepish smile, she willed someone to ride past on a bicycle, someone to drive by in a cart, because despite her headache, there wasn't anything she wanted more in that moment than for him to kiss her.

"Sorry," he said. "Habit, I guess, but it looks like we're alone."

She was tempted to close the distance between them again, but she wasn't sure how he'd react. He had planned the whole day to help her, and he'd just promised to do everything he could to protect her, but that didn't mean he loved her.

She accepted his help up to the cab and squeezed her eyes shut when he closed the door, wishing she hadn't been so clumsy, wishing someone had appeared and given them an excuse to kiss, wishing she knew whether their day together had been a real date.

CHAPTER TWENTY-SIX

IT TOOK BASTIEN A FEW hours to fix the motorcycle Gracie had crashed. When he finished repairing it in the hotel parking lot, his hands were filthy, but he couldn't find his handkerchief to wipe them off. He finally remembered he'd given it to Gracie to use as a bandage. *Maybe I should carry more than one.* He needed to return the picnic baskets to the kitchen but decided to wash up in his room first. When he heard someone whistling "Lili Marlene," Bastien knew Heinie was just around the corner. He waited, his key in the lock.

"Adalard, hello." Heinie looked over Bastien's civilian clothes. "I'm surprised you got leave today. There was a big meeting they wanted everyone to attend about anti-partisan warfare. As if engineers need to worry about that. Wasted day."

Had Bastien known a meeting was scheduled on that subject, he wouldn't have taken leave. "No one told me."

"You're lucky. Most of it was listening to a long-winded Italian talk about coordinating our efforts. His German was horrible, but he wouldn't use a translator. Then he had us all examine those four-pointed nails—as if anyone with half a brain can't tell their primary use is sabotage— and had us look at all the parts of a captured radio set—as if we'll run into those on the street." Heinie rolled his eyes. "If you ask me, the main problem is the Italians. They won't admit it, but their security is practically nonexistent. I guess they're overreacting about a shootout a few days ago. They lost one man, and a second was injured."

"I didn't hear about a shootout."

"Not much to hear," Heinie said. "A pair of agents followed someone they suspected to a meeting with another Gappisti. One of them must have noticed they were being tailed. They led the agents into a building and ambushed them."

"Do they have any leads?"

"Not unless the injured agent recognizes them. He's in the hospital, so he's unlikely to find them anytime soon."

"Did they decide anything about how we're to work with the Italians in the future?" Bastien tried to appear uninterested, but he was cursing himself for missing such a huge intelligence opportunity.

Heinie shrugged. "I almost fell asleep, so I pretended to take notes and wrote a letter to Maurleen."

Bastien laughed, even though he wished Heinie had taken real notes so he could borrow them.

"What did you do instead?" Heinie asked.

"I tried to teach Concetta how to ride a motorcycle."

"How did it go?"

Bastien frowned. "I don't think she likes motorcycles."

Heinie grinned. "Well, nobody's perfect."

"I know, but I was hoping it would go a little better than it did. She crashed hard enough that she'll be feeling it for a few days. I wanted it to be fun for her, but I think I blew it."

"I did that once with Maurleen. We used to go hiking together all the time. Once, I packed egg-salad sandwiches for lunch, and it turns out she hates hard-boiled eggs. But she still let me kiss her good-bye that night."

Bastien nodded. He wasn't sure how Gracie felt about their day off. She'd fallen asleep on the way home and had still been a little groggy when he'd helped her to her apartment. He'd kissed her on the cheek for the benefit of her neighbors, but it had left him wanting more.

Heinie fished in his pocket for his keys. "I doubt she'll hold it against you for long."

Bastien doubted she'd hold it against him at all but still wished things had gone differently.

After washing up, he found the cook, Enrichetta, in the kitchen and returned the baskets. "Thank you."

"How did it go?" she asked. Enrichetta was a short, stout woman with graying hair.

"The food was delicious, especially the pastries."

"And the rest of the day?"

Bastien smiled and changed the subject. "Actually, I wanted to ask a favor. There are certain Italians who don't approve of the alliance with Germany. I don't want anyone to hurt my friend because she chooses to spend time with me."

"You don't want the Gappisti attacking your girlfriend just because she's your girlfriend?" Enrichetta put the baskets away and walked over to a pile of dirty dishes.

"Exactly. I don't think her current apartment is safe. I'm trying to find another one for her."

Enrichetta frowned as she filled the sink with water. "I heard rumors she was in your room most nights."

"I work strange hours. Sometimes I'm up in the middle of the night."

"And she can't go back to sleep?"

"She's a student. She needs a good night's rest, not one interrupted by me."

"Hmm." Enrichetta started scrubbing out a pot with remnants of mashed potatoes in it. "I'll see what I can find."

"If you find something, I'll be sure to show my appreciation." Bastien patted the pocket where he kept his billfold.

The cook smiled and continued with her dishes.

* * *

Gracie met Angelo as planned at the Via Quattro Fontane the Monday after her motorcycle lesson. It still hurt to walk, but she took the long way, doubling back multiple times to be sure no one followed her.

Angelo was waiting. He took her arm, and she felt him slip something into her pocket. "I'm clean today. No one's following me."

"Good. I'm all right too."

"What did you do to your forehead?"

Gracie felt the scab, trying to think what she could tell Angelo without giving too much away. It wasn't that she didn't trust him—she did—but it would be silly to hint that she'd been spending time with a German officer, and who else would have access to a pair of motorcycles? "I fell—it's nothing serious and nothing to worry about. I didn't get it running from the Gestapo or anything like that."

Angelo nodded, then waited, his back slumped against a nearby shop. At their last meeting, he'd said he wanted to show her something, but now there were few people on the streets and it was unnaturally quiet. Then she heard something.

It took Gracie a while to figure out what the sound was once she picked it out. Boots marching and men singing, only the singing didn't sound like a men's choir. There was too much anger in the voices; it was more of a martial chant than a song. A column of soldiers came into view, and Gracie tried to count them as they marched past in their steel helmets. She couldn't get an exact number, but she guessed there were around one hundred fifty of them. Between the strike of their boots against the cobblestones and the song bellowing from their lungs, Gracie felt as though the sound was swallowing her whole. It wasn't until the last of them had marched past that she found her voice again. "Who are they?"

"Eleventh company, third Bozen SS battalion," Angelo whispered. "They're a police unit made of ethnic German recruits from South Tyrol. Still in training."

"What are they singing?"

"It's called 'Hupf, Mein Mädel.' Just a silly song . . ."

"But it sounds terrifying," Gracie finished.

"Yes. For now."

Gracie studied Angelo, wondering what he meant. He'd hinted that the marching would end soon, but it didn't sound like he planned on waiting around for the British or American armies to arrive in Rome and put a stop to it.

He followed the last line of troops with his eyes. "Every day, they go to the firing range. Then they march along the Via Rasella, pass through here, and head to their barracks by the interior ministry. Same time every day. Same song too. Bold but stupid. They've given us the perfect opportunity."

"But there are so many of them—how could you attack them? They'd slaughter you."

Angelo shrugged. "We'll see."

Gracie shivered at the memory of the eleventh company marching past and at the hatred she detected in Angelo. His eyes burned, his jaw was set, and his lips were pulled into a hard, thin line.

CHAPTER TWENTY-SEVEN

ZIMMERMAN BALLED UP THE PAPER he'd just read and threw it across the room. Ever since the disaster at the San Lorenzo church, he'd worried he would be demoted. He was still an obersturmführer, but his assignments had changed. He'd thought being tasked with finding Jews was bad enough. Now he'd been shifted to rounding up black marketeers. He wanted to arrest saboteurs and spies and assassins—real threats. His new assignment wasn't a demotion, but the loss of prestige still made it a punishment.

Ostheim bent to retrieve the wadded report from the floor in front of Zimmerman's desk. "Rough day?"

Zimmerman grunted. "I've been assigned to round up black marketeers. It seems I am no longer trusted to round up hidden Jews and partisans."

Ostheim sat across from Zimmerman and smoothed out the paper. "Sometimes black marketeers know things. Who's working with the Gappisti, for example. Partisans have to eat too."

"No one cares about the black market."

"Obviously someone does, or it wouldn't be illegal." Ostheim read through the paper. "This report says a man is dealing in iron pipes."

"So? Iron's rationed, but does it really matter if we have a few pounds less of it?"

"It does if the iron pipes are being turned into bombs. *Spezzones* is what they call them. All they need is some TNT, a detonator, and a pipe. I had one of my prisoners telling me all about it a few days ago. His little Gappisti bomb factory."

Zimmerman looked at the paper again, wondering how he'd overlooked its significance.

"Do well with the black marketeers, and they'll lead you to the Gappisti," Ostheim said. "We'll work together. Catch me one Gappisti, and

I'll make him tell us who all his friends are. Then you'll be back on anti-partisan duty, and I'll be one step closer to outranking Dietrich."

* * *

When Gracie went to Ley's apartment that afternoon, he took his time closing the door, and while the door slowly inched toward the frame, she found herself torn between wanting it to close instantly and wishing it would stay open forever because as soon as it shut, his kiss would end. What was it about the gentle pressure of his lips on hers, the smell of his freshly washed skin, and the strength of his arms holding her close? It was irresistible and beautiful. Yet it was also painful because it stirred up so many emotions in her heart, and her brain always reminded her it couldn't be real.

She felt a little dizzy when the door clicked shut and Ley slowly released her. The room seamed stuffy—the weather was getting warmer, so maybe that was why. Ley's report was on the table, as well as extra paper so she could encrypt it. "Can I get a little fresh air before I start?"

"Of course." Ley opened the door to his bedroom for her and let her walk past. His face showed concern, but she didn't try to explain what was wrong, didn't even say it in her head because she was afraid she wouldn't like the answer.

From Ley's balcony, she could see a few other hotels and multiple churches. Up that high, it was easy to ignore the dirt and grime and, instead, see just the beauty. The breeze helped clear her head, but she waited, not ready to go inside again. After perhaps five minutes, Ley came out to join her. He stood behind her, slipping his arms around her waist and resting his chin on her shoulder and his cheek against hers. Part of her wanted to sigh with contentment, and part of her wanted to cry because it was all a charade to him but she wanted it to be real.

"Are you all right, Concetta?" he whispered.

She wondered if he could hear the sound of her heart breaking. She didn't trust herself to speak, and she certainly wasn't going to tell him the real problem now that she'd admitted what it was, so she just nodded.

He held her a while longer, then loosened his arms. She turned to go back inside, and his arms fell away, but his face was only inches from hers, and he tilted his head to kiss her again. All the earlier emotions were back, magnified, and so was her certainty that she was falling for someone who would never return her feelings. She heard footsteps below the balcony, so she knew there was a reason behind the kiss, but this time, she couldn't hold back a few tears.

Ley stopped kissing her and stared at her instead. After a quick glance below, he pulled her inside and closed the door to the balcony. "What's wrong?"

Gracie wiped her tears away and tried to control her emotions. Ley waited patiently, giving her the time she needed. "I'm not sure how much longer I can do this."

"Otavia's death was tragic. It will take time to get over it, and that's normal. Add the shootout with your other contact last week and the spill from the motorcycle a few days ago—you've had a rough few weeks."

"No, it's not just that." Gracie met Ley's blue eyes and was sure he knew exactly what she meant, sure his eyes could see directly into her soul and know how much she was drawn to him. She couldn't go on kissing him when each kiss was a game to him and a bit of torture for her. She shook her head and looked away, almost hearing what he was going to say. He'd call her a silly spy for falling in love with her partner, and he'd be right. She met his eyes again, expecting to see a look of triumph on his face or at least a teasing smile, but instead, she saw compassion. "I should have listened to you in Switzerland. You told me I didn't know what I was getting into, and you were right."

"But you're doing a good job."

"No, I'm not. I almost blew things at the train station and when I met Ostheim and then again when we found Otavia. And I probably would have starved to death by now if you weren't giving me food. And pretending to be in love with you is getting a little complicated—" Gracie took a deep breath, then stopped when Ley stepped toward her and gently grasped her wrists. "What are you doing?"

"I just wanted to see if you could talk without your hands."

Gracie's roommates in college had occasionally made fun of her for talking with her hands, but it had always been in good fun. Ley's joke was completely out of place, a distraction from a serious conversation. She studied his face, but though he was smiling, it was without the levity she would have expected. He let go of her wrists, leaving her to wonder why he'd taken them in the first place. Was it a deliberate attempt to sidetrack her? Anger her?

Whatever his motivation for holding her wrists, she needed to encode his report so she could send it in along with Angelo's. She was tempted to take it to her apartment for coding, but if a Gestapo agent stopped her on the way home, having the message in code instead of plain text could buy them a little extra time. Gracie sat at the dining table and worked on the report.

Ley stayed in his room until she was almost finished. "Maybe you just need a break," he said. "One that doesn't involve motorcycles. You've been working hard, and you've had a run of bad luck."

"No, you were right when you told me things would be different in the field. I should have listened." Gracie finished her transposition and set the pencil down. "I just . . . I don't know . . . I thought it would be different."

"You've adapted well."

Gracie shook her head. "No, I'm barely surviving."

Ley sat across from her, quiet for a long time as his leg made the table vibrate. "If you want out of Rome, I know some Italian partisans. I trust them, and I think they could get you to the American lines."

"I can't just quit."

"You can say you were sick and left because you couldn't get proper care here. Leave your radio with me. I'll send a message and explain it before you arrive so it won't be a surprise for them."

"It's not just my orders. I've never given up on something like this before. I couldn't just leave you." As painful as being around Ley was, she didn't want to abandon him in the middle of his mission. What if the Gestapo found him while he was sending in his report—doing the job she was supposed to do?

"You don't have to worry about me. And you don't have to decide right now. Just let me know by Wednesday, midday. That's when I meet my contact again."

Gracie couldn't decide which would be worse: staying and enduring the pain in her heart every time she saw him or leaving and not knowing if he was dead or alive.

* * *

When Bastien walked Gracie back to her apartment, he kept his good-bye kiss gentle and brief. He could sense a whirlwind of emotions starting to build up in her again, but he didn't know what to say to make things better.

She shut her door most of the way, then stopped. "Do you ever work with the SS Bozen battalion?" she whispered.

"No."

The muscles around her lips relaxed in relief. "Make sure you don't start."

"Why?"

She hesitated. "I think the Gappisti are planning something with them, and I don't want you in the middle of it."

Bastien wanted to ask how she knew, but he could guess the information had come from her other contact. "I'll see you tomorrow."

She gave him a sad smile and closed the door.

As he walked back to his hotel, he realized she still hadn't given him a clear answer on whether she wanted to stay in Rome, and he wasn't sure which option he hoped she'd choose. The truth was, she was a good radio operator. His work was easier when he could hand his reports to her and know they would be competently encoded and sent in. He could do it himself, but then he'd be back to where he was in January and most of February—exhausted, barely getting any sleep, on edge. He'd be just like Gracie was now.

Sending Gracie away with Marcello would make his mission more difficult, but he was willing to accept that if it meant she'd be safe. Yet the thought of saying good-bye was a bitter one. As much as he hadn't wanted her to come, part of him didn't want her to leave. He'd miss talking to someone who knew what he was really doing in Rome, and he'd miss her. He thought of her slip, that pretending to be in love with him was getting complicated. He'd tried to stop her before she said something she'd regret, something that would change their relationship and their mission, but if he was honest with himself, it was complicated for him too.

If she stayed, something had to change. The act that was starting to feel real would have to continue, but maybe he could make it less intense.

But if she left and if he lived to see the Allies free Rome, what would happen then? Would he try to find her again, or would he let her go?

CHAPTER TWENTY-EIGHT

ON TUESDAY MORNING, ZIMMERMAN TOOK a pair of enlisted men with him to follow up on a black market lead and investigate where the iron pipes went after they were sold.

The black marketeer didn't want to talk at first. "I sell only legal items."

Zimmerman motioned to his men, and they both leveled their machine pistols at the portly merchant's stomach.

"I only sold pipes once—and nobody told me what they were used for after that."

"Who did you sell them to?" Zimmerman asked.

"I didn't learn their names."

Zimmerman leaned in. "You'd better try very hard to recall both their names and where they can be found. If you can't remember, I'll have to take you to the Via Tasso until your memory improves."

The man swallowed. "They were from a little village north of Rome."

"Möller, go get my map case," Zimmerman ordered.

Möller was quick. When the merchant pointed out the village, Zimmerman recognized its name but couldn't remember why. It was small, insignificant . . . but he had a source there. A young Italian woman, devoted to Mussolini.

"Let's go," Zimmerman ordered his men.

"Good luck," the merchant said.

"Oh, you're coming with us. If you can point out the men you saw, we'll take them to prison. Otherwise, we have a cell waiting for you."

* * *

Zimmerman and his men had changed into plainclothes and found a small café, but the villagers seemed wary, as if they could tell they were really soldiers.

"Möller, find this address." Zimmerman handed the man a piece of paper. "See if you can locate a woman named Isabella. If you find her, have her meet me here."

"Yes, sir."

When Möller returned, he seemed unhappy. "I spoke to her parents, sir. They haven't seen her in almost a week, not since Wednesday morning."

Zimmerman mulled over the information. Isabella had told him she suspected one of her neighbors. He was unemployed but was often away for days at a time, and she'd seen him sneaking inside late at night more than once. Betraying members of the Italian Resistance was a dangerous game. When threatened, they didn't hesitate to defend themselves. *Not so different from us.* Her disappearance made Zimmerman think her suspicion was correct. *Isabella challenged the neighbor, and he eliminated her.*

He led his men and the black marketeer to a modest house across from Isabella's. The residents were surprised and frightened, but he promised them they wouldn't be harmed if they cooperated. Until Zimmerman was done, they were to wait silently in one of the bedrooms.

The afternoon crept by slowly as they waited. A few villagers walked past, but the black marketeer said he didn't recognize them. Not long before curfew, a young man left a house two doors away from where Isabella had lived. An even younger man joined him.

"That's him," the merchant pointed to the first man. "He bought the pipes from me."

Zimmerman smiled. "Wait here," he told one of his men. "Watch our merchant friend, and make sure the family stays in the back room. Möller, come with me."

They followed the two men until they left the village. Zimmerman hesitated, knowing the men would soon notice him, but he wanted to follow them as long as possible in case they led him to others who could prove useful. The older of the two suspects looked around, noticed them, and kept walking.

"Sir?" Möller asked.

"Keep following them. If they run, we shoot."

Not two minutes later, the younger of the two glanced around. He said something to his companion, and they split up.

"Follow the younger one," Zimmerman said. "Take him alive, and meet back at the house in the village."

"Are you sure he's a partisan?" Möller asked.

"If he's not, we can release him later."

Zimmerman followed his quarry for perhaps five minutes before the man slipped into an old barn, out of sight. Zimmerman approached cautiously. Was the man hiding? Did he have a friend there waiting for him? Was he armed and planning an ambush?

Zimmerman reached the barn and inched his way forward, stepping gently with the hope he wouldn't be heard. He paused near the door, checking behind him before taking a deep breath and kicking in the door.

He held his pistol with both hands as he rushed inside, but there was no sign of the man he stalked. He checked the stalls and climbed a rickety ladder to the loft. Nothing but a pile of hay. Zimmerman climbed most of the way down the ladder before he saw the pitchfork hanging on the wall.

I saw him come in, so he must be here somewhere. Zimmerman grabbed the pitchfork and climbed the ladder again. He circled the pile of hay, looking for any telltale signs that someone was inside. The straw looked undisturbed—surely no one was hidden there. Zimmerman began to feel foolish. What if the man escaped while he wasted his time on the loft? He stuck the pitchfork in the hay in frustration, then did it again and again. With the third strike, he heard a muffled cry, and one end of the pitchfork came back tipped in scarlet.

Zimmerman pulled his pistol from its holster. "Out, now!"

Silence filled the barn for a few long moments, but then the hay began to move. The man emerged slowly, bits of straw stuck in his clothes and hair, his face tense as he tried to control obvious pain. A red stain had spread across his left thigh. Zimmerman felt for weapons, but the man was unarmed.

"Down." Zimmerman motioned to the ladder.

The man had trouble moving because of his bad leg, but with Zimmerman's handgun as motivation, he slowly struggled to his feet and started descending the ladder. Halfway down, he fell. His injuries seemed serious enough that he wouldn't run off, so Zimmerman climbed down after him.

As his prisoner writhed on the ground, Zimmerman saw a strange mix of fear and defiance in his face. He almost felt sorry for the man—he was young and wounded yet brave too. But Zimmerman remembered what it had been like to grow up under the oppressive Versailles treaty. He could still taste the poverty, the massive inflation, the utter lack of hope. Hitler had ended those things. *Never again*, his father had said when Hitler was appointed chancellor. *Never again will we let someone hold us down.*

* * *

Zimmerman set aside his report the instant Ostheim walked into view.

Ostheim sat across from him and grinned. "The one you captured is called Roberto. He isn't talking yet. He wouldn't even tell me his name. But his friend Carlo started cooperating about the time I removed his third fingernail. He and Roberto were checking a field that's supposed to be used as a weapons drop. They were to meet Carlo's brother—Giovanni—and another man in a few hours. The other two won't know anything's wrong until their friends don't show up."

Zimmerman smiled. He owed Ostheim something big; if he managed to capture a few partisans and an Allied weapons drop, he might be able to slip away from the disapproval that had shadowed him since San Lorenzo. His eyes paused on the picture of his wife and son, and he quickly looked away. The boy Ostheim had tortured wasn't much older than his own son. *I must ensure victory for the Fatherland*, he told himself, *whatever the cost.*

A few hours later, Zimmerman positioned his men around a dark, open field. Determined to avoid the mistakes he'd made with the San Lorenzo church and the arrest of the women, Zimmerman managed everything himself, making sure each man was sufficiently concealed.

The two Gappisti appeared quietly, like ghosts, cautiously walking to the center of the clearing with something in their hands—*probably signal lamps.* Zimmerman's men followed their orders and waited. The boy in prison had said only two would come, but Zimmerman wanted to be sure. Only when the two separated did Zimmerman give the signal, firing a flare into the air and illuminating the field.

Trapped in the light, the two Gappisti ran. One of them darted right into the SS trap, but the other went the opposite direction. Zimmerman didn't have enough men to surround the entire field, and the Gappisti slipped through one of the gaps.

"Get him!" Zimmerman ordered Möller, who was crouched nearby. Möller and four others moved out as the Gappisti ran over a slight rise and out of sight. Zimmerman wasn't concerned—his men would catch up. A hail of gunfire sounded, and while he waited for his men to trap the runaway, Zimmerman walked over to the one they'd already caught.

He hadn't surrendered without a fight. In the fading flare light, Zimmerman could see blood streaming from the man's nose into a thin mustache and assumed one of his men had subdued him with the end of a rifle. He studied him for a while, wondering what information he held in his head.

The flare had burned out when Möller and the others returned, but Zimmerman could make out shadows—several of his men were carrying bodies. He assumed one of the bodies was the Gappisti, but as they got closer, he realized one of his men was dead, another seriously wounded.

"I'm sorry, sir," Möller said, cradling his right forearm. Zimmerman suspected it was injured, which made two wounded. "He escaped."

Zimmerman felt his anger flash. But his men had tried. And he'd caught three of the Gappisti. That was something. Ostheim would have three of the man's friends, so Zimmerman didn't think it would be long until he rounded up the one who'd gotten away.

* * *

Bastien planned to ask Marcello about smuggling Gracie out of Rome during their Wednesday meeting at the bar, but Marcello wasn't there. Bastien looked around and didn't recognize anyone. He found a corner booth, ordered a glass of cheap wine, and waited.

He'd been there ten minutes when Giovanni slipped into the seat next to him. "Sorry I'm late."

Bastien shrugged and slid the untouched glass over.

Giovanni took a few gulps and looked around, making sure no one could overhear them. "Roberto and my brother have disappeared. Haven't seen them since yesterday. Marcello was arrested at the drop."

"What happened?"

"We were surrounded by a squad of SS troops. I got away, barely. Marcello had sent me to look for the others. I shot a few SS men as I escaped, but there were more troops on Marcello's side of the clearing—he didn't have a chance."

"Is he dead?"

"I don't think so," Giovanni whispered. "He was surrounded before he knew they were there."

That meant someone who knew exactly what Bastien was doing in Rome was in Nazi hands. "Do you know where he's being held?"

Giovanni shook his head.

"Arrested by SS troops?"

"Yes."

"Your brother too?"

Giovanni scowled. "I'm not sure. Is there anything you can do?"

Bastien thought long and hard before answering. Marcello and Roberto could both blow his cover. Maybe it was time for him to abandon his act and head for the American lines. How long would they hold out under torture? Could he do anything for Marcello, Roberto, and Giovanni's brother, or were they lost? "I'm not sure. I'm billeted at a hotel on the Via Veneto. I'll walk along the south end of the street an hour before curfew. Meet me there, and I'll tell you if I've thought of anything."

Giovanni nodded and left.

Bastien wasn't sure what to do about Marcello and the others, but he knew he had to warn Gracie. If he was at risk, so was she.

CHAPTER TWENTY-NINE

BASTIEN SAID A SILENT PRAYER as he knocked on Gracie's door, pleading for her to be home. There was no answer. He rested his back against the door, wondering if he should leave a note. *What would I say? Run?* Could she get out of Rome without his help?

He heard soft footsteps on the stairs, and soon after, she came into view carrying what looked like groceries, but he guessed it was her radio. Her lips curved up when she saw him—the same bittersweet smile she'd had the last week—but it disappeared when he didn't smile back.

She unlocked her door and, to her credit, didn't ask what was wrong until it was closed and they were both inside. "The flat fell through? Or something worse?"

Bastien had almost forgotten the new apartment. Enrichetta had told him about it early that morning, and he'd picked up the key between inspecting a stretch of the Hitler Line and meeting Giovanni. He pulled the key from his pocket and handed it to her. "You can move in whenever you like."

"Then it's something worse?" Gracie set her bag on the bed and gave him her full attention.

"The SS arrested two of the three men who were with me when I became Dietrich."

Her eyes widened. "When?"

"Within the last twenty-four hours."

"Do you think they've talked?"

"If they have, someone will be waiting to arrest me when I go back to my hotel."

"Then don't go back."

That was an option, but Bastien wasn't sure he was ready to give up yet. There was still a war to fight, still a brother to save. "They might not talk. And I might be able to rescue them."

"Do you know where they're being held?"

"No, but I can guess. I'll check at the Gestapo prison on the Via Tasso first. If they aren't there, I'll check the Regina Coeli. If I don't come back, it will be time for you to leave. The man I was going to send you with is one of the arrested men, so you'll have to try getting out alone. I'm sorry."

Gracie glanced at her radio, then back at him. "The building on the Via Tasso—that's where Otto Ostheim works, isn't it?"

"Yes."

"Maybe I can help. I could distract him or something."

"Absolutely not," Bastien said immediately, louder than he'd meant to. "That would be like sending a lamb to play with a tiger."

"What if I slipped a sleeping pill in his drink?"

"Do you have any sleeping pills?"

She looked at the floor. "No."

"Distracting Ostheim is too dangerous."

Gracie shook her head and flung a hand out in frustration. "Everything about this mission is dangerous. We both know Ostheim hates you. If you walk into the Via Tasso, he'll do everything he can to thwart you, even if he doesn't know what you're doing. And he might get suspicious. But if you wait until most of the officers are gone and he's busy with me, none of the other guards will question a captain transferring prisoners or checking the prison roster."

"Have you thought of how you might keep him busy? Because I have a good idea of what he wants from you, and frankly, I'm more concerned about what he can do to you in an hour than I am about what he can do to his prisoners in a week."

"I just want to help," she whispered. "Your friends are being tortured. Otto asked me to supper once. Maybe I can get him to repeat that offer. We'd be in a restaurant, and if he got out of hand, I could break his nose again."

"What if you try to break his nose, and he breaks your neck?"

"He didn't seem so horrible when he was sober. I don't think he wants to kill me."

"And if he gets drunk?" Bastien asked.

"Do you have a better idea?"

"Yes. Pack your things. If I rescue my friends, you join them on their way south. If I don't show up again, you run." Rome was getting too dangerous for Gracie. He wanted her somewhere safe.

"Actually, I had decided to stay. Until the army gets here. Or until we both have to leave, together. If you think you can keep it up, I want to stay and be your radio operator. And tonight, I want to help you rescue your friends."

Bastien tried to decide what to do. She was the perfect bait for Ostheim, but bait usually didn't make it out of the trap in one piece, and he wasn't about to sacrifice Gracie for a chance to free Marcello. Part of his reasoning was personal—he didn't want to see her get hurt. But it was practical as well—Gracie in Gestapo hands was just as big a threat to his mission as Marcello's capture. But what if there was a way to use her without putting her in danger?

* * *

Gracie wore the black dress she'd purchased for the curfew party. She applied her makeup more heavily than usual and left most of her hair down, as Ley had suggested.

Number 145, Via Tasso, didn't look like it housed evil, but Gracie shuddered as she walked up the steps. Ley had told her which way to go, and he'd also warned her that the guards would question her every move.

"What do you want, Fräulein?" a soldier at the entrance asked.

"I'd like to see Untersturmführer Ostheim, please."

His lips twitched to the side. "Why?"

"It's personal."

After a slight hesitation, the guard let her pass. She swallowed as she walked past him and felt her hands grow damp from perspiration. Every step she took into the building was like one more step into darkness. She followed Ley's directions and turned down the correct hallways, closer to Ostheim's lair, until a uniformed clerk stopped her and asked her what she wanted.

"I'd like to see Untersturmführer Ostheim, please," she repeated. There was a tremor in her voice because she was nervous and frightened, but she was standing outside a Gestapo prison, so she doubted the clerk would think her fear out of place.

"What about?"

She hesitated. "I have a personal request for him."

He motioned her to a chair and told her to wait. When he finished his paperwork, he left for a few minutes, she assumed to pass on the news of her arrival. The clock on the wall ticked loudly, but the second hand seemed to take three times longer than usual to make its revolutions. Twice she thought she could hear cries of pain coming from the prison. She tried to think of something other than the likelihood that whoever was making those sounds was one of Ley's friends. Even if they were the cries of strangers, it was horrible, but she couldn't let herself think about that now.

Instead, she remembered the way Ley had looked at her before they'd parted, the way he'd run one of his hands through her hair and stared at her with those piercing blue eyes, asking her if she was sure she wanted to do this. She was beginning to believe there was more than friendship behind his concern, something real in his kisses, and that thought was enough to calm her breathing.

The clerk returned and sat at his desk, then started filling out more paperwork. Gracie waited. When she focused on where she was and who she was about to meet, she had trouble controlling the tremor in her hands. When she focused on Ley, on all the things he'd done for her, on the way he smiled and the way his lips made her feel, she could stay composed.

Ostheim walked into view and stopped. He looked her up and down and raised one eyebrow in question.

Gracie stood. "Otto, I'm sorry to show up like this. I just didn't know where else I could go." She glanced at the clerk and bit her lower lip, hoping Ostheim would read her gesture as a sign that she wanted to talk to him alone.

He stepped closer. She hadn't seen him since the curfew party. If she really had broken his nose, it had healed well. "Concetta. This is a surprise."

Gracie had a hard time maintaining eye contact, so she looked away. "I'm sorry to interrupt you at work. I almost went to the café instead, where we first met, but I was afraid you wouldn't be there and that Adalard might see me."

His fingers lifted her chin so she was looking at him again. "Why do you want to see me?"

"To apologize." Gracie's voice trembled because Ostheim's touch frightened her, but she hoped he would think she was just emotional. "I was wrong about you and wrong about my boyfriend. Adalard's starting to scare me . . ." She glanced at the clerk. He seemed to be working, but she guessed he was hearing every word. "Do you believe in second chances, Otto?"

A smile that made her nervous crept across his face. "I've got a few things to finish up. Why don't you wait here for a bit, and then I'll take you somewhere quiet, and we can talk?"

Gracie nodded as if that was exactly what she wanted. In a way, it was—she was trying to get him out of the Via Tasso—but it certainly wasn't because she was suddenly attracted to him. He kept his fingers on her chin, watching her every breath for several long moments.

"I won't be long." He turned and walked back to the prison.

Gracie sat on the chair again, relieved that the first part of the plan seemed to be working, nervous about everything that could still go wrong, and dreading the next step.

CHAPTER THIRTY

Bastien met Giovanni on the street south of his hotel. "I have a plan. In one hour, be as close to the Via Tasso as you dare. If nothing happens within two hours, it will be time for you to leave. I'm not sure how our friends will look or if they'll even be able to walk, so if you can find some transportation, do it." Bastien shoved a fistful of cash at Giovanni and pointed toward his hotel. "The guard at the back of this hotel is susceptible to bribery, and he has the keys to most of the motor pool."

"Don't you think he'd be more likely to accept a bribe from you than from me?"

"I have something else I have to do." Bastien looked at his watch. Gracie had gone into the Via Tasso a few minutes ago, and he needed to get back there to make sure Ostheim was taking her to a restaurant, not to his bedroom. "I'm sorry. I'd fix a truck for you if I had time."

Giovanni didn't argue. That was something Bastien had always liked about him. Giovanni might be pessimistic, but once he pointed out his concerns, he didn't dwell on them or try to avoid what needed to be done.

Bastien rode his motorcycle to within a block of the Via Tasso prison, praying he wasn't too late. He strode toward the entrance, and from half a block away, he saw a couple leaving together. He'd arrived just in time. Ostheim was recognizable only as an SS officer at that distance, but Bastien knew the woman was Gracie from her dress and the way she walked.

They were coming toward him, so he crossed the street and waited at the side of a building, where they'd only be able to see him if they turned to look back after they'd walked by. He saw them pass and started having second thoughts about Gracie's involvement. *It's too dangerous.* She'd suggested it, but she looked as beautiful as he'd ever seen her, and he knew what that could mean if everything backfired.

Bastien followed them from a distance. Ostheim held the door for Gracie and motioned her into the first-floor restaurant of a hotel. *Good. He's minding his manners. Maybe he'll stay on good behavior for the evening.* Yet when Bastien saw Gracie smile convincingly at Ostheim, he felt a twinge of jealousy. *Don't be stupid,* he told himself. *She's just pretending.*

Bastien and Gracie had assumed that if Ostheim took Gracie out to eat, Bastien would have an hour, maybe more. One hour to free his friends. He hoped it would be enough. And he hoped Ostheim wouldn't try anything in the meantime.

When Bastien got back to the Via Tasso, he took a few deep breaths, trying to banish his nervousness about Gracie and what he still needed to do. At the entrance, he returned the guard's salute and turned toward the prison.

"Hauptmann Dietrich—just the man I wanted to see."

Bastien turned to find Sturmbannführer Scholz. "What can I help you with, sir?"

"Come into my office. I need a second opinion on something."

Bastien sneaked a glance at his watch and hoped whatever Scholz wanted wouldn't take too long.

* * *

"How long have you been seeing Dietrich?" Ostheim asked.

"A month," Gracie said as the waiter brought their drinks and prepared to take their order.

Ostheim selected something with beef and potatoes for both of them. "What happened?"

"Adalard's starting to scare me. He's possessive."

"Yes, I noticed that at the party."

Gracie nodded. "And he's mean when he gets drunk. He pushed me a few days ago." Gracie ran her hand along the cut she'd gotten in the motorcycle crash.

Ostheim's drink was halfway to his mouth, but he stopped and set it down. Gracie was impressed—was he setting it aside for her? She thought she was safer with Ostheim if he stayed sober, but that also meant he'd remember their conversation more clearly. *I might have to leave Rome after all.* What would happen to Ley if he had to encode and transmit his own reports? Would he put his security check in the wrong place again or, worse, be captured? She shivered as she realized the man sitting across from her would probably conduct Ley's interrogation should he be caught.

Ostheim stood and walked around the table until he was standing next to her. He circled the scab with his finger. "He did this to you?"

"Yes," Gracie lied.

He returned to his seat. "It must have been a horrible month for you."

"It has been."

"You know, it's a new month now on the astrological calendar. Aries might just be my lucky sign."

"I hope it's mine too. I could use a bit of luck. I'm terrified that Adalard will lose his temper again."

Ostheim smiled. "I'll protect you, Concetta."

Gracie thought back to Ley's promise out in the countryside when he'd told her he'd do everything he could to prevent her capture. She believed him. Ostheim's declaration, in contrast, seemed liked a slimy attempt to ingratiate himself into her confidence.

"Here are your meals," the waiter said. Gracie hadn't noticed his arrival, but the food smelled amazing when he lifted the metal plate covers.

"Send them to my room, along with a bottle of wine," Ostheim said. "We're going to enjoy them in a more private setting."

"As you wish, sir."

Gracie tried to hide her shock. Ley's warning rang in her ears. *Whatever you do, don't go anywhere alone with him.* But if she refused to go to his room, Ostheim might head back to the Via Tasso, and she hadn't given Ley enough time yet. "You're billeted here?"

"Yes." Ostheim stood and took her hand, gripping it with a little too much force as he pulled her to her feet. "Convenient location, isn't it?"

He kept hold of her hand up three flights of steps and down a long hallway, releasing it only to unlock his door. She instantly wiped her hand against her dress, drying the sweat. She was sure it was partially her perspiration because she was terrified, but part of it was his too. He had damp palms.

"You're quiet. Are you nervous, Concetta?"

"It's just too soon for me to do this, Otto. I need a friend, but I also need some time."

He put a finger to her lips. "We're just eating supper, away from the windows so Dietrich doesn't walk by and start a fight."

That was the exact scenario she and Ley had planned. Ley was to follow her so he'd know where Ostheim took her, and after he freed his friends, he'd come by again. If Gracie was still in the restaurant, Ley planned to pick a fight with Ostheim. If Gracie made it away before Ley reappeared, she'd go wait in his hotel room. They'd hidden the key under a rug in the hallway.

Ostheim pulled her into his room, and Gracie felt a hundred warnings flare up. The door clicked shut, and Gracie swallowed back panic. Ley wouldn't know where she was. He wouldn't be able to come to her aid, and she wasn't sure she could get away from Ostheim without help.

CHAPTER THIRTY-ONE

WORRY ABOUT ESCAPE LATER, GRACIE told herself. *Right now you've got to keep him busy. Eat slowly and ask lots of questions.* But the food wasn't there yet.

Ostheim's room was a studio. A partially opened door half hid a messy bathroom, and the table looked like no one had cleaned it after the last meal eaten there. Ostheim wandered over and sat on the enormous bed.

Gracie struggled to find something to say. "Where did you learn Italian?" Ostheim spoke with an accent but seemed otherwise fluent.

"School. And this isn't the first time I've been stationed in Italy."

She was still standing by the door when someone knocked. She opened it and almost hugged the hotel worker bringing their food. She held the door open while the man came into the room and placed the food and wine on the table.

Gracie glanced at the clock. If she played it right, eating supper might take up enough time. She could leave when they finished, knowing she'd given Ley the time he needed. *If Ostheim lets me leave.* As the waiter walked into the hallway, Gracie was tempted to grab his arm and beg him to stay, but she knew that wouldn't work. She was supposed to encourage Ostheim for a little longer.

Five minutes into the meal, Ostheim put his fork down. "I'm not really hungry anymore. Are you?"

Gracie swallowed her food and dabbed at her lips with her napkin. *Oh dear.* "Actually, this is wonderful, and I'm still ravenous."

"Hmm." He ate for a few more minutes. Then he stood and took her hands, pulling her to her feet so she was only inches from him. "You know what I thought when I came out and saw you waiting for me?"

Gracie wanted to back away, but the chair was right behind her, and she could see the clock over Ostheim's shoulder. She had to give Ley more time. "What did you think, Otto?"

"That I was really going to enjoy doing this." He covered her mouth with his. It was wet and rough, and he tasted like garlic. His right hand dug into her left arm, and his other hand held her, pressing her body into his and moving down her back lower than she was comfortable with. He was stronger than she, and they were alone, and every time she tried to escape his lips, he pulled her closer.

With her free hand, she felt along the table for the wine bottle. She moved it toward her and gripped it like a lifeline. She returned Ostheim's kiss for a few seconds, even though she felt like vomiting, hoping to distract him. In her head, she reviewed her OSS training about the best ways to knock someone unconscious. Then she slammed the wine bottle into the back of Ostheim's head.

He fell to the floor, and Gracie took a few deep breaths before kneeling down to check on him. He was unconscious and moaned as she checked the back of his head and used one of the cloth napkins to tie his wrists behind his back. She wiped the red wine off her hands and dress and glanced at the clock. Ley needed another half hour. She hoped Ostheim would stay unconscious for that long, but she wasn't sticking around to make sure, and she was confident Ley would approve of her decision.

* * *

Scholz asked Bastien's opinion of yet another SS fortification. He was systematically going through every project Heinie had built in the last two months.

Bastien looked at his watch again. Gracie was supposed to keep Ostheim busy until 1830, and it was already 1815. He debated whether he should leave Marcello locked up in his cell or be late picking a fight at the hotel dining hall. *Ostheim won't try anything in a restaurant, will he?*

"Dietrich, you keep looking at your watch. Is there somewhere else you're supposed to be?"

"Actually, yes, sir. If you'd like, I can inspect a few of Obersturmführer Vogel's projects next week."

Scholz frowned. "You and Vogel are on friendly terms, is that right?"

"Yes, sir."

"Perhaps Tuesday we can inspect a few sites together. Come to my office then, and don't say anything to Vogel."

"Yes, sir. Thank you, sir." Bastien stood and saluted.

Scholz waved him away.

Finally. Bastien was worried for Heinie's sake. It seemed Scholz was looking for a reason to question his work. Heinie was a good engineer, but his projects often ended up in Bastien's reports and, thus, on Allied target lists. Bastien hoped he hadn't created trouble for his friend, but right then, he had bigger problems to worry about.

The clerk guarding the prison stood when Bastien approached.

"Heil Hitler," Bastien said, trying to start off on the right foot.

The clerk, who was the equivalent of a sergeant, returned Bastien's salute.

"Is Untersturmführer Ostheim here?"

"No, sir, but he said he'd return later tonight."

Bastien frowned, although inside he was relieved. "And who is in charge until he returns?"

"I am, sir."

"Hmm." Bastien feigned careful concentration. "When do you expect Ostheim to return?"

The clerk glanced at his watch. "I'm not sure, sir. He could be back in ten minutes. Or he might return much later."

"Well, I'm afraid I can't wait. I need to see the prisoner captured this morning and the ones captured yesterday. I'll explain to Untersturmführer Ostheim when he returns." Bastien held out his hand. "Keys, please."

The clerk looked flustered, but after a glance at Dietrich's Iron Cross, he opened the desk drawer and pulled out a set of keys. "Go down the hallway and turn left. The prisoner we took this morning is in the far cell on the right. The men who told us about him are in the wing on the right." He handed Bastien the keys. "I'll need you to sign in." He opened a ledger book and slid it toward Bastien.

As he gripped the pen, Bastien tried to decide how to sign. If everything went according to plan, he didn't want Ostheim to know he'd been here. But if Ostheim returned before he was finished or if the clerk described an army captain with scarred hands and an Iron Cross, it would be hard to explain why he hadn't given his real name. He scrawled *Hauptmann A. Dietrich* in an almost illegible hand and hoped no one would be able to read it.

Another guard stood where the hallway split. Bastien returned the man's salute and went to the left, planning to rescue Marcello first because he knew more than Roberto or Giovanni's brother did. Bastien tried not to think about how each step he took and each second he lingered made it more and more likely that he would end up in one of the cells he passed. He felt cold.

Gracie had asked him once if he was haunted by Dietrich, and he'd told her ghosts didn't bother him. They didn't, but sometimes his memories did, so he tried to block out the sounds from all the prisoners he wouldn't be able to help. He didn't want to remember their cries and feel guilty that he'd left them there.

He reached the cell and unlocked it. When he went inside, he almost didn't recognize Marcello. Instead of the relaxed, confident Italian he'd known, he saw a broken man. Marcello's face was swollen, probably from one of the guard's fists. A smeared trail of blood ran from his nose to his mustache, and his hands looked almost black from dirt or blood or a combination of the two. But the real difference was in his posture—slumped, defeated—and in his eyes—humorless and hopeless.

Marcello cowered in the corner, pulling his arms up to protect his face when Bastien stepped toward him.

"Marcello," Bastien whispered. "It's me."

Marcello slowly lowered his arms and stared.

Bastien glanced over his shoulder, making sure the guard hadn't followed him down the hall. "I'm alone."

Marcello's voice was raspy. "You'd better shoot me before I let something slip. They keep asking me questions. I haven't told them anything yet, but I'm not sure how much longer I can last. Please, put me out of my misery before I betray you and everyone else I work with."

Bastien was relieved Marcello had kept quiet during his interrogations. He hadn't expected him to break easily, nor had he expected him to look so tortured. "I have a better idea. How about I get you out of here?"

"How are you going to do that?"

"Most of the guards are in the mess hall. I outrank everyone here. Prison transfer. Somehow, you're going to escape on the way to Regina Coeli." As he spoke, Bastien handed Marcello Gracie's pistol. There hadn't been any way for her to hide it in her form-fitting dress. And he hadn't told Gracie yet, but he was going to send her away with Marcello, so she'd get her weapon back soon anyway. Ostheim wasn't stupid. It wouldn't take much for him to suspect that Concetta was involved in the prison break. Even if he didn't, his threat to Gracie would increase exponentially by the time the night was over. Bastien planned to stay a little longer, but he didn't want Gracie to risk Ostheim's retribution.

"Hauptmann Dietrich will be in a lot of trouble if he lets a prisoner like me escape."

"Three prisoners, actually. Roberto and Giovanni's brother are down the hall. But if it looks like a Gappisti attack, I'm hoping I'll get away with it. A few minutes ago I managed to pocket a form with a Sturmbannführer's signature on it." At least something good had come of the delay in Scholz's office. "Giovanni's waiting outside. I'll have him forge up a transfer request."

"I knew you were something special when you dropped in, Capitano," Marcello said softly, a hint of his old self showing in his eyes. "The night you became Dietrich confirmed it. But this, this shows more loyalty and courage than I ever expected."

Before he could reply, Bastien heard a soft scrape from the hallway and turned around.

"The night you became Dietrich? That should have been the day you were born." Ostheim stepped into view with his pistol pointed at Bastien. "Who are you, why are you in my prison, and what type of game are you playing?"

Bastien wished he'd kept his pistol in his hand instead of in its holster. He swallowed back the bitter taste of defeat and worry—for himself and for Gracie. If Ostheim was here, where was she? "I'm arranging a prison transfer." Bastien stuck to his cover story, but he knew it was too late to bluff his way out.

"For a friend?" Ostheim glanced at Marcello.

The second Ostheim looked away, Bastien reached for his Luger, but he wasn't quick enough. Ostheim aimed and fired. A flash of pain seared through Bastien's abdomen and knocked him to the ground, and in the same instant, another pistol fired.

Ostheim fell to the floor. "Is he dead?" Bastien gasped.

Marcello was still pointing his weapon at the corpse. "Yes."

Bastien lifted his head to look at the dark pool of blood on his uniform.

"How bad is it, Capitano?"

Bastien inhaled, and the pain was so bad he could hardly breathe. Only the shouts in the hallway kept him from giving up, lying back, and letting the pain engulf him. "Get out of here, and take my pistol because when they come to see what happened, I'm going to tell them you're responsible."

Marcello didn't move.

"Go!"

Marcello nodded and disappeared. More shots echoed through the prison hallway, but Bastien had no idea who was firing. He hoped Marcello would be able to overcome the guard and the clerk, then make it out one of the exits, but even if he escaped, there was no way he could help Roberto and Giovanni's brother. Bastien pulled a handkerchief from his pocket and pressed it into his wound. *I won't be able to help them either.* Bastien winced as the pain flared. His head pounded, his vision blurred, and the pain in his side screamed at him. *Is this what it feels like to die?*

CHAPTER THIRTY-TWO

GRACIE HAD BLOWN HER COVER as Concetta Gallo. When Ostheim woke, he would know what she'd done. If Ley succeeded, maybe she could stay in Rome with a new name and a new address, but meeting him would get complicated. They might be able to set up a dead drop for his reports, but Ostheim's suspicion could easily extend to Dietrich—perhaps it was time for both of them to leave.

Gracie paced around Ley's hotel suite, looking at the clock every fifteen seconds. He'd told her to run if he wasn't back by 1900 hours, and it was 1902. Ley had given her two absolute commandments that night: she wasn't to go anywhere alone with Ostheim, and she was to leave Rome as quickly as she could if he wasn't back on time. *I've already broken one. Should I break the other as well?*

Obedience or patience? If something had gone wrong, how long would it take the Gestapo to search Ley's suite? If they had Ley, she assumed there would be no rush to search his rooms. They'd question him first, wouldn't they? *Ten more minutes.*

She let ten minutes stretch into twenty and knew it was time to leave. *Just because he couldn't make it here doesn't mean he's captured. Maybe he and his friends escaped but couldn't come back.* Despite her mental assurance, she dreaded leaving without him. What if she never found out what happened to him?

Gracie reached for the suitcase containing her radio and some of her clothes and pulled it from under the couch, then slid it back when she heard something in the hallway.

Voices. Loud. German. Agitated. Someone thumped on the door, and she knew she'd waited too long.

"Concetta, are you in there?" It wasn't Ley's voice, but it seemed familiar. "I can't find Adalard's keys."

She hesitated, but it wasn't as if she could escape now—the balcony was too high to jump from, so she was trapped. She opened the door and saw Heinie and another German soldier holding a stretcher while a third man with gray hair looked on. Lying on the stretcher, eyes closed and unmoving, was Ley.

Gracie let out a cry, and her hands flew to her mouth. A wave of dizziness hit her as she saw the dark red stain along his torso. "Is he . . . is he alive?" she asked as Heinie and the other man brought him into the room.

"For now," the third man said as he closed the door. He spoke Italian, but his accent told Gracie he was German.

"Will he be all right?" She felt like a vise was clamped around her chest as she followed the stretcher into the bedroom.

No one replied as Heinie and the other soldier moved Ley from the stretcher to the bed.

Gracie looked at Heinie. "He'll be all right, won't he?" *Please say he'll be all right.*

Heinie took her arm and pulled her away from the bed, making room for the gray-haired man. Gracie hadn't noticed before, but he had a black bag with him. "What do you think, doctor?" Heinie asked.

"I think you should have let me take him to the hospital." The doctor took supplies from his bag and cut Ley's uniform, pulling it away from the wound.

"He told me he didn't want to go to the hospital. There's better security here." Heinie's voice wavered as if he wasn't sure he'd done the right thing.

"He's lost a lot of blood. It would be easier to give him a transfusion in the hospital." The doctor removed the makeshift bandages and examined the damage.

Gracie couldn't help staring at the bloody hole, and what she saw made her lightheaded and queasy. She knew why Ley had said to skip the hospital—a blood transfusion with the wrong blood type might finish him off—but if he needed blood, was he going to die anyway? Ley's wound started bleeding again, and the doctor swore as he used a long set of tweezers to dig into Ley's injured abdomen.

Heinie glanced at her. "Why don't you wait in the other room, Concetta?"

"I'd rather stay."

"Then sit down before you fall down." He pushed a chair over to her, and she took his advice, numb with terror as she took in all the blood and the white-gray shade of Ley's face.

"What happened?" she whispered.

"Someone escaped from the Via Tasso. Shot Adalard, killed three other guards." Heinie manipulated the lampshade on the bedside table to give the doctor better light. "I was finishing up some paperwork when I heard the shots and went to see what was going on. Passed two dead guards and then found a dead officer and Adalard in a jail cell. He was conscious just long enough to make me promise to bring him here instead of the hospital."

"Who was the other officer?"

"Untersturmführer Ostheim."

Gracie wasn't sure if she was more horrified or relieved that it was Otto Ostheim. Dead, he couldn't retaliate for the blow she'd given him to the back of his head. But if he'd made it to the prison cell, that meant she'd failed to keep him from the Via Tasso. Ley was dying, and it was her fault.

She watched the doctor retrieve the bullet and put in about twenty stitches. Ley's face remained unchanged, as if he was too far gone to feel anything. *Please don't let him die*, she prayed. The doctor checked Ley's vital signs and put a dressing over the sutures. Most of the bleeding seemed to have stopped by the time he finished.

"You'll be here all night?" the doctor asked her.

"Yes."

"Good. I don't think he'll wake up, but if he does, give him some water." He took a syringe from his bag. "If it seems like he's in pain, give him this and write down when you gave it to him. I'll be back in the morning." The doctor packed his bag and exited with the other man, leaving Gracie with Ley and Heinie.

She stood and walked to the bed, wanting to get a better look at Ley's face. He seemed calm, but his coloring was all wrong—pallid and gray. She realized she was crying when she felt tears falling down her cheeks. Heinie came up behind her and put his hand on her shoulder. "I'm glad you found him," she said.

"I'm glad he'll have your help while he recovers." Heinie squeezed her shoulder. "I can stay with him part of the night."

Gracie was thankful that Heinie was willing to help, but she knew she wouldn't be able to close her eyes anytime soon. "I doubt I'll be able to fall asleep."

"I'll come by around 0300 and take a shift. Maybe you'll be able to sleep by then. If he needs anything, or if you need anything, I'll be just across the hall." He squeezed her shoulder again and let himself out.

Gracie tugged the boots off Ley's feet and grabbed an extra blanket from the closet to cover him. Then she dragged the chair next to the head of the bed and sat beside him. She felt his face and forehead. He felt a little cold, but his breathing was consistent.

"I'm sorry," she whispered. "I'm sorry I didn't distract him longer, and I'm sorry you got shot. Please get better . . . and please forgive me. I tried . . ." Gracie's voice broke after that. She couldn't talk anymore, so instead, she prayed.

* * *

When Heinie shook her awake the next morning, Gracie glanced at the clock. It was 10:00 a.m. She pushed herself into a sitting position on the couch, where she'd fallen asleep when Heinie had come almost seven hours ago.

"Has he woken up yet?"

Heinie shook his head. "He seemed like he was in pain though, so I gave him that shot of morphine two hours ago."

If Ley was reacting to pain, maybe that meant he was further from death, but she didn't want him to suffer. She smoothed and twisted her hair, then pinned it away from her neck. "The doctor hasn't been by yet?" she asked as she walked into the bedroom.

"Not yet. I have to leave soon, but I thought I could help change his clothes before I go. You know Adalard. He doesn't like to be dirty, and I think that uniform is a total loss."

Ley's face wasn't as gray this morning, and his temperature felt normal, but he didn't look as peaceful. There was more tension in his jaw. "Thank you for sitting with him. You're a good friend, Heinie."

Heinie shrugged. "He'd do the same for me."

Gracie pondered Heinie's statement before agreeing with him. Ley was kind enough to sit with a friend, even one in an SS uniform, as long as it wouldn't endanger his mission.

Gracie pulled the blanket back and took off Ley's socks while Heinie removed what was left of Ley's tunic and shirt. She stared at his lower legs. They were scarred, just like his hands. "How do you suppose he got all these scars?"

"Haven't you asked him?" Heinie seemed surprised.

It hit her then that Heinie and everyone else would expect her to have intimate knowledge of every square inch of Captain Ley's body. "I haven't seen them before. He keeps his socks on most of the time. Something about living through a Russian winter—he said your toes never recover."

Heinie grunted, but he looked confused as he pulled Ley's bloodstained undershirt gently over his head.

Gracie went to the closet to get clean underwear, hoping Heinie would finish undressing Ley without her. *You have two choices*, she told herself. *Refuse to help and blow your cover, or get used to the idea of seeing a man completely naked, and pretend you've seen it all before.*

She was saved from either choice when someone knocked on the door. She went to answer it, leaving Ley in his underclothing. It was the doctor. He nodded to her and went right to the bedroom.

Gracie stood next to the bed while the doctor checked the stitches. She winced as a grimace spread across Ley's face and he grunted in pain. Then his eyes opened. He seemed disoriented, and his breathing grew rapid as he looked from the doctor to Heinie, finally settling on her face.

"Gracie?"

She was flattered that his first thought was of her, but then she realized what he'd done. His voice had been only a whisper, but in the absolute silence of the room, Gracie didn't doubt that both the doctor and Heinie had heard Ley call her the wrong name.

Heinie was watching her closely, the muscles surrounding his eyes crinkled in curiosity. First she'd been surprised by the scars on Ley's legs and now he was calling her the wrong name. She ran a hand over Ley's forehead. He'd already closed his eyes again. "It's his ex-girlfriend's name. I thought he didn't love her anymore . . ." She let her lips tremble and pretended her feelings were hurt, but really, she was scared as she turned and walked to the front room.

One good thing came out of Ley's slip. Heinie finished changing Ley so Gracie didn't have to do it herself. "Don't feel too bad," Heinie said on his way out. "He may have remembered her name, but it was your face he seemed happy to see. The morphine's probably affecting his brain. Do you think you can forgive him?"

"Of course."

"Good, because I think he'll need your help for a while longer."

When Heinie left, Gracie looked into the bedroom again. The doctor felt Ley's pulse and replaced the bandages. She thought Ley was sleeping, but from the doorway, she heard him mutter, "Gracie shouldn't be here," and he said it in English.

On his way out, the doctor stopped and studied her suspiciously. *Does he know?* she wondered. *Did Ley say anything else while I was out of the room?*

"Let me get you something to drink." Gracie grabbed the bottle of liquor that had sat on Ley's wet bar for almost four weeks.

The doctor glanced at the clock but sat in the chair. He didn't complain when the only container Gracie could find was a teacup and didn't seem to mind that she filled it full, even though she thought that type of alcohol was usually served in a shot glass.

"How is he today?" she asked.

"Better than yesterday." The doctor took a sip, examined the teacup's contents with a look of appreciation, and took another swig. "Let him sleep as much as he wants, but try to wake him up this evening and get some food in him. Something easy to digest. Soup. Bread. Milk."

Gracie nodded, glad Ley and the hotel cook were on good terms.

"You'll want to watch for infection. I'll come by again tomorrow, but unless that wound becomes septic, I think he'll be fine. No need to ship him home, but I'd still rather have him in a hospital." The doctor sipped his drink again. "Never seen anyone so insistent as that obersturmführer yesterday, demanding I treat the hauptmann here."

When the doctor left, Gracie sat at the table with trembling hands. *Ley spoke English, and the doctor heard.* Had he understood? Should she leave before the Gestapo came and arrested them both? But she couldn't leave Ley, not while he was barely alive.

When her hands stopped shaking, she went through Ley's things until she found his money. She took some of it with her, thinking she might need to bribe the cook, but when she went to the kitchen, the lady working there seemed happy to help without any monetary incentive.

"How is your new flat working out?" she asked Gracie as she handed her a basket filled with rolls and a large container of broth.

"I haven't made it there yet," Gracie said honestly.

The woman laughed. Gracie could still hear it echoing behind her in the hallway as she hurried back to Ley. *What is so funny?*

Ley's mumbling grew worse that afternoon. She dreaded Heinie returning from duty or the doctor coming to check on him again. She couldn't always pick out what he was saying, could rarely tell what language it was, but she heard her name more than once and wasn't sure how long she could convince everyone that he was talking about an old girlfriend. Gracie wasn't even a German name.

It's the morphine. She couldn't skip his next dose. He'd be in too much pain. But if he kept talking in his sleep, they'd both end up dead.

CHAPTER THIRTY-THREE

Zimmerman walked through the prison with Heinrich Vogel. It wasn't Vogel's job to investigate the shooting, but Zimmerman asked for his help since Vogel had shown up soon after the incident.

"The first guard was here, dead when we arrived." Vogel pointed to the floor where the corridor split. "Then the other lay halfway down the hall. Poor man died in my arms." Vogel frowned at the memory.

When they reached the cell, Vogel showed Zimmerman the final two spots. "Ostheim was here. He was dead when we arrived. Adalard—um, Hauptmann Dietrich—was over here. I wasn't sure he was going to make it last night, but I was with him this morning, and I think he'll recover."

"What was Dietrich doing here?"

"I don't know. He wasn't conscious long enough for me to ask."

"Hmm. Did you see the prisoner who escaped?"

Vogel shook his head. "He was gone before I got here. Most nights I would have been gone by then too, but I was finishing up a report for Sturmbannführer Scholz."

Zimmerman looked around the cell, but it offered him no clues. Somehow, the prisoner had obtained a weapon, and he'd used it effectively. "Thank you for your help, Obersturmführer Vogel."

"Of course. Let me know if I can help with anything else."

Zimmerman nodded, doubting there was much either of them could do to recover the man he'd captured yesterday before dawn. "I will. And let me know if I can ever help you with your duties."

Vogel was in the doorway, but he stopped, hesitating. "Actually, since you work with Sturmbannführer Scholz, I would appreciate any mention of my help. The two of us had a disagreement over SS marriage laws, and he hasn't forgotten it. Any comment showing him I'm still loyal to the SS would be helpful."

Zimmerman had heard about the incident. Most officers who wanted to advance in their careers would instantly drop ties with a girlfriend of questionable ancestry, but Zimmerman could sympathize with lovestruck Heinie Vogel. He knew what it was like to earn a commanding officer's displeasure. And he knew what it was like to fall in love with someone very different from himself. "I'd be happy to."

He walked back to his desk, pausing where Ostheim usually sat. *I can't believe he's gone.* Ostheim had always been so careful with his duties in the prison. Zimmerman couldn't imagine him making a mistake, yet he was dead.

He went to his own seat and thought for a while, unable to concentrate on his paperwork. He was glad for the distraction when Möller rushed over to him. His forearm was bandaged from the raid, but he'd turned down medical leave. "Sir, there's been an explosion in the Via Rasella. Sabotage, they think."

"Drive me there," Zimmerman said.

Möller was enthusiastic behind the wheel—the type of driver who made his passengers fear for their lives—but the streets were mostly empty, and Möller made the drive in record time. The Via Rasella was narrow, surrounded by tall buildings, and positioned on one of the seven hills of Rome. This afternoon, it was a swarm of activity.

Zimmerman stepped from the car and grabbed a distraught German enlisted man's arm. "What happened?"

"They butchered us," he whispered, staring at the blood on his hands as tears pooled in his eyes.

"Who?"

The soldier shook his head. "I don't know." He was distracted by a shadow moving along one of the roofs. He pointed his submachine gun at the top of the building and pulled the trigger, blasting the roof line.

Zimmerman couldn't see anything worth shooting but didn't scold the soldier for his trigger finger. The man was emotional beyond reason. "What unit are you with?"

"SS Bozen 11th company, 3rd Battalion. We were on our way back from training when they attacked."

Zimmerman had heard of the Bozen SS. They were tasked with anti-partisan warfare in Rome, and the 11th company had been on their last day of training. They would have been walking up the street on their way back from the firing range when they were hit. It was the perfect spot for an ambush. *Why didn't their officers see that before the Gappisti did?*

Zimmerman left the soldier to shoot at the shadows of long-escaped adversaries. Bits of stone, stucco, and broken glass littered the bloodstained cobblestones, and the pockmarks of bullets showed on the buildings lining the street. The soldier he'd just left hadn't been the only one firing his weapon, and they'd hit more than just stucco. A female corpse hung over a ledge, and her blood stained the wall below her. *Was she one of the partisans or just in the wrong place at the wrong time?*

As he walked farther up the hill, he saw the huge crater. It had blown open a nearby building's wall and left a massive hole in the ground. Water flowed down the hill, so the explosion must have ruptured a pipe too.

He approached a hauptsturmführer who seemed calmer than the enlisted man had been. "What happened?"

"Not sure. A bomb. Might have been dropped from the windows. It cut through their lines, then a team of gunmen hit the side and rear with mortars and pistols. Most of the men assumed they were being attacked from the apartments, so that's where they fired."

Across the street, a team of soldiers dragged civilians from the building. One of the women was shouting, children were crying, and an old man collapsed in the press of people forced from their homes. A soldier gave him a solid kick, which forced him back to his feet.

"Put them with the rest of the civilians," the hauptsturmführer ordered.

"What were our losses?" Zimmerman asked.

"Sixty percent casualties." He shook his head, disgusted. "Keep your hands on your heads," he yelled at the Italians.

"Any civilian deaths?"

"A few."

Zimmerman saw the soldiers' bodies stacked in a row along the street's edge. He drew closer and forced himself to look at each face. He didn't recognize any of them, but they were his countrymen, his Nazi brothers. Nearby, another soldier sat on the street, weeping, his face buried in his hands. Zimmerman clenched his fists as he looked at the long line of German dead. *Whoever did this will pay.*

More civilians were forced onto the street, and the soldiers divided them, sending the men to one location and the women and children to another. A few of the soldiers were emptying the buildings not just of residents but also of valuables. A jewelry box here, a silver tray there. One of the civilians protested, her cries carrying over the sound of the others. "That's my grandmother's tea set!"

"Keep your hands on your head!" the officer shouted again.

Losing an heirloom tea set is the least of her worries, Zimmerman thought.

He walked up and down the Via Rasella, trying to piece together what it must have been like. The wounded had been taken to hospitals, but the dead still lay in their orderly row. As he studied the crater, he considered what he'd heard—that the bomb might have been dropped from a building. He studied the angle from the nearest blasted-out window to the crater. No one could throw a bomb that big that far. They would have needed special equipment. More likely, the bomb had been on the street. Hidden inside a car? He couldn't see any pieces of wreckage, but the blast was big enough to have incinerated an automobile.

He searched the nearest buildings to be sure of his theory. The civilians had all been removed, and he ignored the looting soldiers. None of the rooms held anything that would launch a bomb, and he didn't think equipment like that could be moved or hidden quickly. He walked outside, planning to ask the civilians if they'd seen anything.

A vehicle pulled up, and Vogel got out, along with a pair of SS engineers. Vogel directed them as they unloaded their explosives.

The hauptsturmführer Zimmerman had spoken to earlier finished his roundup of civilians and approached the engineers. "General Mälzer wants to blow up the entire street and shoot all the civilians."

"What?" Vogel looked at Zimmerman as if asking him for help. Zimmerman turned away. He wasn't going to dispute an order from General Mälzer, the German commandant of Rome. "Were any of the civilians involved in the blast?"

The hauptsturmführer shrugged. "Does it matter? Get ready to blast the buildings."

"But, sir, Mälzer can't have meant it. It's doubtful any of the residents were involved. It was probably the Gappisti, and the guilty ones are far away by now."

The hauptsturmführer glared at Vogel. "Are you questioning your orders?"

Another soldier discovered an unexploded mortar, saving Vogel from having to answer. The soldier who'd found it brought it to the cluster of three officers. Zimmerman took a few steps back, as did the hauptsturmführer. Vogel strode forward and examined the shell. "It's Italian."

"The Gappisti?" Zimmerman asked.

"That would be my guess," Vogel said.

"Then let's shoot these people so the Gappisti lose their support." The hauptsturmführer gestured toward the rounded-up civilians. "Make the population hate them for the retribution they've caused. With no one to hide them or feed them or turn a blind eye when they distribute their propaganda, the Gappisti will be easy to catch."

Vogel handed the mortar to one of his men and gazed at the hauptsturmführer in stern disagreement. "Who do you think the people are more likely to hate? The Gappisti who killed soldiers occupying their city or the soldiers who massacred civilians unconnected with the attack?"

"You better watch yourself," the hauptsturmführer said. "Get those buildings ready for demolition, now." He turned and stalked away.

Vogel watched him go but didn't give his engineers any orders.

"Vogel," Zimmerman whispered. "If you know what's good for you, you'll do what he says."

"Why?" Vogel asked. "It won't bring them back to life." He pointed to the row of dead Bozen SS troops. "The civilians aren't the guilty ones. They don't deserve to be executed, and killing them won't do us any good. It will just cause more problems with the rest of the Romans, with the Pope. This will make the bad press the Americans got after destroying Monte Cassino seem like a picnic."

"Just follow your orders, Vogel," Zimmerman said. "It's not your job to think. It's your job to obey."

"I can't obey an order like that."

"Why not?"

"Because it's not right!"

Zimmerman shook his head in exasperation. Vogel's view of war reminded him a little of his wife's. Neither of them seemed to understand the ruthlessness required for victory. "What's right is following your orders."

Vogel didn't say anything. His engineers waited for direction, one of them staring at the carnage around him in disbelief, the other glaring at Vogel in disgust.

Zimmerman walked away. If Vogel didn't get over his weak stomach, he was going to get in trouble, and Zimmerman thought it best to avoid friendship with someone whose career was about to collapse. He hadn't gone far when the hauptsturmführer came up to him. "New orders. We'll turn the civilians over to the Italians for questioning."

Zimmerman was reluctant to admit it, but Vogel was right—killing the civilians would cause as many problems as it solved. Better to question them and see if they knew anything useful. By whatever means necessary, he intended to find the guilty parties, and when he did, he would show them no mercy.

CHAPTER THIRTY-FOUR

BASTIEN TRIED TO OPEN HIS eyes, but his eyelids felt heavy and dry, as if they were glued shut and had weights on them. His torso ached, especially the left side, and it took him a while to remember why. He tried to rub his face with his hand, thinking it might help him open his eyes, but his hand seemed to take an eternity to move from his side to his face, as if his nerves were no longer connected correctly.

"Are you waking up?" It was Gracie's voice, but he still couldn't get his eyes open.

"Trying to." His voice sounded like a croak. His eyes finally opened, but the light from the balcony window was blinding. He squinted, trying to find Gracie, and saw her only after she pulled the curtains shut, darkening the room.

She came back to a chair by his bed, her eyes searching his face. "How do you feel?"

"Rotten."

"Can I help you with anything? Are you hungry? Thirsty? Do you need more morphine?"

Now that she mentioned it, his throat was dry. "Water, please."

Gracie went into the other room, then returned with a glass of water. She stacked an extra pillow behind his head and helped hold the glass for him. He wanted to do it himself, but his hands still felt uncoordinated.

"Do you remember my name now?" Gracie asked.

What a silly question. "Of course. Are we alone?"

"For now. The doctor said he'd come, but he's late."

Bastien let her help him with another sip of water. "I remember several names for you, Concetta. Or Miss Graziella Begni, or Gladius." He whispered the last options.

A small smile broke out on Gracie's face.

"What?"

"You don't remember waking up this morning, do you?"

I was awake this morning? "I guess not."

"Well, if Heinie asks, you have an ex-girlfriend named Gracie."

Bastien searched his brain to figure out why on earth Gracie would have started a rumor like that, but it just made his head hurt. "What are you talking about?"

Gracie set the glass on the small table by his bed. "You called me Gracie in front of Heinie and the doctor this morning, so I told them you were confusing me with an old girlfriend."

Bastien had slipped in his head before, but slipping out loud was worse than the time he'd fouled up his security check. "Don't let anyone give me any more morphine. I'm sorry."

"No, I'm sorry," Gracie said. "I thought I'd distracted Ostheim long enough. He's the one who shot you, isn't he?"

"Yes, but I was late getting to the prison. What happened with Ostheim?"

"The waiter brought our meals, and Ostheim told him to send them up to his room. He was billeted in the hotel he took me to. I went with him, but when he started kissing me, I knew I had to get out of there."

"Didn't I tell you not to go anywhere alone with him?" The instant the words slipped from his lips, Bastien regretted them. Gracie already looked distraught; she didn't need a lecture. Besides, he'd made several of his own mistakes the day before, and she'd been trying to help him. "Did he hurt you?"

"No, but I was scared, so I hit him over the head with a wine bottle. I thought he'd be unconscious past our deadline, but I guess I was wrong. I'm sorry." She wiped away a few tears. "It's all my fault."

"No, I was late. And I shouldn't have put you at risk in the first place."

Gracie blinked rapidly, as if she was trying to prevent new tears.

"I'm glad he didn't do anything more than kiss you." When Bastien pictured it, it made him wish he'd been the one to pull the trigger and kill Ostheim.

"No, he just shot you instead."

"Let it go. He can't hurt either of us anymore. Unless you believe in ghosts."

Gracie's lips twitched in amusement as she shook her head. "Let me get you something to eat."

"First, could you help me to the bathroom?"

She frowned. "I don't know that you're supposed to get out of bed."

Bastien wasn't sure he was physically capable of getting out of bed, but it was urgent that he make it to the bathroom. "Let's try."

Gracie pulled the blankets back. He hadn't realized he was wearing nothing but his skivvies.

"Let's get you on your side first. Then I'll pull your legs to the edge of the bed and use them to help swing you upright." Gracie rolled him onto his right side so his weight was on the uninjured side of his body. As she gently pulled his legs into position, he had the impression this wasn't the first time she'd helped someone with limited mobility out of bed. "Ready?"

Bastien nodded, but even with Gracie's help, sitting was agony, and it must have shown on his face.

"Are you all right?" she asked.

Bastien took a few deep breaths, hoping the pain would calm down, but it didn't, and it wasn't just his bullet wound. He had a headache and he felt dizzy. He didn't know if he could stay sitting for much longer, let alone walk to the bathroom, even with help.

"Are you ready for me to help you stand?" Gracie was next to him, but the blood rushing past his ears made it hard for him to hear her.

"I don't know if I can," he confessed, hating to admit how helpless he was. Already, his peripheral vision was splotchy, and he was starting to feel nauseated. The left side of his abdomen burned with every breath.

"Should I get a jar?"

"Yes," he whispered.

When she came back from retrieving it, she hesitated. "Can you do it by yourself?"

He glanced at her face, red with embarrassment. "Yes." He wasn't really sure he could, but there were some things he wasn't going to accept help with.

She looked relieved and left the room. When she came back, he handed the jar to her. If she'd ever had any romantic feelings for him, he was sure he smothered them when he handed her the jar full of urine. He would have felt regret, but his side hurt too much.

Gracie set the jar on the floor. "Let's get you comfortable again, then I'll take care of that."

He was grateful for her help because he wasn't sure how much longer he could sit without falling over. But lying down was almost as painful as sitting up had been. Gracie left with the jar, and he heard water running, but he'd dozed off by the time she came back.

"Adalard?"

He blinked a few times, trying to banish sleep again.

Gracie cleaned his hands with a wet towel. "I'm sorry, but the doctor wanted you to eat something. The cook sent up a few things for you. After that, I'll let you sleep again."

As if being unable to go to the bathroom by himself wasn't bad enough, he had to let Gracie spoon feed him his soup. He was like a baby, unable to do anything for himself, only he was twenty times bigger.

"Enrichetta said she hopes you feel better soon," Gracie said, breaking the silence. "She also had a good laugh about how I haven't made it to my new flat yet."

"Hmm." Bastien thought he knew why. "When I asked her about finding a place for you, she seemed to think it wasn't necessary because she assumed you were with me most nights."

She gave him another spoonful. "Most people seem to assume that. Which reminds me: I let something slip in front of Heinie. I was taking your socks off, and I didn't know you had scars on your legs. He seemed to think I should have seen them before."

"Well, that's not as bad as my slip."

"How did you get them?"

"The same way I got the scars on my hands."

Gracie held his gaze, wordlessly asking for more information.

"A fire," he said. "When I was nine."

He felt Gracie's fingers on his right hand, examining the scars there. "It sounds terrifying and painful," she said. "Especially for someone so young. I'm sorry."

She offered him more soup, and he shook his head. "I think I've had enough."

Gracie set the bowl on the end table. "How did the fire start?"

A month ago, Bastien would have told her to mind her own business, but not now. Maybe it was time for Gracie to know more about his past. "My brother, two years younger than me, liked to play with matches. My mom was out with the baby, and my dad needed to help the neighbor with something, so he told me to make sure Hans didn't get into trouble. I got busy building something, and Hans started a fire. I think he was trying to light an oil lamp, but he dropped it, and the oil spread everywhere. All over the floor, all over the curtains. Then he dropped the match." Bastien paused, the memory of the inferno still fresh in his mind. He could still remember his brother's frightened pleas for help and the way Bastien had thought the flames would consume them both. "I got him out, but he died a few days later."

They had been in the same hospital room. As long as he lived, Bastien would never forget his little brother's cries of pain. He had been Bastien's best friend. They'd played together, walked to school together, shared their toys, shared a bedroom. Hans had been a good boy, but he had died an agonizing death of painful burns followed by a raging infection. "It was my fault," Bastien said. "I was supposed to be watching him."

"You were only nine," Gracie whispered, a catch in her voice.

"My dad told me to take care of my brother, and I didn't. Fourteen years later, when my dad was arrested, he entrusted the rest of my siblings to me. I've often wondered why when I failed him so miserably with Hans." Bastien glanced at his scarred right hand. "That's why I have to help win this war, soon, before my other brother joins the fight and ends up dead. I can't lose him too. I can't fail my father again."

CHAPTER THIRTY-FIVE

ZIMMERMAN KNEW IT WAS GOING to be a long night. Orders had come down from Hitler himself: the Italians would pay. Generals Von Mackensen and Kesselring had confirmed it and specified that ten Italians would be executed for every German soldier who had died in the Via Rasella. But it was up to their subordinates to find the needed number of Italians to carry out the sentence.

Calls had been placed to the Italian authorities, giving them specific numbers of prisoners to provide. Twenty-eight German soldiers were dead, so Zimmerman was searching the Via Tasso records for men to add to a list that needed to reach two hundred eighty.

The original plan was to execute those who were sentenced to death anyway, but after a search of both the Via Tasso and the Regina Coeli prison records, that number came to only three. "Two-hundred seventy-seven to go," Zimmerman said to Möller as he brought him another stack of files.

"Another one died of his wounds in the hospital," Möller said. "We've got to find ten more."

Zimmerman frowned. He wouldn't have final say on the list, and he was glad, but finding the needed prisoners would help make up for the disaster at San Lorenzo. He wished there was more time, but Hitler had demanded the reprisal be carried out within twenty-four hours. "Let's see if we have anyone in for a life sentence."

Twenty minutes later, Möller looked up from his stack of files. "None."

Zimmerman hadn't found any either. "Those being held for crimes that could result in capital punishment."

They found sixteen to add to the list.

"Coffee?" Möller asked.

Zimmerman nodded and yawned at the same time. While Möller was gone, he stared at the darkened window. When he glanced back at his desk, he saw the picture of his wife and son. Their eyes faced the camera, as if questioning his actions. He set the picture face-down in a drawer as Möller returned.

"Sir, the death toll is up to thirty-two, with several men in critical condition. We've got to make the list longer."

"Jews? If they're being sent to Auschwitz, they're going to die anyway. Might as well use them to fill our quota."

"Excellent plan, sir."

"And check with the Italians. We turned the civilians from the Via Rasella over to them. They might have something."

While Zimmerman scanned the files for Jews, Möller made a few phone calls.

"The Italians have suggested ten Communists for our list."

"Good."

"What about this man, sir?" Möller asked a few minutes later. "He was in the Italian Army but switched his loyalties during the armistice. Followed the king instead of Mussolini."

Zimmerman glanced briefly at the dossier. "Add him."

"And this one? Similar politically but Carabinieri instead of army."

"Add him too."

Slowly, surely, their list began to grow as they searched the prison files for men who were spies, Communists, Jews, or petty criminals—men to pay Hitler's bill of revenge.

* * *

Friday evening, Gracie put her hand on Ley's forehead and frowned. It had felt warm all day, but now she was sure his fever was rising. She hadn't seen Heinie or the doctor since Thursday morning. It was hours past curfew, but she needed to find help.

"Adalard?" Gracie wished she knew Ley's first name. It seemed wrong to use an alias when he was so sick.

He opened his eyes a crack.

"I'm going to fetch the doctor. I'll be back soon."

His answer was a barely audible grunt, another sign of his deteriorating condition.

As Gracie walked to the door, she heard a knock. *Please let it be the doctor.* When she opened the door, she didn't see the gray-haired man she'd tried to get drunk the day before, but Heinie was the next-best thing.

Usually, she could hear him whistling from several doors away, but today he was quiet. Dark skin shadowed his eyes, dust covered his uniform, and there was a soberness about him that made the air seem heavier.

"Are you all right, Heinie?" she asked.

He shrugged. "I wanted to check on Adalard."

"He's worse—he has a fever. Yesterday I got him to eat a little and hold a conversation, but today he's hardly eaten anything, and he's quiet. The doctor hasn't come, even though he said he would."

"Medical personnel have been a little busy the past few days."

"They have? Why?" Gracie wondered if the Americans were closing in, but last she'd heard they'd made little progress since January.

Heinie either didn't hear her or chose to ignore her question. "May I see him?"

Gracie nodded, then followed Heinie into the bedroom. Ley had dozed off again. The fever had left the roots of his hair damp, but he'd asked for more blankets several times throughout the day.

Heinie sat in the chair next to the bed and felt Ley's forehead. Ley opened his eyes and looked at the two of them but didn't speak.

"When did the fever start?" Heinie asked.

"This morning. At first I wasn't sure, but by this afternoon . . . I'm worried about him, Heinie. Can you ask the doctor to come again?"

Heinie was quiet, staring at his friend.

Ley closed his eyes. "You're acting like I'm a corpse at a viewing. Stop it."

Heinie smiled slightly. "Sorry. How do you feel?"

"Like I caught influenza and got shot at the same time."

"Can you get the doctor, Heinie?" Gracie was hesitant to see the doctor again because he might remember Ley's English slip, but she was far more frightened by Ley's declining health. "I don't know what to do anymore."

"I'll try," Heinie said. "I saw him not long ago doling out medicinal alcohol." He shook his head. "You haven't heard any of the news, have you? About yesterday?"

"No." Something in Heinie's voice made Gracie afraid to ask for details.

"What happened?" Ley asked.

"The Gappisti attacked a column of SS troops. Bozen 11th company."

Gracie inhaled sharply, remembering Angelo's vow of revenge when he showed her those same troops.

Heinie continued. "Thirty-three of them are dead. Hitler ordered ten Italians executed for each German death. The executions were carried out this afternoon."

That made three hundred thirty victims. "Who did they execute?" she finally worked up the courage to ask, wondering if Angelo had been caught.

"Whoever they could find in the prisons," Heinie said. "The Gestapo carried out the executions. They took the men—" Heinie broke off. When he continued, his voice shook. "Some of them were just boys. They took them in groups to the Ardeatina sand pits by the Christian catacombs. I was told it began very orderly. They were taken five at a time, told to kneel, then shot in the head. It was supposed to have been a painless death. More than three hundred unarmed men killed in under five hours. Efficient and secret and . . . and utterly reprehensible."

Heinie rubbed a trembling hand over his mouth. "I was called in to blow up the cave entrances with some Wehrmacht engineers. Bury the evidence. I saw the bodies. Huge stacks of the dead. Their hands were tied behind their backs, and they were shot in the head, but it wasn't always a straight shot. I saw one prisoner who looked like he'd been beaten to death. No bullets." Heinie paused, taking a few deep breaths. "I guess most of the guards didn't want to do it, but they had to. Their leaders suggested they get drunk tonight. They told my men and me the same thing when we finished, but it won't make a difference, not for me. Piles of bodies almost as tall as me. And why? They haven't caught any of the Gappisti who bombed the Via Rasella. It's wrong, and I'm ashamed to have been part of it."

Gracie tried to fathom the murder of more than three hundred people, all of them unconnected to the crime they were being punished for. She didn't know what to think of Angelo. He couldn't have known what would happen as retribution for the attack he'd been part of, but it felt wrong that he was probably still free while three hundred others had died in reprisal.

"Concetta, will you get me some soup?" Ley whispered.

Gracie looked at him in surprise. She'd been trying to get him to eat all day, and *now* he had an appetite? After hearing about a massacre? She finally glanced at Heinie and understood. Ley wanted to talk to his friend in private. Heinie was a wreck, overcome with guilt for something he hadn't planned and hadn't participated in, unless he counted blowing up the cave entrance.

She went to the wet bar and took her time warming some broth on a hotplate. She could hear quiet male voices, and though she couldn't pick

out what they said, Heinie seemed more at peace when he came out of
the bedroom, no longer hunched over with guilt.

"I'll ask the doctor to come by," he said.

Gracie saw Heinie out, then went back to the bedroom to bring Ley
his soup. "Adalard?"

There was no response. He was asleep again.

* * *

Gracie's nerves stretched thin as she walked to her Saturday-morning
appointment with Angelo. She still wasn't sure how she felt about the
attack on the Via Rasella. The Bozen SS troops were a legitimate target,
but surely the attack hadn't been worth it, not when ten Italians had been
murdered for each German soldier killed. She understood now why most
people under Nazi occupation didn't resist. The consequence was slaughter.

When she told Angelo about the reprisals, he squeezed his eyes shut
and bowed his head. "How did you find out?" he asked.

"I can't say. I'm sorry."

"Are you sure it's true? Not just a rumor to make the Gappisti look bad?"

Gracie felt tears forming in her eyes. "I wish it weren't true. You have
no idea how much I wish it weren't true. But I heard it from someone who
saw the bodies."

"They'll pay," he whispered, his hands balling into fists.

"But if you retaliate, won't they just kill more innocent people?"

"We can't let them win by terror, Concetta. We have to fight back, show
them we won't give up until they've been driven from Italy. Rolling over
every time they hurt us will make them think their reprisals work. We have
to continue, now more than ever." Angelo handed her his report and left.

Please let it be over soon, she prayed. She left the piazza the opposite way
she'd come, relieved she was a radio operator, not a soldier or a saboteur.
Maybe Angelo was right. Maybe it would be wrong for the Gappisti to give
up. But she'd seen Angelo's reaction to the news, seen his shock and grief
and desire for vengeance. Were she in his position, she thought she'd feel
the same emotions but also guilt—the crushing, overwhelming kind.

She hurried back to Ley's hotel room. His fever had been worse that
morning, and though the doctor had come, he hadn't given her any
reassuring news.

Heinie was sitting by Ley's bed when she returned. "I think it's down
a little from this morning."

Gracie felt Ley's forehead, but his skin still burned against her hand. "Has he woken up at all?"

"No."

She moved her hand from his forehead to his cheek. He inhaled deeply and turned his face toward her. She held her breath, hoping he'd open his eyes, but he relaxed again without responding to her. *What will I do if he dies?* Gracie knew what she felt for Ley was stronger than the normal camaraderie that came from working on a mission together. She trusted him, she admired him, she depended on him, and most days she thought she was in love with him. She didn't want to bury him here in Rome, especially when it was her fault he'd been shot. She blinked away fresh tears, knowing they were a combination of worry and inadequate sleep.

"Hey, it's just a fever. He'll get over it," Heinie said.

"Are you sure?"

Heinie looked at Ley for a long moment. "I think so."

She wanted to believe Heinie because the alternative was too painful.

* * *

On Sunday, Ley's fever grew worse. Gracie spent all day and all night changing out cool washcloths and trying to spoon water into his mouth. He opened his eyes a few times but never spoke, never seemed to recognize her. Monday was more of the same. His fever dropped a half degree Celsius, but his condition seemed otherwise unchanged.

Tuesday morning, after a few hours of sleep, Gracie checked Ley's temperature again, and he felt normal. She stuck the thermometer in his mouth just to be sure, but his fever was gone.

When Heinie came by, she threw her arms around him. "He's finally getting better."

"I told you he'd be fine." But despite Heinie's prediction from a few days before, he seemed relieved. "I can stay with him a while, if you'd like. I know you haven't had a chance to leave for a few days."

"Thank you. I'd like that." She still had Angelo's report, and it was past time to send it in. She hadn't been in contact with headquarters for a week. They probably thought she'd been captured.

As she walked through Rome, carrying her radio in her suitcase, she felt as if a huge weight had lifted off her shoulders. The city was solemn, the civilians hungrier than normal because the Germans had reduced rations again as punishment for the attack on the Via Rasella, but Ley's body was beating the infection, and the doctor had come by the day before and seemed to think the bullet wound would heal.

The war still raged, and the Allies still hadn't been able to get past the Gustav Line or off the Anzio beachhead, but Ley's condition was something she could hold on to, something positive. If she was honest with herself, Ley's health was the battle she cared about the most.

First, Gracie went to her old flat. She packed extra clothes around the radio and retrieved the spare handgun she'd brought from Switzerland. Then she returned to an abandoned apartment she'd used once before to contact headquarters. She needed to find new locations for her transmissions, but that would have to wait until Ley was healthier.

She wrote her first report since training, explaining what had happened and stressing that Centurion's cover was still intact. Then she encoded it. It took longer than usual to receive a response, and when she'd transmitted her report and Angelo's, there was a lengthy message from Caserta. *Probably asking me all sorts of questions to make sure I'm still free.* When she finally signed off, she felt like she'd been on the air for far too long. She cut her transposition keys from her handkerchief, burned the used pairs along with her transmitted reports, and slipped the rest of her keys into her pocket with the encoded message from headquarters.

Gracie took the radio to her new flat. The one-room suite was nicer than her previous place, with a private bathroom and a tiny kitchen. She smiled. *I'll be able to cook my own meals again. But not today.*

She hung her clothes in the bedroom's small wardrobe and placed the suitcase in the bottom. She was tired, but she vetoed the idea of a nap. Heinie couldn't sit with Ley forever. And if Ley woke, she didn't want to miss it, so she headed back to Ley's suite.

A few blocks from the hotel, she heard someone call to her. "Signorina, a moment please."

Gracie looked behind her to see two men, one of them with a pistol drawn and pointed at her.

CHAPTER THIRTY-SIX

"Is that her?" the man with the Beretta asked.

"Yes," the other one said. "The guard at the hotel pointed her out to me. Hard to miss that birthmark."

Gracie mentally cursed her blemish. She glanced around, but she'd taken a shortcut through a side street, and no one was nearby other than the two men. She considered running, but the men were fewer than ten feet away. The one with a pistol didn't look like he'd miss.

"Inside, please." The man waved his weapon toward a door. When she hesitated, he continued. "If you cooperate, no harm will come to you."

The unarmed man took her elbow and pushed her inside the abandoned shop. She reached into her jacket pocket as the door closed, but her escort was one step ahead of her. He grabbed her wrist and pulled her hand out, then felt the pocket and confiscated her pistol. "Grazie, signorina."

"See if she's hiding anything else, Dino." As Dino looked through her other pockets, the man with the Beretta lowered his weapon but only a fraction. "I'm looking for information on Hauptmann Dietrich."

Gracie was already scared, but the man's question put her solidly in the terrified category. She did her best to breathe normally. "Who?"

"Hauptmann Adalard Dietrich. According to the guard Dino bribed, you're his girlfriend."

"You trust a German guard?"

He raised one eyebrow. "No, but I trust the guilty look on your face. There's no need for concern. We have better things to do than punish Italian women who decide a relationship with a Wehrmacht officer is preferable to starvation. I understand Dietrich was shot recently. Is he still alive?"

Gracie tried to figure out what the man was planning. Was he going to finish Ley off? "That's none of your business."

The man smiled slightly. "I assume if you're trying to protect him, there's still something left of him to protect. Is he going to recover?"

Gracie didn't answer. He raised his pistol, threatening her, but she bit her lip and kept silent. Ley wasn't in a position to defend himself, and she wasn't going to give away any information that might put him in danger.

After several long seconds, he lowered his weapon again. "Your loyalty says something good about you or something good about him. Listen, if he's in the hospital, see if you can't steal his identification tags. They have the wrong blood type on them."

"How do you know that?" Gracie whispered, shocked.

"Are you surprised that it's not a match or surprised that I know?"

Dino handed the man the items he'd taken from Gracie: her handkerchief, keys to her apartments and Ley's hotel room, and the coded message from headquarters.

The taller man looked at her transposition keys and the message, then met her eyes. "You're the radio operator."

Gracie didn't speak, unwilling to confirm his suspicion and afraid he wouldn't believe a denial.

He handed her the paper, keys, and handkerchief. "Return her pistol, Dino."

"But—"

"Now."

Dino handed her pistol back to her, and Gracie slipped it into her pocket, confused and worried by how much this Italian seemed to know.

"I didn't stop you to hurt you. I just have a message I want delivered. Tell Capitano Ley that Marcello made it south and our other two friends no longer need his help. They made their way to Ardeatina."

Gracie gasped. *How does he know Captain Ley's real name?* She got the impression he wouldn't tell her even if she asked. "The two other friends, they died in the caves?"

The man nodded, then jerked his head toward the door. Dino left, and the taller man quickly followed, leaving Gracie alone, flabbergasted.

It took several minutes for her nerves to calm down enough that she felt confident leaving the shop. She walked more slowly than usual and looked around more frequently, wondering if anyone was following her. Instinct told her that despite the heavy-handed method, anyone in Rome who knew Ley's real name was her ally, but she still felt unsettled, especially as she passed the guards in the hotel lobby. *How much did it take for one of them to tell Dino all about me?*

She was glad Heinie hadn't yet left when she arrived because it gave her time to collect her thoughts. Ley's face was still too pale to look healthy, but he smiled when he saw her, and that told her the worst was behind them.

"How are you?" she asked, kissing Ley on the forehead. That was yet another reason she was glad Heinie was around—it gave her an excuse to act like a concerned girlfriend.

"Brain's not so foggy today." Ley's voice was weak and rough.

"How are you, Heinie?"

"I'm all right. You?"

"Fine," she lied. The mysterious gunman had known far too much about both her and Ley.

"Here." Heinie stood and gestured to the chair he'd been sitting in. "Take my seat. I was about to leave anyway."

"Don't let me chase you out, Heinie. I can get one of the dining chairs."

"No, I really was planning to leave. I'm sick of arguing with him. Says he's not thirsty, but the doctor wants him to drink plenty of liquids. It's your turn to try to cajole him into following the doctor's orders." Heinie winked at them as he grabbed his hat and turned to go.

"How are you really feeling?" Gracie asked when she heard Heinie go out into the hallway. She placed a hand on Ley's forehead to make sure it still felt normal and ran her fingers through his hair before remembering she was supposed to act professionally now that they were alone.

Ley closed his eyes. "I feel exhausted and dirty. If I lie perfectly still, the hole in my side is a dull ache, but if I move, it turns into something significantly worse."

"Should I let you sleep?"

"In a while. Have you had contact with headquarters since I was shot?"

"This morning. That's why I left," she said.

"Any news?"

"Yes, but it's still encrypted. And someone here in Rome asked me to give you a message. He said Marcello made it south, but the other two friends died in the Ardeatina caves."

Ley's eyes snapped open. "Who told you that?"

"He didn't tell me his name. He was taller than me by a few inches, medium build, dark hair. Italian. Expressive eyebrows. He was with someone called Dino. And he knew your real name and that you have a different blood type than Adalard's."

Ley frowned. "Giovanni. That means his brother and Roberto were executed in the caves."

"His brother?" Maybe that explained why he'd been so brusque. "How does he know your real name? And your real blood type?"

"He was there the night I became Adalard. So were Marcello and Roberto." Ley was quiet for a while, and gradually his eyes closed, and Gracie thought he'd gone back to sleep. "How did Giovanni know he could talk to you?"

"His friend bribed one of the hotel guards for information about your girlfriend. He recognized my birthmark. Cursed thing."

Ley opened his eyes and smiled lazily as he raised his hand to her face. His fingers caressed her hairline, and his thumb moved on, then off her birthmark. "I think I'd miss your birthmark if you didn't have it."

"That's the most ridiculous thing anyone's ever said to me."

His smile deepened. "No, I like it."

She couldn't figure out why he or anyone else would like her birthmark. She suddenly wanted to kiss him, really kiss him, but that would probably involve enough movement to aggravate his injury, and she wasn't supposed to be in love with him.

"Surely I'm not the first person to admire it."

"My dad called it an angel kiss, but that's different. He started calling it that before I knew it was there, so it doesn't really count."

"He'd be proud of what you've done here. Too bad you'll never be able to tell him. I'm sure it will all be classified."

Gracie felt a catch in her throat, and she shook her head.

"You don't think he'd be proud of you?"

"My father had a stroke. Two days before I found out Michael's submarine was missing. He doesn't recognize me anymore."

Ley put his hand over hers. "I'm sorry."

Gracie tried to blink away her tears, remembering the horrible wait in the hospital and then sitting by her father's bed and having him look past her, seeing her but not knowing her. He hadn't known her sisters or her nephews either and had barely responded to his wife.

Ley continued, his voice soft. "So you lost the two most important people in your life all within a few days?"

Gracie nodded. "Someone asked if I was interested in special government work a couple weeks later. I couldn't stand staying in Salt Lake with my dad there but gone and my wedding dress hanging in the closet. I told myself I wasn't a coward because I was going to do something important, but really, I was running away."

"A coward wouldn't run away to fight a war."

Gracie stared at Ley's blanket, thinking of how she'd tried to stay busy in Salt Lake so she wouldn't notice the loneliness, so she could focus on something other than grief. Aggressive cooking and cleaning hadn't worked, but her OSS training had given her something to occupy her intellect and had provided her with new challenges. Winning the war had become a new, absorbing goal, as had her desire to prove she was capable of the demanding task she'd jumped into. "I might have done the right thing, but I did it for the wrong reason."

"Few people have perfect motives." Ley's vibrant blue eyes stared up at her. "But doing the right thing, even for the wrong reason, is a good start."

"How do you do that?" Gracie asked.

Ley's brow wrinkled in confusion. "Do what?"

"Make everything seem better. You did it last Friday with Heinie, and you're doing it now with me."

"What day is it?"

"Tuesday."

He frowned. "The last few days have all run together." He felt his chin. "I need to shave."

Gracie fingered his six-day stubble. "I shaved my dad's face for him after his stroke. I can give you a shave, if you'd like." She moved her fingers up to his hair. "And wash your hair."

"In bed?"

Gracie shrugged. "There are plenty of extra towels in the bathroom."

He nodded his permission, and she went to gather his shaving supplies. She thought of the last time she'd shaved her dad. The eyes that had always smiled at her had been unfocused and vacant. The voice that had always been encouraging had been unfamiliar and broken. Gracie took a minute to compose herself before returning to Ley. It was time to replace her old memories with new ones.

"You know, it's not everyone I trust with a razor on my neck," he said as she sat next to him on the bed.

She ran her hand along his face and then coated it with shaving cream. "If you don't talk while I shave, I'm less likely to nick you."

"Sorry."

Gracie waited for him to relax his grin before she began, gently running the razor through the stubble and foam. His eyes flickered from her hands to her face. "Nervous?" she asked.

He waited until she cleaned the razor to answer. "No. I've seen you transmit. You have steady fingers. I'm just admiring the view."

She laughed, then focused on his skin, trying not to meet his eyes because every time she did, she had to suppress laughter at the mirth she saw there. When she finished she wiped his face and neck with a clean towel and cupped his smooth cheek in her hand.

Ley felt the result with his fingers. "A beauty, a talented radio operator, and a good barber? I'm lucky to have you."

Gracie felt herself blushing. Her mother might never have called her a beauty, but she knew Ley meant what he said. "You're just trying to butter me up so I use warm water when I wash your hair."

"Is it working?"

She wiped at a spot of shaving cream she'd missed next to his ear. "The water will be the perfect temperature." She stood to take his things back to the bathroom and get more towels.

"Concetta?"

She turned back to him.

"I'm not trying to flatter you. I just thought if your father can't be your champion anymore, maybe I should step in. Someone needs to tell you how wonderful you are."

His face was serious, sincere, his guard still down from his illness. He meant what he said, and she didn't think she could have a better champion.

CHAPTER THIRTY-SEVEN

The rest of March and all of April fell into a routine. Bastien slowly got better over his long convalescence leave, and Gracie was there every time he needed to eat, every time he needed help dressing, every time he needed help to the bathroom. And she was there when he needed to talk, even if it was the middle of the night.

Heinie stopped by most days, but usually it was just Bastien and Gracie, and it had gradually become easier for him to open up to her. They talked about the news from the front, about the bread riots taking place all over Rome, about the massive roundups for forced labor, and about their families. Bastien hadn't talked about his family with anyone since arriving in Europe, but it felt natural to share everything with Gracie. *Almost everything.*

She left at least once a week to meet her other contact and send in his report, but Bastien didn't ask for details. Some days they borrowed Heinie's chess set; other days Bastien drew maps of the front line—or at least the front line as he remembered it.

It was discouraging to be stuck in his hotel room, unable to work. Gracie seemed to sense when his cabin fever was building to the boiling point, and she usually suggested some sort of distraction, but none of the crossword puzzles they found presented much of a challenge, and he could only lose so many chess games before that too grew old.

Gracie handled all the meals, usually picking something up from the hotel cook. Bastien could tell things were getting worse for the German Army as the quality of food gradually deteriorated.

"It's still better than what most civilians get," Gracie said.

"Probably better than what most of Fifth Army is eating too."

Bastien had known Gracie was brilliant when it came to codes and wireless operation, but he was surprised by how gentle and patient she was as he convalesced, even when he grew frustrated with his slow progress. He was even more surprised by how natural it felt to see her every morning and every evening and most hours in between. On the few days when he woke before she did, he'd stand in the doorway to his bedroom and watch her sleep on the couch and wonder why it felt so normal to be sharing his suite with her. And sometimes he'd catch himself thinking about the possibility of sharing his life with her.

On the first day of May, he felt well enough to shave his face in the bathroom rather than having Gracie bring his things to the bed.

She examined the results when he finished. "Maybe I need more practice. I don't think I ever got it this smooth." Her fingers lingered on his face, and he mirrored her gesture, running one hand through her hair and the other along her chin. They were already close to one another, but he leaned closer, then caught himself the instant before he kissed her. He let his hands fall to her shoulders as he straightened and pulled away. She seemed disappointed that he'd stopped, and he felt a stab of guilt that he'd hurt her feelings and a realization that he'd completely lost his focus. *It's time to get on with your mission. You didn't come to Rome to fall in love with Gracie.*

She looked at the floor. "Maybe I should go back to my apartment now."

He didn't want her to leave but knew she should. "I don't really need a nurse anymore."

She didn't immediately move to get her things, but when she did, it was as if she was moving in slow motion. "I'll check on you tomorrow."

"Thank you." The words seemed inadequate—she'd done everything she could to help him for more than a month—but he wasn't sure he was ready to say *I love you*, and even if he was, he couldn't say something like that in Rome.

She slung a bag over her shoulder and ran her fingers along his face again. He closed his eyes, savoring her touch, her nearness. He wanted to ask her to stay, wanted to wrap his arms around her and kiss her, but he'd already let things go too far.

When she left, the room felt empty. *That's how it's supposed to feel*, he reminded himself. He was supposed to be alone. He was supposed to be concentrating on his mission. He wasn't supposed to be letting a good little Mormon girl become the most important thing in his life.

* * *

The bed in Gracie's new flat was far more comfortable than the couch in Ley's hotel suite, but she had trouble sleeping. Ley could walk by himself now and stand long enough to shave, but he was still feeble. What if he needed her while she was away?

She tried to use her new kitchen as a way to pass the time, but most days, she spent hours waiting in line and rarely ended up with more than pane nero, so there was nothing to cook. Some days, if it wasn't for her visit with Ley, there wouldn't be anything to eat at all.

Gracie had been lonely before, but the first few weeks after she left Ley's suite felt far worse than any of the other twelve weeks that had passed since meeting him. She still had a key to his suite, so she let herself in each day when she came to visit. The need for kissing in the hallway had passed, and she longed for physical contact again.

The second Friday in May, Gracie had a meeting with Angelo.

"Have you heard the news?" he asked when they met in the center of a plaza an hour before curfew.

"What news?"

Angelo grinned. "The British crossed the Rapido River yesterday."

"They did?" Gracie's heart beat a little faster. The Rapido was so tiny that it only appeared on the most detailed of maps, but it had been one more obstacle near Monte Cassino blocking half the Allies from crossing the Gustav Line. The other half was still trapped on the beachhead near Anzio.

Angelo nodded. "Maybe they'll show up here before too long."

Please let them make it to Rome soon, Gracie thought. *I don't care which group gets here, but please let them come quickly.*

Angelo slipped her his report, then took her hand and studied her as they strolled through the plaza. "Are you getting enough to eat?"

Gracie gave a short laugh. "Is anyone in Rome getting enough to eat?"

"Doubtful. Maybe German officers and a few of their favorite collaborators." He paused, glancing at her face. "I guess I expected you to be happier about the news."

"I am happy."

"You don't look it."

Gracie sighed. "It's been a rough week."

"Do you want to talk about it?" Angelo asked.

Gracie shook her head. *I should be happier*, she thought. But an hour a day wasn't enough time with Ley, not when she'd grown used to being near him constantly. Other than her loneliness and worry about getting caught, there wasn't anything she could pinpoint as a problem. At least she had Angelo for a few minutes to break up the time until she could visit Ley again. She looked at Angelo more carefully. He seemed skinnier than she remembered, and there was less of a bounce in his step. "Are you all right?"

"I've been worried since the Via Rasella. I feel like half of Rome is searching for me and the other half is judging me." He frowned. "The reprisal was harsh. Just about everyone knows someone who's disappeared, and they wonder if maybe their son or their uncle died in the caves. But I'm not going to let the Nazis win, no matter what they do to us."

Gracie nodded. If the Allied Armies were finally gaining momentum, the Gappisti were more important than ever. But that didn't make the deaths in the Ardeatina caves any less tragic.

Angelo's steady stride skipped a pace. "Let's cross the street. I'd bet my Beretta those two men are some type of plainclothes police."

Gracie followed Angelo, sneaking a glance at the two men walking toward them with squared shoulders and steady gaits. *Definitely police or military.* Gracie glanced over her shoulder and saw another pair of men. "There's another group behind us."

Angelo swore under his breath. "We'll see if we can lose them in that apartment building."

Gracie realized she'd tightened her grip on Angelo's hand, and she forced herself to relax. The building ahead was a large one, and there would be scores of rooms to hide in and probably several exits. Then she looked ahead of her and gasped. "Is that who I think it is?"

"Yes," Angelo whispered. It was the man who'd chased them the day they'd met by the pyramid, the one Angelo had gunned down as they'd escaped. They were surrounded.

"Let's try the side entrance." Angelo pulled her into a narrow side street, and they ran to a door. It was locked. Angelo picked up a damaged brick lying in the gutter and broke out the glass in a nearby window. As he ran the brick along the windowsill to dislodge the remaining shards, three of the men who'd been following them turned into the alley.

The window was three feet off the ground. Angelo nimbly climbed through, and Gracie tried to follow. It shouldn't have been difficult, but she couldn't find a handhold that wasn't covered in broken glass. *You can choose glass in your fingers or bullets in your back.*

"Halt!" one of the men shouted. As Angelo pulled Gracie the rest of the way through the window, she looked back. All three men were armed with handguns.

"Come on!" Angelo ran through the room they'd entered—somebody's living room—and opened a door leading to a hallway. Gracie ignored the stinging in her hands as she followed Angelo down the corridor and up three flights of stairs. The Italian shouts of their pursuers followed them each step of the way.

"Check if any doors are unlocked," Angelo said.

They were in a long hallway with doors on either side. He reached for one on the right, and she began checking the doors on the left. The first knob she grasped was locked, and as she moved to the next one, she saw the red smear she'd left on the doorknob. The third door down was unlocked. She shoved it open, ran inside, and stopped.

A mother and three small children sat around a table, and they looked horrified that a stranger had just broken into their flat. Angelo rushed in after Gracie and closed and bolted the door behind him.

The mother stood and moved between her children and Angelo. The youngest, a little girl of about two, started crying.

Angelo took his pistol from his jacket pocket. "Keep her quiet. Take them into a bedroom."

The woman didn't move, and another child, a boy not much older than his sister, joined the crying.

"Now!" Angelo said. He kept his pistol pointed at the family and one ear against the door. The men following them couldn't be far behind.

The mother glared at Gracie and took her children into another room.

"We can't stay here," Gracie said. The furniture was worn, and the four chairs around the table were mismatched, two of them with obvious repairs. The meal at the center of the table was barely sufficient for one, but it was divided into four parts.

"Why not?"

"What if one of the children gets hurt?"

"I'm not going to hurt them," Angelo said. "If the Fascists do, let it be on their conscience."

Gracie knew if anything happened to the family, it would also be on her conscience. She glanced at her hands. They were smeared in blood, and she could see about a dozen cuts of varying sizes. "I left blood on all the door-knobs. They'll know we're here because the next doorknob will be clean."

Angelo glanced at her hands. He grabbed a pair of threadbare cloth napkins from the table and quickly bandaged her palms. He took a piece of bread off the table when he was finished and bit into it as he jogged to the balcony.

Gracie followed Angelo outside. Each apartment had a balcony with a low wall, and only a few feet separated each one from its neighbor. Down below, the street was emptying as curfew approached.

"We'll go down one floor, then through an apartment, and we'll be on a different level than where they expect us."

Gracie looked at Angelo's suggested path and felt her head spin. The balcony walls were smooth concrete, and they were spaced far enough apart that anyone climbing between them could fall to their death. "But there aren't any footholds."

"Can't be helped. I'll lower you down first. We better hurry."

Gracie took a deep breath, hoping it would give her courage. She'd never been scared of heights before, but she'd never attempted to climb down buildings before either. She swung one leg over the wall where the balcony attached to the building and felt her shoe slipping. Her hands were sweaty and bloody, and she worried the napkins would make it impossible for her to grip anything. Someone pounded on the apartment door, and she slid her other leg over the side. She gripped the inside of the wall with her forearms and tried to balance on the wall's outside surface with her feet. She winced when Angelo took her hands.

"Sorry." He moved his hands to her wrists. "Time to let go."

Gracie hesitated. Angelo couldn't weigh much more than she did. *I'm going to have to trust him.* She eased her forearms off the wall and felt herself falling. Angelo didn't drop her, but his face showed strain. She couldn't see how far she was from the balcony below because her face was right next to the concrete wall.

"You're about a foot from the next ledge. I'll move my grip from your wrists to your hands, but I can't lower you any more than that. You'll have to land and lean forward."

"All right." Gracie's voice trembled. Could she survive a four-story drop if she fell? *If you do survive, you'll be caught, and the end result will be about the same.* Pain shot through her hands when Angelo lowered her down.

"Ready?"

"Yes." She might not have been ready to drop, but she was ready for him to let go of her hands. He released her, and a second later, her feet hit the wall of the balcony below. *Lean forward.* It wasn't graceful, but as she tumbled into the balcony, hitting her back and then her knees, she knew it was better than being arrested and better than falling to the street below.

Gracie pushed herself to her feet and peered through the glass door into the flat. She couldn't see anyone, which was a relief. She looked back where she'd come from, expecting to see Angelo's shoes. Instead, she heard shouting and saw Angelo leap not down but across to another balcony on the same higher level. He was out of sight after that, but she heard two Italian voices, a man she assumed was one of the plainclothes police and a woman, the mother whose dinner they'd interrupted.

"They were right here," the woman's voice said. Gracie crouched in the center of the balcony, where she'd be invisible unless someone looked out from the flat the balcony was attached to.

"They can't have gone far." The male voice grew louder. "Bruno, did you see anything?"

"No." The next voice was male, and it sounded like it was coming from the street.

How did he miss me dangling from the balcony above? He must have been at a bad angle or been looking in the wrong place.

"Keep an eye out."

Bruno would see her if she stood, especially now that he was focused on this part of the building, and the man above would know to look in the bordering flats first. *Where is Angelo?* She waited for what seemed like a long time, then peeked over the balcony wall. She spotted a man in the street, but her face was in a shadow, and he didn't seem to see her. He was too far away for her to be sure, but she thought he was the one Angelo had shot almost two months ago.

CHAPTER THIRTY-EIGHT

GRACIE COULDN'T STAY WHERE SHE WAS. She reached for the latch, planning to go through the flat, when she heard a soft call.

"Concetta?" The voice came from the balcony diagonally above her. "Meet me here." Angelo pointed to the balcony directly below him.

She stared. Only two feet separated each terrace, but she still couldn't get over the long drop down, and there was a man on the street watching for them. *Just one long step*, she told herself. *From one narrow concrete ledge to the next.*

"Hurry," Angelo whispered. "I can hear them in the hallway, and I need your help to get down."

Gracie climbed onto the ledge and tried to ignore the sudden fear that gripped her. *Don't look*, she told herself. *This isn't any worse than when Angelo lowered you down.* Still partially crouched over so she'd be harder to spot, she extended her left leg and shifted her weight forward. Her back leg slipped at the awkward angle, but she managed to tumble into the next balcony.

Seconds later, she saw Angelo's feet dangling from the balcony above. "Pull me in," he said.

She grabbed his leg, then his belt and did her best to keep him from falling backward. He hit the concrete floor hard, but she reached out just in time to keep his head from cracking into the ledge.

"Stop!" a voice from the street shouted. "Down one floor, over two units."

The search must have moved from the mother's apartment to the left while Angelo had jumped to the right.

Gracie yanked open the door and almost ran into the flat's occupant, an aged lady armed with a broomstick.

"Get out of here!" she yelled.

Gracie quickly obeyed, and Angelo stayed on her heels. They ran into the hallway again as noise from the search party sounded in the stairwell.

"Psst."

The sound came from behind her. Gracie turned and saw a wrinkled hand motioning to them from a doorway a few units away. Gracie met Angelo's eyes, and he nodded. They didn't have many options now, so they'd have to trust a stranger. They sprinted for the door, and their unknown benefactor ushered them inside.

The apartment was just as rundown as the others, but the large man who'd saved them seemed less downtrodden than either of the women. He shut the door softly, put a finger to his lips, and pressed his ear to the door.

"How many are chasing you?" he asked.

"Five," Gracie said. "But at least one is outside still."

"They'll probably search each flat, and I don't have anywhere to hide you. If you take the stairwell at the end of the hallway and go to the basement, someone there will be able to help you."

Gracie nodded. She looked at Angelo, and he too seemed willing to follow the man's instructions.

The old man scratched his chin. "We have to hope they all search flats at the same time and don't leave anyone in the hall."

The wait was tense. Gracie was sure both men could hear her heart pounding. *Angelo looks just as nervous as you feel,* she told herself. After a few minutes, the sounds from the hallway grew quiet. The resident softly cracked the door and slowly stuck his head out. He glanced both ways, then motioned them forward and pointed toward the stairwell.

"Good luck," he whispered.

"Thank you," Gracie said.

The man winked at her before returning to his flat.

They had to pass several doors before they reached the stairwell, and as Gracie grasped the lever, one of the Italian plainclothes finished his search and spotted them. Angelo drew his Beretta and fired. Gracie saw the man drop.

"Hurry. They'll all be after us now," Angelo said.

Gracie sprinted down the stairs to the ground floor, and then Angelo caught her by the shoulder and motioned for her to slow. He put a finger over his lips. Someone above burst into the stairwell, and as the rattle of his footsteps echoed through the passage, Angelo and Gracie tiptoed to the basement.

Please don't let the door squeak, Gracie prayed when they reached the basement. She could still hear their pursuer, but he seemed to be stopping at each floor to check if they'd run into the hallway. Angelo cracked the door open, and to Gracie's relief, it didn't make a sound.

She stepped inside, and Angelo closed the door softly. A single dim lightbulb lit a long, dusty corridor lined with mechanical closets.

"Where do we hide?" she whispered.

"He said there would be *someone* to help us." Angelo walked ahead of her and stopped at the first full-sized door they saw. He raised his hand to knock, then looked back at Gracie for confirmation. She nodded.

Gracie heard a shuffling behind the door before a short, balding man opened it.

"Can you hide us?" Gracie asked.

"A man on the third floor sent us," Angelo added.

"My chess partner, no doubt." The man stepped back so they could come inside. "I'm the building's caretaker." He smiled, then let out half a laugh. "And caretaker for any of the Gappisti friends he sends my way." He led them into his living room, past the kitchen, and through a bedroom. He pointed to a short bookcase. "Help me move this."

Angelo stepped forward and helped slide the bookcase to the side. Behind it was a recessed alcove no bigger than a normal bed.

"They'll probably search every flat. I'll let you out when they've finished."

"Thank you," Gracie said.

"Go ahead." Angelo motioned her inside.

The room was only four feet high, so she ducked and crept forward before sitting on the hard concrete floor. Angelo climbed in beside her, and the caretaker slid the bookcase in front of them, enveloping the two fugitives in darkness.

"I feel like I'm in a tomb," Angelo whispered into the black silence.

Gracie was simply glad they hadn't been forced to hide in the catacombs. "Do you think they'll find us?"

"I still have a mostly full clip if they do."

The niche was so small that their shoulders and hips touched. Angelo took her hand and gave it a squeeze. He'd probably meant to comfort her, but she gasped out loud as pain shot through her hands.

"I'm sorry," Angelo said. "I forgot. Are they still bleeding?"

Now that they weren't running, the throbbing in her hands was just about all she could concentrate on, but she couldn't see them in the dark. "I can't tell."

"I'm sorry," he said again.

"Did you get any cuts?"

"No, I had the brick in one hand, and the other never touched the window. I'm sorry I didn't think to offer it to you."

"Well, we didn't have much time to think, did we?"

Angelo put an arm around her shoulder. "There, is this more comfortable?"

His arm was warmer and softer than the wall. "For now," she said.

Time dragged on, and they didn't dare speak above a whisper. They both grew restless, and it was hard to find positions that didn't quickly grow uncomfortable. Gracie shivered in the cold, but the coolness of the walls and floor eased some of the pain in her hands when she rested them against the hard surface.

Eventually, someone came to search. Gracie was afraid to breathe as she heard muffled voices from the other side of the bookcase. Then it was quiet again. She drifted off to sleep for a while—she wasn't sure how long—and when she woke, she had a kink in her neck. Angelo had fallen asleep too, leaning on her shoulder. She couldn't see him, but the slow, steady rhythm of his breathing convinced her he was dozing.

CHAPTER THIRTY-NINE

GRACIE FELT LIKE THEY'D BEEN hiding for hours, maybe all night. Her hands still ached, and she hadn't eaten since breakfast. Finally, a crack of light appeared, then widened. She blinked at the sudden brightness, and Angelo woke and straightened.

"The last of them have gone," the caretaker said.

"What time is it?" Gracie asked.

"Almost three."

They'd been hiding for close to nine hours. She wasn't sure how much of that time had been spent sleeping and how much had been spent staring into the darkness, but she guessed she'd been awake for most of it.

She felt stiff as she crawled into the bedroom. "Thank you for hiding us."

He smiled at her. "You should be fine using any of the ground-floor exits. Just watch for patrols."

Gracie asked to use the bathroom before they left. The lighting was so poor she could barely make out the cuts, and it hurt when she tried to peel away the napkins, so she put off cleaning her hands until she could see better. She left the basement with Angelo and stepped carefully up the stairs, trying to stay silent. She held back a yawn, wishing she was already home so she could wash and slip into bed.

"Let's use the back exit," Angelo said.

Gracie nodded her agreement. If there were patrols out, she thought they'd be on the main road.

As they left, a wave of cool, fresh air helped Gracie drive the lingering fogginess from her head. The waning moonlight reflected off marble and stucco, and Gracie sighed with relief that the evening's ordeal was finally over.

"Which way are you headed?" Angelo asked.

"North."

"So am I." He smiled, letting his guard down as they crossed a street, moving away from the building they'd hid in. "What a night."

A crack sounded, and the window to their right shattered. Gracie spun to the left and locked eyes with the Italian man, Bruno. Then she glanced at his pistol and ran.

Angelo kept pace with her, and Bruno fired another three shots, but he didn't hit either of them. When a second man stepped from the shadows and blocked their path, Gracie suspected Bruno hadn't been trying to hit them. He'd simply been driving them toward his partner.

Angelo yanked on Gracie's arm and pulled her into the recessed doorway of a bakery. He took out his pistol and fired at the nearest man, then shot the lock out of the store's doorknob. "Inside!"

Gracie rushed through the front of the bakery, heading for the back room, where she hoped she'd find another exit. The smell made her stomach rumble, but she knew Bruno wasn't far behind them, and perhaps some of his friends too.

"Here." Angelo handed her the pistol and reached for the padlock on the back door.

Gracie suspected most bakeries had large stocks of ingredients in their storerooms, but not this one. Rome was starving, and the shelves were bare. She spotted a key hanging on a nail behind an empty flour bin and reached for it as the door from the front of the bakery crashed open.

Bruno barged into the room and aimed his pistol at her, so she immediately lifted the weapon she held in response. She pulled the trigger and gasped as the man fell. Angelo quickly kicked the man over and confirmed the truth: Gracie had just killed a man.

"Nice shot," Angelo said.

Gracie could barely breathe as she stared at the corpse. She'd shot him in the neck, and his blood was all over the floor and on two of the walls. It was horrifying, but for some reason, she couldn't pull her eyes away. Bruno had been alive not three seconds earlier. Gracie's hands started to shake.

Angelo took the pistol from her and slipped it into her pocket. "Hide that." He rearmed himself with Bruno's pistol and searched through the dead man's pockets, finding an extra clip of ammunition and Bruno's OVRA ID. "Fascist secret police. That's what I thought. Let's get out of here."

They left the building the back way to avoid more of Bruno's friends. Gracie tried not to think about what had just happened. She had to focus on getting away, had to exercise caution with each street they crossed, checking for patrols and avoiding the moonlit patches of road. After a few blocks, Angelo guided her into an alley and paused, listening for the sounds of anyone following them.

They were close, their bodies touching. She could feel his heart beating and the flow of blood rushing past her ears. She felt physically ill but didn't know if it was because her body was out of adrenaline or because she was having a difficult time wrapping her brain around the fact that she'd just ended someone's life. Was the man she'd killed married? Did he have children waiting for him to come home? *What have I done?*

Angelo's hands gripped her shoulders. "Are you all right, Concetta?"

"I . . . I don't know."

One of his hands slipped to her chin, and he lifted her face into the moonlight. "You're trembling."

"Well I . . . I just . . . I just killed someone."

Angelo's lips pulled into a smile. "He was a pest. You don't need to feel any more remorse for killing him than you'd feel for exterminating a rat."

"But how do you know that? It's not like you talked to him. What if he was a good person?" Gracie could feel sweat beading along her forehead and the back of her neck, and she was starting to feel lightheaded.

"Don't worry about him," Angelo said. "He was trying to shoot us, remember?"

Gracie nodded, but the queasy feeling in her stomach was getting worse.

"You did well tonight," he whispered. Then he pulled her closer and kissed her mouth. She was used to being kissed, but Angelo's move was an unwanted surprise. He was kissing her too hard; he was holding her too tightly. And she still felt ill. She pulled away, but it took a few seconds for her to fully extricate herself.

"What's wrong?" he asked as his fingers found her face and ran into her hair.

"I'm sorry. Now's not a good time. I'm not feeling well."

His face hardened into a frown. "You're overreacting."

Gracie could feel herself shaking again.

Angelo's face softened. "Look, people are dying in Rome every day. But what's rare is almost getting caught like that and surviving. We've been given a second chance at life—or maybe it's a third or fourth chance—and we should celebrate. My place isn't too far away. Come back with me. I'll help you forget about what happened." He kissed her again, a brief but suggestive invitation.

Gracie shook her head, trying to clear away her confusion and the massive headache that was building behind her forehead. "I'm supposed to meet another contact this morning. I don't want to miss his information, and it's a long walk."

Angelo ran his fingers along her jaw, then down her neck, stopping when he reached her blouse and hooking onto the fabric, following the neckline across her collarbone and up to her shoulder. Gracie would have pulled away, but she was standing against a wall. "Maybe you should meet him another time."

Gracie shook her head again. "No, I have to go," she lied. Ley wasn't back at work yet, so he wouldn't have any information for her, but she suddenly needed to see him again more than anything.

Angelo leaned toward her again. Gracie turned her face so his lips brushed her cheek rather than her mouth. He shook his head and walked away. After a few yards, his steps slowed, and he turned back. "I'm sorry, Concetta. You've had a hard night, and I haven't been very understanding." He took a few steps toward her. "Don't worry about what happened in the bakery, all right? I'll see you next week. I wrote the address on my report." He pointed to her pocket, where she'd stored his report hours ago, before turning around again and leaving.

Gracie walked three blocks and then vomited into the gutter. She stayed on her knees for a while, catching her breath, then crept through the dark streets, wondering if she should return to her own apartment. But she was closer to Ley's room than hers, and her desire to see him hadn't diminished. She sneaked past a few guards and entered the hotel through the back door, stepping quietly up the stairs to his suite. She let herself in with her key and closed the door softly behind her. She didn't want to wake him, so she left the light off and felt her way to the couch.

Maybe she just needed time to think. She'd known she might have to shoot someone when she volunteered for fieldwork, but she hadn't realized how dirty she'd feel, how many doubts she'd have. Couldn't there have been some other way?

A sliver of light appeared under the bedroom door, as if someone had just switched on a lamp. Not long after, Ley opened his door.

"I thought I heard someone come in," he said. "Are you all right?"

Gracie opened her mouth but wasn't sure what to say, so she just shrugged her shoulders.

Ley walked across the room, slowly, with one hand over his injured abdomen, as if bracing it. Only half the buttons on his shirt were fastened, and it wasn't tucked into his trousers. His feet were bare. He lowered himself onto the couch next to her and turned to study her face. "What's wrong?"

Gracie hesitated, but when she met his eyes, full of concern, partially lit by light from the other room, it tumbled from her mouth. "I killed someone."

He closed his eyes, and when he opened them again, they were more somber than before. "What happened?"

Gracie took a deep breath and blinked away warm tears. She told him what had happened, from when she rendezvoused with Angelo until Bruno had burst into the back room of the bakery. "He had his gun out, and . . . and I shot him." Gracie finished with a sob.

Ley slipped his arm around her shoulders and pulled her into an embrace.

Gracie cried harder and leaned into him, burying her face in his chest. "I keep wondering if he has a family. What if I orphaned his children or widowed his wife? What if he has a mother depending on him? What if—"

"Shh." She felt Ley's hand on her hair, felt the vibration of his voice when he continued. "Don't go there, Gracie. There's no need to beat yourself up over it."

She sobbed again. No one had consciously called her Gracie since before she'd left Switzerland. How long would this assignment last? It was turning into a nightmare.

"You've been up all night?" he asked.

She nodded into his chest. "Mostly. I dozed off a little while we were hiding."

"You'll feel better after you get some sleep."

"But what if he was a good man?"

"There are a lot of good men in the Fifth Army. Some of them are married, and some of them have children, and most of them have mothers at home praying they'll make it through the war. Your work will save some of their lives."

"I still feel awful about it." Gracie tried to calm her sobs. She was getting his shirt wet.

"I'd be surprised if you just shrugged it off. What you're doing here isn't easy. But it is important, and you're doing a good job."

She listened to his words, but she wasn't convinced. It had taken her a long time to adapt to life in the field, and she'd made far too many mistakes.

As if he sensed her lingering doubts, Ley sighed and continued. "Have you ever heard of Ehud?"

"Who?"

"Ehud, from the Book of Judges?"

"No." Gracie was embarrassed that she hadn't. Of the two of them, she was supposed to be the more religious one, but she'd always preferred the New Testament or Book of Mormon over the Old Testament. They were easier to read, the stories and teachings easier for her to understand.

"What about Nephi, from the Book of Mormon?"

"How do you know about Nephi?" she asked.

"That doesn't matter. What matters is if you've heard of him. I assume you have?"

"Of course I know who Nephi is. Except there was more than one." She felt Ley shift underneath her, and she lifted her head to look at him, studying his stubble in the dim light.

"The first one. You remember the story, how he had to kill Laban?"

"Yes."

"And you remember why?"

Gracie nodded. "There were a couple reasons. Laban wouldn't give them the records they needed, and he was threatening to kill them."

"It was for the greater good. And so was what happened this morning with the police officer you shot. At least he was sober—he had a fighting chance. I imagine Nephi had to second-guess himself a little too, so you're in good company if you're uneasy about it."

Gracie wiped at her tears with the back of her hand.

Ley gently took her wrists and turned her hands palms up. "What did you do to your hands?"

CHAPTER FORTY

GRACIE'S HANDS WERE STILL WRAPPED in napkins, stained now with blood and dirt. "Just some glass. I had to crawl through a broken window."

Ley untied one of the napkins, but she flinched when he started pulling the cloth away from the scabs. He stood, wincing as he walked, and turned on the light over the table. "Come over here. We'll soak them off."

He grabbed a bowl and filled it with water, then set it on the table. Gracie sat down and put her hands in the bowl. The water stung at first, but the coolness was refreshing.

"How brave are you feeling this morning?" Ley held up the bottle of liquor. It didn't look like anyone had touched it since she gave some to the doctor. "This or soap. They'll both hurt, but I think this is more likely to kill off anything septic."

Gracie peeled away the napkins. "I can't get an infection. I need my hands to send in reports." Ley dumped the water out of the bowl and replaced it with alcohol. She gritted her teeth and put her palms into the shallow layer of smelly liquid. It bit sharply into her skin, but she made herself count to ten before she took her hands out.

Ley sat across from her and looked at her palms. "You've still got some glass in there. I'll get my tweezers."

"Let me get them. It hurts you to walk, doesn't it?"

"Not any more than it hurts you to use your hands."

He was up before she could protest. She didn't want to be a burden, but it was nice to have someone take care of her for a few minutes, especially after what she'd been through that night. Ley came back with the tweezers and studied each scratch. He took shards of glass from three of them. Her hands were sore, and the slivers were painful, but his touch was comforting. She liked watching him work, watching him concentrate, and she hoped his gentle care was a sign of affection that went beyond friendship.

He put new bandages on the cuts that still oozed blood, then released her hands. "Why don't you get some sleep?" he whispered. "Everything seems a little worse when you're tired."

Gracie smiled, not sure if Ley meant people in general or Gracie in particular. He was right about her though. She needed sleep.

"You can take the bed. I need to be up soon anyway."

"Aren't you still on sick leave?" Gracie asked.

"I'm going back today."

Gracie remembered the way he'd walked across the room, like he was in pain. "But you're still recovering. Don't you think you should take a little more time?"

Ley looked at his hands. "I'm not doing much to win the war while I'm sitting around here."

"But you aren't healthy yet. What if you make it worse or let something slip because you aren't at your best?"

He rubbed the scar tissue on his right hand with his left fingers. "I didn't come to Italy to sit around in a hotel room all day."

She stared at his hands, remembering how he'd gotten those scars and what might be motivating Ley to get back to work before he could walk across the room without wincing. "How long are you going to beat yourself up over something that happened when you were nine? Winning the war won't bring Hans back."

"I couldn't save Hans, but I can still help Lukas."

"But what about you? Are you ever going to do what's best for you?"

"I promised my father I'd take care of my family. I can't break that trust."

Gracie studied his face, but she couldn't detect any emotion except the firmness of purpose she was so used to seeing there. "You have taken care of your family. You got them out of Germany, and you made sure they had food to eat and a house to live in. You've spent years putting their needs ahead of your own. Your father can't have meant for you to give up your own life when he asked you to look after everyone else."

Ley looked away. Eventually, he got to his feet and went over to his couch. "You've had a long night, Gracie. You should go to bed now."

When she saw the way his face was pinched with pain, she decided right then wasn't the best time to continue their conversation. She didn't feel sick anymore, not physically, but she hurt for Ley. It didn't seem fair that he always thought of others first. If his father was anything like him, he couldn't have meant to extract a promise that would keep his son in perpetual obligation. "I'm sorry," she whispered.

He met her eyes for an instant and then looked away again. "You haven't done or said anything you need to apologize for."

Despite his words, she could tell she'd hurt him, somehow, without intending to. As she crawled into his bed, she tried to think of what she could say to help. But she was exhausted and quickly drifted to sleep, surrounded by the smell of Ley's soap.

* * *

Bastien stretched out on the couch, but he couldn't sleep. A little before six in the morning, he checked on Gracie, opening the door softly so he wouldn't disturb her. She didn't stir. She still looked the same, but he knew she had lost something that night, part of her innocence. He grieved for her loss and was grateful he hadn't been the one to hand her the pistol. *Please help her, Lord. And help me help my brother.*

He returned to the couch and thought back to that night in 1936 and the knock on the door that had changed his life and set him on the road to lost innocence. Two Gestapo agents had burst into his family's apartment and arrested Bastien's father, claiming he'd written editorials critical of Hitler's government and published them in Swiss newspapers. The claims had proven true, and his father's pseudonym hadn't been enough to protect him.

The next year had been a melancholy limbo. When Bastien's brother Lukas wasn't at school or sleeping, he would sit in their apartment's entryway and stare into space, as if waiting for his father to walk through the door and come back to the family. Bastien's two sisters had always filled the house with laughter and music, but the Ley household had turned quiet, except sometimes when Bastien couldn't sleep and he'd hear his mother crying.

Bastien and his mother had spent countless hours waiting in lines to see government officials, asking about the fate of Friedrich Ley. No one would give them details. Twelve months passed before one of Friedrich's business partners learned that he had been sent to Sachsenhausen, where he'd died of typhus. Constantly at the front of Bastien's mind were the final words his father had spoken to him the night he was arrested. "Take care of the family, Bastien."

A knock on the door startled Bastien out of his memory. He looked at the clock. Heinie had offered to drive with him today in case Bastien's strength started to wane. It was time for Bastien to get on with his mission. He had a promise to keep.

* * *

Gracie transmitted Angelo's report in the morning, along with answers to all the questions Caserta had sent in their previous message to confirm she wasn't compromised. She spent the rest of the day trying to forget what she'd done to the Italian police officer and trying not to worry about Ley. He'd been gone when she woke, and she wondered how he was managing his first day back at work and how she could help him when he seemed so intent on sacrificing everything he wanted for the chance to help his family.

She let herself into his hotel room late that afternoon and found him sitting on his couch. His face looked pale and unhealthy, and she wondered if she'd interrupted a nap.

"Are you all right?" she asked.

"Just tired."

Gracie sat next to him. He pulled a folded paper from his pocket and handed it to her. "My first report since that night with Ostheim."

Gracie read through the details. "You've had a busy day."

When he didn't respond, she put the report down and looked at him. His head was resting on the back of the couch, and in the minute she'd taken to study his report, he'd fallen asleep.

She liked the way his face relaxed when he slept. Her eyes focused on his lips. They looked ordinary, maybe even on the small side, but there was nothing ordinary about the way she felt when he kissed her.

She went into his bedroom and retrieved a blanket. She wished she could help him the way he always managed to help her. How many OSS agents would have known to bring up the story of Nephi after she shot the Italian police officer? He had said he knew a few Mormon families, and she assumed he had heard the story from them and hoped his religious beliefs weren't as far from hers as she feared they were. As she spread the blanket across his sleeping form, she couldn't resist kissing his forehead. It woke him, and she felt her face grow warm because she'd been caught.

"Did you encode it already?" he asked with a yawn.

"No, not yet."

He lay down on the couch and was asleep again before she picked out her first transposition key.

CHAPTER FORTY-ONE

ZIMMERMAN LOOKED UP FROM HIS reports to see Möller standing in front of his desk. "What is it, Möller?"

"Do you have a minute, sir? Untersturmführer Richter in signals found something I think you'll be interested in."

It sounded more promising than reading through reports on the black market, so Zimmerman followed Möller upstairs to Richter's desk.

"You found something?" he asked.

Richter nodded. "Yes." He pulled out a chart. "This spring we started tracking a wireless operator. For four weeks straight, he'd go on the air every day, usually for about ten minutes, normally between ten and noon."

"You're sure it was one wireless operator and not several?" Zimmerman asked.

"Yes. You can recognize operators if you listen to them often enough. The length of time they wait between keystrokes, the way certain letters are tapped out. This one's very precise. Quick, but he has a steady hand. Easy to pick out the letters."

"You've read the messages?"

"No." Richter frowned. "No one's broken the code."

"Hmm. So you know he's talking, but you don't know what he's saying. Do you know where he is?"

Richter pulled out a map of Rome, and Zimmerman studied the myriad of circles and annotations. "I started listening for him the beginning of March, tracked the areas he was transmitting from."

"Spread all over central Rome."

"Yes. Unfortunately, he likes to move around. Makes it harder to catch him. Then toward the end of March, he went off the air."

"Did we arrest any wireless operators then?" Zimmerman asked. That was about the time he'd caught a few Gappisti members, but he didn't think any of them could use a radio.

"Not that we know of. I heard him again a few times through April and the first part of May. Then this week. Back on the air every day."

"Can you catch him?"

Richter shrugged. "I've been trying since March. If I can get more manpower, and if I can get him to stay on the air long enough, I might be able to triangulate his position. It doesn't even have to be an exact triangulation. Most wireless sets can be disguised, but they're too big to hide completely. If we get close enough and search everyone with a package, a suitcase, or an overcoat, we might get lucky."

"I could help with the manpower," Zimmerman said. "But how will you keep him on the air long enough to track him?"

"Oh, I know a few tricks." Richter pointed to the map again. "Neighborhoods he's used before. He's got a long list, but he's starting to repeat himself."

Zimmerman took his time looking over Richter's map and chart. "I'll get you the men. Enough to monitor all the locations at the right time. You catch me a wireless operator." *And then I'll make him tell me everyone he's working with.*

***

Gracie pulled the hair off her neck, sweating in the late May heat as she prepared to transmit from a stuffy attic. She pushed open the only window and felt a faint breeze. In this weather, she liked to send her reports in early, so she'd lined up for food as soon as curfew lifted. She'd waited three hours, but the bread had been gone when she reached the front of the line.

Her stomach rumbled as she strung the flimsy antenna around the room and checked all the connections on her radio. When everything was properly set, she sent her initial transmission and waited. Headquarters finally replied and said they had a message for her. She wasn't surprised—ever since Ley's injury, they'd been asking questions only she knew the answers to, trying to confirm she wasn't captured. As she waited for their transmission, the headphones suddenly filled with a high-pitched mechanical screech. She flinched and pulled the headphones away from her ears. *That was loud.*

Hesitantly, she put the headphones on again. She could make out the message from headquarters, but partway through, the screech returned. *Is someone trying to block my frequency?* She took the headphones off and listened, then crept to the small window and peered out, but nothing looked or sounded unusual on the street below.

She was tempted to leave, but Ley's report was about fortifications the Allied Armies could reach as early as this week, and it needed to be sent today. Yet if the Germans bombarded headquarters with noise on the frequency she was using, Caserta might not hear what she was sending. *I've got to try. That's why I'm in Rome.*

She tapped out her message, praying headquarters would be able to understand it. She also requested their earlier message be repeated because she'd received only part of it before the interference. When she finished, she switched from transmit back to receive, and seconds later she heard a response. There was no static, and it was easier to make out than usual, each tap loud and clear, completely opposite what had happened earlier when someone had tried to block their frequency. She scrambled for a pencil and paper and wrote what she heard: *nvhhz tvlun zbmrm vgvvm rmwvx rksvi zyovi vkvzg zglmx v*

Gracie stared at the message. Double transposition wasn't secure if there weren't at least one hundred characters. The response from headquarters was too short, and there weren't enough vowels. *Some type of substitution code?*

Gracie played with it for a while. It didn't take long to figure out that *V* was really *E*. Whoever sent the message was using the most elementary of substitution codes, where the alphabet was folded in half and *Z* replaced *A* and *Y* replaced *B*. *Lazy coder. A German cryptographer would figure it out as quickly as I did.* But when she deciphered the message, her contempt was quickly replaced by shame.

Message of May nineteen indecipherable. Repeat at once.

Gracie had never had an indecipherable and took pride in the fact that her messages were always perfectly encoded and never jumbled beyond comprehension. May nineteenth was three days ago. She'd had no report from Angelo, just from Ley, so she'd been the one who encoded it. When she remembered what Friday's message contained, horror replaced her embarrassment. *German response to the fall of Cassino.*

She'd burned the report as soon as she'd sent it, but she did her best to remember the important points. She would have to find Ley and check that she wasn't missing anything vital, but with a three-day delay, she knew she had to get as much information in as soon as possible. She did her best to reconstruct the report, then encoded it and double-checked her work as the transposition keys burned.

Gracie flipped the switch to transmit and repeated the requested information. Then she gathered up the antenna and started putting her radio away. *I've been in this attic way too long.* As she unplugged the receiver from the transmitter, she heard a disturbance on the street below. She rushed to the window and saw six or seven German soldiers running into the building.

A few coherent thoughts flew through her panicked brain. *If they're here for me, I need to leave now. If they're not here for me, I can come back for the radio later.* She grabbed her handkerchief and papers and unplugged the quartz radio crystal—the set couldn't operate on the right frequency without it—and hesitated for a moment before slipping the items into her pocket and fleeing.

She'd gone down two of the five flights of steps when she saw the soldiers again. They were spreading out, monitoring all the hallways. One of them motioned for her to stop and spoke to her in German. When she didn't respond, he called another soldier over. *Breathe normally*, she told herself. *They may be looking for me, but they don't have a physical description; they're just looking for someone with a radio, and my radio is still in the attic.*

"Do you live here?" the second soldier asked in accented Italian.

If he checked her papers, he'd see she didn't, so she answered honestly. "No."

"Then why are you here?"

"I came to visit a friend. I was hoping she'd lend me some food."

He smiled. "Any luck?"

"No, she wasn't home."

"Try Trastevere or Testaccio. I think they were handing out rice there today."

"Thank you." Gracie continued down the stairs, half expecting the soldiers to call her back, but they didn't.

Outside, another pair of soldiers stopped everyone who passed and checked their bags. They stopped her too, and she repeated her story and prayed they wouldn't find her crystal or her transposition keys. They seemed more interested in the middle-aged man with a briefcase behind her, so they let her go without a pat down.

Even though she'd escaped, Gracie felt sick. *They tracked me.* She was free, but she didn't have her radio, and without it, she was of no use to anyone. She stopped at a café with a view of the building she'd just left and stayed until she saw several of the soldiers exit with her equipment.

Knowing it was pointless to stay, Gracie returned to her old flat. It was closer, and Ley had checked it for her a few days before because a neighbor at her new apartment often met her in the hall and asked awkward questions. As she walked, her legs were shaky with fear and failure, and when she arrived, she sank onto her bed.

What am I going to do without my radio? She couldn't help Ley or the Allies if she couldn't transmit, but if she hadn't left the attic when she had, the Germans would have caught not only the radio but the crystal, the keys, and her. And she couldn't have taken the radio with her—they would have found it in their search.

The more she thought about it, the more depressed she became. Her radio was gone, and Ley's was broken. He still had it for spare parts, but it couldn't transmit on its own. Exhausted and hungry, she buried her face in the pillow and heard a crinkle. She pushed the pillow aside and found Ley's latest report. He had a staff meeting until after curfew, so she wouldn't see him tonight. She'd made a spare key for him so he could drop off his report even if she was gone. Seeing his work, she cried. He was risking his life to gather information, and she'd gone and lost her radio.

When she managed to get her emotions under control, she read his report, wondering how vital it was. At the top of the page, he'd written a warning: *Some associates trying to silence you. Be careful using your tools. Vary time of day and do not revisit past locations.*

Unfortunately, his warning had come a few hours too late.

* * *

Zimmerman paced in front of Richter's desk. "So you caught me a wireless set but no operator?"

Richter kept his eyes on his desk. "I didn't expect him to leave it behind. We searched everyone in the area—no one was carrying anything suspicious. We probably searched him."

"Are you sure you had the right location?"

"Well, yes. We got the wireless set, didn't we?"

Zimmerman stopped pacing. "Can you use the set? Pretend to be its operator? Send in false information?"

Richter frowned. "Whoever receives the reports will recognize his transmission style. I don't know that any of my men can duplicate it. And we don't have the proper code." Richter held up a piece of the wireless set. "Plus, he took the crystal—we can't get the set to the right frequency without it."

Zimmerman swore. All that work for a captured wireless set they couldn't use. *At least the flow of information to the Allies will slow.* But what Zimmerman really wanted was the operator and everyone feeding him his information.

"If by chance he finds another way to get on the air, we can try again and arrest everyone in the vicinity. I wonder if he'd fall for the same trick again . . ."

"What?" Zimmerman asked.

"That's how I got so close. With his first transmission, we figured out the neighborhood. I sent him a request to repeat a previous message. I encoded it but left it simple enough for him to figure out. It kept him on the air long enough for us to track him down."

"You think the same thing would work again?"

Richter shrugged. "Depends on who we're after. It's unlikely he has a spare wireless set anyway."

Zimmerman walked slowly down the stairs and back to his own desk. He shook his head in frustration and started looking through a list of leads for possible Jewish refugees.

* * *

Bastien was exhausted after his marathon meetings, but he was also worried about Gracie. During breakfast he'd overheard an SS untersturmführer discussing plans to track a prolific wireless operator, and although there might be other prolific wireless operators in Rome, he'd thought instantly of Gracie. She had been in Rome thirteen weeks already, and the average radio operator lasted only six. He'd left warnings at both her apartments and stopped by the Via Tasso on his way home. She hadn't been arrested, so he assumed she was fine, but he wanted to double-check. And he hadn't seen her since yesterday. He missed her.

He put a box of raisins and a chocolate bar in his pocket. They were American rations found on the black market and confiscated by another German officer. Bastien took it as a sign that the army was getting close. They weren't very impressive gifts, but he thought Gracie would like what they represented. Rome's liberation was near.

And what will Dietrich do when the Germans leave Rome?

He tried to ignore the twinge in his side and went to Gracie's first apartment. He'd checked it carefully a few days before, and since her other contact was still free, they assumed the apartment was safe. When he arrived, he knocked softly on the door before unlocking it and going inside.

It was late, so he'd half expected to find Gracie asleep, but she was sitting on her bed, fully dressed, with her knees pulled up to her chest. She watched him come in but didn't say anything.

"Are you all right?" he asked after he'd shut the door.

"I lost my radio." Her whisper sounded lifeless. She held her hand out to him, and he reached for the small object she was giving him: a square metal box with two prongs. Her radio crystal. "That's all I have left of it. I walked right into their trap."

"You didn't get my warning?"

"Not until I got back." She inhaled deeply, her breath ragged.

Bastien sat beside her and put his arm around her. "I'm sorry. I wish I'd found out sooner."

Gracie leaned into him and sighed. "I was stupid. I should have left when they started jamming me—found a different location. And the more I think about it, the more I'm sure the request I heard to repeat Friday's message was from the Gestapo, not from headquarters. It was a different code. And the signal was the strongest I've ever heard—probably being sent from a block away. I should have known." Her voice cracked. "I've got to be the most gullible radio operator who's ever lived."

"Gracie, you've been amazing here in Rome. You didn't have time to analyze everything while you were sending a report, and the Gestapo is very good at what they do. That you managed to escape and leave them with nothing but a radio they can't use is a credit to your skill."

"But what good is your information if no one ever hears it?" Her hands flared in frustration. "I've ruined your mission."

"Nonsense. If you really want your radio back, I can walk into SS headquarters and get it for you." And he would if it would make her happy.

She jerked her head around to face him. "Don't you dare. If you got caught and it was my fault, I'd never forgive myself."

"Fine. If you don't want me to get yours, you can borrow mine."

"Yours?" Gracie's brow wrinkled in confusion. "I thought yours was broken."

"The crystal is broken. The rest of the radio is fine."

Gracie shook her head. "I'm such an idiot. I should have asked what was wrong months ago. When you said it was broken, I assumed it was something bigger."

"You're not an idiot. You're a brave, brilliant woman who's been under enough stress to paralyze most other mortals." There was just enough light for him to watch her face soften into a smile. He ran his fingers through her hair and felt an overwhelming urge to kiss her. But he couldn't do that, not while they were completely alone in her dark bedroom. He slid her radio crystal into his pocket and pulled out the American rations. "Did you get much to eat today?"

"No," she whispered.

"Well, the army has to be close because these were being sold on the black market." He handed her the chocolate and raisins. She looked at the American labels and grinned. "Thank you."

"I'll bring my radio over tomorrow. Maybe I should come with you the next time you send something in."

"I'd like that. Thank you."

He brushed his fingers along her cheek, pausing at her birthmark, wishing they were somewhere other than Nazi-occupied Rome. Then he pulled his mind back to the mission. "Tell them you need to vary your transmission schedule."

Gracie nodded.

He stood to leave and turned back before he closed the door, letting her image sink into his memory. As he walked to his hotel, he knew exactly what he wanted to do: finish the mission and, when Rome was out of Nazi hands, end his charade as Adalard Dietrich and take Gracie on a real date. *Or a few dozen.* But he also knew his duty to his new country and to his family, and he had every intention of fulfilling it. He would see Gracie to safety, and then he'd carry on as Hauptmann Dietrich for as long as it was feasible, even if his role took him to Berlin.

CHAPTER FORTY-TWO

GRACIE FELT A MIX OF emotions as she walked to her meeting with Angelo the Friday after she'd lost her radio. The Americans had finally broken out of the Anzio beachhead, and the excitement on the streets was contagious. Their arrival in Rome was just a matter of time. *Not long now*, she told herself. *Then Ley and I will be done, and Angelo will be free.* She felt a stab of pain that Otavia wouldn't get to see Rome's liberation, something she'd sacrificed so much for.

But the festive atmosphere she walked through couldn't completely mask a growing worry. What would happen when the Allies arrived? Would she receive another assignment? And what about Ley? His reports had grown longer this month, full of details on how the Germans were reacting to the Allied advance. She doubted the Allies had many sources as useful as Ley, and she worried what his next assignment would be. Would Colonel Ambrose and OSS expect him to continue on as Dietrich?

Angelo surprised her, slipping out from a side street and kissing her on the cheek. "*Buongiorno*, Concetta." He put his arm around her waist and matched his pace to hers. "Beautiful day, isn't it?"

"Yes."

He grinned as he looked around to make sure no one was close enough to overhear him. "One of my friends passed by the German embassy in the Villa Wolkonsky this morning. Smoke. They're burning their papers. I guess they don't think they'll be here much longer."

Gracie felt him slip something into her pocket, and his fingers lingered on her hip. She was tempted to push his hand away, but they looked less suspicious if they acted like a couple.

"There's my report," he said. "Are you busy tonight? I found some prosciutto on the black market and real flour. You and I could celebrate

Rome's liberation a little early. Then I'm going to sabotage a few German retreat lines. We can always use an extra hand if you want to join the Gappisti."

"I can't," Gracie said. "The Gestapo almost caught me on Monday. They were tracking my signal. So now I have to transmit at different times, and I have another contact who's going to keep watch while I'm on the air in case they track me again. We have an appointment, and it's too late to change it."

"I'd be happy to stand guard for you while you use your radio."

Gracie wasn't sure how to politely decline Angelo's help. She couldn't tell him Ley was a more effective escort because he wore a German uniform, nor did she want to say anything that would suggest she trusted Ley's security more than she trusted Angelo's. "He'll have more information for me to include."

Angelo was quiet as they walked past another couple. "Is it always the same man, that contact you keep running off to?"

Gracie nodded and tried not to blush as Angelo studied her face.

"He's a lucky man. If the Germans are still here next Tuesday, I'll meet you at the flower stalls near the Spanish Steps. If they leave before that, maybe I'll see you sooner." He stopped walking and pulled her around to face him. Then he leaned closer and kissed her firmly. He was a skilled kisser, but something was missing. She felt his kiss with her mouth, but it didn't stir anything deeper than her lips, and she was overwhelmed with relief when she finally pushed him away.

Angelo looked hurt, but she didn't want any more of his kisses. Hesitantly, he ran his hand across her check. "Remember, Concetta, he's not your only option."

She watched Angelo stride away. He was handsome, brave, and fighting for a noble cause, but Gracie didn't need more than one option. She only wanted Ley.

* * *

Zimmerman looked up to see Richter standing in front of his desk. "Yes?"

"He's back on the air," Richter said.

"Great. We'll try again tomorrow morning."

Richter sank into a chair. "It's not quite that simple. He's been transmitting at a different time every day. New locations. If you can give me enough men, I think we can pull it off, but we'll need at least twice what we had before, probably more."

Zimmerman frowned. Providing a few dozen men for a few hours was one thing, but Richter was asking for more than fifty for the entire day. "I'll have to think about it. We've been busy preparing for the withdrawal. And we've had good luck lately picking up the Gappisti."

Something similar had happened the week the Americans and British invaded Anzio. The Gappisti suddenly thought they'd be rid of the Germans in a few days, and they'd let their guard down. Zimmerman had never yet matched the number of arrests he'd made that week, but now, as the Allies advanced again, he was coming close. He wanted the wireless operator, but more than that, he wanted all the saboteurs and double agents his men were tracking down. Even if he could get the number of troops Richter was requesting, he wasn't sure it would be worth it to pull them away from their current work—not when they might catch a dozen Gappisti in the same amount of time.

Richter walked away with shuffling footsteps and hunched shoulders. Zimmerman glanced at the clock and stood. He had Italian scum to arrest—an informant had overheard a friend bragging to a girlfriend about his work with the Gappisti and about a rendezvous to take place in an hour. Zimmerman planned to be waiting with Möller when the Gappisti arrived.

Zimmerman changed into civilian clothing and met Möller at the door. "Do you want anyone else?" Möller asked.

Zimmerman shook his head. His men had other leads to pursue, and Zimmerman was confident he and Möller could handle a group of three. He'd brought a submachine pistol as backup but thought his Luger would be enough firepower.

It was past curfew, so the streets were deserted. The neighborhood they went to smelled of inadequate plumbing, rotting garbage, and cheap bread. *The smell of poverty.*

The garage where the Gappisti were supposed to meet was across from a run-down apartment building. "Find a room with a view of the garage and wait there," Zimmerman ordered.

Möller nodded and crossed the street. Zimmerman located a back entrance and waited inside the garage, behind a dilapidated fire truck. While he waited, Zimmerman thought of his other leads. He was neglecting them because this one offered him the chance to collect three Gappisti. But as time crept by, he wondered if he'd invested his energy in the wrong project. The crack in the garage's side entry grew darker. He couldn't see his watch, but it seemed like he'd waited an eternity.

Eventually, the door opened, and a shadow came inside. "Mario?" a male voice whispered. "Are you there?"

Zimmerman crouched down, peering up through the truck's windows while the man lit a lantern, leaned against the truck, and took out a cigarette. Zimmerman tried to control his breathing to make sure the Gappisti wouldn't know he was there—not until his friends arrived. As the Gappisti neared the end of his cigarette, two others joined him.

"You're late," the man with the cigarette said.

The shorter of the new arrivals smiled. "Sorry. I was celebrating with my girlfriend."

The first Gappisti groaned. "Don't rub it in."

"Things didn't work out with that girl, then?"

"No. She wasn't interested in promises of prosciutto or sabotage."

"I thought everyone was hungry," the taller man said.

The man flung his cigarette stub to the ground. "She lost weight in April, same as everybody. She's got something going on with another contact. She'll change her mind, or I'll find somebody else."

"Is that any good?" One of the newcomers gestured to the cigarette.

The first Gappisti pulled out his pack and offered some to his friends. "Bought them at the black market this morning. American."

"I've never had an American cigarette." The shorter man reached for one.

"Did you bring the maps?" The first man put the cigarettes away and reached for the papers when one of the newcomers pulled them out. "So this road here, that looks like the best. Stop the first car in the convoy with our nails, then ambush anyone who tries to clear away the wreck. Maybe confiscate a few weapons. This could be our last chance to hit them before the front lines change, eh?"

Zimmerman had heard enough. He straightened and stepped away from the truck, keeping his machine pistol pointed at the Gappisti trio. "You're under arrest, all of you."

The men froze for an instant, then the short one reached for his pocket. Zimmerman shot him. The other two dove to the ground, and one of them got off a shot that whizzed past Zimmerman's ear. He'd planned to take them alive, but he shot another one in the confusion, hitting him as he pulled the door open. The third man escaped.

Zimmerman swore under his breath and ran out the door after him. He could see his quarry running away on the dark street, but Zimmerman knew something the Gappisti didn't. Möller was one of the best marksmen in Rome. Zimmerman heard the crack of a rifle and saw the last Gappisti fall.

Möller left the apartment, and Zimmerman waved him toward the man he'd just shot. Zimmerman went back into the garage to check the men he'd gunned down. They were both dead. In the lantern light, their young eyes stared up at him. He wished he would have planned things differently so they could have been captured rather than killed. Dead, they wouldn't lead him to any of their friends.

He went outside again as Möller marched the third man back. It was the Gappisti who'd arrived first at the garage, the one who'd been shopping at the black market and had unsuccessfully wooed a woman that day. He had his hands on his head and dragged his left leg. When he got closer, Zimmerman noticed the gunshot wound in his thigh. And there was something else too—his clothing hung strangely, and there was a wet mark on his abdomen. When the man was close enough, Zimmerman pulled on his jacket just to confirm his guess. The man winced.

Zimmerman laughed. "You know the great thing about these four-pointed nails?" he said to Möller. "If you're chasing a Gappisti with a pocket full of them and he falls, he's always going to impale himself."

CHAPTER FORTY-THREE

WHEN THE BODIES HAD BEEN collected and his latest catch brought to the Via Tasso, Zimmerman went with the new interrogator to visit the injured Gappisti. The man was obviously in pain from Möller's bullet and the nails, and Zimmerman could almost smell the fear.

"I want your real name, and I want the name you go by with your partisan friends. Then I want to know who supplied you with the nails and who supplied your friend with that map. And I want to know all your other contacts."

The skinny Gappisti didn't answer, and Zimmerman would have been surprised if he had right away. Ostheim's replacement, Untersturmführer Koch, hadn't started working on him yet.

"I'll be back later, and you can tell me then."

Three days later, the Gappisti still hadn't given anything away, but the Allied Armies were getting closer. Zimmerman had no choice but to go through his files and either pack or burn them. He didn't want anything useful to fall into Allied hands if he had to leave. And he would have to leave—soon. It was May thirtieth. Zimmerman wasn't sure he'd be in Rome when June arrived.

While going through his paperwork, he came across his report on the prison escape the night Ostheim was killed. He flipped through it, and a question that had nagged him then returned, stronger than before. *What was Dietrich doing in the prison that night?* Ostheim would have found out. Ostheim had wanted to look at Dietrich's files after the curfew party. It had seemed petty at the time, but if army headquarters was anything like Gestapo headquarters, no one would miss one little file amid the packing and burning.

An hour later, Zimmerman returned to his desk, Dietrich's folder in hand. Remembering Dietrich's Iron Cross, Zimmerman searched the file. Dietrich had done something impressive before, and Zimmerman wanted to know what it was. He skimmed through Dietrich's military career until he found the citation. The Soviets had overrun the German lines, including a group of engineers. Dietrich had climbed on a T-34 tank, dropped a grenade through its turret, and single-handedly killed its entire crew. Then he'd machine-gunned down two squads of Soviet infantry.

Zimmerman put the file down, searching his memory. At the curfew party, Dietrich had said he owed his Iron Cross to his men, but according to the write-up, he'd acted alone.

Zimmerman found more papers—and the answer to a question Ostheim had asked months ago. The SD investigator who'd come to Rome in February had been following up on Dietrich's erratic behavior during his recovery in Berlin. While serving on the Eastern Front, Dietrich and his men had been involved in the severe mistreatment of Soviet civilians. Cruelty to Russian peasants wasn't worthy of an SD investigation, but bragging about his exploits in the presence of Swiss diplomats had been sufficient reason for someone to make sure Dietrich was being more discreet in Rome.

The next page was a letter dated in early March from an Untersturm-führer Fritz Meyer complaining that Dietrich had interrupted his men at a train station in Lombardy, intervening on behalf of an Italian woman handing out potatoes to a train loaded with Italian prisoners.

Atrocities for Soviet civilians and mercy for Italian ones? It was possible but seemed strange. Zimmerman dug through his desk drawer, past postcards he'd been meaning to send his son, past the picture of his family. He finally found a blank piece of paper and began a list.

Iron Cross citation

Meyer's letter and the SD report

Zimmerman thought a while longer, then added two additional lines.

Unexplained presence in prison during jail break

Knew of planned raid on San Lorenzo church

Something was off about Dietrich. Zimmerman wondered why he hadn't connected the dots before. He folded the paper and stuck it in his pocket, then went to find more information. Scholz and an aide were in his office, digging through paperwork.

"Sir?"

Scholz looked up. "Yes, what is it?"

"Could I look at some of your reports? The ones on all the engineering projects?"

"Take whatever you like. Destroy them when you're finished." Scholz motioned for his aide to find the relevant files, and Zimmerman walked back to his desk with a six-inch stack of reports. He spent the next hour shifting through them. By the time he was finished, he had another line on his list.

Highest percentage of damaged projects of all engineers

Zimmerman wasn't sure that counted as a reason for suspicion. Surely Allied airplanes didn't know whose projects they were bombing, and other engineers had percentages nearly as high—Heinie Vogel, for example.

"Sir?" Koch stood before his desk. Zimmerman had been so absorbed in his thoughts that he hadn't heard the new interrogator approach.

"Yes, what is it?"

"The Gappisti you arrested last Friday. He's finally talking."

Zimmerman motioned for Koch to sit down.

"Born Antonio Russo. Goes by Angelo among the other Gappisti. And he told me all about his friends."

Koch handed over his notes, and Zimmerman glanced through the list, his eyes stopping on the second name: Concetta. He read the description: *Italian, five feet eight inches high, long black hair, birthmark on her right cheek. Operates a radio.* It even described where she lived.

"He's supposed to meet the female contact just before curfew tonight," Koch said.

"Keep him talking. See what else he knows." Zimmerman checked his watch. "And leave word at the front entrance for Möller to see me as soon as he arrives."

Koch left, and Zimmerman searched until he found a copy of Richter's report on the wireless operator he'd tried so hard to capture. Sure enough, the transmissions tapered off the day Dietrich was shot in the Via Tasso prison. They began again when he went back to work. Zimmerman remembered Neroli's description of the two women who'd thwarted his San Lorenzo roundup. *One looked like she was expecting a baby; the other one had dirt or something on her cheek.* It hadn't been dirt; it was a birthmark.

Zimmerman's list was growing, but it still wasn't watertight. Had Concetta been using Dietrich, or was he part of the plot? Recalling how distracted Scholz had been with preparations to withdraw from Rome, Zimmerman thought he had better know for certain before he accused Dietrich of anything. At the very least, he should arrest Concetta and the rest of Angelo's contacts. But he didn't have much time—he needed to know at once, before he was forced from Rome.

Zimmerman stared at his list, formulating a plan that would prove where Dietrich's loyalties lay. He walked beyond Scholz's office and found who he was looking for. "Obersturmführer Vogel, may I have a minute?"

CHAPTER FORTY-FOUR

Whenever someone knocked on his door, Bastien found himself wishing it was Gracie and hoping it wasn't the Gestapo. This evening, Heinie stood outside his room.

"Adalard, are you busy?"

Bastien wasn't, not until late that night when he was supposed to help Gracie with her transmission. He had a long report for her, full of information on retreat routes and reinforcements. "No, come in."

Heinie came inside but didn't take the offered seat. "I was at the Via Tasso today. Zimmerman's been looking for a wireless operator, been obsessed with it the last few weeks."

"I'd heard," Bastien said, thinking of Gracie's narrow escape.

"He caught someone. A Gappisti who's been passing reports to the wireless operator. And the Gappisti told Zimmerman who he's been working with." Heinie looked at the carpet as if he didn't want to continue.

"And?"

"It's Concetta."

"What?"

Heinie looked up, his face pained. "I'm sorry to be the one to tell you, Adalard."

Bastien grabbed his holster belt and strapped on his pistol and knife. "Have they arrested her yet?" If he could warn Gracie before Zimmerman found her, they could both leave at once. The front line wasn't too far way. He'd take his report directly there.

Heinie put a hand on Bastien's shoulder. "She's gone, Adalard. You can't do anything for her now. And it gets worse. Zimmerman studied that old report I wrote for Scholz—the one about air raid damage on engineering projects. Everything you've touched has been bombed. She used you,

Adalard. She got information from you and gave it to the enemy. I thought I should warn you . . . because I don't know what the SS is going to think. You might want to come up with a good explanation for telling your mistress all about your job."

Bastien stood there, unable to move. "You know what they do to prisoners in the Via Tasso?"

Heinie sighed. "Yes. Maybe she escaped. I shouldn't say it, shouldn't even think it, but I hope she did."

"When did Zimmerman leave?"

"Adalard, you have to let her go."

"But I . . ." Bastien let his thought trail off. He had to play his role a while longer.

"You really loved her, didn't you?"

Bastien had never admitted it to himself, but he nodded at Heinie's question. He did love Gracie, more than he'd ever loved anyone.

Heinie walked over to the wet bar. "I've only gotten drunk once before in my entire life, but I think tonight might be a good time to try it again." He poured a drink and set it on the table by Bastien. "I know you don't normally drink, but you should make an exception tonight. Maybe she got away. Or maybe she'll cooperate, and there won't be any reason to torture her."

The Gracie Bastien had brought to Rome in February might have crumpled in a Gestapo interrogation, but after three months in the field, he knew she wouldn't say anything, not anytime soon. "I've got to see if there's something I can do."

"Don't be stupid, Adalard. If you interfere, you might end up in the cell next to her."

I might end up in the cell next to her anyway. Bastien grabbed his boots and slid his feet inside.

Heinie was quiet for a while, for too long. When Bastien looked over at him, his left hand held Bastien's broken radio crystal. Bastien had hidden it in a teacup in the cupboard when he'd given the rest of the radio to Gracie. Heinie's right hand held his pistol, and it was pointed at Bastien.

"You haven't been sleeping with her; you've been working with her," Heinie said.

Bastien didn't reply. He was tempted to grab his own pistol, but Heinie might fire if Bastien reached for his weapon, and he wasn't sure he could shoot Heinie.

"And she wasn't using you; you've been using me! Zimmerman said that other than you, my projects had the highest percent of bombing damage. I suppose you were the one telling the Allies all about my work?"

Bastien still didn't say anything.

"Why would you betray the fatherland?" Heinie whispered.

"Our fatherland was hijacked by the Nazi Party, Heinie. They've corrupted Germany, and they're destroying Europe."

"Are you confessing to *treason*?" When Bastien stayed silent, Heinie set his jaw and lifted his pistol higher. "Why?"

Bastien spoke, not because Heinie was aiming a pistol at him but because Heinie was his friend, and despite his uniform, he was a good man. Silence might be the wiser course, but he wanted Heinie to understand. "The Nazis murdered my father at Sachsenhausen in 1936. His only crime was disagreeing with them and writing it down with a convincing pen."

"Zimmerman had your file on his desk. It said your father died when you were ten."

Bastien took a miniscule step toward the door.

"You aren't Adalard, are you?" Heinie's mouth opened in a gasp of surprise, and his right arm relaxed slightly. "Of course you're not. And Concetta . . . Her real name is Gracie, isn't it? What you called her when you were sick . . . Who are you working for?"

"My new country."

Heinie's arm tensed again. "I think I deserve a better explanation than that."

Bastien swallowed and shifted closer to the door. Everyone despised a traitor, but Heinie might respect an enemy, even one who'd been playing a role. "After the Nazis killed my father, I took my family to America. I joined the US Army, and when I came across Adalard's body and saw a chance to shorten the war, I took it."

"Of all the despicable things—"

"Heinie, you know the Nazis are evil. They're controlling your life, telling you who you can and can't marry. You saw the bodies in the Ardeatina Caves. You know it was murder. What do you think will happen to you and your family if the Nazis stay in power? What do you think will happen to Maurleen?"

"You leave her out of this."

"Why? The best thing that can happen to Maurleen is for this war to end, soon, in an Allied victory."

"That's not true!" Heinie shouted.

"Yes, it is. The longer this war goes on, the more likely it is she'll be killed, and as long as the Nazis are in power, she'll never get to marry you." Bastien took another small step toward the door, hoping Heinie wouldn't pull the trigger. Bastien had two choices: escape or death. He wouldn't allow himself to be captured alive, especially now that Heinie knew he wasn't Dietrich.

"Don't move, Adalard, or whatever your name is."

"Are you going to turn me in, Heinie? For doing something you know is right?"

Heinie's eyes were pinched, and his jaw trembled. "I have my duty. You know that. And you know what would happen to me if I let you go."

"No one has to know you were here. Put the radio crystal back where you found it and go to your room."

Heinie's arm shook as he kept his pistol aimed at Bastien. He gripped it tightly, his finger on the trigger for what seemed like a long time. "If I ever see you again, I'll have to shoot you."

"I understand."

Heinie lowered his arm. "I hope you find her before Zimmerman does."

Bastien took the final two steps to the door. "Thank you, Heinie." Before his friend could change his mind, Bastien stepped into the hall and ran for the back exit.

CHAPTER FORTY-FIVE

GRACIE WAS NERVOUS TO SEE Angelo again after she's snubbed him at their last meeting, but when he didn't show up at the Spanish Steps, her apprehension turned to worry. The atmosphere around the flower stalls was one of cautious celebration, but all Gracie could think about was what had happened to Otavia when she'd missed an appointment. Gracie was supposed to meet Ley that night—maybe he could find out if Angelo had been caught. In the meantime, she went back to her new apartment, the one Angelo hadn't been to and couldn't compromise if something had gone wrong.

There was no food to eat, and the bed looked dusty, so she stripped the sheets off the mattress and took them to the kitchen sink. If she washed them now, they might be dry by the time she got back from her meeting with Ley. Maybe a little spring cleaning would distract her from her empty stomach.

She was searching for soap when a loud rap shook her door. It was the type of knock that caused instant fear in habitations all across Europe. Gracie ripped the handkerchief with her transposition keys from her pocket and shoved it into her bra. Then the knock sounded again, and the door burst inward. Two SS men entered, one of them an officer with a small suitcase, the other an enlisted man with a rifle pointed at her.

"Concetta Gallo, I presume," the officer said.

Gracie backed away, almost tripping over the sheet trailing from the sink.

The officer set the suitcase on the kitchen table and lifted the top. "I believe this belongs to you."

Gracie forgot to breathe. Inside the suitcase was *her* radio.

"Möller, search her apartment," the officer said.

Möller obeyed, starting with the kitchen cupboards, then moving on to the sideboard and couch, then the bedroom. She heard several crashes, as if he was knocking over furniture, and he returned with one of her batteries. She wasn't surprised that he'd found it. She kept it out of obvious sight, but the apartment didn't have many hiding places.

The officer examined the battery and set it next to her radio. "You came well prepared. Further evidence, I suppose, that you're one of the best wireless operators I've ever listened to. I almost didn't believe Zimmerman when he told me you were a woman. I'm delighted to meet you, signorina."

Gracie wasn't sure how to respond, so she kept silent.

"I'm Untersturmführer Franz Richter, and I'm here to offer you a deal." He looked at her as if he expected her to answer. "Don't you want to know what type of deal I'm offering?"

"I suppose so," she whispered.

"Your life for your cooperation." He waved his hand over the radio. "I can't duplicate your code or your keystroke, but if you transmit exactly what I tell you to the Allies, we won't execute you."

"I'm not willing to make a deal like that."

Richter studied her for a few long moments. "And if we agreed to spare Angelo in exchange for your cooperation? Unfortunate man's lost most of his fingernails and half his teeth at the Via Tasso. Work for me, and I'll see his torture ended."

Gracie squeezed her eyes shut, imagining Angelo's pain. But she thought of his willingness to risk reprisals on innocent civilians in his fight against the Nazis and of the three hundred thirty-five men and boys who'd been shot in the Ardeatina caves. Angelo understood sacrifice for the ultimate goal. She couldn't spare him if it meant giving the Allies false reports, information that would lead to greater casualties. "I can't work with you, not even for him."

"And what about Hauptmann Dietrich? Has he been working with you? What would you do to spare him?"

She focused on his questions. Richter didn't know who Ley was, not yet, and wasn't sure if Dietrich was a willing participant or a tool. She'd do what she could to give Ley more time and hope he'd figure out she was arrested while he could still escape. "I seduced Dietrich because I thought he'd be a useful source." Then she added a partial truth. "He talks in his sleep."

"Then I suppose his future career is of little interest to you."

"No, Herr Richter. Dietrich's future won't be a useful bargaining chip. Nothing will. I'll never work for the Nazis."

Möller took a step toward her and struck her across the face with his rifle butt, knocking her to the floor. He brought his boot back like he was preparing for a kick, and she instinctively moved her arms in front of her face to block it.

"That's not necessary, Möller. Tie her to the chair, but leave her hands free so she can operate the wireless set. Then go keep watch. If Dietrich shows up, it means he's more involved than Signorina Gallo's admitting, and we'll want him for questioning."

Möller's strike had left Gracie's head spinning. He pulled her roughly to her feet and pushed her toward the heavy dining chair. Then he tied her ankles to the chair legs and looped a rope around her waist, pulling both so tight she knew she'd have bruises.

When Möller left, Richter handed her a handkerchief. "Your cheek's bleeding."

She accepted the cloth and wiped her cheek. Her entire face still stung, and her ankles were already numb.

"Now, let's see if we can come to some sort of arrangement," Richter said. "Have you heard what happens to women in the Ravensbrück concentration camp?"

* * *

"I'll take the key to Signorina Gallo's apartment now," Zimmerman demanded of the landlord.

"But why, sir? I must give my tenants a reason when I allow their rooms to be searched."

Zimmerman didn't have time for this. He aimed his pistol at the old man's head. "My actions are not your concern. The key. Now."

The man's hands trembled as he retrieved the key and gave it to Zimmerman. Remembering what the interrogator had learned from Angelo, Zimmerman walked to the fifth floor. He kept his pistol out in case Concetta was inside. If she was gone, he'd have to trust that Richter and Möller had followed her from the broken rendezvous with Angelo.

He unlocked the door and shoved it open. The door smashed into the wall, but the small apartment was empty. Zimmerman looked out the window, but there was no one in the fire escape. He didn't mind so much that he hadn't found her. He was disappointed in himself for meeting her twice and never guessing who she really was, but finding the wireless operator was Richter's obsession. He could have her. Zimmerman was more interested in knowing if Dietrich would come for her.

He searched Concetta's room. In the bottom drawer of an old dresser, he found a wireless set and a pistol hidden under worn clothing. Nothing else was of interest to him. He left the room and headed down the stairs. On his way from the third to the second floor, he heard someone coming from the other direction.

He continued slowly, hoping the rapid footsteps from below would drown out any noise he made. On the second floor, he stopped and hid in the hallway, his pistol aimed at the stairwell. When Hauptmann Dietrich bounded into sight, Zimmerman felt an overwhelming anger. For some reason, he'd hoped Dietrich was a stooge, that he'd been giving his information to the Allies unwittingly. His appearance proved he was an active member of Concetta's network, and he'd fooled Zimmerman for far too long.

Zimmerman pulled the trigger.

The blast reverberated through the old apartment building, and Dietrich collapsed. Zimmerman didn't want him dead, yet. He needed answers first, so to keep him from running away, he'd shot him in the lower left leg. When Dietrich reached for his Luger, Zimmerman stepped forward, covering him with his weapon. "Don't touch it. Hands on your head."

Dietrich pushed himself into a sitting position and obeyed. He was breathing hard, but despite the blood soaking through his pants, his face was unreadable. Zimmerman couldn't detect any fear, and it enraged him. He took Dietrich's Luger and struck him under the chin with it, but even that didn't seem to faze his prisoner.

"She's not here," Zimmerman said.

That got Dietrich's attention. His eyes flew to Zimmerman's face.

"You came to save her?"

Dietrich nodded, once.

"Hmm." Zimmerman glanced at Dietrich's wound, then back at his face. "When her name came up in an interrogation, I wasn't sure at first. Was she your partner or your lover? It seems the answer is both."

"Where is she?"

Zimmerman shrugged. "I sent some men to follow her from a meeting with another contact. She's probably on her way to the Via Tasso by now. And I don't have to tell you what will happen there."

Dietrich was quiet, looking beyond Zimmerman.

"I thought Heinie might warn you. That's why I told him about the report. If you'd been quick to denounce her, I might have believed you— had you said it was all a mistake, that she'd somehow tricked and used you. But now I know better. And now I get to capture one of the biggest traitors in all of Rome. Win for me. Could be a win for Heinie too. Best-case scenario, he loses his commission and gets to marry his girlfriend. Worst-case scenario, he gets executed. I think the most likely outcome is he'll be transferred to the eastern front, but maybe he can get married on his way to Russia. A small victory for him. But someone has to lose. You. And Concetta."

Dietrich frowned but still didn't speak.

"What I want to know is why. Why did you tell the Allies where all our defenses were? Why did you warn the Jews that I was planning to round them up in San Lorenzo?" Zimmerman pointed his pistol at Dietrich's head. "I want answers. Now!"

Dietrich looked away. "Because I'm not one of you. I'm not a Nazi."

Zimmerman felt a new wave of rage surge through him. He could take it from his wife, the weak stomach for war's requirements. He had even tolerated it from Heinie that day in the Via Rasella. But he wouldn't take any self-righteousness from a traitor. Wehrmacht officers were sworn to obey the Führer. Yet Dietrich had been playing a double game since arriving in Rome, maybe longer. "You'll pay for what you've done," Zimmerman said. "For the rest of your life—however short that may be—I want you to remember that in the end, I beat you. Even if you somehow escape the firing squad, I want you to forever regret the day you dared challenge Obersturmführer Kornelius Zimmerman, the Schutzstaffel, and the Third Reich."

Zimmerman moved his aim from Dietrich's forehead to his kneecap. A shot there would cripple him permanently. He squeezed the trigger, and Dietrich's cry of pain echoed through the hallway.

CHAPTER FORTY-SIX

GRACIE SAT AT THE KITCHEN table and stared at her fingernails, wondering how much it would hurt when Ostheim's replacement at the Via Tasso ripped them out. The handcuffs Richter had added to Möller's ropes bit into her wrists as she balled her hands into fists so they wouldn't shake so much. She'd heard most of what Richter had threatened her with during training or in Switzerland, but until today, it had never seemed inevitable.

In training, they'd been told that if arrested, they should hold out long enough to give their contacts sufficient time to discover something was wrong and change their location, their code name, and anything else they needed to adjust if the person in custody said too much. Angelo was already captured, and Ley would know something was wrong when she missed their next meeting. *Will he search the prisons again?* But he couldn't do that. Ley's only chance for survival was immediate flight.

Gracie wished she could warn him somehow. She wasn't sure how long she could keep secret the fact that he was really an American spy, especially once she was tortured. To give Ley a chance, she would have to remain silent. Her head ached from Möller's single strike. How would she handle a few dozen strikes? She was terrified of what lay ahead but prayed she could hold out long enough for Ley to escape.

In addition to protecting him, she needed to make sure the Germans didn't use her to send misleading information to the Allies. In her head, she made up a false security check, so if she was forced to transmit, headquarters would know she was under duress. She heard a ripping sound from her bedroom, where Richter had gone in search of her codes. He'd already torn open the mattress. She guessed he was now checking her extra clothing. *I have to get rid of my transposition keys before he searches me.* If she could resist torture long enough for Ley to escape, and if she could somehow destroy her keys, maybe her mission wouldn't end in complete failure.

The matches she kept in a drawer by the kitchen sink would incinerate her handkerchief if she could get to them. Her feet, still tied to the chair legs, didn't touch the floor, so they couldn't help her move, but her manacled hands were in front of her. She couldn't pull them more than a few inches apart, but she could still reach her handkerchief and light a fire. Using the table as leverage, she pushed herself back toward the drawer. The chair dragged a few inches across the floor, screeching horribly. It was heavier than she'd thought. And louder.

Richter came back from the bedroom with his pistol drawn. "Trying to escape? I doubt you'll get far, not tied to that." He returned his pistol to its holster, leaving the flap unclasped, and rested his hands on the table, leaning closer to make his point. "But, my dear wireless operator, you don't have to escape. You just have to cooperate. Why don't you tell me where your codes are?"

Gracie didn't trust her voice not to shake, so she looked away instead of answering.

Richter grunted in disapproval and went back to her bedroom. The noise from his search grew louder, and she guessed he was checking for loose floorboards. Trying to time her movements with each bang coming from the other room, Gracie pushed herself farther from the table, then grabbed the countertop to spin herself around and pull herself to the right drawer.

At last she could reach the matches. She'd gone through about half the transposition keys, so it was only half a handkerchief that she retrieved from her bra. She struck a match and pushed the silk into the flame, breathing a sigh of relief as the fabric caught fire.

"No!" Richter's voice startled her, and she dropped the half-burned silk. Why couldn't he have searched the bedroom for just a few more seconds?

Richter grabbed her by the arms and pulled her out of the way, tipping her chair into the table. Gracie grasped at the wood with her shackled hands but gripped the suitcase instead and couldn't stop herself from tumbling. She put her hands out to catch herself and slowed her fall, but she still knocked her head on the floor as pieces of her radio crashed all around her. Her vision swirled, and a wave of nausea spread from her stomach up to her throat.

When her head cleared, she looked at Richter. He had saved most of her transposition keys and was studying them with a smile of satisfaction. She'd failed again.

Then she noticed the sheet she'd put partially into the sink earlier that afternoon with plans to wash it. She'd never gotten it wet, and the bottom edge, resting on the floor, was smoldering because she'd dropped the burning handkerchief onto it. As she watched, a small flame grew into a larger one, and soon the entire sheet was engulfed.

Richter turned and cursed. He ran past her and took a cushion from the sofa to smother the fire. As scary as it was, a raging fire would accomplish both her final goals: destroy her transposition keys and keep her from breaking under torture. When Richter ran back into the kitchen, Gracie grabbed his ankle and yanked as he stepped past her. He lost his balance and fell on top of her.

Gracie's receiver lay on the floor, within reach. She grabbed the five-pound box and tried to smash it into Richter's face. He blocked her and gripped the receiver, ripping it from her hands. He glared at her, no longer the calm, reasonable officer who'd prevented Möller from kicking her. Gracie gulped, knowing his survival instinct would show her no mercy.

He clenched her neck with his hands and slammed her head into the floor. She almost lost consciousness as the pain exploded in her head and went down through her spine. If he killed her, she wouldn't have to worry about breaking under torture, but what if she could somehow escape? As Richter drove her head to the floor a second time, she reached for his pistol and jerked in desperation. She found the trigger as it slipped from his holster, and she squeezed.

Richter's grip fell slack with the blast. She pushed him away and gasped for air. Her throat burned from Richter's hand, her head throbbed, and a cloud of smoke was filling the apartment, obscuring her vision and making her eyes water. The fire had reached the kitchen cupboards. She retrieved her handkerchief from the floor, where Richter had dropped it, and wrapped it around one of the transmitter knobs before hurling both toward the flames.

With her keys destroyed, she turned her focus to survival. She tried to scoot along the floor but could move only an inch or two at a time. *Keep moving.* She had to fight for each breath and coughed constantly, each cough pulling at the ropes around her waist and making them cut deeper into her skin.

The smoke grew thicker. At the door, Gracie reached for the doorknob, but it was too high. She tugged at the rope around her waist, trying to twist the knot forward so she could untie it, but it wouldn't move. Möller must have tied it to one of the rungs. *Maybe if I can get the handcuffs off.* She pushed herself back toward Richter. He was dead. Sorrow-induced tears joined the smoke-induced ones—she'd killed another man, but if she didn't find the handcuff key, she knew she wouldn't have long to feel guilty about it.

She searched Richter's clothes, wrenching at his uniform so she could reach each pocket, then pulling herself around the corpse to try the other side. She found a set of keys, but none of them unlocked the handcuffs. She shoved them into her blouse pocket and searched Richter's clothes again but came up empty-handed. He didn't even have a knife. She assumed he'd left the handcuff key in the bedroom, but the bedroom door was on fire.

She coughed again, so hard it hurt, and every breath only made her weaker. She tried pulling herself to the front door again, but each try took more effort and earned her increasingly small advances. She felt dizzy, and it was getting difficult to string together a coherent thought. She told herself that it didn't really matter if she died, but the light of flames flickering through acrid smoke filled her with terror.

When Gracie had received news of Michael's death, she'd come to the conclusion that the worst way to die was on a submarine, trapped at the bottom of the ocean, crushed by pressure from the sea, drowning in darkness. She'd been wrong. Burning to death was going to be worse.

CHAPTER FORTY-SEVEN

BASTIEN TRIED TO FOCUS ON something other than the overwhelming pain in his left leg. It was worse than when he'd been shot in the Via Tasso, much worse, and Zimmerman seemed to be enjoying every moment of it.

"I should have listened to Ostheim," Zimmerman said. "He felt something was off about you. I brushed it away as jealousy."

Bastien covered his shattered knee with his hand to slow the bleeding. He concentrated on each breath, attempting to block out the pain as he waited for his chance.

Zimmerman stood over him, tall and triumphant. "So, Dietrich, what really happened outside Leningrad?"

Bastien squeezed his eyes shut. It was a wonder no one had picked up on that before—a miracle he'd lasted as long as he had. He'd done his part to end the war, worked as hard as he could to help Lukas. If he only knew Gracie was safe, he could die in peace.

"You don't deserve to wear that Iron Cross, not anymore." Zimmerman leaned closer and gripped the decoration hanging around Bastien's throat. He paused, fingering the award, and then he yanked.

As Zimmerman pulled the medal away, Bastien brought his right hand up and chopped it into the side of Zimmerman's neck. With his other hand, Bastien grabbed the knife he kept in his holster and plunged it into Zimmerman's throat. Zimmerman struggled for a few seconds, but Bastien caught the wrist that gripped the pistol and held it so Zimmerman couldn't aim. The Nazi officer kicked Bastien's injured leg, and the pain shook him to the core, but it had been Zimmerman's death struggle.

His body hit the floor.

Bastien trembled from the last influx of pain, feeling weak and sick. He took a few deep breaths and stripped Zimmerman of his pistol belt to use it as a tourniquet around his leg. He stuck Zimmerman's Luger back inside the holster. He might need the extra weapon. He found his own pistol too and retrieved his knife, Zimmerman's car keys, and a handkerchief. He tied one of his handkerchiefs around his knee and tied Zimmerman's around the hole in his calf, hoping that between the bandages and the tourniquet, further blood loss would be minimal. He left Dietrich's Iron Cross lying on Zimmerman's chest. Perhaps he'd earned it. The man had, after all, proven his loyalty to the Third Reich, maybe at the cost of his soul.

Bastien tried to stand, but he couldn't put any weight on his left leg. Even the gentlest of movements caused agony. He hobbled to the stairs and clung to the railing, slowly easing himself down one step at a time. He would never have guessed that walking down a flight of stairs could be so difficult, so excruciating. *You have to turn in your report. And you have to find Gracie. Make it that far, then you can quit.*

When he reached the bottom stair, he pulled out his pistol. The landlord cowered in the corner. "I need you to drive me," Bastien said. But he wasn't sure where. South, to the front line? To the Via Tasso? To Gracie's other apartment? "And I need you to help me walk."

The landlord hesitated. Bastien lifted his pistol, and the man hurried over. Bastien slung his left arm around the man's shoulders, and together they made it across the entryway. Zimmerman's car was parked nearby. Bastien had noticed it on the way in, but he'd dismissed it as unimportant. German personnel vehicles were common sights on the streets of Rome, but he cursed himself for not being more cautious.

"You'll have to drive," Bastien told the landlord.

"Where shall I take you? The hospital?" The man looked ready to bolt, but he eyed Bastien's pistols and helped him into the passenger seat.

Bastien was torn. Should he escape and fulfill his mission or rescue Gracie? He wasn't sure where she was, but he gave the man her other address. Surely she would have headed there if her other contact missed their meeting. *But is she still there?*

As the man drove, Bastien dug through what looked like confiscated black market material in the back of Zimmerman's car and found an American first-aid kit. He pulled out a morphine syrette and jabbed the needle into his left leg. Even with the morphine, each pothole aggravated his leg and left him in so much pain that he was tempted to look for another syrette, even if it left him unconscious. *Hold on a little longer,* he told himself.

He directed the landlord to the back entrance of Gracie's ground-floor apartment. Two motorcycles were parked outside. He prayed that Gracie and whoever Zimmerman sent were still there, rather than at the Via Tasso, or that she'd somehow escaped. Bastien had the landlord help him to the door. The old Italian man opened it for him, but as soon as Bastien was inside, the landlord slammed the door shut and ran for the car. He was behind the steering wheel before Bastien could get his pistol out. He cursed and let him go.

Using the wall for support, he pushed down the hallway and noticed the smell of smoke. With each forward hobble, it grew stronger. By the time he reached Gracie's door, he knew for sure. *Why does it have to be fire?* He forced himself forward, told himself not to look at his hands, not to think of the fire when he was nine. He reached for the knob, but all he really wanted was to turn and run.

The doorknob to Gracie's apartment was warm but not so hot he couldn't turn it. Smoke seeped from the crack under the door, and when he pushed the door in, thick black clouds billowed out. The smoke was so thick he couldn't see a foot ahead of him.

"Gracie?" What had happened to her apartment, and what had happened to her? He wanted to leave when nothing but the crackle of flames answered him, yet something told him he had to go inside. He couldn't let Gracie share his brother's fate.

Bastien prayed for courage. Then he tied his last handkerchief over his mouth and got down on his hands and right knee and crept into the hot room. The smoke made his throat and eyes burn, and dragging his left leg was almost unbearable.

He stumbled into an SS officer, who stared lifelessly at the ceiling. He looked familiar, but Bastien didn't spend more than a second looking at him. He could see and hear the fire to his left, where the kitchen had been.

Not far from the corpse, he found her. "Gracie!" he shouted. He felt for a pulse and thought he located one, but it was so weak he couldn't be sure. He pulled her toward the door, but she barely moved. It took him a few tugs to realize she was tied to one of her chairs. He used his knife to cut the rope around her legs and waist, freeing her from the chair, but left her hands cuffed. He could worry about the chain later. For now, it was useful. He threaded her arms around his neck and shoulder and crawled for the door. He couldn't see the door, but his injured leg had left a blood smear he traced back to the hallway.

He wasn't sure how he found the strength to drag Gracie out of the apartment and through the hallway. His arms trembled and then collapsed as he pushed into the fresh air of the back alley. He rested for a few seconds, then took a closer look at Gracie. The side of her face was bruised, and so was her neck, and there were soot smears around her eyes, mouth, and nose. Her face was tinted blue, but as he watched, she began to cough.

Someone would notice the fire soon, but his adrenaline was gone, and he was feeling the morphine. He couldn't carry Gracie any farther, the car was gone, and he wasn't going to leave her. So he stayed where he was, praying she would wake up soon. Seconds turned into minutes, and gradually her eyelids flickered, and he felt her muscles tense.

* * *

Gracie heard a sharp crack and struggled to open her eyes. She'd never had such a horrible headache, and her throat was itchy and dry. She coughed, gasping for air, and felt someone holding her. When her eyes finally focused, she realized she was in the dark alley behind her apartment, in Ley's arms. "Adalard?"

The faintest of smiles pulled at his lips. "Not anymore."

She struggled to piece together what had happened. Her mind was a swirl of confusion, but she gradually remembered the fire, remembered looking for the keys, remembered her certainty that she was going to die. "How . . . how did I . . . Did you get me out?"

"Yes," he whispered. His face was smeared with sweat and soot, and he had blood all over his uniform.

She held up her wrists. The handcuffs were still there, but the chain was broken, no longer connecting the cuffs.

"I shot one of the links out."

That was the sound I heard. She nodded, but that made her head swirl again. "You should have left without me."

He grunted. "We can leave now. Let's go." But he didn't move.

Gracie sat up, and her headache sharpened. Her throat started itching again, and she coughed until her side hurt. She felt Ley's hand on her arm and turned back to him as she caught her breath. "All right. How?"

"One of the motorcycles, if we can find keys."

Gracie took Richter's keys from her pocket and handed them to Ley.

"You're driving," he said as he picked out a likely key.

She felt a knot form in her stomach. "But you remember what happened last time I drove a motorcycle. And that was when I was fully conscious and it was light outside." Her brain still felt foggy, and each breath with her scratchy throat was an effort.

"Gracie, Zimmerman shot me in the leg twice. I can't switch gears, can't operate the kick start."

She glanced at his leg. A holster belt acted as a tourniquet, and a few handkerchiefs served as bandages. Everything from the tourniquet down was bloody. As she turned to the motorcycles, her head pounded, and her throat grew even more dry. "Isn't there some other way?"

He didn't answer immediately. "You can go on foot. Take one of my pistols." He reached into his tunic and pulled out a paper. "My report too. Wash your face and change your clothes as soon as you can, but don't go near either of your apartments or my suite. I won't be able to come with you."

Gracie put his report in her pocket but didn't move. "I can't leave you."

"Then I suppose we'll die here." He reached out and cradled her face in his hand. "There's no one I'd rather spend the last moments of my life with."

Shouts sounded from the front of the building. The fire had been discovered, and they didn't have much time. Gracie didn't want to get on a motorcycle again, but if Ley could save her from a burning building even though he was scared of fire and injured so badly he couldn't walk, surely she could help him escape on a motorcycle.

She draped his arm over her shoulder, then they struggled to their feet. He winced as his left foot touched the ground, and he leaned heavily on her as he hopped toward the motorcycles. As they got closer, she recognized them as DKWs, the type Ley had borrowed on the trip to the countryside. She took him to the right side of the motorcycle, even though the kickstand was on the left, so he wouldn't have to put any weight on his injured leg.

He settled on the back of the seat, balancing with his good leg. "I'll walk you through it, Gracie. Turn on the petrol cap and push in the tickler."

Gracie followed the instructions, trying not to think about how much her head hurt and how exhausted Ley sounded. He took the keys, picked one that fit, set the throttle, and switched on the ignition. "Try the kick start."

The engine purred to life on her second try, then immediately stalled.

"I bet whoever was riding it left it in gear. Check it, will you?"

Gracie moved the lever from first gear up into neutral, then tried starting it again. She climbed onto the motorcycle, and Ley's arms slipped around her torso.

"You can do this, Gracie," he said.

She gently let out the clutch as she gave it gas. It was a jerky start, but they were moving.

"Switch into second." His voice guided her each step of the way, telling her when to slow, when to shift gears.

As they turned onto the main street, Gracie saw Möller out of the corner of her eye and panicked. She'd forgotten about him, but he hadn't abandoned his post, and his rifle was aimed in their direction. She heard the shot and held back a scream. Ley jerked, and she almost lost control of the motorcycle.

"Are you all right?" she asked.

"Just keep going. South. Fast." He tightened his grip around her waist.

She obeyed, driving past block after block of Roman buildings. Civilians, out after curfew, quickly got out of their way. She saw a few men in uniform, but they all seemed preoccupied, until a convoy of German trucks came into view. She rode onto the sidewalk and shot past them at full speed, disregarding the shouts and the gunshots.

"Turn right at the next street. Slow down a little but not much because there's a checkpoint just after the turn. Remember your countersteering. To go right, push the right bar forward."

She took the turn quicker than she was comfortable with, but Ley helped her balance, and she kept the motorcycle upright. She repeated what she'd told herself every block. *You can do this. You have to do this.*

They sped around the checkpoint and into Rome's outskirts, but then she heard the sound she'd been dreading since Möller. More motorcycles. She felt Ley look behind them. "Keep going. Only two of them so far."

Only two? It sounded like a crisis to her, but she kept riding because every yard meant they were that much closer to freedom, that much farther from the Via Tasso and the Gestapo.

They were nearing a straight stretch of road, so she pushed the DWK to its maximum speed. The other motorcycles were getting louder, but she couldn't make hers go any faster. She felt Ley turn behind her and heard his pistol.

"Got one," he said. "But a personnel vehicle is coming up behind us. Armed men in the passenger and rear seats. Slow down and cut into the field so they'll have a hard time following us."

Gracie nodded and shifted down a gear. She felt and heard Ley fire again, then the road ahead of her seemed to come alive with tiny bursts of dust. Someone was shooting an automatic weapon at them. She forced herself to ignore the bullets as she turned into the field.

The other motorcycle and the personnel carrier were catching up. Ley shot again. Gracie started picking up speed, turned to avoid an olive tree, then skirted around a boulder.

The other motorcycle chased them into the field, and Ley fired until his first pistol was empty, then switched weapons. In her periphery, she saw the other motorcycle draw parallel to them. She opened the throttle completely. As the weeds whipped past her legs, the rider on the other motorcycle raised his pistol and fired. Ley jerked again, and she heard him groan, but he lifted his arm and shot back. The other driver jerked abruptly and crashed.

"Are you all right?" she asked.

"Just keep going." She could barely make out his voice.

Gracie glanced around. The personnel vehicle still followed them in the distance. She kept to the field until their pursuers no longer seemed likely to catch them. "Should we stop and bandage you?"

"No. Head for Mount Artemisio. The Caesar Line seemed thin there last time I saw the map."

CHAPTER FORTY-EIGHT

THE MOON SANK TOWARD THE horizon on Gracie's right. In the distance, the countryside moved past slowly, but when she looked down, she was reminded of how fast she was going and how badly it would hurt to fall. They weren't even wearing helmets. *Falling would be the easiest thing we've done today.* Gracie would never again take for granted the ability to breathe without her throat hurting, and she wasn't sure how many bullets were in Ley's body.

She drove back onto the road and headed for the Alban Hills. They passed a few farms, then came over a gentle rise, and Gracie felt her heart stop. At least three dozen German infantrymen were below, and there was no way they hadn't heard the DKW.

"It's all right," Ley said. "I'm still in German uniform. Follow the road to the right. That will take us away from the main group. I'll say I'm a courier and we ran into some Gappisti."

"A hauptmann for a courier?" Gracie didn't know if it would work, but it sounded better than riding through the middle of a German platoon. Maybe they wouldn't notice Ley's rank or the blood in the dark.

A soldier at the checkpoint held up his hand.

"Do I stop?" she asked.

"Yes."

The soldier approached Ley and saluted. Gracie couldn't understand most of their conversation, but the man seemed adamant that they weren't to go past him.

"He said if we keep going, we'll end up in a combat zone," Ley explained in quiet Italian.

The soldier insisted they turn around.

"What should I do?" Gracie studied the nearby men, all foot soldiers with light arms and no mechanized support. The men looked as if they'd been in hard battle—they were dirty and unshaven and weren't paying much attention to the checkpoint.

"We need your fastest start yet," Ley whispered.

Gracie put the motorcycle in first gear, then jammed the throttle open as she let out the clutch. Ley's arms tightened around her waist as the motorcycle jerked forward, and he kept holding her as she moved quickly into second, then third gear. The soldier shouted at them, and she heard rifles firing, but she knew they'd be hard to hit, especially as she switched to fourth gear.

Ley kissed the back of her neck. "You're wonderful, Gracie."

She smiled and sent a prayer of gratitude heavenward. Maybe they were going to make it after all.

She had to slow her speed as the road became less defined, then slow it further as the terrain steepened into hills. Ley wasn't guiding her through the shifts and turns anymore, but she could handle it now. He moved behind her, and she almost lost her balance. "You're tilting to the left," she said.

She felt him straighten. "Sorry." He was leaning on her, so she felt the vibration in his chest more than she heard his voice.

"Are you all right back there?"

"Mmm."

"Should I stop?"

"No."

They passed the outskirts of a village, and Gracie drove into the vineyards. Ley's uniform was so dirty and bloody she doubted anyone would recognize it, especially in the dark, but she didn't want to take any chances. She thought it best to avoid both Fascists and Italian Resistance.

Ley shifted again, this time to the right.

"You're leaning again."

He didn't answer, and a few yards later, he fell off completely. Gracie couldn't counterbalance his weight, and the motorcycle tipped, stalled, and slid out from underneath her. She banged her head and scraped her legs, but it only took her a second to untangle herself from the grapevines and crawl back to Ley.

"Captain Ley?"

He didn't answer. She found a pulse and checked his tourniquet, but the blood on his legs didn't seem any worse than it had been in Rome. Then she turned him over and saw the holes in each shoulder. *One from Möller; one from the other motorcycle.*

Ley groaned softly. She ripped the bottom of her already-torn skirt and wrapped the fabric around his injuries, but she knew he needed better care immediately. When she'd bandaged him, she turned him to his back and looked into his face again. "Captain Ley?"

His eyes opened, and he stared at her for a long moment. "Addio, Gracie."

Gracie's breathing grew ragged. *Addio* wasn't the normal Italian good-bye. People usually said *ciao* or *arrivederci*. They only said *addio* when they were saying good-bye for a long time or giving their permanent farewell. "No! Don't say good-bye yet!" She put a hand on each side of his face. "I want you to fight for your life. I don't care how much blood you're losing or how many people are waiting for you in heaven—it's not your time yet." Her voice shook as she spoke. "Don't you dare give up and leave me here without you."

His lips parted, his words mere whispers. "Gracie, I . . ." Then his eyes squeezed shut, and his face twisted in a grimace of pain.

"Stay with me; please stay with me."

"I'm trying." And he was. She could tell by the way he focused on her eyes, but each time he blinked, it took a little longer for him to open his eyes again, until eventually, they wouldn't open anymore.

"Captain Ley?"

He didn't respond.

Gracie felt the same overwhelming, paralyzing horror and grief that she'd felt when her father didn't recognize her, when she'd heard Michael was dead, when she'd found Otavia's body, and when she'd killed the Italian police officer. It consumed her, and all she wanted to do was throw herself on Ley's chest and sob until someone from the SS found her and put her out of her misery.

Her mind was waging a war. *He's not dead. He's just unconscious.*

But he's dying.

Find someone to help you!

It's too late. No one can save him now. Those you love are always taken from you, and he'll be no exception.

No! Gracie stumbled to her feet. She wasn't going to give up, not yet, not this time. She couldn't get him back on the motorcycle by herself, but she could go to the village they'd just passed. Surely someone would be able to help. She couldn't do anything more for Ley's wounds on her own, so she slid the motorcycle away from the grapevines, pushed it upright, and climbed on. It started for her despite the crash. She looked back at Ley's outline and said a quick prayer for him before heading toward the road. When she reached it, she heard several shots, then a voice telling her to halt.

Gracie stopped the motorcycle. Even a German patrol might have a medic or at least a first-aid kit. Ley was still in his uniform. Maybe they could keep the ruse going long enough to get him stabilized.

Someone shone a flashlight in her face. "Who're you?"

Gracie squinted past the light. It took her a few seconds to realize the man had spoken in English. "You're Americans?"

"Yeah."

Gracie sobbed with relief. "One of your officers is injured over in the field. You have to help him."

"Medic!" someone called. Gracie climbed off the motorcycle, so exhausted she could barely get the kickstand down.

"Where'd ya get that?" one man asked, helping her with the kickstand.

"It's a long story."

"You speak pretty good English." The soldier had a Southern accent and seemed to be their leader. "I hope that means you ain't a Fascist about to lead us into an ambush."

"No, I'm American. And Captain Ley needs your help. Please!" Gracie's plea was cut off by a coughing fit.

Another soldier joined the group of five she'd run into. He had a Red Cross brassard around his bicep and a stretcher under his arm. "Who's wounded?" He glanced around.

"He's in the vineyard." Gracie took a step toward the grapevines, hoping the medic would follow. "He's been shot four times. Both shoulders and his leg."

"Can you spare a man to help?" the medic asked the patrol leader.

"Brown, grab the other end of that stretcher and come with me."

Gracie led the medic, the patrol leader, and Brown back to Ley's body. She found him just as she'd left him, unconscious between the grapevines.

The medic bent down and checked his vital signs. "He's alive."

Gracie sighed with relief and blinked back a few sudden tears, hoping Ley would stay alive now that the medic was here to help.

Brown shone the flashlight on Ley's shoulders as the medic examined him. "That looks like a Kraut uniform to me, Sarge," he said.

"He is wearing a German uniform," Gracie said. "But he's American. We've been in Rome on assignment for OSS."

"What's OSS?" Brown asked.

"I've heard of it," the sergeant drawled. "But how do we know that's who you've really been working with?"

Gracie panicked. They'd come all this way, and now they might get shot by their own side? "I promise. Just don't let him die," she sobbed. "If I'm lying, you can shoot us both in the hospital."

The sergeant chuckled. "We don't shoot people in hospitals, ma'am. But I'll have to take those Lugers as a precaution." He took the pistols and held them in the light. "Been looking for a Luger since Salerno. Brown, help with the stretcher."

Gracie followed behind the litter, watching Ley's head bounce from side to side as the medic and Brown walked over the uneven ground. When they got to the road, the sergeant led his patrol forward, leaving Brown and the medic to take Ley farther back. Gracie stayed with them, but soon she began stumbling. Even though she wasn't carrying anything, she had trouble keeping up. Her head ached, her throat burned, and she was terrified that Ley would die.

Put one foot in front of the other, she told herself. She wasn't sure how long they walked along the narrow mountain trail before they finally reached a flat road and a waiting American jeep. Brown and the medic loaded the stretcher on the hood, and the medic changed places with the driver. Gracie climbed in, and the medic turned the jeep around and drove to the nearest aid station. Gracie studied the sky until she found the north star. They were headed south.

As the medic drove, he gave Gracie a curious look. "You really a spy?"

"I was." It still hurt to breathe, and the stench of smoke had followed Gracie all the way from Rome. She worried that Ley could feel each jerk as the jeep drove over the rough road. She fought to stay awake until the medic parked outside a group of tents.

Two orderlies came and unloaded Ley, and Gracie scrambled to keep up with them.

"Surgery room's empty. Let's take him straight there," one of the orderlies said.

"You'll have to wait outside," the medic told Gracie.

She nodded, even though she would have preferred to stay by Ley's side. Then she remembered something. "He's not wearing his own dog tags. He's blood type A."

The medic raised an eyebrow. "That's a funny thing to know about someone."

"We worked together for a long time." Maybe fifteen weeks wasn't so long, but after all they'd been through together, she didn't know what she'd do without him. *Please let him be okay*, she prayed.

Ley disappeared with the orderlies, her last glimpse of him revealing a motionless face covered in dirt and blood. "Will he be all right?" she whispered.

The medic considered her question. "I'd give him a one-in-three chance."

Gracie squeezed her eyes shut. A one-in-three chance wasn't as high as she'd have liked, but it was something.

"Do you want me to clean that cut for you?" the medic asked.

Gracie put her hand to the gash in her cheek. She'd forgotten all about it. Then she felt in her pocket for Ley's report. "After I find someone to give these papers to."

CHAPTER FORTY-NINE

GRACIE HAD TRIED TO VISIT Ley every day since they'd left Rome. She'd understood when the hectic field hospital turned her away, but he'd been transferred to a station hospital ten days ago, and he still wasn't allowed visitors. One of the overworked nurses had explained the official reason: Ley was talking in his sleep, and someone was worried he'd mention something classified. But Gracie suspected it had little to do with morphine-induced mumbles and everything to do with Captain Vaughn-Harris.

Gracie wore the same outfit she'd been wearing all week—a maroon skirt and jacket with a matching hat and black heels. Maybe she should have been embarrassed to wear the same thing day after day, but she'd thrown away the clothes she'd escaped Rome in, and her luggage from Switzerland was missing. "Excuse me," she said to the Red Cross lady outside the ward. "Is Captain Ley receiving visitors this morning?"

The petite woman she'd seen every day for the past week glanced at the head nurse, who shook her head no.

Gracie frowned. "What about this afternoon or this evening?"

The head nurse pursed her lips into a thin line. "Not today, Miss Begni."

"But I'm sailing back to the US tomorrow. This is my last chance to see him."

"I'm sorry, but I've been given very clear instructions, and I'm not risking my position for you."

Gracie's throat tightened at the prospect of leaving with no good-bye, and she fought the urge to cry. Colonel Ambrose had told her Ley wouldn't die from his injuries, but she was afraid she'd never see him again if she didn't see him here in Italy. She still didn't know his first name and wasn't sure she'd be able to track him down without it.

Someone called to the head nurse, who followed an orderly down the hall.

The Red Cross lady watched the nurse walk away, then turned her attention to Gracie. "Of course, Captain Ley is still not receiving visitors, but he's in the farthest room down the left hall, and his room is on the right. It's one of the few private rooms we have." She picked up a newspaper, unfolded it to its full breadth, and proceeded to ignore Gracie from behind the latest headlines.

Gracie quickly got over her surprise and rushed down the hallway to the left, mentally wincing with each clack of her shoes. When she reached the end of the corridor, she glanced over her shoulder, half expecting one of the nurses to be chasing after her, but the hallway was deserted.

Even though she knew she'd be kicked out if anyone other than the Red Cross lady saw her lurking in the doorway, Gracie hesitated when she reached the small hospital room and saw Ley sitting in his bed, looking out the window with a blanket pulled to his waist and a folded newspaper on his lap. She still wasn't sure what she'd say, but she knew how she felt, how she'd felt for months despite her best efforts to feel otherwise.

She brushed her hand along her hair, hoping it wasn't out of place, and adjusted her hat. Then she walked in, softly shutting the door behind her. At the slight click, he turned from the window.

He saw her and smiled, but the smile didn't reach his eyes. "Miss Begni, it's good to see you again."

Gracie was halfway across the room when he spoke, and she paused. Why was he being so formal?

"How are you?" he asked. "Colonel Ambrose said you were in good health, but I still wondered."

Gracie pulled a chair from the wall and turned it around, placing it next to the bed so she could face him while she sat there. "I'm all right. You?"

He shrugged.

She studied the bandages around his shoulders. "I was worried about you. I wasn't sure you'd make it after everything that happened that night. Neither were the medics."

"Well, I'm not going to die. Not from this, anyhow."

"How bad . . . ?" She stopped, trying to come up with a more delicate way to ask, but she couldn't think of anything. "How bad is your leg?"

Ley hesitated, then reached for the blanket and pulled it off his legs—or pulled it off what was left of them. Gracie couldn't hold back a loud gasp. The bottom half of his left leg was gone.

She took a few deep breaths, trying to absorb what it meant. There would be no more skiing, no more dancing. Would he ever walk without crutches?

Drive a car? His injury would change his life, yet as Gracie thought about it, she knew it wouldn't change how she felt about him.

"I'm sorry," she whispered, wondering what he'd gone through since waking up to life without a leg. She reached for his hand, but he busied himself replacing the blanket, so she let her hand fall away. "Will they get you a prosthesis or something?"

"Eventually. In the States."

"Does it hurt?"

He shrugged again, retreating behind some invisible barrier. "Will you be in Italy long?"

She shook her head, more to clear it than as an answer. She wanted to ask more about his leg but respected his apparent desire to change the subject. "I'm sailing back to the US tomorrow."

"Heading for Utah?"

"No, Virginia. I'm going to help train recruits."

"Well then, all future OSS radio operators will be in good hands." He leaned back into a pillow propped against the headboard. "Virginia? That's where my mother lives. You could take my motorcycle for a spin. I doubt I'll be using it." He gestured to his leg and frowned.

"Will you go home soon?"

"Probably by the end of the week, but if I'm delayed and you'd like to borrow my motorcycle before then, feel free. I can send a note so my mom unlocks it for you."

Gracie heard footsteps in the hall. She turned to check the door, but the sound stopped before reaching Ley's room. "I will come visit you, but I have absolutely no interest in riding your motorcycle."

"I'm offering you my prized possession, and you don't want it?" The slightest of smiles tugged at his lips. "I threatened my little brother with serious injury if he so much as touched it while I was gone. I should have just handed it over to him when I left." The newspaper had been pushed to the side of the bed when Ley showed her his leg. He gathered it up and handed it to her. The front page headline was about the liberation of Rome. It was an old newspaper; all the headlines now were about the invasion of France. "Did you read this? General Clark let most of Kesselring's army escape so he could have a photo op in Rome. Idiot."

Gracie could imagine Ley in five, ten, and even fifty years still second-guessing the military when they made mistakes. And she supposed she would agree with him in the future just like she agreed with him now. The Germans were out of Rome, but Kesselring's men were still in Italy, fighting at another line of defense. "Maybe they should have made you a general."

"Hmph. That's not likely. But they should have focused on engaging and destroying the enemy and let the race for Rome wait. Now they'll have to fight them again."

Gracie handed the paper back. "As conceited as he is, I'd rather see pictures of General Clark than the ones I looked at a few days ago. When the Germans withdrew, they loaded up the prisoners from the Via Tasso into two trucks. They took the men in the first truck a few miles from Rome and shot them in the back of the neck. The second truck wouldn't start, so those prisoners were returned to their cells and freed along with the rest of Rome. Some OSS men wanted me to see if I recognized any of the slain men as Angelo."

"Did you see him?"

"No. I suppose he was one of the lucky ones." Gracie's relief had been almost palpable when she'd finished searching the OSS photographs. Even though he'd succumbed to torture and revealed her identity, she wished him well.

"They've had me looking at lists instead of pictures."

"What type of lists?" Gracie asked.

"Captured German prisoners. They asked me to see if I recognized any war criminals among their catch. While I was searching, I found Heinie's name."

"Is he all right?"

"The list said he was wounded but ambulatory, so it can't have been too bad. In most ways, I think he's better off. He's safer in a POW camp than in Hitler's army, and now he won't have to battle his conscience. In some ways, I envy him. Waging war with your conscience is the worst kind of fight." He studied her for a moment, then reached for her chin and gently held it, lifting it into the light from the window. "That cut is healing nicely." He guided her face to the side so he could see her bruises. They were almost gone—she'd barely been able to pick them out in the mirror that morning. "You're glorious in the sunlight, Graziella. Remember that when you get back to Utah. Sit in the sunlight, and some good Mormon boy will snatch you up in no time."

Her breath caught, first with the warmth of his compliment, then with concern that he didn't want her beauty for himself. "I'm not sure I want some good Mormon boy to snatch me up."

He frowned and released her chin. "Have you lost your faith?"

"No. If anything, it's stronger now."

"Then what happened to your dream of marrying a nice Mormon boy?"

Since leaving Rome, Gracie had spent every spare moment thinking and praying about what to do next. When she pictured a future with anyone other than Ley, she felt unsettled and anxious, but when she imagined a life with him, she felt at peace. She hadn't expected to feel that way, but each day, the impression grew stronger. It was painful to risk her goals, but she couldn't let him go. She looked right into his blue eyes. "I fell in love with someone else."

"Oh?"

He wasn't making this easy for her, but she didn't have time to beat around the bush. "I didn't want to fall in love with you. I tried not to. But the truth is, I stopped pretending to be in love with you months ago because I didn't have to pretend anymore; it was just there, every time I saw you, every time I thought of you."

"You're not in love with me."

"Yes, I am."

He folded his arms across his chest. "Your mother wouldn't approve of me."

"I don't care what she thinks anymore." As Gracie said out loud what she'd gradually realized over the past few months, she felt liberated. She would always love her mother, but her mother's opinion didn't matter anymore.

"Don't you know what I've done? How many men I've killed?"

"Yes, I know, and I understand the guilt and the nightmares because I've done the same things."

He met her eyes for an instant, then looked away. "Gracie, you don't even know my first name. You don't know me well enough to be in love with me."

"I love the parts I know."

He shook his head slightly. "Graziella Begni, you deserve better than a cripple. So go away and forget about me."

Was that why he was being so difficult? Because of his leg? "I don't care that you're crippled. And you lost your leg saving me."

"You don't owe me affection just because the SS shot my knee out."

"My affection for you began long before you were wounded."

He sighed. "I'm not right for you, Gracie. Eventually, your memories of our little charade will weaken. Your whole life you've wanted someone else. In a few months, you'll realize you still do."

She felt her breath catch in her throat again as he called their time in Rome a charade. Was that all it had been to him? "So you were pretending the entire mission?"

He looked out the window again. "We were supposed to be pretending."

Tears stung her eyes. Humiliation, disappointment, and heartbreak all engulfed her. She sat there for a while, staring at the ground, not ready to give up but not knowing what else she could say. There had been so many times she'd thought his feelings for her were real. Had she misread him so completely? Or had his feelings for her somehow vanished with his injured leg?

She looked at him again, studying his face. It was handsome and sad, and the thought that it might not be part of the rest of her life caused pain more intense than anything she'd ever felt. "Will you at least write to me so I know how you're doing?"

He nodded. The hope of a letter was better than nothing, so she took a paper from her pocket that listed the apartment OSS had arranged for her in Virginia and set it on the small table beside his bed, next to a pile of letters. She picked them up, staring at the address on the top one, written in loopy cursive handwriting. *Captain Bastien Ley.* "Bastien?" she whispered.

It caught his attention, and Bastien turned to eye the pile of letters in her hand.

"Now that I know your first name, can I be in love with you?"

"It's just a name."

"It's *your* name."

"It doesn't change anything. The smartest thing for you to do now is to put those letters down and walk away."

"You taught me to never ignore a good intelligence source."

One side of his mouth pulled into a lukewarm smile. "That only counts at curfew parties. Here, it's tampering with another person's mail. That's a federal crime, certainly beneath the dignity of a good little Mormon girl like you."

"What are you hiding, Bastien?"

He reached for the letters, and she pulled them away. She felt a little guilty taking advantage of his limited mobility, but she was desperate to extend her time with him or at the very least learn his address so she could track him down in Virginia.

"Gracie, give me my letters."

She flipped through them, looking at the postmarks—the oldest had been mailed last August. She felt a flash of pain for Bastien—he'd been out of touch with his family for almost a year. "Why didn't Colonel Ambrose bring these when we met in Switzerland?"

"Colonel Ambrose isn't very sentimental, is he?"

She snorted. "No. He didn't even tell me about your leg. And I've been pestering him daily—Captain Vaughn-Harris anyway—to get permission to see you, and he keeps brushing me off."

Bastien crossed his arms again. "You needed permission from Vaughn-Harris?"

"I thought it would help. The nurses won't let anyone visit you. Didn't you know?"

His face slackened, and his lips parted slightly as he shook his head no.

"You mumble in your sleep when you're medicated. I guess they're afraid you'll reveal something you shouldn't. I told the nurses and Captain Vaughn-Harris that I preferred to see you awake anyway, but the nurses wouldn't budge, Captain Vaughn-Harris was probably turning me down out of spite, and Colonel Ambrose wouldn't listen. A hospital visit isn't going to help win the war, so why should he bother?"

"Am I allowed visitors now?"

Gracie glanced at the door. "No."

"Then how are you here?"

"One of the Red Cross ladies felt sorry for me and looked the other way so I could sneak back."

Bastien smiled. "Gracie Begni, you're breaking all sorts of rules today. Disobeying the nurses, committing mail crimes. Next thing I know, you'll be bringing me a beer and splitting it with me."

"Do you drink? I never saw you take so much as a sip, and the alcohol in your hotel room was never opened until I gave some to the doctor. Good thing I did. I think it helped him forget the English words you mumbled last time you were on morphine. That and a night full of casualties from the Via Rasella."

"What? When was I mumbling in English?"

"After you were shot. Heinie had just left, and the doctor was changing your bandages. You said 'Gracie shouldn't be here,' and I suppose I thought if I was on your mind then, maybe I meant something more to you than just someone who operated the radio." He didn't respond, so she randomly picked one of the envelopes she still held and pulled out the letter. A piece of newspaper came with it, and when she unfolded the clipping she realized it was a wedding announcement. The headline read *Harold Carson to marry Stefanie Ley.* "Your sister?"

He nodded and reached for his letters. "Give them back, please."

She handed him the letters but kept the clipping. The young couple looked happy, and Stefanie looked a bit like Bastien. *Harold Carson, son of Robert and Susan Carson of Manassa, CO, will wed Stefanie Ley, daughter of Ursula and the late Friedrich Ley of Fairfax, VA. The couple met while Petty Officer Carson, US Navy, was stationed in Washington, DC, and will wed on March 17 in the Salt Lake Temple . . .*

The announcement went on, but Gracie stopped reading and stared at Bastien, shocked. "Your sister is a good little Mormon girl, and she's marrying—" Gracie checked the date. "And she *married* a good little Mormon boy in the Salt Lake Temple?"

Bastien's lips turned up ever so slightly. "Yes."

Gracie had trouble controlling her breathing, a swirl of possibilities suddenly spinning around in her head. "Is . . . is she the only member of the Church in your family?"

"No."

She tried to hold back the burgeoning hope that was quickly forming. Having Bastien share all of her beliefs was too good to be true. But he only used alcohol when he was disinfecting cuts, he didn't smoke, and she'd never even seen him drink coffee. Could it be because he followed the Mormon health code? He believed in an afterlife, his family was the most important thing in the world to him, and he knew scripture stories from the Book of Mormon. Was it possible? "Your two years in Switzerland—not with the military?"

"A Church mission."

"Why didn't you tell me?" she whispered.

"What, and have you making self-righteous judgments the entire operation about what I was doing in regard to our shared standards?" He paused, looking at the blanket. "Only you aren't self-righteous; I just thought you would be. And then I thought telling you would complicate things."

"How would my knowing more about your religious beliefs complicate things?"

Bastien still wouldn't meet her eyes. "I guess I thought it would be easier—for both of us—if we knew our relationship would end with our assignment. Our job was supposed to be our top priority, not each other."

"But you came for me when you should have left with your report. Why?"

He ran his fingers along the blanket, hesitating. "I didn't think I could live with myself if I didn't try to help you. And I guess I wasn't sure where the line was between how you felt and how you were acting . . . But then I woke up here, alone, without my leg. For some reason, I thought you'd be waiting when I woke, but you weren't. I still thought you'd come, but days went by, and I didn't see you, and Colonel Ambrose said you were only hospitalized for a day. And then I realized I was wrong to hope that maybe some of your feelings for me went deeper than our assignment."

Gracie reached out and put her hand on his. "I wanted to come. I tried to come."

Bastien lifted his hand so their palms touched and their fingers tangled together. They'd shared more kisses than she could count, but they'd never held hands. Gracie didn't ever want to let go.

"What would you have said if I had been here when you woke up?" she asked. "Would you have told me to go away and forget all about you?"

Bastien shook his head. "I would have asked you to forgive me for being so rude during most of the assignment, and I would have asked if we could try it again, without any pretending."

"And when I didn't come, you thought I didn't love you, and you changed your mind?"

His voice was quiet. "It wasn't just that you didn't come. The more I thought about my leg, the more I realized it would be unfair to ask, no matter how I feel. You deserve someone who's whole, and I'm damaged."

"I don't care about that."

Bastien sighed. "This isn't like the last time when I was out for a few weeks and made a full recovery. This isn't going away."

"Then let me help."

"Gracie, since I was little, I've been terrified of two things: fire and being permanently crippled. I'm not going to drag you through the nightmare I woke up to. You deserve better than that."

Her heart ached at the desperation in his voice. "You don't have to face this alone, Bastien. We can do it together, just like we managed curfew parties and jail breaks and crossword puzzles and DKWs. I'm just the right height when you need help learning to walk again, and we've been through hard things before." Gracie swallowed back a sob. "I can't believe you never felt anything in those kisses you gave me."

"It's not that I don't care for you, Gracie. The truth is I fell in love with you a long time ago. But I'm not sure I can make you happy."

Gracie glanced at their hands, threaded together, then back at his face. "Bastien, you're the good man I've always looked for, and you're the hero I fell in love with, all rolled into one. Even if you are missing part of a leg, you're more than I ever hoped for, and I love you."

His hold on her hand tightened, and he stared at her for a long time, his face showing a myriad of emotions before he finally spoke. "Then maybe we do have a future together."

Gracie took a deep breath—one of relief and hope and joy. "Good, because I'm not sure what I'd do without you."

Bastien smiled, the gloominess in his face finally gone.

Footsteps sounded in the hallway. Gracie turned in panic, but whoever it was must have gone into the room across the hall.

Bastien was frowning when she turned back to him. "I guess you'll have to say good-bye soon."

"We'll see each other again before long."

"I know, but now that I've stopped battling my heart, I'm not sure I want to say good-bye. At least not yet." He glanced pointedly from her eyes to her mouth.

Gracie stood and leaned over him, meeting his familiar lips for a long, slow kiss. She'd missed his kisses, and this one was better than any of the others because she knew he wasn't pretending. It was deep and sweet, and she knew more than ever that they belonged together. Every inch of her skin tingled with delight as his mouth moved with hers and his fingers caressed her neck and face. A powerful connection had overwhelmed her during their first kiss, and now it was stronger, cemented by their time in Rome. She felt blissfully happy, in a way she hadn't known was possible.

Then the door crashed open, and the head nurse started yelling at her. "What are you doing here? I told you Captain Ley isn't allowed visitors. Out! Now!"

Gracie pulled away, but Bastien wrapped his arms around her and pulled her closer, kissing her mouth again for a few hungry moments.

"If you don't leave, I'll call security."

Bastien relaxed his arms and ended his kiss, but as Gracie moved to face the nurse, he whispered in her ear. "I love you, Gracie."

"I love you too," she said as the nurse tried to shoo her from the room.

"Gracie?" he asked when she reached the doorway.

"Yes?"

"I don't know if I'll ever be able to get down on my knees—knee— to ask you to marry me. Would you consider a proposal from someone who can't kneel?"

She smiled. "Yes."

"What about from someone in a hospital bed?"

Ignoring the evil look from the nurse, Gracie let her smile turn into a grin. She nodded.

"Will you marry me, Gracie?"

The nurse called to a military policeman, and Gracie wondered what Vaughn-Harris had said to make the hospital staff so intent on keeping Ley alone. Gracie's visit, like her life up to that point, hadn't gone exactly as planned. It was turning out much better. She looked at Bastien's face. She loved that face, loved him, loved the mix of hope and uncertainty in his eyes. He had a rough road ahead of him, adjusting to life without a leg and moving past his memories of war. She wanted to help him with every inch of his journey. She smiled and wondered why she was crying when she was happier than she'd ever been before.

"Gracie?"

She laughed, realizing she still hadn't answered him, and then she said, "Yes."

EPILOGUE

Dear Captain Vaughn-Harris,

I'm writing this letter for two reasons. First, I have to confess to lying to you. When you came to visit me just before I sailed home, I told you I never wanted to see Agent Begni again and couldn't think of anything worse than being on the same ship with her all the way across the Atlantic. My real feelings were opposite of what I said, which brings me to the second reason for writing this letter.

I owe you my hearty thanks. Thank you for pulling strings and calling in favors to ensure that Gracie and I were on the same ship for our journey home. In a peaceful world, Gracie and I would have preferred to get married in Utah, but given Gracie's demanding work schedule, my uncertain health, and wartime curtailment of travel, we didn't see how we could make it across the country to a temple anytime soon, probably not until the end of the war. The war might be over in four months, or it could stretch on another four years, so we decided not to wait. A chaplain married us before we left port, I managed to arrange a private cabin, and the voyage back to the United States was our honeymoon. Even though I'm missing a leg, I've never been happier. I don't suppose we'll ever want to see each other again, but please know that when I think of you, I will smile in gratitude.

Regards,
Captain Ley

NOTES

THIS BOOK STARTED WITH THE vague concept of two agents trying very hard not to fall in love with each other, mixed in with some cool motorcycle scenes. When I started planning the *where* and the *why*, I thought Rome before the Allied liberation would be a great place for a pair of American spies. Allied intelligence had the same idea, only they had it seventy years before I did. Though the specific information Bastien and Gracie provide the Allies was made to fit this story, there were several real OSS agents in Rome in the spring of 1944 and many Italian nationals working for their country's liberation. Otavia and Angelo are fictional, representing examples of the real Italians who worked against the Nazis. Throughout the book, *partisan* is used as a general term for armed resisters, as opposed to the word's use in Yugoslavia (and in my last novel, *Deadly Alliance*), where *partisan* refers to a member of a specific guerilla group.

Bastien's opinion of Allied leadership on the Anzio beachhead is perhaps overly harsh. Most historians today conclude that there simply weren't enough men to be effective at Anzio, but Bastien's condemnation was mirrored by contemporary intelligence officers and frontline soldiers.

Prior to the offensive in spring 1944 that culminated in Rome's liberation, rumors circulated that the Allies had given up taking Rome from the south and were planning another amphibious landing north of Rome, near Civitavecchia. This deception, planned by the Allies, helped keep German forces spread out while the British, Americans, and other Allies massed enough manpower for successful breakthroughs through the Gustav Line and past the Anzio beachhead.

Descriptions of civilian life in occupied Rome are accurate, including the dirt, the hunger, the huge roundups, and the commonplace torture at both the Via Tasso and the Regina Coeli. The water supply in Rome at that time was inconsistent, affecting fountains and drinking water. It's also true that for a small percentage of the population, luxury and curfew parties were the norm until the German evacuation.

In the spring of 1944, a pregnant woman named Teresa Gullace was shot dead by a German soldier while she tried to throw a package of food to her husband, who was locked in a train as part of the large March 1 roundup of seven hundred Italian men for forced labor. She left behind five children. While Otavia is a fictional character, I felt her story showed how even those most deserving of mercy were often denied it during the harsh occupation.

The various German defensive lines mentioned in the book are factual, as are events such as the Gappisti attack at the Via Rasella and the subsequent massacre at the Ardeatine Caves. Though the Via Rasella bomb was hidden in a garbage can, those investigating immediately after the explosion assumed it was dropped from a window or rooftop. General Mälzer did order the block destroyed, but fortunately for the rounded-up Italian civilians, the orders were changed. Zimmerman's participation in the events is fictional, of course, but the methods and inner justifications he used as he assembled his list of victims is in line with what actually happened. Readers may have noticed that the number of victims killed in the Ardeatine Caves is first stated to be three hundred thirty, then three hundred thirty-five. Due to a miscount, five extra men were executed.

Differing accounts of the Via Rasella attack and the Ardeatine Caves massacre give conflicting details. In this novel, I chose to go with the time line Robert Katz described in *The Battle for Rome*, but other accounts place the demolition of the cave entrance by German engineers days later instead of immediately after the executions. There is also conflicting information about when the final Bozen SS troops died of their wounds and how many civilians were killed in the blast on the Via Rasella.

OSS employed many women during WWII. Most of them didn't work behind enemy lines, and of those who did, most were residents of the occupied countries. Women like Gracie, Americans citizens sent into the field, were rare but not unheard of. Though Gracie's story isn't based on the work of any one agent, there are parallels between her and the real-life tale of Noor Inayat Khan, a British SOE agent ruled unsuitable for espionage but sent to France anyway because she spoke the language and SOE was desperate for wireless operators.

At 11:00 p.m. on March 30, 1944, members of the 36th Infantry Division, a Texan National Guard unit, set out for Mount Artemisio. Before dawn, they had surrounded Velletri, and the Caesar Line that had held the

Allied Armies on the beach at Anzio was finally breached. Gracie meeting an advanced patrol on the night of May 30/31 has her running into the Allied line at the earliest possible time.

The Americans were in Rome on June 4, but most of the German forces they fought were able to retreat, regroup, and fight on for almost a year. Most historians agree with Bastien's conclusion that more of the German Army could have been captured with better Allied strategy.

ABOUT THE AUTHOR

A.L. SOWARDS HAS ALWAYS BEEN fascinated by the 1940s, but she's grateful she didn't live back then. She doesn't think she could have written a novel on a typewriter, and no one would have been able to read her handwriting if she'd written her books out longhand. She does, however, think they had the right idea when they rationed nylon and women went barelegged.

Sowards grew up in Moses Lake, Washington. She graduated from BYU and ended up staying in Utah, where she enjoys spending time with her husband and children or with her laptop. She does not own a typewriter. She does own several pairs of nylons.

You can visit her website, ALSowards.com, for social networking links, deleted scenes (good ones!), pronunciation guides, and more.